YOU SPIN ME

a nostalgic romantic comedy

Boston Classics
Book 3

KAREN GREY

Published by HOME COOKED BOOKS

A division of Jasper Productions, LLC

Copyright © 2021 by Karen Grey

All rights reserved. Printed in the United States of America.

Cover art and design by Lana Pecherczyk.

Subjects: | BISAC: FICTION / Romance / Romantic Comedy.|

FICTION / Romance / Historical / American.|

First edition, April 2021

This is a work of fiction. Names, characters and events are either a product of the author's imagination or are used fictitiously.

No part of this book may be reproduced in any form or by any electronic or mechanical means, including information storage and retrieval systems, without written permission from the author, except for the use of brief quotations in a book review.

Content guidance for this book can be found at www.karengrey.com/contentguidance

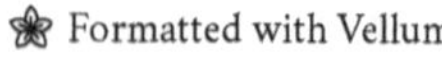 Formatted with Vellum

Praise for the Boston Classics series

★★★★★ "This author is truly a master at creating likable, three-dimensional characters." *Laurie Reads Romance*

★★★★★ "I'm always happy to read Karen's books that transport me back to the 80s and 90s. I love her snippets of music, TV, and current events of that time period sprinkled throughout the book for that hit of nostalgia." - *Pixie Dust Reads*

★★★★★ "I am loving this series, each book is entertaining and contains plenty of laugh out loud moments and heartfelt ones." *Bookbub review*

★★★★★ "Karen Grey has a lovely, deft touch with her characters, the plot, and with the world she's created." *Bookbub review*

★★★★★ "I love these retro romance reads!" *Bookbub review*

★★★★★ "I need more! This series is amazing!" *Bookbub review*

★★★★★ "Karen Grey has become an auto-buy author for me. I like her writing style/voice. She writes go-getter female characters and awesome male characters." *Bookbub review*

★★★★★ "I'm all about this semi historical genre. The music, the radio, the phones with cords. Every bit of it." *Goodreads review*

Content Guidance

The content notes below are meant to give readers a generalized view of potentially triggering subjects within this novel.

- Use of expletives: frequent but not mean-spirited
- Sex/Nudity: several sex scenes
- Violence: none
- Death: none
- Other: major traumatic events in main characters' pasts including severe burns and an eating disorder

If you'd like a more detailed list of content warnings (which may include spoilers) they are available at: https://www.karengrey.com/contentguidance

To anyone and everyone who has suffered loss,
faced pain and found unexpected gifts.

"Love looks not with the eyes, but with the mind,
And therefore is winged Cupid painted blind."
—William Shakespeare, A Midsummer Night's Dream

Prologue

Once upon a time, there was a beautiful princess.

She was a tad vain and spoiled, but aren't all princesses?

To be honest, she wasn't a princess per se, she was just an upper-middle-class Jewish girl from a little town outside of Boston.

But she was beautiful. And it wasn't exactly her fault that she was spoiled. From the moment she popped out of her mother's womb, everyone oohed and ahhed at her perfectly formed features, her dark curls, her thick lashes and her expressive eyes. By the time she could speak, she'd been praised for that beauty more times than anyone could count. Who could blame her for trading on those looks?

If you could have every wish granted with a sweet, dimpled smile or a demure flutter of lashes, wouldn't you?

The problem, of course, is that beauty fades. Skin wrinkles, breasts sag, curls lose their gloss, and the plumpest of lips thin.

If a girl truly believes her worth to be a function of her outward appearance, what is she to do when the mirror cracks?

ONCE UPON ANOTHER TIME, *there was a beast of a little boy.*

He hadn't started out that way. He was his family's darling. Everyone adored his wide smile, his sweet nature and his big brown eyes that flashed with humor.

Unfortunately, our little hero was impatient. He wanted to be like his older brothers, to stay up late and watch movies and eat popcorn.

One night, he was awakened by moonlight shining on his face. He couldn't yet tell time, but he knew that it must be very, very late—so late that everyone had finally turned off the television and trooped off to bed. The huge round moon gave him an idea. He knew where the popcorn was kept. He knew how to turn on the flame. Just like in the commercials, he would make the foil rise to a shape like the moon.

If he did that—all by himself—he'd never be treated like a baby again.

His skin prickled with cold when he pushed the bedcovers aside. He didn't like the tight pajamas his mother tried to put on him every night, so he slept in his undies. He did love his Superman cape, however, so he slipped it over his head. The cape warmed him and made him feel brave.

He crept downstairs, pushed a chair across the kitchen floor, climbed onto the counter, opened the cabinet and stretched his pudgy four-year-old arm until he grasped the metal handle of the magic popcorn maker. He crawled over to the stove and sat down next to it. He hesitated, unsure. He couldn't quite remember what came next. He just wanted to watch the foil rise and to hear the kernels pop.

Finally, he remembered: the knobs! Reaching across the burners, he turned the one closest to him.

There was a whoosh.

Sadly, what happened next turned his life into a living hell.

Chapter 1

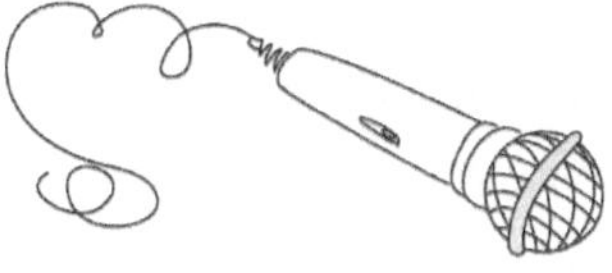

JESS

When I get home from work at four-thirty in the afternoon on December 1, 1988, having spent the day teaching dance and aerobics to rich kids at a posh private school, it's already dark outside. It's as cold inside my apartment as it is outside, which means the furnace is on the fritz again.

My thirtieth birthday just gets better and better.

No messages on the answering machine, which means no auditions for me tomorrow. Nobody told me that ad agencies go into hibernation from Thanksgiving to New Year's. I was really hoping for a chance to book something this month. Even doing background in a commercial would help pay the bills.

At least my heating oil charges will be low. Just as I find the super's number in my day planner—which I should have memorized by now, I have to call him so often—the phone rings and I pick it up, hopeful for some good news. "This is Jess."

"Hey, it's Will. Happy Birthday."

Will's my best boy friend. Not boyfriend. We've played lovers at Shakespeare Boston too many times to count, but he's as much of a brother as my real brother is. Plus, he has a pretty serious girlfriend.

"Thanks, but can you keep that under your hat? Last thing I need is everyone in town asking how old I am now."

"So, old woman, did you get a call?"

"You mean about *Hamlet?*"

"Well, yeah. Duh."

"Uh, no. I didn't." But he probably did. "Are you telling me you're playing the Prince of Denmark?"

"I am." The pride in his voice is laced with concern. "But I didn't get to ask about the rest of the cast. Did you check your machine?"

"I'm standing right here looking at it. No messages."

"Maybe they haven't called everyone yet."

"When did they call you?"

"This morning."

Which means there's little chance I'm in the show. Pacing, swinging the phone cord, I have to work hard to keep the bitterness out of my voice as I congratulate him. "I'm really happy for you, Will."

Part of being an actress is rejection. I've been lucky enough to avoid it at Shakespeare Boston. Until now, it seems. "Either way, it's fine. Ophelia's no Juliet. I mean, the part's a challenge but mostly because there's not a lot to work with. You just have to choose which kind of crazy to play her."

"Well, you'd be great. I don't know what they're thinking."

"That I just turned thirty? That I'm too ethnic for what they're going for? Both, probably."

"I can't see anyone at Shakespeare Boston saying you're too ethnic."

Noting that he doesn't say anything about the fact that I'm aging out of ingenue roles, I have to force the corners of my mouth up so I don't sound angry. "Sometimes it's about the picture, Will. And there are a lot of girls in town who can play Ophelia."

"Yeah. I… it'll be weird if you're not around."

"Well, maybe it'll force me to stretch my wings. Good thing I sent out my headshot to all the theaters this fall like a good little actress."

"Speaking of which, I heard there's an open call up at Chichester Rep tomorrow."

"An open call? Waiting all day for a two-minute audition where if you're lucky they'll be eating something smelly, and if you're not, they'll be asleep?"

"I'm going. Every audition is another chance to perform."

"Make me barf, man."

"Jess—"

"I know, I know. Kidding. Sort of."

Sucking it up, I get the details. Chichester is a bit of a haul, but Thursday is a shorter teaching day for me, so I can probably get up there before the five o'clock deadline. Unfortunately, Will and I can't drive together because he has to bartend in the afternoon.

"Well, I should go. I have a class."

While I do teach dance some evenings at a studio nearby, I don't actually have to tonight, but I can't take more of Will's sympathy right now.

"I'll make this quick, then." He clears his throat. "Are you in town for New Year's?"

"No. My family always spends it down in Florida with my grandparents. Are you having a party?"

"Yeah, but it's more than that. We're… kind of making an announcement."

I know all the colors of this man's voice, so I can tell this is good news. "Since I can't be there, will you tell me now?"

"If I do, you have to keep it to yourself. Kate wants this to be a big surprise."

"Oh my god. You're not."

"We are. We're engaged."

"Damn, Will. I didn't think you had it in you."

"I didn't either, but when it's right, it's right."

"Well, congratulations. That's awesome news."

"Nineteen eighty-nine. I think that's a good year to get married."

"I have to go, but… good job, man. She's a keeper. And congrats on *Hamlet* again."

"Thanks. Bye, J. Let me know if they call."

Proud of myself for mustering the goodwill to wish my friend well when I'm losing out on every front, I stare at the phone on the wall for a few minutes. I am truly happy for him and Kate. They're great together. I mean, a part of me is a weensy bit jealous since I can't seem to find a guy I'd actually want to spend more than a few nights with.

Maybe it's like that Groucho Marx joke. I don't want to be a member of a club that'll have me as a member.

At the same time, it kind of pisses me off that I'm too old to play Ophelia, but Will's not too old to play Hamlet.

My headshot stares at me from my desk, where the tools of my trade sit in neat and organized piles. A box of stationery, big brown envelopes, and my cute Apple computer. Everything's set for me to send out the 8 x 10 photos of my carefully made-up face and painstakingly styled hair, the attached resumes—which I spent hours cutting down to size and gluing to the backs of photos—formatted in neat columns stuffed full of Shakespeare heroines.

It's all a waste, all the time and energy and money I put into making this face as presentable as it can be, this body as attractive as it can be.

It doesn't matter. I'm thirty. I can't be an ingenue anymore. Yet I'm not old enough to play a matron, so I may as well not exist.

It's too late to go to law school or med school, even if I didn't have a learning disability which would make those pursuits impossible. My brother (lawyer) and sister (doctor) have both covered, anyway. I guess I could join the Peace Corps or something, but I doubt they'd have much use for a dyslexic actress.

Enough, Jessica.

I may not have a class to teach tonight, but there's always a dance class to take. Better than staying home in this cold apartment, where I'd probably stress-eat. I may no longer be an ingenue, but if I want to have a chance at any acting work at all, I sure as hell can't let myself go.

When I check the dance studio's schedule stuck to my fridge, the date on the calendar brings back memories.

On my twelfth birthday, I got to start pointe classes in ballet.

On my eighteenth, I went out clubbing in downtown Boston with my drama-geek college buddies with a not-fake ID.

On my twenty-first, I finally got rid of my virginity.

On my twenty-fifth, I landed my twenty-fifth professional theater role: Hermia in *Midsummer Night's Dream* (my fourth time playing the role).

I guess my thirtieth is when I stop celebrating birthdays.

IT'S A MUCH LONGER DRIVE to Chichester from Boston than I calculated—I probably didn't add up the little red numbers on the map correctly—so it's almost five by the time I step inside the theater. Even though it's the end of their day, there are still plenty of people waiting to audition. When I sign in, I'm dismayed to find sheet after sheet filled with the names of actors who got here before me. They must've seen hundreds of people today. If I hadn't driven over an hour to get here, I'd turn right back around and go home. The casting director must be in a coma by now.

Worse, the gatekeeper hands me a selection of scenes to choose from, explaining that even though the audition notice said they wanted to hear a comedic monologue, the director wants us to read from the play he's casting. Since I decided to do this last-minute, I didn't have time to get a copy of it. All I know is that the playwright is known for farcical comedies and there's a role for a woman in her thirties. A good little actress would have read the whole thing a few times so she could make informed character choices. Looks like I'm winging it today.

Since a quick read of the scenes is impossible for a dyslexic person like me, I give the woman my most conspiratorial smile and ask which scene fewer people have read today. She gives me a knowing nod and hands me a scene which is blessedly short.

After a quick scan of the room, I find a guy sitting by himself and looking bored. I sit down next to him and lean over, squeezing my boobs together with my upper arms. If I have to carry around these jugs, I may as well get something out of them. "I am such a silly goose; I left the house without my reading glasses"—a bald-faced lie, but whenever I tell people I have a reading disability, they treat me like an idiot—"so do you think you could read the scene with me?"

Man-gaze drops to cleavage first, then meets eyes. *Score.*

"Uh, sure," he mumbles.

Pressing my palms together, I recite, "'I can no other answer make, but thanks, and thanks.'" When he gives me an odd look, I clarify, "That's from *Twelfth Night*." Snuggling in closer, I add, "If you can read both parts the first time through, that'd be so totally awesome."

He gives the tatas another appreciative glance. "No problem."

Cue dramatic sigh. "You're my hero."

You may be wondering: How exactly does a girl who can barely read end up an actress who specializes in Shakespeare? Well, this particular dyslexic girl is a whiz at memorization. Taking one final deep breath—this time to clear my head rather than lure in my prey —I focus all my brain cells on listening as he reads through the scene.

The gods must be smiling on me because my buddy doesn't get called before I've got the words locked in. Now I can use the rest of my wait to analyze the scene and make a few choices. Instinct tells me to play this character straight so that the humor comes from the degree to which she takes herself seriously.

When I hear my name, I follow the assistant into the room wearing my most winning smile because before I get to play the character, I have to play the role of easy-to-work-with and accomplished actress.

"Good afternoon, I'm Jessica Abraham. So nice to meet you." Handing over my headshot and resume with my left hand keeps my right free to shake the director's hand. Such a little thing, but it makes a difference to not start the whole thing off with an awkward fumble.

"Thanks for coming in, Jessica. I'm Miles Jacobs, and this is Carol, our stage manager, and her assistant, Larry." The director is younger than I expected. Mid-thirties, maybe? Short with a pale, rarely-sees-the-outdoors complexion, he's got kind of a nebbishy air about him.

Either Carol just took a vacation to Florida or she's got a tanning salon membership, because there's no way she's maintained that golden skintone and blonde highlights through a Boston winter. By the way she's tapping her pencil on the schedule, I'm guessing that she's dying for a cigarette. She smiles politely and tips her head at Larry, a younger looking black guy. "Larry here will read with you."

Larry waves. He's the only one who gives me a real smile.

Miles takes a moment to scan my resume. "You've done a lot of classical theater."

"I've been fortunate at Shakespeare Boston."

He taps a finger on his temple. "That's why I recognize you. I saw both shows this past summer." He flips the resume to study my head-shot before making eye contact again. "You seemed much younger as Juliet. And you made some choices that surprised me."

I smile, deciding to take both comments as compliments. "Juliet has a lot more layers than most people think. I tried to find as much humor as I could in the early scenes."

His attention drops back to my resume.

"I did quite a few more contemporary shows in college," I mention.

"Brandeis. Cool. My older sister went there."

"Mine too." We spend a few minutes playing the do-you-know game. Turns out our sisters were in the same sorority. Always good to make a personal connection, especially in an open call like this one.

Carol doesn't let us stray too far from the business at hand, however. "Sorry to interrupt, Miles, but you do have a design meeting at seven and you said you wanted a dinner break before that." *Plus, I need a smoke*, I can practically hear her saying.

"Right. Thanks, Carol." When he turns back to me, the relaxed smile I'd coaxed out of him has sadly disappeared. "Alright then, so let's take it from the top. Whenever you're ready."

Even though I have the scene memorized, I hang on to the photocopy. An acting teacher once said that no matter how well-prepared you are, it's best to have the words at hand. Even if it's useless for me, it lowers expectations for my audience. The paper reminds them that what I'm performing isn't a finished product.

My choices seem to play well—I mean, I even get a laugh from Carol—until Miles interrupts me. "Great, thanks. We'll be in touch."

Painting my professional smile back on, I do a little curtsy to make things fun. "Right, thank you."

Once I'm out of the room, though, I can't help but push my lips out in a pout. I drove all the way up here for that? I didn't even get to finish the scene! As I layer back up to head out into the cold, I remind myself that it's important to get out and meet new directors. Even if he doesn't like me for this part, maybe there'll be others in the future.

I'm exhausted by the time I get back to Boston, but I drive straight to the dance studio. Two hours of sitting in the car means my body needs to move. By the time the jazz class is over, I'm sweaty and the stress is gone. When I get home to a blinking red light on my answering machine, I don't even stop to stress about what news the thing might reveal before punching the button. I hope it's not the guy I went out with last weekend. He was an even bigger jerk than the one in the scene I read this afternoon.

BEEP. Jess, this is mom. Don't forget, I'm hosting Shabbat dinner tomorrow night. Everyone's hoping to see you to celebrate your birthday.

She whispers the last word like it's a state secret. I wish it were so secret that it could be erased, but I dutifully circle the date in my day planner and send up a prayer to the gift gods that my parents will actually give me the Macy's gift card I asked for. Turning thirty means I need to invest in some serious face creams.

BEEP. Jessica, this is Dr. Robertson. Can you come speak with me tomorrow morning before your classes? Thank you.

Oh dear. Getting called into the principal's office. Even though I'm a teacher now, it's as unappetizing a prospect as it was when I was a student. I make a note about that too.

BEEP. Hi, um... this is for Jessica... uhhh, Abraham? This is Court-ney? I'm an intern up at Chichester Rep?

Even as my heart beats fast in anticipation, I can't help thinking that this girl needs a voice coach. Her habit of turning every sentence into a question makes her sound like she's unsure of her place in the world.

I'm, um, scheduling callbacks for Beyond Therapy? *So can you call me at the theater to... do that?*

After taking a moment to recite the phone number along with her, I let loose with a little pirouette. Then I pick up the phone to call right back.

Mellow-voiced Larry answers instead of the up-talking Court-ney. He lets me know the other scenes I need to prepare, gives me a time for a Saturday-morning callback and tells me to dress frumpier. Translation: the director wants me to cover up the knockers.

I make a few calls to try to track down a copy of the play. Will has one, of course, so after a quick shower, I head over to his house, where I spend an hour hanging out with him. He didn't get called back, but since he's one of the few people who know about my dyslexia, he very kindly gives me a rundown of the play's plot and reads through the scenes with me. Then other friends show up—Randall and Mike and Deb and Pam—all of whom will be working on *Hamlet* this spring. Without me. Normally, I'd stay and gossip but it's been a long day and I'm not ready to hear all about the play I won't be in.

Back home, even though I'm wiped out, I make myself cleanse and moisturize my face. When yawning makes it impossible to continue counting the new lines on my face, I give up and fall into bed so I can wake up tomorrow in time to talk to the principal before Friday's long day of classes.

Not that beauty sleep will do me any good. Now that the crinkles next to my eyes have become permanent fixtures, it's all downhill from here.

THE BOSTON TRAFFIC gods smile on me the next morning, and I'm able to make it to school with enough time to speak to the principal before classes begin, as requested. After nodding to the school administrator, I stick my head inside the scary office. "You wanted to see me, Dr. Robertson?"

"Yes. Have a seat, Jessica." The tall, intimidating woman gestures at the tiny chair across from her equally imposing desk. Dance-teacher me would like to suggest that letting energy extend past her wrist and through her fingertips would bring more grace to the movement, but that is not the kind of comment you make to your boss.

"I know you have class shortly, so I'll make this brief." She clears her throat. "As I mentioned this fall, we are facing both financial and" —she pauses, the smile that never sits comfortably on her face shifting into something more grim—"*other* pressures to restrict our arts programming while increasing our physical education offerings. The good news is that your Jazzercise course has proven so popular that parents are demanding that we add more aerobics to the sched-ule. Unfortunately, that means that we will be eliminating ballet."

"But what about the students who want to take it? I have some very promising—"

She raises a hand. "I'm afraid that this is not a negotiation, Jessica. For serious students, our families can well afford to take their girls to a private studio. *After* school. And please don't take this personally. We are making these adjustments across the board."

The clock is literally ticking on the wall above the principal's head. I have class in a few minutes. Ballet I, in fact. Kindergarteners and first graders, a group of excitable girls and boys. The discipline of ballet is perfect for them. None of them will likely dance professionally, but their teachers tell me that participating in my class first thing in the morning helps the students focus.

Before I can open my mouth to make this argument, Robertson's smile turns into an actual grimace. "I regret to tell you that we've found someone who is a certified aerobics and primary school phys ed educator, so we won't be renewing your contract next semester."

Even though the thought of teaching aerobics day in and day out turns my stomach, I'm still shocked that she's just letting me go. I've been here for four years. Kids love my classes.

For once, I have no words, so I simply nod, stand and turn on my heel to exit before I burst into tears. An invisible hand between my shoulder blades propels me down the hall away from the administrative offices and toward the elective classrooms.

After I open the door to the dance studio, I pause on the threshold before entering. Taking in the shrouded piano in the corner, I realize that I should've known this day would come when they stopped paying for a pianist for my classes. This beautiful studio will never again be filled with graceful port de bras accompanied by resonant trills teased from ivory keys. Instead, sneaker-clad feet will thud to the beat of a boombox.

I won't be here to witness it, but it's still a loss.

For the kids.

And for my checkbook.

Chapter 2

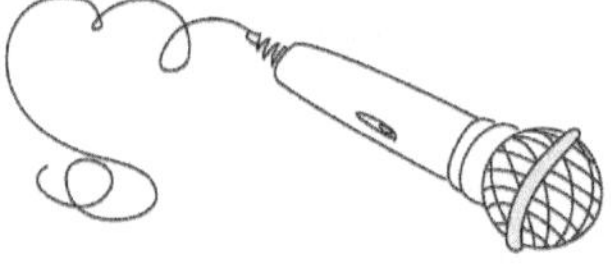

At the sound of the roaring tiger, the time will be nine o'clock. ROARRR. YEE-OUCH! Get that thing outta here! Phew, that smarts. Don't worry, Boston, we won't let the cat out of the bag. Not as long as you keep listening to Grace Traynor on WBAR, 101.7 FM.

CAL

Hoodie in place, head down, stride as even and long as I can make it —despite the nagging stiffness in my left hip—I take my usual route to WBAR's Boylston Street studios: down a back alley, avoiding human traffic.

Only a few people have a key to the rock station's back door—the janitor, the general manager, and me. The other DJs enter through the front door, but going in the back way allows me to avoid the station hangers-on that congregate in the lobby.

Once I'm in the music library, I can relax. Not that I take my hoodie off. Instead, I pull the strings tight so it snugs close to my chin. The soft fabric is comforting. You wouldn't think being reminded of the bandages that covered the left side of my face and neck for so long would be a good thing, but the hood, like the bandages, hides the ugly. People might stare, but they don't know what I'm hiding. They can only imagine.

And I doubt any of them could invent a mental picture as gnarly as my reality.

Anyway, enough of that.

Time to make the donuts.

After setting the crate on the beat-up table, I unhook Blondie's leash. A retired police dog, she's so well-trained that no one minds having her here, even though she's almost as scary-looking as me.

At the table, I create my set list. My crate holds EPs and singles that the station doesn't own yet. There's an upside to spending most of my time alone: It gives me time to write letters. At this point, I have pen pals at stations all over the world. We keep each other informed about local bands that haven't yet made it big. Since I don't have an over-the-top on-air personality and nobody wants my face on any posters, breaking unknowns is what keeps my listeners tuning in.

There's an art to introducing new music. You can't only play stuff nobody's ever heard of or just local bands like Human Sexual Response or The Atlantics. Even in my late-night slot, I have to mix in songs people can sing along to. Knowing where and when to slip in a new track—in a way that sets it off without jarring the ears— takes experience. Maybe even talent.

That said, sometimes you *want* to shake people up. Especially in the transition hours. Ten to eleven when the partiers are hitting their stride. Then again after midnight, when shift workers are commuting.

My job here in the library is to pull all the possibilities for the evening so I'll have them at my fingertips. Which are intact. It'd be hard to do this job without the use of my digits. Unlike many survivors with facial burns, I didn't lose an ear, so wearing head-phones isn't a problem.

Things I do my best to be thankful for.

AN HOUR later I'm in my favorite place in the world. The six-to-ten-slot DJ leans away from the mic so I can say the words that signal the beginning of my time on-air. "Say good night, Gracie."

The statuesque blonde sing-songs "Good night, Gracie" into the mic before letting fly her signature cackle.

We switch places so I can take over and finish the routine. "Boston, give a big nighty-night to your *second*-favorite alt-rock jock, Grace Traynor."

As I say the last syllable of her name, I punch the button to play the cart recording of a crowd shouting, "Good night, Gracie." As the roar echoes in my headphones, my fingertip releases the disc so the turntable can spin my first pick of the night. My patter continues over the opening bars. "Your late-night DJ Callihan here at ten oh two p.m. on WBAR 107.1. I'm not taking prisoners, but I *am* taking requests. But first, it's 'Crash and Burn' from Boston's own 'Til Tuesday."

Yeah, yeah, it's weird that I like to play songs that mention fire. What can I say? I have a sick sense of humor. As I'm lining up my picks for the next hour, evening producer Talia Cruz sneaks in with the commercial notebook. "You got three spots to read this hour, doll."

"Got it. Jimmy feeling better?"

I pull promo and ad carts from the carousel, checking them off in the log as I listen to Talia's expletive-filled report on her teenage son, who broke his arm skiing over Thanksgiving. Until she stops her own monologue mid-rant. "Shit. I forgot to pick up the weather." Turning to exit the booth, she points at the phone next to me. "You got a call light lit up."

When I pick up the receiver, a listener line volunteer lets me know there's a caller named Jane with a request. As I fade the music, I punch the telephone button. "This is Cal at WBAR FM. You're on the air, Jane. What's your request?"

A breathy giggle precedes her voice. "Man, thanks for taking my call, Cal. You're so chill."

"Thanks for listening, Jane."

"So, um, can you play 'Night on the Town' by the Del Fuegos for my friend Brenda? It's her twenty-first birthday tonight."

"Will do. Is there a certain time you were hoping for?"

"I'm picking her up in like an hour so if you could play it at eleven fifteen, that would be killer."

"No problem. Hey, you want to do a favor for me, Jane?"

"Sure." Her giggle is adorable.

"I'm about to play 'Answering Machine' by the Replacements. You want to do the intro for it?" She's got a fun voice, so I also ask if I can record her doing it. Sometimes the station cuts stuff like that into promos.

"Fer sure!" More breathy giggles.

"You ready?"

"Oh yeah, I'm totally amped."

After I start the intro of the song, I push record and cue her. "Take it away, Jane."

"Next up it's the Replacements with 'Answering Machine' on WBAR Boston 107.1 FM!"

I punch out my mic as well as the phone's as I slide the volume up on the song.

"Great job, Jane. Happy birthday to Brenda."

"Thanks so much, Cal! I love you!"

"Have a great night, Jane."

I wonder if Jane'd be so happy to talk to me if I ran into her on the street. I can just see it. Sweet, innocent girl screams in horror.

I take the phrase "a face for radio" to a whole new level. That's why I'm here. I get to make people happy without having to witness their revulsion—or worse, pity—when they see my messed-up mug.

A FEW WEEKS BEFORE CHRISTMAS, station general manager Richard Jones pokes his head into the music library while I'm prepping. "Evening, Cal. Can I talk to you before you go on?"

It's unusual for him to be here this late, but I can guess what he wants. "Don't worry, I'll take on any extra shifts over the holidays. Except Christmas Eve." I'm not married or anything, so I often work holidays. But I like to hang with my nieces and nephews on the night before Christmas.

"That'd be great, but I need to talk to you about something else."

"What's up?"

Jones sighs heavily as he parks his butt in a chair. Since they moved him up from program manager to general manager three months ago, I swear he's aged five years.

He cranes his neck to look down the hall before kicking the library door shut. "So, here's the thing. We have the enviable problem of having too much success. Corporate went on a buying spree all over the country, and now we have to bring in more ad revenue while they turn around all the new stations they picked up."

"Smart," I grunt. "Kill the one successful station to save the others."

He continues without acknowledging my comment. "Which means I have to get our numbers up in every slot so we can raise airtime prices in every slot. That includes the sleepy ones—yours especially because WBST is stealing males eighteen to thirty from you."

"But I own women eighteen to ninety. Doesn't that count for anything?"

"You want to run tampon ads?"

"Sure, I don't care."

"I was kidding. Owning women doesn't count. Young men is the demographic corporate wants, so we have to get them. In every slot."

"So what do you want me to do? A publicity stunt? How about I invite some young assholes in and see what they have to say when they see my face?"

I swear there's a light in his eyes for about two seconds, but he shuts it down quick. "Of course not. But you can't be completely invisible anymore. If you're out there promoting the station like the other jocks do, it'll get your on-air numbers up."

"Jones, you do not want me out in the world. I fucking scare people."

"I think you over—"

"Jones." Interrupting him, I pull my hood down. "You're used to me. Think back to the first time you saw me. What was your first reaction?"

Jones should never play poker.

"You know I'm right," I say.

He rubs his newly lined forehead. "All right. I wouldn't put you through that kind of thing, but we have to do *something*. Like, maybe we can play up your invisibility, the mystery of who you are. The Invisible Man or something. You could wear a mask."

"And then what? You can't build that kind of thing up without a reveal at some point."

"Maybe by then the pressure will be off and you can go dark again."

I push my creaky body out of the chair and finish loading the albums I pulled onto the wheeled rack. "I gotta get in there."

"Yeah, yeah." He gets up to open the door. "Think about it okay?" As I push out the door, he adds, "Unless you want to move to the slot after yours, the two to six a.m.?"

Wheeling to face him, I don't even try to hold back my temper. "I like my slot. I earned it. People are used to me being there for them. They like the music I introduce them to. I mean, isn't that what we do here?"

"Yeah." He sighs, his head dropping heavily. "You're right. Go rock their worlds. But we'll talk later, right?"

I shoot him the bird as I roll the rack down the hall.

He knows I don't mean it.

Not really.

Chapter 3

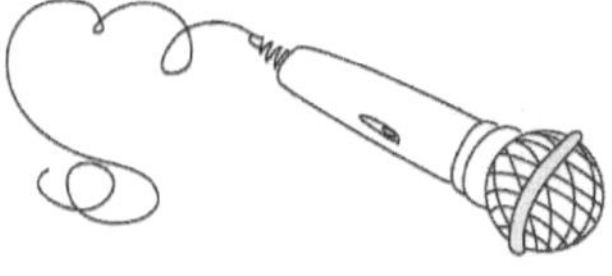

Hey, Boston, Nigel gave up his paycheck this week so you people can have commercial-free rock and roll all weekend. So maybe bring him a snack or something.

JESS

When I get to the theater for my callback Saturday morning—only fifteen minutes late, not too bad for me—I'm glad to see that the room isn't crammed full of actors. It's nice when they've actually whittled down their choices for the second round. Scanning the room, I home in on a tall, good-looking, white guy sitting in one of the chairs.

"Excuse me, are you by any chance called back for Bruce?" When he smiles, I continue. "I'm reading for Prudence, and I was wondering if you'd like to run through the scene with me?"

"Uh, sure." He moves a briefcase to the floor to create space next to him. "I feel like I've seen you before."

I tip my head to the side as I try to place him. "Were you at that Duncan Hines callback right before Thanksgiving?"

"I was." He holds out a hand to shake mine. "Jack Wells."

"Jess Abraham. Nice to meet you."

"I did not get the frosting job," he says. "Did you?"

I drop my purse on the floor and sit sideways on the chair facing him. "Nah, they said I was too ethnic."

"What?" His light brown brows scrunch together over light brown eyes. Everything about him is kind of light brown, but there's an intensity in his voice that's compelling. "What does that even mean?"

"Not blonde." Shrugging, I paw through my bag looking for my script.

He holds up the play. "Anyway, shall we?"

Having found my makeup case as well as my own copy, I open my compact. "Let me check my face real quick, in case they call us in."

He scans my face, his assessment—refreshingly—more professional than personal. "You look good to me."

With a polite smile, I clarify, "Thanks, but I'm actually not supposed to look *too* good."

He tips his head to the side. "Maybe take off the lipstick, then?"

"You think?"

He nods curtly. "Definitely."

After I scrub my lips with a tissue and then reapply lip balm, we run the scene. While Jack plays it broadly, I do my best to keep my character Prudence low-key and uptight. It isn't easy. When we finish, I let out an exaggerated, "Phew! I almost Harvey Korman'd about three times. You're hilarious."

"Thanks." He seems truly pleased. "You're an awesome straight man. Or woman."

"You don't think I'm coming across too bitchy?"

He shrugs. "Whatever you want to call it, it worked for me—gave me a lot to play off of."

"They do say it's better to make a big choice and let them rein you in." I flip through the pages to expel a bit of nervous energy. "The play is pretty ridiculous."

"Yeah. But you still have to ground it in reality. Can't find the farce without it."

"So true." I point to the other scene in my script. "Are you doing this as well?"

I end up having such a good time with Jack that my usual anxieties fade, which is good, since I worked myself into a tizzy on the way up here. Being desperate for the job is the best way to lose one, but it's not easy to drop.

Once we're in the theater, we have them laughing within minutes. And when Miles makes a few suggestions, I'm able to shift gears without overanalyzing everything.

Things don't go as well when they have me read with a different actor in the role of Bruce. This guy doesn't introduce himself, as if he's so famous I should know who he is. I can't get eye contact during the scene, and he doesn't react to anything I'm doing. It's so extreme I decide to roll with it and let being ignored get to Prudence. It's a completely different tack and feels wrong after the fun I had with Jack, but what can I do? I have to work with what I'm given.

When they dismiss us without any notes, I'm relieved, even as I hope that I didn't just shoot myself in the foot. Out in the lobby, I'm surprised—and dismayed, if I'm honest—to see Rhonda Williams. She played the other heroine in *Two Gents* this fall, and Will told me that she won the role of Ophelia.

Instead of me.

"Hey, Jess! Are you called back for Prudence too?"

"I am." I nod, trying not to let my disappointment show. Rhonda is uber-talented. Could she possibly do this show as well as *Hamlet*? Or would she turn down *Hamlet* to do this?

"Miles directed me in a musical over the summer," she continues. "He's really great to work with."

Rhonda's sweet smile and enthusiastic hug make me feel guilty. It's not her fault I'm getting old. I put on my coat and gather my things to make a dignified exit before I say something crabby, but as I reach the door, I hear my name.

"Jess, can you hang on a sec?" Larry calls. "We'd like to read you with someone else, but he's running late. Can you stay?"

I check my watch. "Um, sure. How long do you think? I might

grab something to eat." I don't want to hang around and run into other potential competition.

"We just got a message that he left a shoot down in Needham, so it'll be a good hour."

I hike my bag back up on my shoulder. "Great. I'll be back at noon."

"That'll work. Thanks for being flexible."

"Of course." I finish buttoning up my coat. "Good luck, Rhonda."

"Thanks, you too!"

Not gonna be a bitch. Not going to resent her unlined face. But seriously? Why would they call her back for Prudence, who's supposed to be a Jewish New Yorker in her thirties?

I'm too nervous to eat now. Coffee'd be even worse.

When I step outside, I'm hit with a brisk wind. Snow might be on the way. Wrapping a scarf around my neck and pulling on my hat, I head downtown. At least I don't have to worry about my hair frizzing. It might even help. May as well get as far from Rhonda's cherubic good looks as possible. A red runny nose and Rosanne Rosannadanna hair might be selling points.

Keeping up a brisk pace to warm up as well as walk off the nerves, I remind myself that every audition is a chance to practice my craft, whether I get the part or not. I can't control the director's choices; I can only control the choices I make.

Just as the biting wind has me thinking about turning back around, a softly lit shop window catches my eye. Stepping inside the cozy interior, I'm rewarded with a wide selection of tea to choose from. My hands around a steaming mug of peppermint, I sit down and breathe in the bright scent, consciously erasing my worries.

Just because I'm newly and unexpectedly unemployed, just because I lost the last role I went for, just because my life is starting to feel out of control. Doesn't mean I have to give in to the negative obsessions that plagued me when I was a teenager.

After all, this is supposed to be fun. It's called a play for a reason.

HOURS LATER, by the time I drop my bag and shuck off my shoes inside my crappy little apartment, I am wrung out. But in a good way, like I've played through every emotion in my range, and then some.

The guy they had me wait around for was super fun to read with. Thankfully, he isn't competing with Jack. Seriously, if they don't hire Jack for the role of Bruce, they're idiots. Instead, this other guy, Timothy, was up for Stuart, a therapist who sleeps with his patients. He was perfectly nice when we chatted in the lobby, but man, could he play a slimeball. Grease practically dripped out of his mouth when he talked.

Miles stopped us to give direction over and over again. At first I was worried, like we weren't getting it right, but then it was like we had the parts and rehearsal had begun.

Yet again, it's too cold in my apartment to take my coat off. Two calls to the super haven't resulted in a working heater. My sister says that I wouldn't be so cold all the time if I had more body fat. She is a pediatrician and would probably know, but what she doesn't get is that actresses can't be fat. Especially actresses like me with outsized knockers that make me look heavier than I am. Heading to the kitchen to make hot tea, I side-eye the blinking answering machine. It may be small, but it has the power to change my life. Or at least my plans for the next few months. Not quite ready to face the unknown, I turn on the kettle and the radio and dance my ass off while I wait for the water to boil.

Two songs later, I've Flashdanced myself around the apartment long enough that I can take off my coat. After I pour the hot water over a tea bag, I take a deep breath and press the play button.

BEEP. Jess, this is Esther. We're doing the last night of Hannukah here Sunday, and the girls are really hoping you'll be there. Gabe and Rachel are coming, and Mom and Dad of course. So we'll see you? Call me.

Hannukah at my sister's tomorrow. I jot that down in my calendar. Since my brother and his fiancée will be there, I can't skip it. Good thing I thought ahead and picked up some presents for my nieces.

BEEP. Hi, this is for Jessica Abraham. I'm calling from Jay Fowler's office. We want to bring you in for a commercial next week. I have you slotted in for Monday at noon. Please call to confirm.

Well, that's good news. A break in the drought. And I can usually squeeze in a noon audition over my lunch break. Guess I won't have to worry about that anymore come January.

BEEP. Hello Jessica, this is Carol from Chichester Rep. I'm happy to say that we'd like to offer you the role of Prudence in Beyond Therapy. Rehearsals begin after the new year, but please give me a call Monday to confirm and go over details. Congratulations. We're looking forward to working with you.

Glee races through my torso. Fuck the neighbors and these paper-thin walls. I turn up the music and let my limbs celebrate this win all over the apartment.

Maybe this old woman's career isn't over after all.

Chapter 4

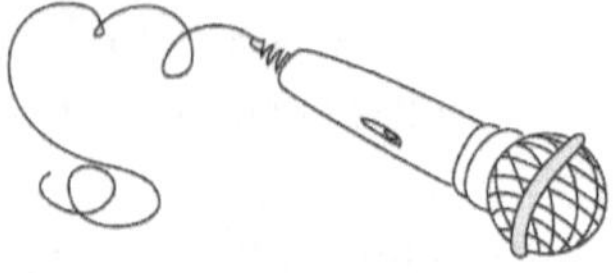

**It's Tuesday, January third in the last year of the eighties.
Still getting used to that. Cal Alonso here at WBAR to keep
you night owls company. Weatherman tells me the skies
are clear but the roads are still icy from the weekend
storm, so be careful out there kids.**

JESS

By the time I get on the road after my first rehearsal at Chichester
Rep, the highway's free of cars. The trip back is shorter than the trip
up, but it feels longer. My day started way too many hours ago. I'll
miss the kids when my job ends in a couple weeks, but it'll be nice to
get to sleep in a bit.

At least the good radio station's signal sticks with me for the
whole trip. Singing and car-dancing keeps me awake, and the sexy-
sounding DJ is an added bonus. This guy rocks.

Just as I pull into my apartment parking lot, he asks a trivia question that I actually know the answer to. I figure the odds of winning
are low, but the cold night air has me sprinting from my car to my
apartment anyway, so I may as well try for it.

"Come on, come on, you stupid door." Sticky lock conquered, I race to the phone. The station's phone number was seared into my memory the moment his growly voice recited it, so I punch in the numbers with confidence. When I get ringing instead of the usual busy signal, I do a little battement dégagé in celebration.

"Yello, it's WBAR." The guy who answers is definitely not the DJ. He sounds like he's about twelve. "What's the pencil sketch technique used in the 'Take on Me' music video?"

"Rotoscoping."

"Righteous. You won the Tower Records gift certificate."

"Awesome! I've never won anything before."

"Tight." He doesn't sound anywhere near as excited as I am. "Okay, uh... I need to get your name and address so we can send it to you."

After I give him the info, I ask, "Hey, can you give the DJ a message for me?"

"A message?" I sure hope he's not twelve. He sounds totally stoned.

"Can you thank him for me? He totally saved me from crashing into a ditch or something tonight. I have this new, long commute, and—"

"You know what? You tell him. Hang on."

The heat is supposed to be fixed, so I try to reach the thermostat while I'm on hold. Unfortunately, the phone cord doesn't quite reach. I'm about to put the receiver down when the voice from the radio lands in my ear.

"Cal here."

"Oh, hi." My heart jumps along with my feet as they fly into a changement. "You're really... Callihan?"

"Speaking."

"Thanks for—Um, aren't you, like, on the air?"

"There's a song playing right now."

"Oh, duh. I get it. I was listening in the car, but I ran into my apartment to call in for the contest." *Why am I being such a Joanie right now? Boys never make me nervous.* "Anyway, I wanted to thank you. I have this new job an hour's drive away and I hate driving at night and you totally kept me from falling asleep on the way home and crashing my car on Route 3. So… thanks. I just wanted to say that."

"I'm glad you did." There's a smile in his voice. Hopefully, he's not laughing at me. But I wouldn't blame him.

"Okay, well." A ridiculous-sounding giggle chirps out of me. "Thanks again."

"Wait. Do you work this late all week?"

"Um, yeah. Tuesday to Friday."

"So you'll call again tomorrow."

"What if I don't know the answer?"

"The answer to what?"

"To the trivia question."

"That doesn't matter. You can call anytime."

"Even if there's not a contest?"

"Even if there's not a contest." When I don't say anything, he adds, "If you don't call, I'll worry."

"Oh, gotcha. Well, good night."

"Wait—what's your name?"

"Jessica. Jess. Either one."

"Good night, Jess. Sleep well."

"You, too. I mean, when you get to. Not now. Silly me. You're working."

"Doing what I can." When he laughs, the rumble rolls into my ear and rushes all the way to my lower belly, flooding me with… I don't know. The vibrations are like a massage from the inside.

Damn. Now I'm more riled up than when I ran in the door. As I skip across the room, the hum of the dial tone makes me realize that I've still got the receiver pressed to my ear.

After setting it back in its cradle, I move through a series of pliés, kicks and extensions to wind down as well work off the time I spent sitting at rehearsal and in the car. When my teaching job ends, I'm going to have to try and pick up more classes at the studio where I teach jazz on Monday nights—both for the cash and to stay in shape. Meanwhile, I may not have normal furniture, but I do have a beautifully crafted ballet barre in my living room, which I use more than I'd ever use a couch.

Discipline, my constant companion, guides me through my bedtime routine.

Skin care. Water. Sleep.

As I slide into dreamland, a question pops into my mind. *I wonder if that DJ looks as sexy as he sounds?*

THE NEXT NIGHT, the drive home from Chichester seems shorter, maybe because I'm jazzed about how well rehearsal went. It's so different working on a contemporary play—less time sitting at the table parsing words and more time on our feet trying stuff out.

I must admit, I'm also looking forward to talking to Cal again. I may have pretended I was talking to him on the way home. Every time he asked a question on air, I answered him out loud. As if he could hear me.

But when I get back into my apartment and turn on the radio and shimmy around my kitchen as I wait for the apartment and the kettle to heat up, I lose momentum. He was probably just being nice last night. He doesn't really want me to call again. He probably tells girls that all the time.

I've convinced myself not to do it when I hear him say my name.

"Hey, Jessica. Jessica who won the trivia contest last night? You need to call me so I know you're not in a snowbank on the side of Route 3." Then he rattles off the station number.

I guess he did mean it. I should let him know I'm not dead. When I get through this time, a woman answers.

Suddenly, I'm not sure what to say. She sounds older and a lot less friendly than the kid last night.

"Anybody there?"

"Sorry, uh. This is Jessica? I'm calling because Cal asked me to?" *Now who's doing the uptalking?*

The woman barks out the dry laugh of a lifetime smoker. "Thank god you called, hon. He's going nuts here. Hang on."

Seconds of hold music later, he picks up. "I thought you were dead."

The tension in his voice squeezes my chest so tight I have to force out my answer. "I thought you were kidding."

"Why would you think that?"

"Because, I don't know, you're working?"

"You don't talk to people on the phone when you're at work?"

"Not really?"

"Well, not knowing if you're alive or not is really distracting. So, you're going to have to call." He clears his throat. "You didn't get your license last week or something, right?"

"No. I'm, uh, a few years beyond sixteen."

He must hear annoyance in my voice because he comes right back with, "I'm going to worry either way. I just want to know how *much* I should worry."

"You don't have to worry. I grew up in Boston, and I've been driving in the weather for some time. I'm legal, but I don't drink and drive. But wait, what if I go out after work?"

"Use a payphone."

He's obviously very serious about this. "Do you worry about every girl who's out driving late?"

"I worry about everybody out driving late. I feel like part of my job is keeping everybody awake who needs to be." His sincerity softens my skeptical heart, but before I can promise that I'll call again he says, "Uh, I have to cue up some songs but I'll be back. Can you hang on?"

"Um, okay."

I guess instead of hold music, the station somehow plays what's on air because I turned down the radio before I called but now I hear not only music but Cal's patter through the phone. Even though I'm feeling the long day, my hips keep time to the beat as I wait.

"Still there?"

"Still here," I answer over a stifled yawn.

"Am I keeping you up?"

"Sorry. Kind of."

"No problem, I'll let you go."

The candid disappointment in his tone has me switching gears. "Well, I can talk for a bit. I do have to get up early for work but I'm also pretty buzzed when I get home. It takes me a while to wind down."

"From the drive?"

"The drive and, like, being on."

"What is it you do up there an hour's drive away?"

"I'm an actress. I'm rehearsing a play up in Chichester."

"Oh, I thought you were a nurse for some reason. On a split shift."

"Ha. Nope. Nobody would want me to be their nurse."

"Why not?"

"I can't deal with hospitals. I had some… icky experiences when I was younger."

"Huh. Me too." There's a long silence before he speaks again. In the background, the song ends and a commercial starts. "So, how do you usually wind down?"

"Um… have a cup of herbal tea." Holding the phone cord out of the way, I do a few développés as I comb my brain. "Watch stupid TV. Read a book. Sometimes I work on choreography for my classes till I'm exhausted. I also teach dance to kids. For the next couple weeks, anyway."

"How come only for a few weeks?"

"I got fired. They replaced me with an aerobics teacher." I'm talking about myself too much. Guys don't like that, so I switch lanes. "Long story. What do you do after work?"

"That's another long story, maybe for another night. I gotta go spin some records now."

"Okay. 'Play "Misty" for me.'" It's weird flirting when I can't see how my words land, but I'm rewarded with a groan at my silly joke. "Sorry, couldn't resist."

"Seriously, any real requests?"

"Hmm. How about 'Like to Get to Know You Well' by Howard Jones?"

A surprising bellow of laugh lands in my ear.

"What's so funny?"

"Oh, it's something about my sister and her husband. They were dating when that song was getting a lot of play. Every time it came on, they'd race to say, 'I'd like to get to know you' with a pause before the 'well' as if they were having second thoughts."

"But they did?"

"Did what?"

"Get to know each other well?"

"I hope so. They have a baby now."

"Okay. Play that song for me."

"I will. And you'll call tomorrow? Or I'll be forced to play every song with the name Jessica in it until you do."

My words ride a laugh as I promise to call. "Good night, Cal."

"Good night, Jess."

After I hang up, I turn the radio back up—not so loud that it'll wake the neighbors, but enough so I'll have a chance to hear his voice again.

Then it hits me. He has no idea what I look like. He never even asked anything like *What are you wearing?*

I can't conjure a picture of him, either. But Cal's voice? It sneaks down my nerve endings and stirs up some serious giddiness. A feeling I could get addicted to.

CAL

I'd like to get to know you well, she said.

Same here is what I should've said. If I knew how to talk to a girl. Instead, I told her some stupid-ass story about my sister.

"Am I an idiot or what, Blondie?"

One thing about having visible scars? Sometimes you can get away with shit other people can't. Like bringing your dog to work.

Or to the bar around the corner, which is where the two of us are headed right now.

At the end of every shift, we head over here. By the time I push open the heavy door, the place is officially closed, but the owner's an old friend who lets us in anyway. I take my usual seat at the far end of the bar where a sweating beer glass waits for me.

"Hey, Phil."

"Morning, Cal. Got a nice brisket sandwich tonight."

I nod. "Sounds great."

He nods back. "And you're up for taking the leftovers again?"

"Yep. The guys count on me."

"You know I like that the food's not going to waste, but you don't have to—"

"It's not like I have anything else to do right now. I'll take them."

Phil shrugs and pushes back into the kitchen. I sneak a few pretzels to Blondie. Once she's wolfed them down, she settles onto the floor with a grunt.

So, this girl. Jess.

People call. Sometimes people call a few times, even call back after a few weeks, and I remember them. Sometimes they need to talk, to tell their stories. I'm a good listener.

But this girl? I want to tell her *my* story.

And believe me, that never happens.

Who'd want to hear my story? My sad sack of a story? Nobody, that's who.

Phil slides my dinner across the bar. I share it with the dog. After I finish my beer, we head out. Since my hands are full, I don't bother with a leash. Blondie knows the routine, anyway.

I've always walked her after my shift. One night last summer, I saw a couple of cops hassling a panhandler. It bothered me, so I asked Phil what he did with his food waste at the end of the night.

Throw it away, he sighed. *Then chase dumpster divers away from it.* I figured I could kill a couple of birds with one stone by delivering the leftovers to people who are hungry. So far, the system seems to be working. We do have to make sure the health department doesn't hear about it because they'd shut the thing down.

Blondie shadows me as we head down an alley between Fenway Park and the gardens to a spot where a group of homeless guys regularly set up. I leave a couple bags with Walt, who'll share the food with warier guys. We chat for a few minutes, and I ask if he needs anything. Like always, he says no. I carry the others up to a camp under the Storrow Drive underpass to leave them with the usual suspects, and then Blondie and I walk home.

It's wicked cold tonight. I wish these guys would go to a shelter, but I get it. Some people just don't fit in. At least when I go back to my warm loft, I know they have food in their bellies.

Back at my building, Blondie and I take the elevator instead of the stairs since there's no chance of meeting anybody at this hour. Another beer for me, fresh water for her, food for the cat and I flop on the couch. I should go to bed, but that girl Jessica's voice won't stop tickling my brain. Something about it. It's musical, but not in a fake way. A rollercoaster of expression. I can't even imagine the face that'd match that voice. Full of life. Meeting the world head-on.

Blondie's wet nose worms its way under my wrist. She knows the spots that get my attention, that I can feel without her having to press through scars.

Stroking her soft fur, I mumble, "Yeah, okay. Bedtime." She steps back, wiggling, and bumps into the coffee table. "You goon. You've got to be careful when you only got one eye."

My body practically creaks out loud as I stand, slowly stretching tight skin, hoping to avoid shadow pain. A yawn takes over. Maybe I'll get to sleep quickly tonight.

Jessica's voice in my ear soothes my soul in a way not even music can is my last thought before I slip into sleep.

Chapter 5

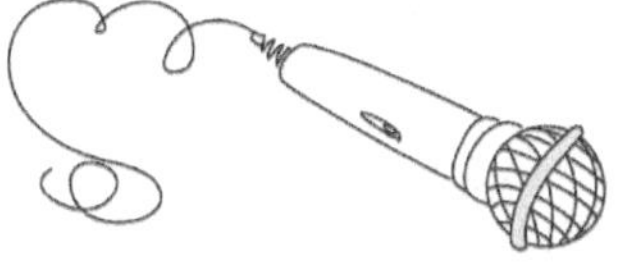

**Warning-warning-warning. You've entered the CAL-zone.
BWAH-HA-HA-HA. Cal Alonso, rocking your Friday night.
It's ten fifteen at 101.7. Up next, I've got the live version of
U2's "Bad" from the *Wide Awake in America* EP. Get ready
for a full eight minutes of a band on fire.**

JESS

I swear Cal plays upbeat songs from ten to eleven for me—to keep me awake as I drive home—but maybe that's being a bit too self-centered.

"Hey, who was singing that song with the 'Deh-buh-bee-buh-bop?' Is it called 'Don't Let's Start'?" I ask when he gets on the line.

"Yeah, that was They Might Be Giants."

"Oh man, I wish I'd known about them earlier. I think the kids in my classes would've liked them."

"Their lyrics are pretty silly."

"It's so fun. A bit different for you, right?"

"You've been paying attention."

"I might be analyzing your choices, yes." I put on a fake Austrian accent to play psychiatrist. "Tell me about your childhood. Vaht made you vant to be a… disc yawkey? Iss dat how you say?"

He snorts out a laugh. "My life isn't that interesting."

Dropping the accent, I switch tacks. "To you, maybe. Probably a lot of people think that. But I'm a Sag so I'm curious."

"Sag?"

"Sagittarius."

"How did you get into acting?"

"Nope, no fair. No throwing it back to me." I swear I've never known a guy who talks about himself less than this one. "It's all Cal, all the time, on this call. Come on. You're a DJ. That is very cool."

"Nah, it's just a lot of pushing buttons."

"You have to know a lot about music."

"Yeah, but that's easy. I'm interested in it. Anybody could do what I do."

"Not me."

"Why not?"

"I'm sure I would push the wrong buttons. I can't even get the stereo at the school to play half the time. At least I don't have to worry about that anymore."

"You're finished?"

"Yep. Today was my last day."

"Is that a good thing or a bad thing?"

"I don't know. I mean, I cried. I cry at everything, though. The huge bouquet of flowers that some of the moms got me is sitting on my kitchenette bar right now, and I can't even look at it without my eyes leaking. Even though it was mostly aerobics this year, I'm really going to miss the kids."

"What will you miss about them?"

"Kids are refreshing. They say what they think."

"Yeah, that's the problem." His voice shifts into a new gear and I think I hear a note of bitterness. "Kids can be cruel."

"It sounds like you speak from experience."

"Yeah." Definitely bitter. "Uh, hang on. I'll be back."

I'm wondering what nerve I hit as I listen to Cal talk—not to me but to all of Boston. I'm still not used to the transition when he switches from one mode to the other. When he announces that the next song is "If You Were Here" by the Thompson Twins, his voice still sounds a bit off, but he doesn't miss a beat.

"Hey, I'm back. Sorry."

"Don't apologize. I mean, I hope I'm not distracting you."

"It's fine."

Definitely not fine. "So, you were saying?"

"I… don't remember. We were talking about your teaching job ending."

"Right." Interesting sidestep. "Well, something I learned from teaching is that the meanest kids are usually the ones who are hurting the most."

"Huh."

"Kids don't cover up their feelings, at least the younger ones. When they're excited, it's full-on. Or sad, or mad. I love getting them to channel all that energy into dance. Even the shy ones, the ones who don't talk. They might not have words for their feelings but their bodies express it for them. I had choreography and a plan for every class, but half the time I'd make something up on the spot to, like, move the feelings around. Does that make sense?"

"Not really, but… well, maybe. I mean, I think I get what you're talking about, but I can't even begin to imagine how you do that."

"Well, do you spin at clubs too?"

"Yeah, some."

"You probably go in with a plan, right?"

"Right."

"So if people are really into a vibe, you don't take a left turn into another one just because that was the plan."

"I guess not."

"That's what I mean."

"I guess I do—Shit. Something's—Fuck. Something's, uh, wrong on one of the meters. I have to go. I've got a problem here I have to figure out. Call me tomorrow?"

"Are you working tomorrow?"

"Oh, right. No. Uh. Shit, I really have to go. I guess I'll talk to you Monday."

"Okay, bye."

Seems like something I said really threw him off.

Makes me wonder what names little Cal got called.

And if they were similar to the ones hurled at me.

SATURDAY MORNING I have to skip my favorite ballet class so I can get to the theater for a costume fitting before rehearsal. Not an equal tradeoff. Not only do I hate missing the workout, but costume fittings are never fun. Either they treat you like just another dress dummy or they fawn over you with fake compliments. When I walk into the costume shop only a few minutes late, the frowns on the faces of the designer and head seamstress threaten to turn this one into a death spiral.

But a genuine smile blooms on the face of the older woman when she sees me. "Come in, my darling. I am Anya." The seamstress's Russian accent is as charming as her sparkling blue eyes. "Welcome to my domain." A gnarled hand tucks a lock of steel gray hair behind her ear before sweeping over the well-organized room. From the sewing machines to the cutting tables, from dress forms to neatly labeled boxes stacked on shelves, everything seems to be in order.

Wanda, the designer, looks up briefly before tracing a finger over one of the sketches on the table. "We have a challenge here." Her already strained smile presses into a flat line. "Make you plain."

I shrug out of my coat and give it to Anya when she holds out her hands. "What do you mean? Miles didn't say anything about that. I mean, I know he doesn't want Prudence to be too sexy, but... plain?" I aim for a light laugh as I step closer to get a look at the sketches, but even I can hear the panic rising in my voice.

Wanda adjusts the scrunchie holding flyaway blonde hair in a high ponytail, obviously a nervous habit. "We had a design meeting this morning. He thinks you'll be funnier if you're not quite so attractive."

Bile rises from my empty stomach. Going onstage without the armor of good makeup and a nice costume to prop up my appearance feels worse than going onstage naked. People don't come to the theater to see ugly women.

Wanda groans from behind a rack of dresses. "Believe me, I'm not happy about it. We'd already done some shopping for you." She pulls a dress, shakes her head, puts it back. "Now I have to start from scratch."

Anya waves an elegant hand, her voice riding a resigned smile. "Me too."

"Me three." I can't keep the growl out of my voice.

It's still early in the process, so I don't quite feel like I own the character. When I try to picture Prudence, it's like she's across the room, rather than in the mirror. Closing my eyes, I try to picture her the first time she walks into the restaurant for a blind date. Is it that Prudence thinks she's attractive but she's not? Or does she try too hard and make choices that don't work for her?

Or is she brave enough to be who she is? I'm not sure I can wrap my head around that point of view. To leave the house without applying makeup and styling my hair, without covering my room with discarded outfits because nothing can ever quite fix my body's silhouette...

But that's me, not Prudence.

I take a deep breath. There's no way out of this but forward. "Okay. What's she going to look like?"

By the end of the fitting, I'm actually kind of excited. Anya clucks a bit, saying it's a sin to cover up such a perfect figure. I don't contradict her, even though I know she must be lying. My tits are totally out of proportion to the rest of my body. When Anya finds a dress for me to wear at rehearsals that fits all wrong, along with a sports bra that makes my breasts spread out, the look is so far from my own that it kind of feels safe, like a full body mask that hides my flaws by creating different ones.

Then there's my hair, the one part of my body that I love. The hair that more than one acting teacher has called a crutch. One even went so far as to challenge me to cut it off to see if I could act without it.

Anya, Wanda and I head into a dressing room to try out some options. We all agree that a bun and glasses are too cliche. When Anya separates my curls to create a thick braid down my back, her touch is comforting, reminding me of my mother's. She slides a wool cap on and off a few times, and the frizz it creates is classic. Suddenly I'm awkward-looking in a way that I can see supporting the humor of the play. I promise to play around with makeup, too, to go for the *Don't* choices in *Cosmo* instead of the *Dos*.

My acting job starts here. I need to pretend that I feel good about this choice. It might pay off, anyway. Maybe I'll actually have a success based solely on my craft. And if I fail, well, I doubt anyone but locals will see the show. Nobody of importance is going to make the trip up here from Boston, especially in winter. "This could be fun."

Wanda taps Anya on the shoulder. "I win. I told you she wouldn't be a diva about it."

Anya gives me a nod of appreciation. "I admit it, I am pleasantly surprised." She pats me on the shoulder. "No actress wants to look bad onstage. But you get it. We all want the look to work, to make your job easier."

Standing, I check my unfamiliar profile in the three-way mirror. "As Hamlet says, 'There is nothing either good or bad but thinking makes it so.'"

Wanda winks at me before closing up her portfolio of drawings. "Miles was afraid to tell you himself. He made us do it."

A flash of anger sparks, but I extinguish it with a sigh. "I can hardly blame him. I spend an awful lot of time and money on my appearance." When I check my reflection in the mirror, Prudence's poor choices distract me from zeroing in on my wrinkles and breasts. I have to admit it's a bit of a relief. "Maybe this old dog can learn some new tricks."

Anya laughs. "Pah! Old dog. Get out of here, you spring chicken."

A little shiver of anticipation mixes with fear of the unknown and zips through me. Unchartered territory.

Kind of like what's going on between Cal and me.

THERE'S a different DJ on WBAR as I drive home from rehearsal late Saturday afternoon. I never paid much attention to the person talking between the songs before, but I miss Cal's voice. Turning off the radio, I try to talk myself into calling one of my friends to see what they have going on tonight, but once I'm home staring at my phone, I can't quite get myself to do it. In the past we'd all head out together at the end of a day of rehearsal, making plans as we went.

I could call my friend Bella. She's not in *Hamlet* either, but she does have a kid and would have to pay for a sitter.

While I'm wishing I knew how to contact Cal and wondering what fabulous plans he might have tonight—probably at some club or concert—the phone rings. Thinking that Cal might have somehow gotten a hold of my number even though it's unlisted, I pick up instead of letting the machine get it first.

Unfortunately, it's not Cal. It's this guy Charles that I met at a bar when I was out with teacher friends back in December. He's hot. He likes to say I'm hot. He has work contacts that get us into the hottest restaurants.

Everything else between us is ice cold, however. I slept with him after the first date because, you know, a guy treats you to a meal at a fancy place and you feel obligated to put out.

Plus, I usually like sex. I didn't with Charles. He took the quid-pro-quo thing to a whole new level, like I was literally there to service him. I don't know why I slept with him a second time. I guess I'm a Pollyanna that way. I like to give people the benefit of the doubt. Maybe he'd had a bad day or had performance anxiety the first time. It was marginally better, but only because he came so fast and was out the door even faster.

Normally I wouldn't go out with any guy on such short notice, but Charles can be persuasive. He says something about a guy from work who had reservations at this new place that it takes months to get into but his girlfriend got sick. Probably whoever Charles asked out first got sick, but whatever. It's not like I have other plans.

Later though, in the car on the way back from the restaurant, I'm wishing I hadn't said yes. Wishing I'd pushed through the awkwardness and called a friend instead.

It's not like I could even eat half the food. Charles must've mentioned my "hot bod" about fifty thousand times, which made me feel self-conscious, like I shouldn't eat because thin girls don't eat, so I only took two bites of everything.

Hearing that I'm hot or sexy or gorgeous—those words have always been so important to me. The power of seducing a guy has always been intoxicating.

Something's changed.

And it's not just about turning thirty.

As we take the Allston exit from the Mass Pike, a warm, masculine voice breaks into my thoughts, and it's not the guy driving me home. Without asking permission, even though Charles is ridiculously protective of his car stereo, I turn up the volume on the radio.

"It's a nippy twenty-five degrees under clear skies right now, or so they tell me. Your weeknight jock Callihan here, subbing in on a Saturday night. So tell me: What's happening, Boston? Are you heading to Spit or leaving the Bruins game? I'll keep you company whether you're staying in or going to a party. Let's kick it off with 'Rescue Me' by the Alarm."

I'm wishing Cal would rescue *me*, when I realize he already has. The sound of his voice makes me realize that not only do I not owe Charles anything, I don't particularly like him.

The moment we pull up in front of my apartment building, I open the door before Charles can even get the car in park. "Thanks, man. That was great."

His lips flatten into a thin line. "I don't get to come in? What the fuck?"

"Sorry, I'm super tired and I have an early call tomorrow."

"Can't we have sex? I'll leave right after."

Pushing the apology trying to escape past my lips to the side, I make myself say, "Nope. Gotta go to bed. Good night."

Unfortunately, my clean exit is foiled by a tangled purse strap. When I turn around to free it from the car, Charles grabs my wrist. "Come on, Jess. You're so smokin' in that dress; you've had me riled up all night."

"I said no. No, thank you," I add with a forced smile. When he doesn't let go, I enunciate even more clearly. "Did you not hear what I said, Charles?"

"But I'm hard as a rock," he whines. "You dress like you do, a guy expects to get laid."

"So I'm a call girl now? You bought dinner, so I owe you sex? If that's the situation, I'm going to have to raise my prices."

"Jesus, you don't have to be a bitch about it." Tightening his grip, he twists my wrist to pull me back into the car.

"Let me *go*." Yanking back so hard that both his grip and my purse strap break, I almost fall off my heels. Once I've caught my balance, I growl, "Don't call me again. Ever."

After slamming the door in his face, I race up the steps and into the building. I don't stop until I'm inside my apartment, deadbolt locked. Heart thudding in my chest, legs shaking, I drop my ruined purse on the floor and struggle out of my coat.

Heading straight to the bathroom, I turn the shower on full bore, needing to get the stink of Charles off me. It's only when I collapse onto my bed in my flannel pjs that I hear Cal's voice again, coming through the tinny speaker of my clock radio. Pulling a blanket around me, I turn it up and let the tears flow.

I can't call him now. I don't want him to hear me like this. I can keep listening to his soothing voice, though. As the sobs subside, I silently thank him for watching over me.

Chapter 6

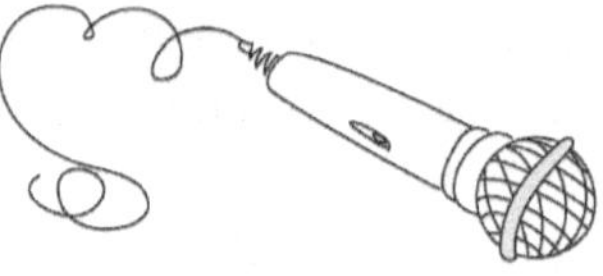

Nigel here this Sunday afternoon on WBAR and I've got the Beatles' "Every Little Thing" for your listening pleasure.

CAL

Driving home from Sunday dinner with my family, it occurs to me for the first time how alone I am. I've always felt cocooned by my family, but in a good way, not an isolating one.

Neither my parents nor my siblings have ever shown the tiniest bit of resentment toward me, even though I sucked up way more than my share of attention and resources growing up. It took hundreds of hours and thousands of dollars to get me through surgery after surgery. At some point, the Shriners began picking up my bills, but the nurses always had to kick my parents out of my room in the hospital to make them go home and rest. At school, my brothers did their best to protect me from bullies. I'm more of the family baby than my baby sister.

My family is everything to me.

For the first time, I'm wondering if that's a problem.

My siblings have all paired off and have their own families.

They're adults. I may have the body of a thirty-two-year-old man, but inside? I'm a little kid who never really left the nest.

I don't think they worry about me. It probably seems like I'm doing well enough. I make a decent living at a job that I'm good at in a hugely competitive field. I've got a big loft apartment in downtown Boston, great co-workers, and friends all over the world, if you count pen pals.

So far, I've had no reason to leave the comfy cocoon that is my life. I mean, I know better than most that when bandages get ripped off before the skin underneath is fully healed, the pain is horrendous.

Unfortunately, those wounds might get exposed sooner than I'd like. Jones is still bugging me about stepping up my game, adding something to my slot that'll attract more listeners, but I don't know what someone like me can do. Grace practically hosts a party during her shift. Drive-time DJ Motor trades jokes with the headlining comics who visit him when they roll into town. "Morning Guy" Guy does massive promos, like last summer when he gave away a car by broadcasting from said car while it dangled from a crane hundreds of feet in the air over the Charles River.

How do I compete with that?

I can't see myself getting up in front of hundreds of people like Special Kay and Nigel do when they introduce bands at live shows, but according to Jones, I have to do something to up ratings.

The other change I never saw coming? Jess. I've never been so nervous and excited about anything as I am about her call each night. It's all I've been thinking about since Friday. I even took the extra shift last night, hoping she'd call. And you wouldn't believe the what-ifs buzzing around inside my skull, taunting me. *What if there's a chance she and I could actually have something together? What if I could have a real relationship like my siblings and parents do?*

The only way I can see that happening? Get her to fall in love with me on the phone. If I can be her knight in shining armor five nights a week for long enough, then maybe by the time we meet and she finds out I'm a prince stuck in the body of a frog, she'll accept the real me.

Yeah, I know.

Who am I kidding?

"ALL RIGHT, you assholes, I don't have all day here."

That's how Jones kicks off the music meeting every Monday morning. Or afternoon, rather. It's two o'clock, but it feels like morning to me. Attendance at the meeting isn't required and Weird Wayne rarely shows because of his two-to-six-a.m. shift time, but I make it a priority to be here so I can have some influence on what gets played across the station's programming.

It also makes me feel like I'm part of a team. The DJs in this room are a relatively diverse group, not only diverse in musical taste—though we do challenge each other and cover the whole spectrum of rock music—but also by gender, race, sexuality and even generation. Not many rock stations have a woman with her own slot—they're usually a sidekick—but we have two and they couldn't be more different. Special Kay (call her Karen, her given name, at your peril) has helped make the careers of female-fronted bands like Roxette. Right now she's all about some group from the Midwest nobody's heard of called Babes in Toyland.

A Red Sox cap frames Kay's pale face and stringy brown hair. Like most of the guys, she's always in jeans and band T-shirts. Gracie's style is at the other end of the spectrum. She's a Deborah Harry-inspired party girl with bleached hair, funky glasses and funkier outfits. Then there's Motor, who's never not in a suit. Not the stuffy-old-man kind, though. He dresses in homage to his hero, David Bowie. Motor's a people collector, so it's a party during his drivetime shifts, from an evolving crew of pretty young things—both male and female—to the comics who stop by. This week he interviewed local Paula Poundstone and an up-and-coming comic in town on tour. I think his name was Jerry Steinfeld. Or Seinfeld? I don't pay much attention to the comedy circuit so I've never heard of him, but Motor says he's got a boss new style.

Nigel, who came to the States from England to study and never got around to leaving, is the darkest skinned of us all. I'm probably next in line on that scale. What's left of my original skin color is the swarthy brown of my Portuguese and black Irish heritage. Nigel's also the most well-spoken and definitely the smartest at the table. After he and Jones made a sensation at Northeastern University's radio station, they quickly climbed the ranks here. Most people have no idea that Nigel's black because he sounds like he was raised by the Queen herself. Elizabeth, not the band. At the moment, he's impatiently flipping through a stack of albums—probably new music he can't wait to bring to our attention.

Finally, an enthusiastic whoop from Guy followed by a groan from Big Bob means that the hallway whiffle ball game is over, so the meeting can begin.

When the players enter, Jones rolls his eyes. Guy—aka "Morning Guy" Guy—high-fives everyone within reach before taking a seat. You'd never know the guy is almost forty with a wife and kids. He *is* a big kid.

Grace leans back in her chair and props her thigh-high boots on the table. Jones gives her a look but doesn't say anything. Instead, he hands out the week's playlists before reading a memo from corporate re keeping the on-air shenanigans rated PG.

Guy nods enthusiastically and straightens the satin station jacket he's never without. The WBAR logo is emblazoned across the back, and his name's embroidered over his heart. I have one too, but I never wear it. Too likely to garner attention. Motor grumbles about how the shock jocks on our rival station manage to get away with all kinds of R-rated crapola. He has a right to be pissed. They've done a number on him lately—outing him as gay and stirring up hatred about it. No one here gives a shit about his sexuality, but he's been getting ugly letters and phone calls.

I can't even imagine what those jerks over there would say about me.

My contemplation of that scenario is interrupted by Gracie's hand waving in front of my face.

"Earth to Cal?"

"Sorry, what'd I miss?"

"I said, aren't you, like, pen pals with Joe Berg from that Canadian band?"

"Uh, sort of. A Toronto DJ turned me on to them several months ago. Why?"

"Why Not Happiness is playing at The Paradise this week," Jones says, tipping his head toward the window, which has a great view of Lansdowne Street, where it seems like half the clubs in Boston are located. Spit, Metro—they're all within walking distance. We moved to this location from a high-rise further downtown a year ago, and management's been on us to get bands in here to chat or play acoustic sets. Jones knocks on the table. "Think you can get them for an interview?"

The egg sandwich I wolfed down before the meeting turns to cement in my gut. Jones's lifted eyebrows remind me that I need to step up to keep my shift.

I rub the scarred edge of my left eyebrow. A nervous habit. "I'll see what I can do."

Jones smiles. "Great. Keep me posted."

There's no way I won't get the interview since the station has such a good reputation for putting bands on the map. Thing is, I've never done one before. Sinking into my seat, my mind churns with dread while a typical meeting continues around me. Impassioned arguments about songs moving in and out of rotation are punctuated by various objects flying across the table, from plush puffins—our station mascot—to balled-up food wrappers.

Big Bob and Special Kay are laughing so hard that they're falling off their chairs when Jones gives up and ends the meeting with his usual call to action. "Get out of here, and don't come back until you've discovered the next big thing."

He catches me in the hall before I can escape to the gym. "You're spinning at Metro this Saturday; don't forget."

I side-eye him. "Can I forget it if I get this interview?"

He shakes his head. "No way. We need all the jocks on tap for this marathon. It's a big publicity opp as well as a fundraiser."

I give him my scariest half-grimace. "Don't worry. I'll be there."

He claps a hand on my shoulder. The right one. Nobody ever touches me on the bad side. "It'll be chill, Cal, you'll see."

"Eat my short, Jones." And then I escape before he can ask me to do anything else.

I GOT the shit beaten out of me on a weekly basis in ninth grade. In fights I picked. When it was kids bullying me, that was one thing. I'd heard all the taunts on the playground all through elementary school. But when my younger sister joined me in junior high, kids picked on Penny because of me. I couldn't have that, so shit went down. I'd go after the tormentor and get walloped. Over and over again.

Against my mom's wishes, my dad took me to the boxing gym his friend Sam ran, and I learned how to fight. I got good. The bullying stopped.

Usually hitting the bag makes me feel good. Even when it hurts.

Some days—like today—I need to feel fresh pain. It cuts through the static of my fucked-up nerve endings. Makes more sense than phantom pain. Clarifies things.

It doesn't make sense to some in my family—in particular, my sister and my mom. They can't believe that I want to inflict pain on myself. But like getting tattoos, this is pain that I get to choose.

After only twenty minutes of punching the bag today, I've had enough. Normally, I go at it until I'm on the verge of getting over-heated, but today I can't seem to focus.

Jones and my boxing coach going at it inside my head probably isn't helping. They're like an angel and devil, one on each shoulder. Except they're both devils.

You can't be completely invisible anymore, Jones says.

Again, Sam bellows. *I don't have time for whiners.*

It'll be chill, jabs Jones.

Turning to the speed ball, I try to show Jones what chill looks like, but Sam doesn't let up.

What I want to see is your fucking elbows up while you hit that bag another fifty times, he yells.

My head drops. My lats scream.

Jones: *We have to do something.*

Sam: *I ain't got all day. I got other assholes to train.*

Drilling into the bag until I'm breathing so hard I taste blood—my fucking elbows high—still doesn't chase away the fear. When I try picturing the band members I have to interview on the surface of the uppercut bag, they laugh at me or turn away in disgust. Like the teenagers did after I shut them up with my fists.

Usually, hitting things eases my rage. Rage at the unfairness of the world—a world that can take away my childhood with a single mistake. A world that would give me a job I love, only to take it away again. A world that teases me with the voice of a woman that I can't stop thinking about, even as I know that there's no way I'll ever be able to meet her in person.

If I'm too chickenshit to interview the members of a band I know everything about, how will I ever summon the courage to meet the girl I've been talking to for a week? A girl who's woken me up like I'm Sleeping Beauty and she's the prince?

That's a good one.

At least I can laugh at myself, right?

I'M STILL GETTING SETTLED behind the mic Monday night when Talia pops up in the window, holds up three fingers and mouths "Jessica."

Surprised that she's calling when it's only just after ten, I can't punch the button fast enough. "Hey. You're early."

"I forgot to tell you we don't rehearse Mondays, so I didn't have to make the drive."

"Oh, good."

"I was just calling to let you know you don't have to worry, so you don't... worry." All it takes is the trill of her laughter to lighten the burdens I've been lugging around all day.

"I'm glad you called. Not because I'd worry. Talking to you is... getting to be one of the best parts of my day."

"Aww, really?"

I can't tell if she's flattered or embarrassed. It would be easier to tell if I could see her face, but then I'd have to deal with her seeing mine. "Yeah, really. Especially today. I'm a little frustrated."

"About what?"

"Hang on a sec, okay? I'm not quite organized here."

"Well, actually, I just got in from teaching dance classes, and I should take a shower."

"Okay, I get it." I suppose I should know better than to tell a girl how much I like her so soon. A cool guy would probably say something about imagining her in the shower, but that feels kind of gross. "I'm sure you have all kinds of things you could be doing other than sitting on hold."

"Believe me, with anybody else's hold music, I can't get off the phone fast enough. I like listening to your music, but I don't want to get chilled. Should've thought of that before I called, I guess."

This time her laugh is definitely embarrassed. Maybe she isn't blowing me off. "Do you want to call back?"

"Yes. I want to call back. In, like, forty-five minutes?"

"Sounds good."

"'K, bye."

It takes me a few moments to come back to earth and remember what it is I'm supposed to be doing here. When I do, I feel the need to change up my plan for the evening. Rereading the list I put together an hour ago, I cross off one angsty song after another. I mean, it's not like I'm going go all Debbie Gibson or Duran Durn here. But instead of "Under the Milky Way" and "A Forest," I'm going to slot in U2's "Desire." I could maybe even get away with Bobby McFerrin and "Don't Worry, Be Happy" on a Monday night. That's the mood I'm in, knowing that Jess wants to be here with me.

Chapter 7

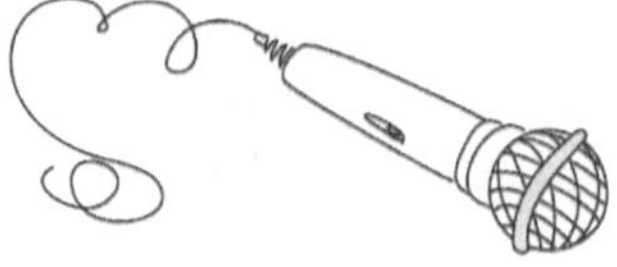

This week on *Hawaii Five-O*, Jack Ward gets his hair shellacked. On *Dallas*, Miss Ellie gets waxed. Or is that whacked? Whatever, all you have to do right now is stick with rock scientist Cal Alonso and his mute sock-puppet sidekick. They'll be back right after this station identification.

JESS

I've decided that Cal and I need to get to know each other. Part of me wishes I knew what he looks like, but at the same time it's nice that he can't see me. Like, right now, my makeup's gone, my hair's in a messy bun and I'm in my rattiest sweats—the ones I can't wear in public because of the mysterious stains on the backside. On the phone with Cal, I can stretch on the floor in comfort while we chat instead of pretending to look interested while a guy talks endlessly about himself. I can be myself.

I play so many roles these days, both on and offstage, that I'm actually not sure I know how to be that girl, but on the phone with Cal feels like a safe place to try.

Cal seemed wary when I suggested we play twenty questions, but

I'm going to do my best to make it fun. "Okay, I'll start. Nothing huge. Just the basics, like what's your favorite TV show? Do you watch TV? Maybe you don't since you work nights."

"I watch sports on weekend afternoons."

"Ugh, sports. Such a guy." I make sure I put a tease in my voice because I know how guys are about their teams. "What about Sunday night? I'm guessing *MacGyver*."

"Actually, I'm kind of a *Moonlighting* fan."

"Really? That is interesting."

"What's so interesting about that?

"It's, you know, romantic." I'd never admit it, but I love a guy with a romantic side.

"Romantic? It's a mystery show."

"Uh-huh. You keep telling yourself that."

"I most certainly will. What about you?" I've always loved how you can hear emotion in a person's voice, but with Cal, I depend on it even more since I can't picture him. Right now, I'm getting a flirty color from him that makes me want more.

Not only is it distracting, I'm stumped for an answer. "I don't know why I asked this question. I barely watch TV because of my schedule. I get home too late."

"Can't you tape shows you want to watch?"

"I could if my VCR wasn't broken. Now I have to wait for my brother to decide he needs the latest model so he'll give me his old one. Meanwhile, I'm stuck watching whatever's on if I want to watch anything."

"What would you be watching if you weren't talking to me?"

"Um, tonight, probably *Thirtysomething*, but I would've missed the first fifteen minutes, so maybe not. I'll have to catch up on the reruns this summer. Otherwise, I'll never know if Hope has another baby or if Nancy and Elliot go through with their divorce, or—"

After his snort of laughter, I go for playful defensiveness. "Are you laughing at me?"

"Of course not."

"Yes, you are."

"I'm not. I have no idea who those people are."

"They're my TV friends. Don't you have TV friends?"

"Yes, but…" Trailing off, he clears his throat.

"Oh, ho. Cal has TV friends he's ashamed of."

When he doesn't say anything, it's my turn to laugh.

Joining me he asks, "Who's laughing at who now?"

"Come on, you have to tell. Is it Big Bird? Oscar the Grouch? I could totally see that."

I have to wait for the answer while he puts me on hold to do his actual job, but when he returns, he jumps right back in. "When I was little, I definitely identified with both of those guys, but I have managed to move on from *Sesame Street* since then."

There's still a smile in his tone, so I press on. "Then are your TV friends game show people or soap opera people?"

"Can I plead the fifth on that?"

"Mm-hmm. Soap opera people, then. Which show could it be? Hang on. I'm grabbing my *TV Guide*."

"It was *As the Earth Revolves*, okay? I used to watch the soaps with my mom."

"Aww." Very cute. As long as he's not still living with his mom. That would be problematic.

"She called them her stories."

"Weren't you in school when that was on?"

"I was home sick a lot."

"Oh, that's too bad." He doesn't elaborate, and I think I've pushed far enough. "One more: *Lassie* or *Mr. Rogers*?"

"Definitely *Mr. Rogers*. *Lassie* was too scary."

"It was for me too, but I love dogs, so I'd make my sister watch with me. You were a sensitive little guy, huh?"

"I guess I was."

"I love that. I'd like to see a picture of you as a little kid." Even though talking like this is cozy, my brain still craves an image to go with the voice.

"Yeah, there aren't many of those." Something beeps in the background. "Listen, I should go. But thanks for talking to me instead of watching *Thirtysomething*."

"You're welcome. You're better than TV friends."

"Good night, Jess."

"Good night, Cal."

I totally forgot to stretch after class I was in such a hurry to call Cal, so I'm a bit stiff as I get to my feet to hang up the phone. Carefully lifting my leg to the barre, I try to picture him. A guy with a voice that masculine and sexy has to be good-looking, right?

But what if he isn't? Am I that shallow? Ticking through an imaginary slideshow of all the guys I've ever gone out with, I have to conclude that I am.

Not to mention that my vanity has me doing everything within my power to enhance my good bits and hide the bad. So much about attraction has to do with appearance. Right?

Could I fall for a guy who isn't handsome? I'm attracted to Cal when we talk, but what if we met and one, or both, of us were disappointed in what we see?

What would we do then?

CAL

Wednesday morning a phone call from the PR guy for Why Not Happiness wakes me up at nine a.m. Though I'm barely awake, I manage to take in the information. Their tour schedule is tight. They don't get into Boston until right before sound check, but lead singer Joe can talk to me on the phone before they get on the bus. In less than an hour. It'll be an exclusive, so I make myself say yes.

An hour is not much time to get ready. I take Blondie out to pee, shower as fast as I can and haul my ass to the station. I find an engineer to set me up to record the phone call, and I manage to scribble a few questions on a piece of paper before it comes in.

"Hey, Joe, thanks for taking the time to call."

"Sure, man. Uh, like we don't have a lot of time, but yeah, like, thanks for, uh… promoting the tour."

"Happy to do it. How's it going so far?"

"Good. Yeah. Good."

"Good. Great."

"So, uh…" I scan my notes. My questions all seem pretty lame. But we can't have dead air. Hopefully, this can be edited.

"So, how's the weather there in Boston right now?" Joe finally asks.

"Oh, yeah. It's cold."

"Probably not as cold as in Ottawa."

"Right, yeah. You guys are Canadian. The Great White North, eh? You like those guys? Bob and Doug?"

"Yeah, we don't really talk like that."

"Right." Feeling like a total idiot, I search for a question that isn't insulting. "So…"

"Yeah, so we're playing at the Paradise…"

"Right. The Paradise. Great venue."

"Yeah, we'll be there tonight."

"At, uh… nine o'clock. So be there or be square."

"Yep. Okay, I gotta go man, but, uh… thanks."

"Thank you, Joe. Oh, whoops, I forgot to introduce you. That was Joe Berg, front man for Why Not Happiness."

"Okay, gotta go."

"Bye, now."

He hangs up, and I just sit there, the dial tone thunderous in my ears. That could not have gone worse. When the booth door squeaks open and Jones steps in the room, all I have is, "Well, that sucked."

He shakes his head with a wince. "I don't think we can salvage it. The weather? Seriously, Cal. You didn't even ask him about working with Todd Rundgren."

My head, heavy as a cannonball, drops into my palm. "I'm an idiot. I forgot… everything. My mind went blank."

Jones sighs. "I guess we'll have to come up with another kind of gimmick for you."

You can't say *I told you so* to your boss, even if he is your friend. "Yeah, I guess we will."

The words of the band's hit single, "We're All Adults Now," mock me the entire way back to my apartment. Am I? Am I really an adult? Jury's definitely out on that one.

WHEN JESS CALLS THURSDAY NIGHT, I've prepared a few stories. I may have lost out on being a talk show host, but I am not going to lose her. On our Wednesday call, I was still in a funk from the interview failure, and I don't want her to get bored with me.

I'd be happy to listen to her talk about the weather. Or read the phone book. Just the sound of her voice is entertainment enough for me. A mellow caress when she recites Shakespeare, a sharp prick when she's moved by a friend's troubles. When she imitates members of her family or other actors in her play as she tells a story, she never fails to make me laugh.

That's something I've done more in the past couple weeks talking to her than I have in years. I'm determined to do the same for her with the stories I've saved up.

"So, since tomorrow's Friday the 13th, nobody's releasing anything new, but I called over to Fort Apache studios in Cambridge earlier and talked a guy I know into getting us a copy of a single from the album that Throwing Muses is releasing next week."

"Oh, I think I heard you play that."

"Yeah, it's a great track. I'm looking forward to hearing the whole thing. Anyway, when the bike messenger dropped it off a couple hours ago, he accidentally let a few people in, and they've been partying in the station offices since then."

"You didn't hear them?"

"They're at the other end of the building. Talia—the night producer, you've talked to her—"

"Right."

"Anyway, she went to get a soda, and there they were, sprawled all over the cubicles where the ad sales people work. They'd broken into the vending machine and made a huge mess."

"Like what kind of mess?"

"You know, wrappers and cans everywhere. I think maybe some-body threw up in a trash can."

"Ew."

Good job, Cal. Gross the girl out. "Yeah, the office guys are going to be pissed tomorrow." Now I'm questioning my choice of stories.

"Do a lot of people just show up at the station door?"

"Yeah, they push the buzzer over and over until someone answers. Talia breaks it every once in a while, but someone always fixes it again. A volunteer will usually take their requests off the squawk box out there, but they have strict instructions to never let anyone in who doesn't have a badge. Unless they're actually some-one's friends. Gracie brings people in all the time."

"Do you?"

"Nah, too distracting."

"But it's not too distracting to talk to me?"

I can't help but grin. "I'm sure if you were here in person, I'd be very distracted."

"I could figure out some ways to distract you."

The tease under her words tempts me with possibility, but I can't get my hopes too high. "Anyway, there are fewer people here this late to keep an eye on things. I don't want to be responsible."

"Oh, before I forget, I'm done with rehearsal early tomorrow, so I'll probably go to my family's for Shabbos. I won't be driving home late."

"Shabbos?"

"You might have heard it called Shabbat? It's the beginning of the Jewish sabbath. We light candles and have a special meal at sundown on Fridays."

"Right." The thought of going three whole days without talking to her has me scanning my brain for ideas. The flyer for the DJ marathon this weekend catches my eye. "You know, I've got some extra tickets to a club where I'm spinning Saturday. Do you want some?"

"So we could meet up?"

Shit. I have got to learn to think before I speak. "Well, I can't guarantee that. It'll be kind of crazy. But I can give you a bunch. You can bring friends."

"That'd be cool. But if it works out, I'd really like to meet in person."

O Positive's "Walk Away Renee" is winding down, giving me an excuse to say good night—as well as a reminder of what I should do with Jess. After quickly giving her the details for Saturday, I say, "Call me tomorrow night if you can, okay? But if not, I'll have tickets in your name."

JESS

I'm quite proud that I've chosen Shabbat dinner at my sister's house for my Friday night entertainment instead of a date with a jerk.

My family isn't particularly religious, but Shabbos is an important gathering time. Since I was little, the scents of chicken soup bubbling on the stove and challah baking in the oven have always wrapped me in the comfort of family. I miss the traditions of the meal when I'm in a show and have to perform every Friday night.

Rehearsal ends at three-thirty, but it gets dark at five, so I don't have time to go home and change after rehearsal. Instead of the sparkly tops and short skirts I usually wear, I'm in one of the Prudence outfits I've come up with from my closet: a maxi skirt from my high school wardrobe paired with low-heeled boots and a long sweater. I'm getting quite comfortable in this character's look, which is a big change for me.

When I walk in the front door, I'm greeted by the yapping of my sister's two little dogs followed by the squeals of my two little nieces. I squeeze the girls together, inhaling their sweetness. Someday I'll have this, too. Even if the price is gaining fifty pounds like my sister did, it'd be worth it.

Somebody'll have to do some serious tutoring before I can make a Shabbat dinner, though. As my sister has so helpfully reminded me when I've tried to help her, you're only supposed to burn a *chunk* of the challah as a mitzvah, not the whole thing. And that was when I was just heating up bread from the bakery. Luckily for all of us, I don't have to get anywhere near the kitchen this Friday because my nieces take my hands and drag me up to their room.

On the way, nine-year-old Abigail complains, "Jessie, you haven't been here in so long!"

Seven-year-old Tamara chimes in, "Yeah, you haven't even met Fluffy."

My sister usually keeps me up to date on family news, but she hasn't said anything about a Fluffy. "I am so embarrassed. Here you have an exchange student visiting from Siberia, and I haven't even met him."

Tamara stops halfway up the stairs. "What's an exchange student?"

"She's kidding, Tami." Abigail rolls her eyes at her sister before narrowing them at me. "You don't even know who Fluffy is."

I shake my head and pull them along. "Of course I know who Fluffy is. I was pulling your leg." I stifle a giggle when Tami looks down to check the leg in question. Seven-year-olds are so literal. Tickle-fighting our way down the hall, I race them to their bedroom. Once inside, I scan the chaotic scene until I locate a new cage in the corner. Their pet mouse died a few months ago, and they must have been ready to replace it. "Fluffy is"—whatever it is, it's well named because all I see is ball of fur—"this new pet!"

Abigail carefully opens the lid and takes out the furball. "Fluffy is a silkie guinea."

I nod vigorously. "Of course he is."

Tamara balls her fists on her non-existent hips. "Fluffy is a girl, duh."

"Duh, I knew that. Can I hold him? Her? It?"

"After me. It's Abby's turn to hold her first this time. Then me. *Then* you."

"No problem, I can wait." I flop down on the lower bunk, kick off my boots and curl onto my side. The girls show me all the exciting things Fluffy can do, and I join in by coming up with a voice for the furball. Since her tricks mostly involve eating and running away from them, the dialogue isn't hard to come up with. "Oh, you can't catch me" and "Who knew carrots were so darn yummy?" Things like that.

Next thing I know, my sister's voice is waking me up. "Girls, it's almost dark. Time to light the candles."

"Shh. Aunt Jessie's sleeping."

"Not anymore," I croak.

"When did you get here?" my sister asks.

"Um, a while ago? Sorry, ladies. I must've fallen asleep."

Esther claps. "No time for naps, let's skedaddle downstairs. Tamara, you're on the challah cover. Abigail, you set out the Kiddush cups." She points at me. "You, tame that hair so mom doesn't have a cow when she sees you." She looks me up and down, a flicker of surprise crossing her face. "Nice outfit."

As she follows me down the stairs, she tsks, "You've lost weight, though."

Ever since my anorexia diagnosis at the age of fifteen, Esther has worried way too much about my weight. Pulling my hair into the braid I've been wearing at rehearsal, I sidestep the comment. "Is Gabe coming?" I can't even remember the last time I saw my brother.

"No, just mom and dad. He's out of town for work." She hugs me from the side and kisses my cheek when we hit the landing. "It's nice to have you here. I miss my baby sister."

Soaking up the coziness of my sister's comfortable home as we make our way to the dining room, I squeeze her back. "I've missed you too."

I hope my parents don't ask about what's happening at the school. If I tell them I'm not working there anymore, they'll freak out and bug me to find another teaching job or something else they can understand. Of course, my dad would also sneak me some cash before I go home, which I could use. I really have to figure out a way to support myself doing what I love.

Sooner rather than later.

CAL

Friday night when I hit line three expecting Jess, all I can hear is coughing. "Hello?"

More coughing.

"Jessica?"

"Sorry," she answers, her voice scratchy.

"You okay?"

She gulps something. "Just having a coughing fit."

"I noticed. Are you sick?"

"I don't know. I might be coming down with a cold."

"That would suck."

"Happens. Especially when you burn the candle at both ends, as my mother says."

"Do you still want the tickets for tomorrow?"

"Oh yeah. Dancing is good for you."

"Is that a prescription?"

"Of course. Haven't you ever had a doctor tell you to dance more?"

Under the raspiness, there's a giggle in her voice that has my heart rolling over and begging for more, so I go for a joke. "When you're as clumsy as me, most doctors tell you to dance less. In consideration of others. To avoid injuries, you know."

"Nobody's that bad."

"You haven't seen me dance."

"Will I get to Saturday? Am I going to get to meet you, finally?"

The flirt in her tone, it's like the melody in a romantic comedy soundtrack. It may be for me, but how long can I keep stringing her along? "Things get pretty crazy in the booth, but I'll put your name in for—do you know how many people?"

"Four, if that's okay. Including me."

After double-checking that she has directions to the club, I make my escape before she can ask more questions. "I'm going to have to go; I've got stuff stacked up here. But I'll see you Saturday."

I'm playing with fire here.

She wants to meet. I want to see her.

I know she's got to be gorgeous. She's an actress.

There's no future here.

Especially once she sees me. Pity or revulsion. I can't take either. But I guess there's a part of me that holds out hope.

If I see her, watch her with other people, maybe I'll get enough of a sense to know if she'd be okay with dating someone like me. Maybe I can somehow woo her enough with my voice that—

Who am I kidding? I just want to watch her dance.

JESS

Saturday night my friends and I navigate the creepy downtown area where abandoned buildings seem to outnumber places still in business, only to find that the line leading to the club is so long it snakes around the corner.

Randall moans. "That is one long line."

Mike, full of energy as always, bounces on the balls of his feet. "Don't be a wuss. We're on the list. Jess here knows somebody. We can cut."

Becky, wide-eyed as ever, asks, "Is that fair?"

I hook one arm in hers, one in Randall's. "Cal said he'd get us in. If we can't skip the line, we'll do something else. I've missed you guys." I shiver, wishing I had the confidence to choose warm tights and boots instead of heels and stockings.

Randall puts an arm around me and pulls me closer. "You forget it's winter?"

"I'll warm up as soon as I'm dancing."

"If we get inside."

"Enough with your whining, old man," Mike turns around and walks backward a few steps as he taunts Randall.

I stick out my tongue at him. "Enough with your talk about old men. I'm as old as he is."

Becky stops short, throwing me off balance. "What? No way."

"Way." Have to own up to it someday.

"Well, you don't look it. Oops, sorry Randall. I didn't mean you're old or anything. I'll shut up now." Becky's cheeks, already rosy from the cold, are now fully flushed. She sounded a little surprised on the phone when I asked her to come out with us. She's been assistant stage manager for Shakespeare Boston from the beginning, but maybe she still feels like an outsider.

Glad I asked her, I whisper in her ear, "It's okay; he is old."

Randall rolls his eyes but takes the teasing in stride. "Hey, I heard you quit teaching at that private school."

"More like they quit me. I got replaced by an actual aerobics teacher."

"That sucks. But you're doing that play up north?"

I laugh. "Yes, an entire hour outside of town." Randall's from Boston too, so he thinks anything outside of 128 may as well be in New Hampshire. "Anyway, the money's not horrible, and I'll get the weeks for my health insurance."

"Nice. Well, I can put a word in at the restaurant if you want."

"I might take you up on that if I don't book anything else soon."

Mike claps his hands. "Get a move on, folks."

I squeeze Randall's arm. "He's right; let's get inside."

We catch up with Mike as he trots up to the dude guarding the door. Mike's on the shorter side, but he puffs up his chest and flashes his wide smile. "Hey, my man. Jess Abraham here should be on your list."

Standing, the bouncer is monolithic. "List?"

"Yeah." Mike takes a step back. "You know, the list?"

"I don't got no list."

I go up on tiptoes behind Mike. "I'm a friend of the DJ's."

The guy's face may as well be carved of granite. "There's five DJs spinning right now."

I untangle myself from Becky and Randall and raise my hand. "I'm a friend of Callihan's."

"Callihan's, sure." The sarcasm in his tone is not encouraging.

Two people exit, and he checks the IDs of the next two people in line. After frowning at me, he follows them inside, shutting the door behind him.

Mike turns to face me. "What the fuck, Jess? Do you know this guy or not?"

"I do. We're friends." *Friends who've never actually met*, I don't say. "If this is a bust, I'm buying everyone a drink." I wrap one leg around the other in an attempt to warm up. "So, what's the *Hamlet* gossip?"

Mike's eyes light up. "I think something is going on with Eva Marie and the guy playing Horatio."

"Really?" I squeak. "Is he for real, Becky?"

She flashes an impish grin. "All I can say is Dave is pretty mad."

"I always wondered if those two had a thing. How old is the guy playing Horatio?" I couldn't tell you if Eva Marie was forty or sixty. Dave's probably in his forties, but... "A guy young enough to play Horatio—that's cradle robbing."

"Give her a break. She's still got it going on." Randall smiles at a cute guy in the line behind us.

Mike shakes his head. "It's too weird. She was my teacher. She can't date anybody."

The giant reappears, interrupting our gossip. "All right. You're in."

He doesn't sound happy about it, but when he lifts the velvet rope to let us pass, he gives me a nod. "Sorry about the wait. Cal never has guests, so I had to check."

CAL

As expected, it is chaos up here in the booth with multiple jocks coming and going, so I'm relieved the bouncer caught my attention to ask about my guests. It's ridiculously important to me that I don't let Jess down. Her voice in my ear is like a drug I'm addicted to.

Gracie's spinning at the moment—it's a crazy setup tonight where we're tag-teaming in fifteen-minute sets—so I find a spot in the shadows and scan the dance floor.

There she is, a voice crows in my head. It makes no sense, but somehow I know. The woman spinning in the center of the dance floor, graceful arms snaking over her head. The crowd makes space for her, not because she's out of control, but because her presence demands it. Her movement is mesmerizing, her hips and feet keeping beat with the bass while her upper body draws the melody in the air.

It has to be her. She glows. Not just because her dress is neon green. Her smile is contagious. The way she moves has everyone around her dancing more… everything.

Even though I'm afraid of dimming that light, I'm drawn to it like a moth to a flame. Or like a four-year-old to a flame.

And just like that, it's like a needle scratching across a record. *That* radiant girl falling for me the way that I've already fallen for her? It's a total fantasy. A fairy tale, not like in a Disney movie with a happy ending, but like in the olden days where kids get stuffed into an oven and everything goes up in smoke.

"Hey, man—"

My protective instincts and boxing training kicking in, I counter-block the hand on my shoulder without even thinking.

"Whoa!" The guy stumbles back, hands high. I blow out a breath, tightening the string on my hoodie before mirroring him. "Sorry, you startled me."

"Yeah, yeah, it's all good. I wanted to let you know that you're up in two." The guy from the club takes another step back when I turn around. "Also, there's a VIP room in case you want to hang there between sets. I heard you had some guests. You can invite them up too."

"Thanks, man." After edging past him, I step onto the platform next to Gracie. From up here, we can see the whole floor, but the way the club is lit, they can't see us. Just as well.

Time for me to disappear into the music, where I belong.

JESS

"You're sure you want to leave with us?" Becky asks as we wait for service at the club's coat check. "You don't want to stay and hang out with your guy?"

"Nah, he's really busy. I'll probably see him tomorrow," I fib. It's kind of embarrassing that they think I'm dating a guy that I don't even really know but I can't seem to rework my story.

At one point, Mike and Becky and I were dancing pretty close to the booth where the DJs were working, but it was too dark to see faces. I was unreasonably convinced that I'd recognize him, but when I got closer, I chickened out and reversed course toward the middle of the dance floor, convincing myself that I was just there to dance.

It did feel so good to let the music move me. All that disciplined work at the barre and in class turns to pure joy when I let my hips swivel, my arms swirl and my entire being spin. Later, after I took a break to go to the bathroom, I told my friends that I'd talked to Cal and he sent his apologies, but it was too crazy for him to stop and meet them.

Our coats appear and Randall, ever the gentleman, holds mine up for me. Mike does the same for Becky, asking, "When do we get to meet this mystery man? They usually swoop in and pick you up in fancy cars."

"Well, if we were rehearsing the same play, that might happen." Since I don't even know if this guy has a car, let alone where he lives or what he does with himself other than watch sports and play excellent music, I need to change the subject before I tell more stories than I can keep up with. "Anyway, free night of dancing. Good tuneage, fun crowd. Not too shabby, right?"

Once everyone's bundled up, we head outside and speed-walk to stay warm, laughing and teasing each other all the way back to our cars. On the way home, I try to figure out why I didn't try harder to see Cal. Or why I lied to my friends about who he is to me.

I guess it's because I don't really know.

All I know is that I can't seem to stop calling him. I really hope he's not avoiding meeting up in person because he's with someone else or even married. *Something* seems off, and with my track record, it's probably not something good. If I had any sense, I'd tell him I'm done—but not only am I not known for my good sense, I'm not quite ready to do that.

Chapter 8

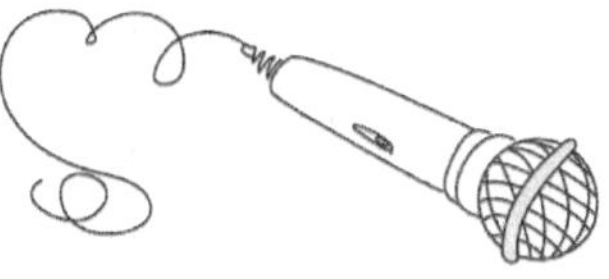

Hello Boston, this is Chevy Chase—the actor, not the city in Maryland—suggesting that you listen to Special Kay—the DJ, not the cereal—every weekday afternoon at 101.7 FM, WBAR Boston.

JESS

Since I have neither school, rehearsal, nor an audition Monday, I call Bella to see if she wants to hang out. Spending time with a small cohort of the Shakespeare Boston gang Saturday made me realize how much I miss my friends. It's never been easy for me to keep girlfriends—I'm too competitive, I guess. But I've had kind of a girl crush on Bella since the moment I met her, probably because she's a soap opera star and she deigned to hang out with little old me. Now, I just love *her*, despite the fact that she's got the svelte figure I wish I had. Her goofy sense of humor and her straightforward honesty are an irresistible combination. Plus, I have no idea how she manages the single mom thing without being stressed out about everything, but I'm always hoping her chill attitude will rub off on me.

The weather's decent, so we decide to meet at a park near her place in West Newton after she picks her daughter up from preschool.

Once Delilah runs over to the climbing structure to play with some other kids, I can't stop myself from sharing my current obsession. "So, I met this guy."

Brows up, she says, "I thought you weren't dating anymore."

"Well, I didn't say I'd never date again." I'd called her to vent after that last date with Charles. "I just want to stop dating assholes."

She laughs her big belly laugh, which so doesn't match her refined Nordic looks. "When you figure that out, tell me how. I'll write a book and make millions." Like a guard dog, her attention snaps to the playground. "Delilah, that's too high, honey."

Delilah, a tiny replica of her mom, pauses halfway up a ladder. "It's not that high."

"I am not going to spend the rest of the day in the emergency room." Bella's tone is a perfect mix of *It's your funeral* and *I'm your mom; of course I worry about you.*

"But other kids are up higher." Delilah lets go of a metal bar to point at the boys on top.

"They're not my kids," Bella replies with impressive calm.

"Mom." Delilah manages to squeeze four or five syllables out of the word. After a brief glare at her mom, she climbs down.

I suppress a laugh. "She sounds like she's twelve instead of five."

"Can't wait for twelve when she tries to act like she's seventeen."

"Like you did, you mean?"

Bella smirks at me. "Are you saying you didn't?"

"I did not. I loved being twelve." Picturing my preadolescent, string-bean self, my hair smoothed into a high bun, I sigh. "I had the perfect ballerina body then."

"Dammit." Bella launches herself off the bench and stalks to the edge of the sand pit. Delilah has climbed around to the other side of the structure. She must think we can't see her. I trot behind Bella, catching up as she deposits her daughter back onto the sand.

"Hey, Delilah." My sister's a fan of the diversionary tactic, so I ask, "Will you swing with me?"

After fifteen minutes of that, Delilah decides to ride her bike. We trail her as she pedals ahead on the sidewalk that loops around the park.

"Where were we? You met a guy."

Uncomfortable with my lack of honesty at the club Saturday, I lay it out straight for her. "I haven't actually *met* him, met him. I mean, I feel like I have because we've talked on the phone so much, but I haven't seen him face-to-face."

"Is this through a personals ad?" She grabs my forearm, her face a mask of mock-concern. "Don't tell me you've signed up to be a mail-order bride."

I laugh. "No, it's weirder than that. A couple weeks ago I called in to a contest at WBAR right after I got home from rehearsal up in Chichester—"

"I thought it was *Chi*-chester."

"That's how you spell it, but they say 'Chister.' Like they do Worcester."

"Of course. Yet another ridiculous Bostonian pronunciation."

"Anyway—"

"Sorry, J," Bella interrupts me. "Delilah, circle back, honey. You're too far away." Turning back to me, she says, "Continue, please."

"So I called in to try to win—"

"What was the question?"

"It was, 'What's the pencil sketch technique used in the "Take on Me" music video?'"

"What *is* the pencil sketch technique used in the 'Take on Me' music video?"

"Rotoscoping."

"How the heck did you know that?"

"I don't know. Why can I remember half the stuff Shakespeare wrote? Shit sticks in my head."

Delilah zooms past on my left. "Miss Jessica! You said a bad word."

"Whoops." I clamp a hand over my mouth. "Sorry, Delilah."

Stopping, she turns around to point at me. "You owe me a quarter."

"Okay."

"Watch me go real fast."

"Okay, but not too fast."

"I won't. If I do, Mommy yells at me."

As she peels off, I say, "Smart kid."

Bella laughs. "Too smart for me most of the time. So what did you win?"

"Oh, like a ten-dollar gift certificate to Tower Records. But this is the important thing—I asked the kid who answered the phone to thank the DJ for keeping me awake during my drive home from Chichester, and he said, why don't you thank him yourself." I pause and catch her eye. "We've been talking every night since. I mean every night that he works. So, like, five nights a week."

"What? Why?"

"I don't know. At first, he said he'd worry if I didn't call in when I got home from the commute. Now it's, like, what we do. Sometimes we end up talking for an hour or more."

"While he's on the air?"

"Kind of. He talks to me while the music or prerecorded stuff is on."

"It's impressive that he can keep it all straight."

"I guess he's been doing it for a while."

"Wait. WBAR? Are you talking about Callihan?"

"Yeah."

"Oh my god, I love that guy. His voice is so mellow." She arches a brow. "Sexy, even."

Not sure what else to say or why I'm even telling her this, I just shove my hands in my coat pockets.

"Is he—I mean, has he asked you out?"

"No. I'm not sure it's like that. Every once in a while he'll sound like he's flirting, but mostly he sounds… interested. Curious. Like he actually wants to know what I think about shit. Shit, I mean stuff."

She elbows me. "Now you owe *me* a quarter."

"Get real. If we played that game, you'd owe me fifty bucks by now."

"Don't tell Delilah."

I hook elbows with her. "I won't. I'll keep your naughty side a secret."

"Thanks." Her head whips up. "Dammit, she fell."

Since she isn't crying, I bellow, "Down goes Frazier!"

Bella looks at me like I'm nuts.

"My brother-in-law yells that whenever my nieces fall down. I think Howard Cosell said it." I point at Delilah. "See, it worked. She's up, no tears." Cupping my hands around my mouth, I yell, "Good job, Lilah!"

Bella hip-bumps me. "You'd be a good mom."

"Eh, I'd be okay."

"Do you *want* to go out with him?"

Talking with Bella is like talking with my sister, so I get how to keep up with the zigs and zags of mommy logic.

"I thought I was going to at least meet him Saturday night. He invited me to this club where he was spinning. I had a great time dancing with Randall and Mike and Becky, but…" I'm not sure how to explain what happened because I still don't really get it.

"But what? He was there but didn't want to meet in person? Do you think he's messing with you or something?"

"There were so many people, and the place where the DJs were spinning was like"—I gesture with my hand—"up high and dark. It was some big event, so there were a bunch of them working together. I could've pushed my way in, I guess, but I got shy all of a sudden."

Her brows come together. "That doesn't sound like you."

"I know. I worked myself into a tizzy about it."

"Like maybe he's married or something?"

"That's what I'm worried about."

"I wonder how you could find out." She rubs her hands together and waggles her eyebrows. "Field trip to the downtown courthouse?"

Laughing, I shake my head. "You're a nut."

"Which is why you love me."

"So true."

Eyes tracking the pink bike, which is about to disappear behind some bushes, Bella yells, "Lilah, turn around."

"I actually think I like getting to know him on the phone. It's been nice to feel like a heterosexual guy likes me for what's in here"—I knock on my head—"rather than because of these girls." I point at my chest. "It feels really different because he hasn't seen the whole package."

Isabelle shrugs. "It is a nice package."

"You know what I mean, though, right?" I'm nowhere near as pretty as Bella, so I hope she does get it. "Your package is exceptional."

She sighs. "It was once upon a time. Now I have these." She draws a squiggly line in the air in front of her stomach.

"What are those?"

"Stretch marks." She groans. "And you don't even want to hear about what pushing that girl out did down there."

I can't help but grimace. "Really?"

"Really." She matches my expression. "Some parts don't stretch back all the way."

My jaw literally drops. "I did not know that."

"The things they don't tell you about being a mom." She shudders, but when she looks up, a huge smile takes over her face. Delilah's pumping her little legs as fast as she can, heading straight for us. Bella gives me a conspiratorial grin and grabs my hand, and—screaming in mock horror—we pretend to run away.

CAL

I guess the listener line volunteers have figured out that Jess is a regular caller because when I catch movement in the window at 10:10 p.m. Monday night, a piece of poster board with "JESSICA" printed in black marker waves in the window. The volunteer also holds two fingers in the air—meaning Jess is on line two. I give him a salute to let him know I got the message as I call out the titles of the tracks I just played. Jess doesn't have rehearsal Monday nights, so I don't have to worry about her making the long drive. It makes me ridiculously happy that she's calling anyway.

Eager to hear Jess's voice, I slide the headphone off my left ear, pick up the phone and punch line two. "Hey, you."

"Hey yourself," she says, a bit out of breath.

"You okay?"

"Yeah, I was dancing to that last song while I waited. It had its way with my body, and I was all over my living room."

Swallowing what I really want to say in response to *anything* having its way with her body, I say instead, "Hang on for a sec? I wanted you to know I know you're here, but I have to take care of a couple things."

"Of course."

As I go through the motions of calling out the FCC-mandated station ID and playing the next song, an image flashes into my mind from Saturday night. The girl in the short neon-green dress, her hair dancing in the air around her like her curls had their own agenda. She moved with the music like nothing I've ever seen. Like instead of muscles and bones inside her skin, all she had was space for the music to fill.

Something tells me it was her.

I'm dying to know.

I'm afraid to know.

I have to make myself pick up the phone. "I'm back. Sorry about that."

"I should probably say good night, anyway. Long day tomorrow."

It's now or never. Ripping the bandage off quick worked earlier today. May as well try it again. "I did want to ask—did you guys have fun at the club the other night?"

"Oh my god, yes. Sorry, I forgot to thank you. We all had a great time."

"Good, great."

"I'm still sad that I didn't get to see you." There's a pout in her voice, and I picture green-dress girl's lush lips pressed together. "We danced for hours. You could see the dance floor, right?"

"Sort of. It was more crowded than usual. Maybe I saw you though. What were you wearing?"

"Oh, you know, a black dress and black tights. Like half the girls there." Her tone is off somehow, but the disappointment echoing inside my skull has me at a loss for words.

"I really only saw one DJ's face," she continues. "He leaned out of the booth and was talking on a mic. That wasn't you?"

I know who she's talking about: a guy from a rival station. Gracie thinks he's fabulous. I think he's a showboat, but he is good-looking. I have to paste a smile on my face as I answer. "Nah. I keep to myself back there."

When she doesn't say anything, I add, "Anyway, I'm glad you had a good time."

"Thanks again for getting us in."

"Anytime. I know you have to go, so, uh, call me when you get home Tuesday, okay?"

"Okay. Good night."

"Good night, Jess."

I don't know why I'm disappointed. That girl in the neon green would never even be seen with a guy like me.

JESS

I don't know why I lied.

Actually, I'm still lying because I do know. I want him to like *me*, not the breasts or the butt or the painstakingly made-up face, but me.

The me nobody really knows.

Least of all myself.

Ha-ha. I crack myself up.

But if that is how I really feel, why did I dress up that night? Maybe I should've worn a black dress and tights and combat boots like Becky. No makeup. Hair pulled into a ponytail.

What keeps me from going out in the world like that?

I work so hard on polishing my surface, put so much energy into hiding or camouflaging my flaws, maybe that's all I am. Maybe there's nothing to know beyond the shiny outside I've spun for myself.

Chapter 9

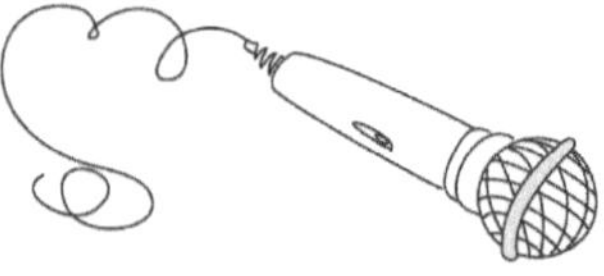

In case anyone's driving home late, I've got some songs to get you car-dancing—and to remind you to stay safe out there. First up, "Motor Crash" from the Sugarcubes. That'll be followed by the Pogues' "Bottle of Smoke."

JESS

As I accelerate to get onto Route 3 for the drive home Tuesday night, I'm so thankful that the run-through at the end of tonight's rehearsal went well. The day off at this point in rehearsals was just what we'd needed—time for everything to settle in. I think we're almost ready for an audience. In fact, I hope we haven't peaked too soon, because we have more than a week to go before opening.

Before I can go down that path, I turn the radio on and am rewarded with Cal's voice. My worries about whatever it is that's going on between us are drowned out by the tunes that keep me alert the rest of the way home. My own private DJ has me so high on life by the time I walk in my front door that I don't care that the heat isn't working again. After making tea and a healthy snack, I call in. Despite the fact that things were a bit awkward on the phone last night, we quickly fall back into our new getting-to-know-you routine.

"Me first," he says as soon as he gets back from doing whatever he has to do so he can talk to me for a chunk of time. "Favorite movie? I'll bet it's *Flashdance*."

"Are you kidding me?" I squawk. "It's not even my favorite dance movie. That movie is one long male fantasy."

"Okay, then. Um, how about *Footloose*?"

"That one's problematic for me because of all the Christian stuff. Sorry if that offends."

"Nah, not much offends me. I was raised Catholic but no one in my family believes in that god anymore. So, what *is* your favorite dance movie?"

"How much time do you have? Because, really, I have a different one for every mood."

"I've cued up four songs in a row, so…take it away, J."

"Okay, when I'm happy, *Singin' in the Rain*." Even the thought of it has me tapping out a little traveling time step.

"Did I just hear you tap-dance?"

"You did."

"You are one talented lady. Okay, what about when you're sad?"

"*West Side Story*."

"Because Natalie Wood died?"

"Because I'll never play that role."

"Why not?"

"I'm not a soprano. It's way too high for me."

"Didn't stop Natalie Wood."

"Harder to fake it onstage than in a movie."

"Good point."

"Then when I'm *really* depressed, it's either *White Nights* or *Turning Point*."

"I can't even imagine you really depressed."

"Oh, it happens. They're both ballet movies, and I… wallow. And lament the state of my—" *Shit.* I forgot I was talking to a man. Very few people get why I hate the shape of my body, but men *really* don't get it.

"Your...?"

Oh, what the hell, can't stuff the toothpaste back in the tube; may as well spit it out. "My boobs."

He chokes out a laugh. "You're going to have to explain that one."

"This girl's knockers are too damn big."

"I didn't think that was possible."

"From your point of view, maybe, but ballerinas can't have boobs."

"I'm sorry to hear that."

The grin in his voice? He's probably staring at a pinup calendar right this minute. Despite how they disgust me, despite the fact that they're at the very bottom of my list of erogenous zones, no guy has ever been able to resist my sweater stretchers. "No, you're not."

"You're right. I cannot lie about something this important. I like big boobs. But really, I like all kinds of boobs."

"Now you have to tell me yours."

"My boobs are sadly—"

"Pretty small?"

"Yeah, it's tragic. I'm forced to enjoy other people's boobs."

"I *meant* your favorite dance movie, you horndog. It's *Fame*, right?"

"Yeah, right. I want everyone to know my name." His tone makes it clear that it's the last thing he wants.

"Well, don't you?" *Doesn't everybody?* is what I almost add.

"Just enough people to sell the advertising."

And then he jumps back on the air before I can dig further on that one.

CAL

A few minutes into my shift the following night, Talia sticks her head inside the studio door. "Hey Cal, I got a fresh one."

One of her responsibilities is to vet and train listener line volunteers. After a girl fainted at the sight of me, Talia created a whole routine to introduce them to me.

"Hang on, this song's about to end. Let me cue up a long one." I've already got "The Flame" by Cheap Trick ready to go from the Heavy section of the play box. One nice thing about this shift, I only have to play from the Heavy and Medium the first two hours. Then, it's one per hour from the whole box. I pull *Failure*, the self-released album by a band called the Posies. A jock I know out of Seattle told me about it and it's been getting good responses. I'll play something from it as soon as the *interview*, as Talia likes to call it, is over with. I've never been sure who's interviewing who.

Once the song's playing, Talia enters the booth followed by a slouchy guy with a purple-tipped mohawk. Talia usually gives them the third degree before bringing them in here, so I take off my hoodie entirely. I'm wearing a sleeveless shirt underneath it, so the scars on the left side of my face, neck and left arm are revealed in all their glory.

Looking the guy dead in the eye, I give my spiel. "I was in a fire when I was four." Mohawk nods slowly, probably stoned. I turn my head to the right, then hold out my arms, left covered in scars, right covered in tats. His eyes widen slightly. "Everything works. I don't need your help. Or your pity. All I need is for you to answer the phone. You get three questions now, and that's it."

He nods slowly. "Do we get free tickets?"

I swallow my surprise. They almost always ask if it still hurts. I almost always say sometimes. "That depends on how many we get. Your shift manager will tell you. Anything else?"

"Yeah." He points at my right forearm. "Who did your tattoos? They're rad."

It's my turn to nod slowly. "Guy in Worcester."

"Can I have his number?"

"Sure. I'll write it down for you later."

"Awesome."

Talia puts a finger on his bony shoulder to herd him out.

I call out to stop them, even as part of my brain registers that the current song is winding down. "That it? You get one more question."

"Nah, this setup is choice. I'm just here to meet girls."

"Fair enough."

He slouches outside and Talia turns a cat-that-ate-the-canary smile on me. "I know. Try and not tell me how good I am."

"Talia, you are both awesome and rad. Now get outta here. I got work to do." I was going to play the Posies' "What Little Remains," but now I'm in the mood for "Believe in Something Other."

After I slip-cut into it, I check the clock. Ten forty-five. Jess should be most of the way home. I bet she'll be car-dancing to this one.

WHEN I PICK up the line to talk to her later that night, she's out of breath. "Were you running up the stairs to call me or dancing again?"

"Both," she pants. "I ran from the car to get out of the cold, but I also didn't want to miss the rest of this song. It's awesome."

"Yeah, that song's hitting big right now. Again. It's a re-release. Playing it's a little like penance for me at the moment."

"Penance? What do you mean?"

"Don't you have penance in the Jewish religion?"

"Kind of. Repentance. Like, you know, everybody sins. So you reflect on yours and try to do better in the future."

"That sounds healthier than having to give things up, like for Lent."

"I don't know; from what I've heard, Jewish guilt and Catholic guilt could go a few rounds in a ring. But what's that song have to do with penance?"

"Ugh. I did an interview with the band that plays it when they came to town last week."

"And?"

"And it sucked."

"I must've missed it. Did you play it before my drive home?"

"No. It didn't air. It was terrible."

"It probably wasn't that bad. I know I'm my own worst judge."

"The station manager agreed. We literally talked about the weather, and I made fun of Canadians."

"And they're Canadian?

"Yep."

"Ouch."

"Yeah, I need to work on my interview skills."

"You could practice with me. I mean, playing twenty questions is kind of like doing an interview."

"I've never had the same feeling with you. When I was on the phone with the lead singer, my brain was… like I'd recorded over my favorite shows with static."

"Hm. Were you nervous?"

"I didn't think I was, but I guess—I did feel rushed because I didn't have much time to prepare. But also, when the guy got on the phone with me, he sounded irritated, like he didn't want to be there."

"And that shut you down?"

"Maybe."

"Most people like to talk about themselves, especially the kind of people who get up on stage. You might have to give them a starting point, though."

"The questions I came up with were all so lame."

"Maybe you were thrown off by his tone. Hey, I know—I'll pretend to be a diva for you so you can practice talking to rock star jerks." She clears her throat. "Hang on a sec; I'm getting into charac-ter," she whispers.

Noticing that the last song's winding down, and remembering that I've got to do some ad spots, I say, "While you do that, I'm going to catch up on a few things."

By the time I get back, I have a couple questions ready for her, but when I let her know I'm back on the line, I can practically hear her eyes roll as she says, "Listen, I don't have all day here."

Her voice is pitched higher, and she's added a squeak to it. I clear my own throat to cover my amusement. "My apologies. So, your play is a comedy, right?"

"Yes. I believe that was in the materials you received. Did you not read them?"

"Uh, I did. I wonder, how do you know if it's funny?"

"By people laughing, my dear. Of course, before we get to that point, we have to go through the rehearsal *process.*" She lengthens the last word dramatically, so I jump on it.

"Can you share a bit of that process, *princess?*" It's the perfect name for the self-involved character she's come up with.

She clears her throat primly. "One find's oneself so deep into the character's journey—what she wants and is trying to do—that thinking about comedy is inappropriate. *She* doesn't think she's funny. Additionally, the only audience reacting to the work at this point in the *process* are the director and the stage manager and the other actors. They've heard the words so many times that it's not funny anymore."

"That must be frustrating."

"It *is.* But when you get a new audience and the people laugh, it is such a relief. For instance, last night we had a handful in to watch a run-through."

"And did they laugh?"

"They did. Especially at me." My sides are splitting trying not to laugh at this character she's created on the fly. "Then one has to simply keep the faith until there's a paying audience and pray that they laugh, too."

"When do you get the paying audience?"

"Well, we have technical rehearsals this weekend, which I *hate* because none of the focus is on *me.* Hang on." She breaks character suddenly, jarring me out of our little improvisation. "Sorry, but I don't want to forget. I won't be able to call Friday. Rehearsals go for twelve hours a day, so I'm staying overnight up there."

"But you could call anyway."

"But it's long distance. And you don't have to worry. I won't be driving home."

"I'll miss talking to you."

"You will?"

"I will. Even if I have to talk to the princess."

"Well, I do have a calling card. I guess I could make a quick call."

"I'd like that."

"Okay. I will."

There's a shift in her voice, a new color, making me want to see her face, see the shy smile that my words painted there. Before I can venture into that territory, she jumps back into her diva character.

"To answer your question, opening is the next weekend and then it runs for five weekends. Six, if they decide to extend. Everyone will have plenty of chances to come up and see it."

"And I'm sure all of Boston is eager to do so," I finish in my best fake DJ voice."

"That wasn't so bad, was it?"

Her voice is back to the Jessica I know and love, and the whole thing puts a smile on my face. "It was definitely better than what I did last week. Thanks for the interview practice."

"You can interview me anytime. I'll be even meaner next time."

"I'll prepare myself. Talk to you tomorrow?"

"Definitely. Good night, Cal."

"Good night, princess."

JESS

By the time I get home Thursday night, I barely have the energy to make it up the stairs to my apartment. I haven't done much physically today, but emotionally I've been wrung out and left to dry too many times to count. The drive home gave me time to relive the humiliation and second-guess everything.

I need to call Cal so he won't start playing Jessica songs, but I don't have it in me to practice interviews with him tonight. I'm so tired I couldn't play another character right now if my life depended on it. I'll let him know I'm home safe and that I need to get to bed. One nice development: my brother came by this morning and gave me his old cordless phone. Not the VCR I'd hoped for, but beggars can't be choosers. Anyway, the new phone means I can talk to Cal while snuggled in bed instead of having to be tethered to the ancient wall phone in my kitchen, so I get ready for bed before calling. By the time Cal picks up, I'm half asleep.

"Everything okay? You sound like somebody stole your sparkle, princess."

"You could say that," I say over a barely suppressed yawn. "Sorry, but I don't think I can be a tough interview for you right now. I can barely keep my eyes open."

"I'll let you off the hook tonight, though I did come up with some good questions."

"I'm sorry. Maybe tomorrow."

"Did something happen at rehearsal?"

"Well, I did kind of have a breakdown. Or maybe a breakthrough? I'm not sure."

"Do you want to talk about it?"

"I don't know. It was embarrassing enough when it happened." Just thinking about it has my face heating up and my throat tightening. "But…"

"If you want, I'll just sit here with you. Speaking of phones, Talia got me a new headset so I don't have to put you on hold. I'll have you in one ear and what I'm playing in the other and my hands can be free. Let me put it on…" After a couple of clicks, he's back. "Can you hear me?"

"Hmm. You sound different. Closer."

"Hold on one sec." He goes on to announce some concert happening over the weekend and then introduce a song by the same band.

There's a click, and then he's back to me. "Pretty cool, huh?"

"That is cool. I feel like I'm sitting right next to you while you work."

"Yep. I can talk to you and still keep everything in order." He blows out a breath. "And I'm listening if you want to tell me what happened."

Maybe it'd help if I talk it through with him. "Well, tonight's rehearsal was either the worst or the best I've ever had. All I know is that it was painful."

"You didn't actually hurt yourself, did you?"

"Well, my ego took a sound beating."

"I know what that feels like."

"I don't know if anyone knows what this feels like, unless you have my"—*spit it out, Jess, you did it once already tonight*—"my disability. I have a learning disability."

"What do you mean?"

"I mean my brain doesn't work normally."

"I have a hard time believing that. You quote Shakespeare left and right."

"Cal, I didn't learn to read until I was practically in *junior high*. For most of elementary school, I was in remedial classes. Teachers thought I was slow. My classmates had harsher names for me. Remember how we talked about kids being cruel?"

"Yeah."

"Kids called me stupid in so many different ways that I believed them."

"Obviously, they were the stupid ones. I mean, you went to college, right?"

"Yeah, after I finally got a diagnosis. Dyslexia. I wasn't dumb; my brain just processes things differently. But that didn't happen for years. Even after I'd learned some workarounds, I was behind. I had to explain it to new teachers every year. It was always so embarrassing. So, since I got out of school, I don't tell people."

"Why not?"

"I don't want their pity. Or their accommodations. I have strategies now, and it's really not anyone's business."

"Makes sense."

"Unfortunately, sometimes I get thrown for a loop. Then everything falls apart. Like tonight."

And I'm back in that horrible moment, my heart trying to claw its way out of my chest.

"You don't have to tell me, princess."

I *think* he's trying to get me to smile with the nickname, but tonight, more than ever before, I wish I could see his face. One of the ways I coped as a kid was learning to quickly suss out who was a potential bully and who was a potential ally. A flicker in the eyes or the set of a mouth often told me what I needed to know.

Then I remember our conversation last night. Something he said pokes its way into my skittery thoughts. "Um, that thing you said about the static in your head? When you did that interview? It's kind of like that. When I have to read something new with other people watching, I get a staticky sound and the words literally move around on the page. That happened tonight. The director wanted us to try an exercise to shake things up, 'try an experiment,' he said, like it was no big deal. He wanted me and Jack to switch roles, for me to read Bruce's lines and he would read Prudence's. And it wouldn't have been a big deal—it probably would've been fun—for anyone who can read like a normal person."

Tears fill my throat, but they're not sad tears. They're angry.

"I *hate* not being normal."

"Believe me, I know."

"But you can't know. In that moment, every taunt I'd ever heard filled my brain, so loud and so mean and so true. Not only could I not read, I couldn't breathe—I couldn't stand. I melted into a blob on the floor." I'm too loud, I know, but what I couldn't say earlier needs to get out of me. "Like a weak, stupid, brainless, backward, moronic dummy."

"You forgot chowderhead."

His words knock me back for a moment, but then I hear the smile behind them. And I laugh. "And dunderhead."

"What about dope?"

"I like dolt better." Another laugh scrapes past my tight jaw. "Obviously, nobody called me any names tonight. Everyone was all worried and caring."

"Which is sometimes worse?"

"*Yes.* Exactly. I almost pretended I was sick, but I didn't want to lose the rehearsal time. And I figured, what the hell, they probably already think I'm a freak at this point. So I told them how my brain is broken. And then Miles—the director—made everyone else say something embarrassing about themselves so we'd be even."

"Did that help?"

Suddenly I'm giggling, remembering Jack's story about how he got lost on the way to his own wedding. "It actually kind of did."

"Then what happened?"

"Miles came up with a different exercise, and we all got super silly. Maybe in the end it shook things up in the way that he wanted. But I can't shake the humiliation." A shiver runs through me at the risks I'm taking with this man, but something keeps me going. "I don't like not being perfect."

"You don't think you can be perfect and flawed at the same time?"

"Uh, no."

"Maybe 'perfectly suited for what you're doing' is more like what I mean."

"I don't know." It's a bit too New Age for me, but I'm suddenly too exhausted to argue. "Thanks, Cal. Thanks for… listening. And just being there."

He doesn't say anything for a beat, but when he does, he sounds almost teary. "Being here for you is the best part of my day, J." Another pause, and then I can almost hear him shift gears as he goes on. "Thanks for the interview practice. How'd I do?"

"Pretty good, actually. You got an exclusive. Shakespeare actress confesses she can't read."

"I just want you to have good dreams."

"'And then in dreaming the clouds methought would open and show riches ready to drop upon me, that when I waked I cried to dream again.'" I sigh, but it's a grateful one rather than a frustrated one. "That's some Caliban for Callihan. Good night," I whisper.

"Good night, princess."

Thankful that I'm already in bed under piles of covers, I press *End* and drop the phone onto its base before I roll over and drop my head onto my pillow.

Chapter 10

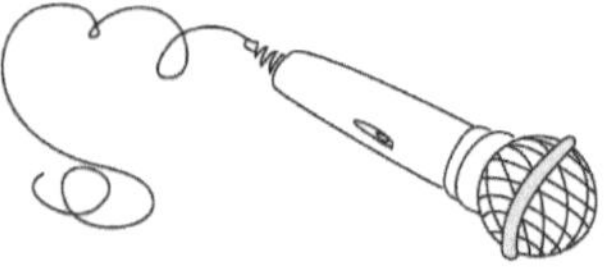

This hour of Friday afternoon, commercial-free radio is brought to you by Nanticket—sorry, Nantucket Nictars, I mean, Necktick—tuck neck. Oh, for crying out loud. Just buy the juice.

CAL

The ringing of a phone wakes me up Friday morning. My phone. In my apartment. Ringing too early in the morning.

By the time I get to the kitchen to pick it up, my heart's in a panic. "Hello?"

"Hey, it's Penny. I—"

"What's the matter?"

"Nothing's the matter."

Rubbing sleep from my eyes, I stumble to the couch, my scars complaining because I got up so fast. "Why are you calling me so early?"

"It's after two, lazybones," my sister says. "In the afternoon."

"Whoa. I guess I slept late." When I turn on a lamp, the dog and cat stir in their beds and begin to yawn. They must've given up on waking me. "Did you want something?"

"Who's the girl?"

"What girl?"

"The girl you talked to on the radio last night."

"What are you talking about?"

"You got some girl to tell you her troubles on the air last night."

"What the fuck are you talking about?" Rocketing to my feet, I startle the pets. They're taking their time stretching awake, but they'll be whining and yowling any second. Meanwhile, my sister's words knit together some sense from the cobwebs of my brain, but I don't like the story they're spinning.

"I was up with the baby, like usual, listening to you, like usual, and the girl told you about her learning disability. It was weird but kinda cool. Is that a new thing you're doing?"

"Fuck." As I struggle to get dressed with the phone crooked in my shoulder, I'm also struggling to figure out how this happened. "Shit. No. That was a mistake."

"Well, she sounds… It sounded like you like her. Like, *like* her, like her."

"Don't be stupid."

"You're the stupidhead."

"You can't win that battle with me."

"Yeah, you're right. Dunderhead. That was pretty funny when you called her that. Or was it chowderhead?" She laughs, like this is all no big deal. "Hey, I know. Why don't you bring her to dinner Sunday?"

"I can't do that."

"Why not? Is she in a mental institution or something? Is that what she was talking about? It was a little confusing."

"No, you idiot. I've never met her. We just talk on the phone."

She sighs. "Who's the idiot in this scenario? Why haven't you met her?"

"Do you really have to ask that?"

"You have got to get over yourself already. Your scars are hardly noticeable now."

"That's because you're comparing them to when they were brand spankin' new. Plus, you see them every week. Believe me, people still notice them."

"So, whatever. If she's a cool chick, she won't care."

"And if she does care?"

"Then why are you wasting your time talking to her?"

"Yeah. Well. I gotta go. The dog needs a walk."

"Yeah, well, your nephew needs both my hands." She grunts, and I hear baby gurgles. "Danny says hi."

"Hi, Danny. Bye, Danny. Bye, Penny. See you Sunday."

"Let me know if you want to bring her—"

I hang up before she can say it.

WORRY about what I've done dogs me the rest of the day, through my workout, through a trip to the post office to mail letters, through the routines I have to rush through because I slept so late. I even make a half-hearted attempt to find Jessica by calling the Chichester theater. Unfortunately, they won't give me her home number.

Jones usually takes off early on Fridays since he spins for the station on the weekends, so I'm half relieved, half anxious when I find him in his office. "Why are you still here?"

He just looks at me.

Fuck. Penny was right. "Listen, I don't know exactly what happened last night, but I was using some new headset so I could…" No way am I telling him about what Jess means to me since I can't even figure it out myself. "So it's easier to take calls. I must've pushed some wrong button when I broadcast that call, but I'll figure it out."

He still doesn't say anything.

"Or I'll chuck the headset. I'm not sure where Talia got it. It's not her fault, though. I asked her to get it for me."

"Are you done?"

"Am I in trouble?"

He takes a deep breath and blows it out again before answering. "The answering machine blew up last night with requests for more about the girl with the learning disability. Calls have been coming in all day long too."

Rubbing my eyebrow, I have to stifle a growl. "It was a fucking mistake, Jones."

"That's not the point." As he paces back and forth, his words gain speed. "I mean, of course I'm not happy you made a mistake, but it might be what you need right now. You didn't even say anything censors would've dinged us on. This is it, Cal. You don't have to go all shock jock. Instead, we go the other direction. We get the girls—all the girls—with this." He pops a cassette into the player on the table. "Listen to the promo we cut."

I couldn't tell you what I actually said to Jess on the phone last night. All I wanted was for her to feel comforted, to know she's perfect as she is. In any case, I'm not taking advantage of her, so I press the stop button. "No."

"Cal, you—"

"No, Jones. I don't want this used like... Anyway, she's an actress."

"So what?"

"She probably has an agent or something you'll have to deal with. You'd have to sign a contract."

"So we'll sign one."

"I don't want you to use it." I shove my hands in my armpits. "It's weird."

"Shit." His finger finally moves from the play button. "Are you seeing this girl?

Thankfully, a sharp laugh barks out from my chest, masking everything I feel about her. "Oh yeah, I'm dating an actress. Me. Have you even met me?"

"Has she?"

Suddenly my skull feels like it weighs a thousand pounds. Eyes on the floor, I mutter, "Only over the phone."

"Do you have a better idea? I'm not sure you get how important it is for you to pick up more market share here, Cal."

"Let me think about it." Grabbing my box, I push past him.

He follows me down the hall. "In the meantime, I need you to call her. We have to get permission to use her voice. Retroactively."

"I don't have her number."

"What do you mean? According to Talia, you talk to her every night."

"She always calls me. Here, at the station."

Jones riding my tail as we pass through the lounge has Blondie jumping up from her bed in the corner. When she advances, obviously sensing my distress, he finally backs off. "Well, find her. At the very least, she's got to come in and sign a waiver—since it already aired."

Instead of escaping into the safety of the booth, I make myself face him. "Got it. Now can I go do my job?"

"Cal, seriously. Think about it. I'd hate for you to lose your slot." When he reaches out to touch my arm, Blondie utters a low growl. Taking a step back instead, he says, "Don't give me that look, man. I'm on your side."

"Yeah, right."

As I turn the booth's doorknob, he clears his throat. "Hey, can you call off your dog?"

JESS

Friday night is our last chance to really work on the show—after the tech weekend, we'll go straight into dress rehearsals and then opening—so after we do a run-through of the whole play and get notes, Miles dives back in to tweak a few things. I'm not needed for every single scene, but I have to stick around for the ones I am in.

I don't mind watching. Miles is really good at teasing out issues and guiding actors through the process. He's so calm and self-effacing that he manages to create a truly safe space where actors will try anything, even the ridiculous—which is what this play needs. We have to find an outrageousness that somehow makes its own brand of sense. Watching the others take chances gives me the courage to play and not worry about results when I'm called up, even though we have to have a show that delivers in days. Some things work, some don't, but Miles makes trying anything and everything seem worthwhile.

Even so, I'm exhausted by the time Carol calls time at 9:59 p.m., so I'm planning to go right to bed as soon as I get to the actor housing.

Jack catches up with me in time to open the door leading to the parking lot. "I'm glad you're staying this weekend."

"Me too. I'll see you back at the house." Shivering, I head for my car, but then I realize that I forgot to memorize the directions. Turning to walk backward, I yell to him across the lot. "Actually, can I follow you?" Since Jack lives in Rhode Island, he's been staying up here for the whole rehearsal period.

"Sure. I'm in the little red Toyota. I'll wait for you by the exit."

The house where the theater puts up actors is only a few minutes away, so my car's heater is still blowing cold air by the time we arrive. Jack unlocks the front door and ushers me inside, where it's not much warmer.

"Did you guys not leave the heat on?"

"We did, but it's pretty useless. We're not living in the lap of luxury here."

I follow him down the hall and drop my overnight bag as he turns on the kitchen lights. "Okay, then. All I need is a bed and a teakettle. Maybe an extra blanket."

"Tim's got some nice whiskey. We usually have a drink at the end of the day. You should join us."

The front door opens and closes, and the man in question yells, "Are you giving away my liquor, Jack?"

A shit-eating grin on his face, Jack yells back, "You know I am."

Both Tim and Earl, the two New Yorkers in the cast, burst into the kitchen, full of post-rehearsal energy—part adrenaline, part whatever it is that makes actors crave the spotlight. As tired as I am, I can't walk away from it, so before I know it, I'm seated at the kitchen table with a glass of brown liquid in front of me.

Raising it to three men I've grown quite fond of in the past few weeks, I say, "To getting through tech weekend."

"Hear, hear," the guys chorus as we clink all around. Tim plops down next to me and tugs on my braid. "Will you let this mane free for the opening night party? My boyfriend's coming, and he will die when he sees this gorgeous hair. He'll want to do highlights, but don't let him. Your color is perfect."

"Don't worry," I laugh. "I couldn't afford it anyway."

"Oh, he'd give you the Tim's-friend discount. You'll need them someday." He nods sagely. "According to Gary, everyone needs highlights in their thirties and forties to get back to the colors of their teens and twenties."

"What about when you go gray?"

Tim shudders. "We don't think about that."

"Why not? Men are distinguished with gray hair. Women are just old."

He pats my hand. "Gay men are just old too, honey."

Earl raises his glass. "Sing it, sister."

Earl is well over six feet tall and must weigh at least 200 pounds, most of it muscle. His deep, resonant voice amplifies his stately presence, but his laugh and his silly personality melt it all into goo.

It's cozy here in the kitchen with this new set of theater brothers, so I let myself relax into their storytelling, bickering and laughter. Until I look at the clock, which seems a little fuzzy, like my brain. "You guys, iss almos' midnight! How did that happen?"

"Relax, sweetie," Tim says. "You don't have to drive home, and our call isn't until ten."

"I jus' have to make a call." When I stand, my joints seem to be made of Jell-O. "Woo."

Earl jumps up to guide me back down. "Maybe you'd better sit here to make that call. Unless you need privacy?"

Blinking, I wonder if I do. "Uh, nooo? Have to check in with my... my..." I shake my head but the word to describe what Cal is to me doesn't fall out of my mouth. "I don' know what he is, but he worries about me." For some reason, this statement is incredibly funny. To me and to the guys. "Everybody laugh!"

Jack appears next to me, phone in hand, the cord stretching across the kitchen. "You sure you want to make this call? You're kind of wasted."

"Oh, yeah. He'll be mad if I don't." Still giggling, I look around for my purse. "I haf to get my calling card."

He pats my shoulder. "Don't worry about it. As long as we don't abuse it, the theater covers our long-distance calls."

"Thass so nice." The numbers are swimming around on the receiver, so I close my eyes and let my fingers do the walking. I'm still giggling, walking my fingers across the table when someone picks up.

"It's Jess! I'm here!"

"Hang on."

Holding up the receiver so the guys can hear the song playing, I explain. "He's working."

The guys nod slowly, like three wise men.

When I finally hear Cal say my name, he sounds very far away. "Hii."

"Jess?"

"Thas me."

"Are you okay?"

"Yep. Sssorry I din' call ear—earl... Ha-ha! Earl. That's you! I'll rest on you for a minute. Your arm is hard, Earl."

"Jess?"

"Hi, Cal! How'r you?"

"Are you drunk, Jess?"

"I am," I whisper. "But don' worry. I don' haf to drive, and these boys will take care o' me."

"What boys? Where are you?"

Cal sounds mad. "Don't be mad. I'm good. I'm a gooder girl than you think."

"I'm not mad, I'm—fuck. I have to fix something. Don't go anywhere."

"I tol' you I don' have to go… Here." Push phone out of my way. Nestle into hard, warm pillow. "You tell 'im."

CAL

It takes way too fucking long to reset everything after one of the ad carts refuses to play. By the time I get back to the phone, my heart is racing and I'm wondering if I can get one of my brothers to find this theater and rescue Jess.

"Jess? Are you still there?"

"No, uh, this is Tim."

"Where's Jess?"

"Jess seems to have passed out."

"Listen to me, Tim. If you do anything to hurt her, I will find you and make you regret the day you were born."

"Whoa, man. You need to calm down. Jess is fine. We've all had a long day. She had some whiskey—probably more than she should've—but we'll get her to bed, and she'll sleep it off."

"By herself," I growl.

"Yes, by herself, Mr. Jess-doesn't-even-know-who-you-are-to-her. If you're going to be such a protective dick, maybe you should let her know you're in love with her. Maybe you should trust her not to get drunk with assholes. Good night."

And then he hangs up on me.

And I throw the phone across the room.

AT THE END of my shift, I'm still so agitated from the phone call with Jess that I take the long way home with Blondie. I don't usually visit the homeless camp with food on Friday nights because it's such a busy night for Phil that his leftovers are minimal, but my feet take me in that direction anyway. Thankfully, we're having a little January thaw, so I won't have to worry too much about the guys. Phil said something the other night about looking into other options for them. Not sure what he was talking about, but getting more people indoors for the winter would be good.

There seems to be a fire lit under the bridge where Walt and crew hang out—probably not a good idea. Not safe, and it'll draw the attention of the cops. When I get closer, I can see that it's a few young men I don't recognize who've lit a fire. Then Walt steps into the circle of light, pointing at the fire and shaking his head.

When one of the guys pushes Walt, I don't even think. I go straight for him. Blondie at my side, barking like she's going to kill the assholes. They scatter, except for one who's too busy going through Walt's shopping cart. The fucker.

Blondie keeps the others at bay while I haul this jerk up by the scruff of his neck. "Drop it, you asshole."

"Mind your own business, dude," he begins.

But when I shove him up against a concrete pillar, the light must hit my face in just the right way because he blanches when I growl, "You and your friends bug my friend Walt again, and your face'll look much worse than mine, I promise you."

He just blinks, so I lift him off the ground. "Did you hear me?"

"Uh, yeah," he squeaks. "Okay, yeah."

Tossing him to the side, I spit, "Get out of here, then. And don't come back."

After he takes off, I keep watch while Walt gets his belongings back in order. He finally shoos me away, but even after the walk home, I'm still agitated.

How can I protect Jess if I don't even know where she is?

And then I realize that I still don't have her fucking phone number, so I'll have to wait all the way until Monday when she calls into the station to hear if she's okay.

It's going to be one long weekend.

SUNDAY AFTERNOON, as I'm closing my eyes for a much-needed post-dinner nap on the couch in my parents' den, someone sits on the cushion by my feet. "I can't talk right now," I moan. "I'm too full."

My mom's hand lands on my right ankle to give it a squeeze. I can tell it's her without opening my eyes. She squeezed me in that spot in the exact same way every time she came to see me in the hospital. "Are you okay, honey?"

"Why wouldn't I be okay?"

"You were a bit grumpy with the kids at dinner."

Grunting, I throw a forearm over my face. Of course I'm grumpy. It's been a totally fucked-up weekend. Jess is getting drunk with strange men, I still have to confess that I exposed her secret to half of Boston, and I'm getting in fights like I'm back in junior high.

Worst of all, the words of the guy who picked up the phone after Jess passed out Friday night won't stop echoing in my ears. *Maybe you should let her know you're in love with her.* If this guy can tell how I feel about Jess in one short phone call, she must know, too. I know I don't deserve her, but something has me hanging on to a thread of hope.

As if that weren't enough, I've got to figure out how to hang on to my job, the one thing I thought I could count on.

It's too much to even try to explain to my mom, and she doesn't need to take on my crap anyway. If I'm going to figure out how to be a grown-up, I have to do it myself.

She squeezes my ankle again. "Cal. You're never grumpy with them, especially not with Robbie."

My nephew Robbie is four. He looks exactly like I did at that age, before the accident. I love that kid more than anything. "I'm sorry. I'm… There are some complications in my life right now and they're a little distracting."

"Does one of these complications have the name Jessica?"

Grabbing a pillow to cover my face, I groan. "I'm going to kill Penny."

"Don't blame your sister." When she pushes my lower leg, I bend my knees so there's room for her. "I listen to the radio too."

"You stay up for my show?"

"Sometimes, while I'm ironing or finishing cleaning up the kitchen."

"When you're avoiding going to sleep, you mean?" After the fire, my mom had insomnia for years. I peek out from under the pillow and, seeing an opportunity to sidestep the sideshow that is my life, I go on the offensive. "I hate it when you look at me like that."

"Like what?"

"Like I make you feel guilt. Or regret."

"But I do feel guilt. And regret."

"Well, stop it. It makes me feel worse."

"I'll stop it when you let a girl kiss you on that cheek"—she points to my scarred side—"as well as the other one." She grips my ankle again. "When you let someone love you more than I do."

"You didn't kiss that cheek for two whole years," I mutter.

Her breath hitches. "You remember that?"

"Of course I remember that."

A sob shudders past her lips as her head drops like a rock. "I'm so sorry, Cal."

Shit. Now I've made my mom cry. Could I be more of an asshole? "Stop it, Ma. *I'm* sorry. It's not your fault."

Nodding slowly, she lifts her chin, but her smile is wobbly. "You're right. I didn't kiss the left side of your face. Not because I didn't still love it, or you, but because I was afraid I'd hurt you. But one day I noticed you resting your cheek on your hand, like anyone would. I called the doctor to make sure I wouldn't make things worse by kissing the healing scars, and he said of course not. So I decided to make sure you knew that I loved every bit of you. I still do. Even when you're grumpy."

Back then, I was afraid to ask why things had changed, why she suddenly started kissing my scars. I was afraid if I did, she might stop.

She squeezes my ankle one more time before standing. "I want you to be happy, Cal. You deserve to be happy. You know that, right?"

Making myself smile as I meet her gaze, because I've caused her enough pain as it is, I serve up a bald-faced lie. "Yeah, of course I do. Now let me take a nap."

FIVE MINUTES into my shift Monday night, Talia slaps the Jessica sign on the window. I take a deep breath before answering with the regular old phone. I don't trust myself with that headset. "Cal here."

"Cal, I am so, so sorry about Friday night. The guys told me that I called you, but I don't remember any of it." She groans. "And let me tell you, I paid for drinking that whiskey the whole next day. Never again."

"How much did those guys give you?"

"They said it was just one shot."

"And you believe them?" When the receiver squeaks in my hand, I realize I've got it in a death grip. "No one did anything? I mean, you were alone up there with three men, and I—"

"It's okay, Cal. They're good guys, they're all in relationships. I've met their partners. I'm just a lightweight."

"Okay." I take a deep breath to try and slow my heart. "I was worried."

"I'm so sorry. And then I didn't have any way to call you all week-end, so—"

"Yeah, about that. Maybe we should exchange numbers. I've needed to tell you something since Friday. I actually owe you an apology."

"I'm sure whatever you're sorry for has nothing on a girl passing out on you mid-telephone call."

"Don't be so sure." I hate to risk dimming the light in her voice, but I may as well get it over with. "During our phone call last week, when you told me about what happened at rehearsal and your dyslexia—"

"Man, was that just last week? It seems forever ago."

"Yeah, well, it was Thursday, to be exact. Thing is, I accidentally played you live. I'm so sorry about that, but I need your retroactive permission to play your voice on the air."

"Wait, what?"

"When I plugged in the new headset, I hooked you into a live feed."

"So all of Boston knows I have a learning disability?"

"Well, lucky for you, my audience isn't quite that big."

"Lucky for me?"

"Jess, I'm so sorry. Obviously, I would never share things we talk about—"

"Except you did."

"I did but it was a total accident. I'm not using that headset again, at least until I know I have it figured out."

She sighs on the other end. "This is crazy."

"Thing is, some people did hear it, and they called in. They want more."

"More? More embarrassing things about me?"

"No. I don't know. Forget it. I said no anyway. My boss is pushing me to add something—anything, apparently—to up my ratings."

Her silence is has my gut tightening. "I swear it was a mistake. I'm not a shock jock. I would never—I value our friendship too much to—"

"Listen, I need a little time to think about this."

"I get it, but since we already played it, my boss needs you to actually come in and sign something."

"Okay, I guess I can do that."

Her tone has gone completely flat, which kills me, but I can't blame her for pushing me away. "Can you call the station tomorrow during business hours and ask for Richard Jones? He'll take care of it."

"That's it?"

"Yeah, that's it."

"Okay, then. Well, good night."

"Good night, Jess. Again, I'm really sorry."

After she hangs up, I just stare at the receiver, playing the call over in my mind. I don't think I could've fucked that up any more thoroughly.

Oh yeah, turns out I could. I forgot to get her number. Again.

Chapter 11

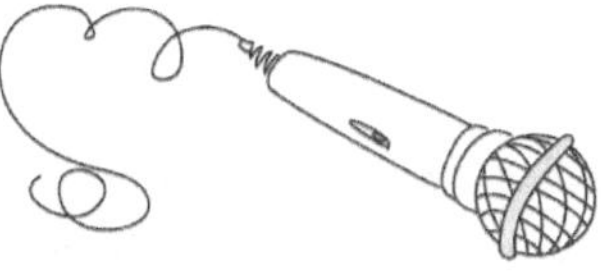

Psst. Boston, it's Abbie. Abbie Hoffman. When I'm on the run and find myself in Beantown with a little time on my hands and nothin' better to do, I listen to WBAR.

JESS

The moment the station receptionist leaves me alone in Richard Jones's office, I'm up and searching the photographs that paper the walls for Cal's face. It's silly, but my gut tells me I'll recognize him. Why I even want to, at this point, I have no idea. After we talked last night, I did my best to convince myself that I should walk away from the endless set of games he seems to be playing.

I let myself believe in the fairy tale for a couple of weeks, but come on. Maybe I've played too many tragic heroines, but the idea that there's someone out there I'm meant to be with who will complete me? Utter bullshit, obviously.

We're animals with a drive to survive and procreate. That's it.

Survival first. I'd choose career success over romance any day, so why should I expect anything different from Cal? He needs a gimmick to up his ratings. Why not get a girl to expose an embarrassing moment live on air?

Experience tells me that men take care of themselves first. Cal seemed like he might be different, but that's probably too much to hope for.

If I'm not going to cut him loose altogether, we need to talk in person. I need to see him to know if I can trust him. I need to be able to read his face.

Jessica's words from *The Merchant of Venice* echo in my head. "Love is blind, and lovers cannot see the pretty follies they commit."

I'm definitely blind in this scenario. But to what? To a man who took advantage of me? Or to my own heart?

The energy shifts in the room, and a masculine voice interrupts my thoughts. "You're not going to find him."

Whipping around to face the speaker, I do my best to pretend I wasn't snooping. "Excuse me?"

"He's not in any of the pictures." The tall, stylishly dressed man extends his hand. "Richard Jones. We spoke on the phone."

His hand is cool and dry, like his voice. "Jessica Abraham. Nice to meet you, Mr. Jones."

He shakes his head. "Just Jones. That's what everybody calls me."

"Got it." I gesture at the photos. "The receptionist told me to wait for you here, and I was…"

"Looking for Cal?"

"Guilty as charged." Hanging on to my purse strap like it's going to escape, I search for a way to ask what I really want to know. "So, what, he's a vampire? Works at night, can't be photographed?"

He doesn't bite.

"Seriously, why wouldn't he be up here?" I scan the array of pictures again. "These are station DJs posing with musicians, right?"

"They are, but"—hands shoved in his pockets, he tips his head to one side—"Cal avoids the spotlight."

"But why?"

"You'd have to ask him."

"I feel like I have. He's very good at dodging that question."

Jones skirts around me to the other side of his desk. "It takes time."

"For what?"

"For him to trust people."

"I don't get it."

A sharp bark of a laugh escapes his mouth. "Believe me, it's not you. It's him."

My harsh laugh matches his. "Yeah, I've heard that one before."

"Have a seat, Jessica." He slides a stack of papers across the desk, likely whatever it is he needs me to sign, but instead of addressing them, he swivels his chair to look out a large picture window. "Don't give up on him, okay? I can tell he really cares about you."

"How would you—"

His hand makes a stop sign in the air between us. "Listen to this."

Rolling his chair over to a stereo setup, he hits the play button on a cassette deck. It takes me a few beats to recognize my own voice. I sound so sweet and innocent. When I hear Cal's voice, an image rears up in my mind—a guardian angel with a fierce but desolate face, like the character in that movie, *Wings of Desire*. There's an ache, a desire to join, but he can't. He has to be separate.

But why?

I'm not sure how long I've been staring at the tape deck—or even if he played our entire conversation—when Jones taps the back of my hand to get my attention. "Like I said, it's his story to tell. He will tell you. He's already started."

Nodding dumbly, I sign the papers in front of me without even reading them because, dammit, something about Jones's words have tears threatening. Swallowing them back, lifting my chin and the corners of my lips in a professional smile, I shake his hand and let him usher me out.

I'm almost out the door when he says, "You have a wonderfully expressive voice, Jess. Do you have a voice-over reel?"

Since this is the last thing I'm expecting to hear, I mumble a no and keep walking. By the time I'm back in my car, my heart feels like a too-full balloon that'll pop if I even breathe wrong.

Despite the humiliating things I revealed to the world, all I heard in my voice on that tape was how much in love with him I already am. Like Juliet, I let him—and the world, for that matter—"over-heard'st, ere I was 'ware, my true love's passion."

In my opinion, Romeo was wiser about romance before he met Juliet, when he called love "a smoke raised with the fume of sighs." A madness that we fuel with our own imaginings.

How can I be half in love with someone I've never met? Obviously, it's more of an obsession, which probably would end as quickly as it started if we actually met. If I cut him off now, he can remain a perfect guardian angel who really only exists in the space between my ears and my heart and I can be the sweet princess that he rescued. He'll never have to know how fucked up I really am.

If I never let him see me, never let him touch me, never hear him lie to me, he won't find out I'm not the sleeping beauty he thinks he's been whispering to.

Who needs that sniveling wannabe, anyway?

I'm a working actress. That's the dream I've pinned everything on; there's no way I'm risking my heart just when things are falling into place.

I listened to Romeo "seal with a righteous kiss a dateless bargain to engrossing death" too many times last summer to avoid the lesson that love is nothing but dangerous.

SOMEHOW, I manage to get through the rest of my day without obsessing further. A challenging dance class with my favorite teacher consumes my focus and whips my butt. Over a late lunch, a couple of women from class distract me with their own dramas.

On the drive up to Chichester, I listen to a mixtape I put together to get me in the mood for the show. I should probably make another one for the drive back if I'm going to stop listening to Cal on the radio.

After my vocal warmup, the show's dresser braids my hair. A careful application of makeup and donning my first costume completes the Prudence mask as well as the preshow ritual that gets me in the headspace to perform this wacky play.

We make it through the dress rehearsal with only a handful of technical mishaps. The director's notes for me are all reasonable and fixable, so I should be over the moon that everything's going well. I'm only staying overnight in Chichester over the weekends, so on the way back to Boston, I try to think about career plans, like a mailing I can do if reviews are good for the play.

Despite my best efforts, I listen to Cal as I drive. When I hit the Mass Pike, I have to force my car to drive to my apartment in Allston instead of continuing on to the station. Showing up and demanding to see Cal is not the way to stay focused on my work.

I should really end this thing—call him, tell him that with my schedule changing, it won't work for me to call anymore. Which is true. We have preview tomorrow and opening Thursday. I need to sleep at night, not talk on the phone with a man who's probably manipulating me.

After I dial the station number and make small talk with the volunteer, I repeat *I do not need a man in my life* over and over in my mind as I wait for Cal to pick up.

"Jess? Were you talking to me?"

His voice in my ear instead of on the radio startles me back to the present. Guess I was saying that mantra out loud. "Um. No. Well, yes. Listen. So, after the show opens, my schedule will be different. I won't be making the long drive home at night anymore."

"Oh. When does that happen?"

"This Friday."

"Well, but you could still call."

He sounds like I'm taking away his favorite toy. But I am not a toy. I am a successful career woman. "I could. But I don't think I want to. I think this—whatever this is—has played out for me."

"What are you—Dammit. Hang on. Please don't go yet. I have to read this commercial, but I'll be back."

When he returns, tears are streaming down my face, but I do not let them color my voice. "I can't keep doing this, Cal."

"I get that your schedule's changing, but—"

"If you wanted to meet in person, I would consider it. After my show opens. But I'm not interested in being your—I don't know—your latest distraction. I can't afford distractions."

"What does that mean?"

"I mean you keeping me at a distance tells me that you're hiding something. And I don't need drama in my life. I get that enough at work."

"Is this because I played our conversation last week?"

"No." I wish I had a script to keep this conversation on track. "Well, maybe. It did kind of wake me up to how weird this is."

"If we meet, you won't want to see me again." His voice sounds like he's a million miles away.

"How do you know that?"

"I speak from experience."

"You mean every girl you pick up from the listener line drops you once she meets you in person? You really know how to make a girl feel special."

"Can't we just do this for a while longer?"

The raw need in his voice pulls at my heart, so I ratchet up the logic. "Cal. I'm sorry, but if you really think I'm the kind of person who'll judge you for—I don't even know what—then why would you want to keep talking to me?"

"You won't like what you see."

Jumping to my feet, I pace the very short length of my kitchen, my hand gripping the phone cord like a lifeline. "Why would you want to be with someone who's so superficial? I don't want to meet you to check you out, make sure you meet my standards. I want to be in a room with you, see your expressions when you talk to me, your body language."

"I think you might have a hard time doing that."

"So you really are the invisible man?"

"I do my best."

"Okay, well. This is it for me. Goodbye, Cal."

After I hang up, it takes everything I've got to not call back.

If only I could forget the number.

UNFORTUNATELY, giving up calling Cal has not helped my sleeping patterns or my ability to get out the door on time, so I'm late to an audition Thursday morning when I literally run into my friend Ben as I rush in the door of the Newbury Street casting office.

Pulling me into a hug, he says, "Hey, Jess. Long time no see."

"I know, but I'm already late for my appointment so I can't stop." After giving him a quick peck on the cheek, I say, "Give Lucy my best."

"Tell her yourself if you want. We're meeting at the Coffee Connection down the street. Join us when you're done."

After promising to see him shortly, I sprint up the stairs and sign in, doing my best to calm a spike in nerves. I really need to book something—anything—soon. After I made myself go through my bills and my bank statement yesterday, it was all too clear that the loss of a regular paycheck from the school is hitting me harder than I'd expected. I need another source of income, and I need it now.

Between a heart that's missing a certain DJ's voice more than I'd like and a head that's desperate for work, I am in pretty much the worst headspace for an audition. So when the casting director hands me an extra scene to read, saying, "You can read it cold," it takes everything I've got to keep my feet in the room and not running out the door.

Taking the paper from his hands, I stare at it, but no matter how many deep breaths I take, the letters refuse to stop doing the cha-cha over the page. Instead of what I'm supposed to be reading, words I seem to be saying a lot lately leap past my lips. "I have a reading disability. It will take me some time to go over this on my own before I can read it."

Time stops as I watch the director's face, steeling myself for his response. My heart's pounding so loudly in my ears I have to concentrate on the movement of his mouth to get what he's saying.

Something about how I can take it home and prepare the scene for the callback.

Moments later I'm back on Newbury Street with an appointment for next week. Who knows? Maybe confessing my deep, dark secret makes me more memorable. Maybe it's better to be the girl who can't read than the vaguely ethnic-looking girl with all the hair.

Nerves are still buzzing around my belly when I find my friends in the coffee shop, but Lucy's warm embrace calms me. No wonder dogs do whatever she tells them to. On top of that, this pair and their second-chance love story almost has me believing in romance.

After hearing all about her growing business and the play that Ben's about to start rehearsing in New York, I tell them what happened at my audition.

Apparently, once I start confessing about my dyslexia, I can't stop. *Maybe it's a good thing Cal shared it with the world.* Hm. Need to file that thought for later.

Lucy takes my hand and gives it a squeeze. "Good for you. My brother Sal is dyslexic. It took us forever to figure it out, and the poor guy was in remedial classes all through elementary school."

"Yeah, that was me. I can still hear girls hissing 'retard' at me when they'd march the so-called slow kids into the so-called normal classroom."

"Kids can be such assholes," Ben says.

As they tell a story from their shared childhood, words Cal said on one of our first phone calls echo in my mind. *Kids can be cruel.* Remembering how he suddenly shut down during that conversation has me wondering what it was about Cal that invited such cruelty.

By the time Lucy and Ben stand to get ready to leave, the all-too-tempting idea of giving Cal another chance is pirouetting through my mind. We're hugging goodbye when Richard Jones from WBAR walks in. As he passes our table on his way to the counter, he notices me. "Jessica. Nice to see you again."

After I introduce Ben and Lucy and they head out the door, after telling myself that my inquiry has nothing to do with Cal and every-thing to do with my career, I ask him for some advice. "You said something about my voice being expressive, and I do have voice training. So far, I've only done theater and on-camera work, but voice-over work is an area I'd be very interested in pursuing."

His brow furrowed, he jingles coins in his pockets as he considers the question. "WBAR has an in-house crew, Rocket and Porky, and they do most of our promos. But every once in a while I do get a demo in the mail that sounds interesting, and sometimes I'll bring someone in for a special piece." After explaining what's usually included in a demo, he offers to send a copy of the recording of me and Cal to Marnie Farrell. "She and I worked together a few years ago, and she could give you some pointers."

After thanking him for the referral, I seal my lips closed before I can ask anything about Cal. If I'm going to capitalize on this contact, it's best if Jones thinks of me as a professional, not some station groupie.

WHEN WE TAKE our bows at the end of the opening-night show, I'm flooded with relief as well as post-performance adrenaline. We did it. We made an actual paying audience laugh.

I'm still riding the addictive high of escaping into a character's mind when I step into the dressing room I share with Lanie, the other actress in the show. To my surprise, I find a bottle of Champagne in a bucket of ice sitting on the dressing room counter next to my things. My parents sent flowers with a promise to see the show at tomorrow's matinee, but an extravagant gift like this is not their style. When Lanie enters moments later, I point to it. "This yours?"

"Not that I know of." Lanie plucks a card from the bucket and reads it before handing it to me. "It's for you. Good show, by the way."

"You too. I think it went well," is my automatic answer. Doing my best to breathe deeply so I can ease my brain into reading the words printed on the tiny card, I remember that I don't have to pretend. "Could you read it to me, Lanie? My brain, you know."

"Sure. Sorry, I forget about your"—she draws a circle in the air in front of my eyes—"reading thing. Um, it says, 'Jess, I'm sorry I can't be there for you. Someday I hope you'll understand. Break a leg.'" She looks up. "Now I want to know what it is you need to understand."

"You and me both." Pulling the bottle out of the ice, I look around the room for glasses. "Not letting it go to waste, though. Should I open it here or wait for the party?"

Laney whips off her costume and swings it stripper-style. "I say we get the party started here and now." Wishing I were as unselfconscious as she, I turn away to pop the cork.

Mindful of how drunk I got last weekend, I only have half a glass before getting in the car to drive the short distance to the actor housing. After dropping my bag in my room, I join the party in the kitchen.

Taking in the sea of now-familiar faces, I give myself a mental pat on the back. Not only did I venture out beyond the safe boundaries of Shakespeare Boston, I took risks with this character that seem to have paid off. I've made new friends as well as work connections.

And, I recite dutifully to myself, I ended an unhealthy obsession with a guy who's probably married or unavailable in some other fucked-up way. Was it thoughtful of him to send the Champagne or was it manipulative?

Still, I'm awfully tempted to call and thank him, especially when I walk into the living room where all of my fellow actors are snuggled up with significant others. Before I take another sip of alcohol— determined to avoid acting on the unhealthy impulse—I squat next to Jack to whisper, "Don't let me near the phone tonight, okay? No drunk-dialing DJs for this girl."

Jack considers me carefully before agreeing. "If you're sure."

"I'm sure," I say, clinking glasses with him. "You're the best bad boyfriend."

"And you're the best bad girlfriend," he replies. "Onstage, at least."

"Where it counts," I say, before taking a healthy swallow.

Chapter 12

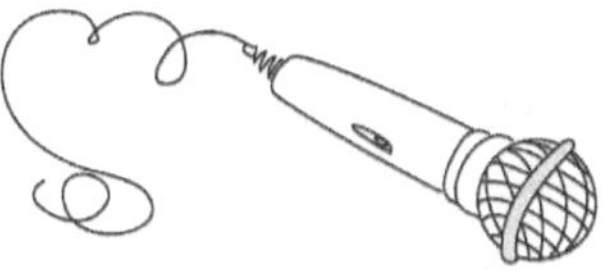

BRRRING. WAKE UP! It's Monday, Monday, Monday FUN day with your WBAR morning jock, Morning Guy Guy.

JESS

Opening weekend goes off without a hitch. Two shows on both Saturday and Sunday keep me busy enough that I'm able to push thoughts of Cal to the back of my mind, but the long drive back Sunday night has me thinking about him. Good thing he's not spinning songs tonight, or I'd have a hard time keeping myself from calling in the moment I get home. Despite an extra-long workout at my barre, I still spend a restless night going over and over our talks and wishing things were different. Monday morning, I get my sleep-deprived body to a much-needed ballet class first thing. After class, as I sit down to try and wrestle the pile of bills on my desk into some sort of submission, my phone rings.

"Good morning, I'm looking for Jessica Abraham?" The voice is businesslike and unfamiliar.

"This is she."

"This is Marnie Farrell from Boston Casting. Richard Jones sent me a tape and said you were interested in voice-over work?"

Well, this is unexpected. "Yes. Yes, I am."

Wishing that I'd done a bit more homework, I hope I can sound like I know what I'm talking about. All I know is that Marnie gets the best on-camera jobs in town. Will has auditioned for her, but I've never been able to get in there. There has to be a way I can leverage this. "I've been doing union stage work since college and on-camera work for the past couple of years, but Jones felt that I had potential in the voice-over arena." At least I hope that's what he told Marnie.

"Mm. I do like what you did with that character in the recording he sent over. I'm casting a commercial that's kind of similar. Could you come in tomorrow?"

"Of course."

She gives me an appointment, tells me to come in early to get the copy, and gives me their address. When I hang up, I squeal and do a series of *chaînés* around my living room. If I were to add voice-overs to the on-camera work I've begun to pick up, I'd have even more chances to earn decent money as an actress. Theater may be my first love, but even with the higher rates at Chichester Rep, it literally doesn't pay the rent.

It's a good thing that I never got Cal's home number because I'd be tempted to call him and thank him for playing my voice on air by mistake. Instead, I do what I should've done after I ran into Jones last week—I get on the phone to do some research.

CAL

Even though I played songs with Jessica in the title every night I worked the past week, she never called in.

I'm still trying to figure out what exactly went wrong, questioning my own grasp on reality in the process. It feels like Jess broke up with me, but how is that possible when our "relationship" only existed along the thousands of feet of cable and phone lines that connected us? Now it's like she never existed except in the space between my ears.

I've tried to go over our last phone call so many times—wishing

I'd recorded that one—because when I try to recall what she said, all I get is a roar in my ears.

I *think* it was about trust. No doubt men have deceived her in the past, strung her along with lies, even. We can be assholes. And I did violate her trust by sharing her secrets without her permission.

Would she have broken up with me eventually anyway? Did I save us both more heartache? Was the interest I heard in her voice a figment of my own imagination?

I can chase my tail about this all I want, but if I'm honest with myself, I lost her because I didn't want to see the look on her face when she saw mine. And believe me, the irony of the fact that I lost her because I was afraid of losing her is not lost on me.

It's driving me nuts. And I need my focus these days since now both Talia and Jones are on me. They quickly dropped the idea of me talking to girls about their problems during my shift when legal pointed out the liability issues, but now they have a new idea. They're determined to get me interviewing bands with the same "emotional intensity" that I brought to my conversation with Jess.

When I step into the library to do my prep on Monday, Talia's waiting for me.

"Hey, Blondie." She's got a nice head scratch for my dog, but all I get is a piece of paper. "Jones and me put together this list of local bands that you've actively supported over the past couple of years by playing their shit way before anybody else did. I know any one of them would be happy to do an interview with you."

"Have you already forgotten the crash and burn of my interview with Why Not Happiness?"

Wincing at my choice of words, she shakes her head. "No, but I also haven't forgotten how often you screwed up your first week on the air. Or how many mistakes I made when I first started this job."

"That wasn't a mistake, Tal. That was a humiliation."

"Jesus, I feel like I'm talking to my kid here," Talia says to the ceiling. "People make mistakes, you lug. Now are you gonna just quit? Or are you going to learn from the experience and do it a little better the next time?" Slapping the list of bands with the palm of her hand, she says, "Pick one, do the research, and I'll set it up."

"In person or on the phone?"

"Either way. You can take it in baby steps. Whatever you have to do to keep this job because I don't want to have to break in a new DJ."

She pauses on the way out the door. "Same could be said about that girl, you know."

Either figure out how to fix what I broke or move on.

If only it were that easy.

AFTER SPENDING SO many hours on the phone with Jess, losing her is actually painful. Like, my heart actually hurts. I thought I knew all the kinds of pain a body could suffer, but this is a new one to me. Not the throbbing, insistent pain of healing donor sites. Not the searing, screeching pain of bandage changes. This is a black hole of ache in the center of my chest.

Maybe something can come from this new brand of misery. I am a good listener, but I have to figure out a way to get over the fear of saying the wrong thing and being bullied by the cool kids.

I can't lose my job and the woman who feels like the best thing that's ever happened to me all in one week.

So I go back to basics. The reason I have this job is that I love music. I have contacts all over the world that share that love.

I spend every free moment the next week writing letters and even making phone calls to other DJs, from college stations out west to small cities in Europe, telling them about up-and-coming Boston bands like Del Fuegos and the Lemonheads and asking what's new out in their worlds. I spend hours poring over my collection of music magazines as well as the press bibles in the library—notebooks full of PR releases and articles put together by station volunteers. Reading interviews of other bands and cataloguing every bit of background on the bands on Talia's list helps me put together a decent list of not-too-boring questions.

People like to talk about themselves, Jess said. I don't, but maybe that's because my story is only interesting if you're a sadomasochist. But the people who make music, they have stories I want to hear. It's likely my audience does too. If I do enough research, I'll have enough questions to get the ball rolling. If there are some awkward moments, they can get edited out as long as there's more than enough good stuff to balance them out.

I just have to remember that it's about *them*, not me. I'm just the vehicle that gets not just the music, but what's behind it, out to the world.

JESS

Tuesday I somehow manage to get to the casting office earlier than early, so I have plenty of time to learn the copy. When my name is called, I'm surprised that it's Marnie herself who not only ushers me into the tiny recording booth but also adjusts the mic and hands me headphones. She smiles when I put them on backward, explaining that the cable is always attached to the left can. Feeling like a total rookie is no fun, but once we get going, her clear direction in my ears has me too busy playing to worry.

The best part? For once in my life, nobody cares what I look like. I'm not too dark, too ethnic, too pretty, not pretty enough, too short, too chesty, too old, not old enough. All that matters is the story I tell with my voice. I could be anyone in here.

Thankfully, Marnie seems to like what she hears. I guess all those college voice classes were good for something besides Shakespeare.

After she decides she has enough options to send to the ad agency, she meets me outside the booth. "You really need a demo to showcase the range of characters you can play, Jess. I'll keep bringing you in to audition, but sometimes a client wants to listen to demos first. Just don't lose that freshness."

Like I'm going to go stale? I'm not sure exactly what she means, but I do know that I had so much fun in that dim little booth all by myself that I can't wait to do it again. Having someone pay me to do it? That'd just be a bonus.

On my way out, Marnie's assistant gives me a list of people she recommends for demo production, which includes prices. It's expensive, almost as much as a month's rent. But when I get home and look up voice-over rates in my union handbook, they're really good. I'd only have to book a day of work to cover the cost.

My heart pounding, I call demo producers, thinking maybe I can figure out some sort of barter. Not sure what, since I doubt sound engineers have much need for a choreographer or dance classes.

I guess I could ask one of my siblings for a loan. Not my parents, though. I need them to believe I'm surviving on my own, or law school brochures will magically show up in my mailbox. Or worse, they'll fix me up with nice Jewish boys fresh out of law school themselves.

CAL

Tuesday evening, I'm in the library prepping when Talia pops in, expression dialed to hopeful.

"I've got the promoter for the Sprytes on the phone. They can squeeze in an interview with you tomorrow afternoon. Their show isn't until the weekend, but they're laying over in Boston for a couple of days."

Big breath in, big breath out. "Okay."

"Thing is, they want to do it in person."

"In person," I repeat.

"That's what I said."

Closing my eyes, I picture front man Gray Thompson's face and imagine the sneer when he sees mine. Redirecting my focus to the notes I've accumulated on the Boston-based band that's been taking over Europe for the past year while failing to get traction in the U.S., I remind myself that they need me as much as I need them.

"I'll do it."

"You're sure?"

"I'm sure."

When Talia's hand lands on my shoulder, my eyes pop open to take in her proud smile. "You'll do good, Cal."

After letting my face crack its half-smile for a beat, I swipe her hand away. "Get outta here. I'm not your kid. I got work to do."

I get a whap on the back of my head in response, but I'm grinning as I pull the folder I've compiled on the Sprytes from the pile in front of me and start editing my questions.

JESS

Wednesday, as I'm about to head out the door to drive to Bedford for dinner with my parents, my phone rings. I check my watch. I'm already late. Traffic will only get worse with every passing minute, but the call might hold good news that'll counter the bad news I turned up calling demo producers, where I learned that rates have skyrocketed since Marnie's assistant put together that handout.

When the machine picks up and I hear Jones's voice on the line, I don't hesitate; I grab the receiver. "This is Jessica."

"Jessica. It's Jones. From WBAR?"

My heart skips. I haven't talked to Cal in over a week. "Is Cal—is Cal okay?"

"Oh yeah, he's fine. At least I think so. He hasn't come in yet."

"Right. Of course."

"So listen, I've got a few promos I need recorded. Since we chatted the other day, I've been wondering if we need to add a female voice to our talent pool. You interested?"

My feet do a jeté and I have to clamp a hand over my mouth to stifle a squeal of joy. Before I speak, I shake it all off so I can play the role of a woman that does this all the time. "That sounds like an excellent idea."

"Great. Can you come in tomorrow? Say, two thirty?"

"I can make that work if I can be finished by four."

I give him my fax number and calmly thank him for thinking of me, as if this isn't the best news I've heard all day. After the call comes in, my feet are batting out entrechats of impatience as my fax machine slowly spits out its missives.

Picking up the sheets from the floor and holding them by the edges to avoid the icky feeling of the slimy paper, I mumble the king's words from *Midsummer*: "What revels are in hand?"

After a few slow breaths, I'm able to read the spots, which are indeed about revels, announcing the station's annual anti-Valentine's Day concert called Bleeding Hearts. It makes sense to have a woman read them, I guess, but you'd think one of the female jocks could do it.

But hey, I'm not complaining.

I float through the drive to my parents' house, riding the wave of hope that maybe I can keep this career going through my thirties without asking anyone for a loan.

After a lovely dinner with my parents and a few rounds of gin rummy with my dad, I head back to my little grotto. On the way home, Cal's voice is like a warm arm curled over my shoulder. I really, *really* want to call him to tell him all my good news. But I made my position clear, and I need to stick to my guns.

CAL

This time around, I'm not only prepared for the interview, I'm amped. Reading up on the part of this band's story that's already been told has me wanting the world to know more. I'm not a writer, but if I can be a music journalist in my own way, I'll at the very least broadcast something better than the spiteful, lowbrow humor peddled by the jerks at the station across town. Proving that my listeners want more—deserve more—has consumed me for the past twenty-four hours. So much so that there's no space left in my brain for nerves.

Plus, if I forget everything, I've got notes. It's chicken scratch, but I can read it.

I'm at the station early, I'm wearing my favorite hoodie, and we've got beverages and snacks set out. I'm as ready as I'll ever be when Talia ushers the four band members into the large studio we use to record acoustic sets. I swear she's more nervous than me. Her hands are flapping around like birds, so I step in to introduce myself to the band's leader.

"Gray? I'm Cal Alonso. Thanks for coming in."

"Hey, thanks for having us." As the baby-faced rocker shakes my hand, his gaze flickers from the left side of my face down to the tats on my forearm and then back to my eyes, but all he says is, "Good to be here."

The engineer gets him settled in front of a mic as I introduce myself to the rest of the band. Only bass player Kate Dale seems to even notice my scars. Something about the way she peruses them— more curious than pitying—makes me want to explain.

"I was in a house fire when I was four. Had to go through a lot of surgeries to repair the damage." Sliding the hoodie zipper halfway down, I let the hood fall so she can see my neck. "Some were more successful than others.

She nods. "That sucks."

"Yeah, pretty much."

We both nod in tandem for a couple beats before Talia calls Kate over. Feeling lighter than I have in months, maybe years, I grab my notes and sit down in front of my own mic. After we get the go ahead from Talia, I jump right in.

"So, first question. When you guys left Boston a year ago, you'd established a name locally. Were you expecting to have such enthusiastic crowds on your European tour?"

Gray shakes his head. "Not at all. I mean, I'm kind of an idiot, so I didn't even know that people over in Germany and Holland and France speak English better than we do."

"Speak for yourself," Kate cuts in.

"Anyway, I knew our songs were getting play over there. I mean, that's why we could do the tour in the first place. But to have all these people in other countries across the fucking ocean—Oh shit."

Talia's voice crackles over the speakers from the booth. "Don't worry, we're not live; we can bleep you."

"Oh, good. Anyway, these fuckers knew all the words to our songs."

"Better than I did, sometimes," Kate says with a throaty laugh. Then she leans toward me. "Hey, can I smoke in here? I mean, will it bother you?"

I shrug. "You can light up if you want. My fire wasn't a cigarette incident, it was a popcorn incident."

She starts to laugh but covers her mouth. "I'm sorry, I swear I'm not laughing at you. It's just, I don't know which would be worse to have to live without—cigarettes or popcorn."

Suddenly, I'm laughing, too, because this is what I've always wanted—to be able to hang out with the cool kids. Not the stuck-up bullies from junior high, but the kids who rocked out in their garages. Which brings me to my next question.

"So, you guys literally started as a garage band, right? For all our listeners who are plugging away in their parents' garages, what's the secret to getting from there to where you are now?"

"Well, first of all," Gray says, puffing up his chest, "it was our own garage. We had moved out of our parents' houses."

"I hadn't," the drummer chimes in.

"You still haven't," Kate clarifies.

He shrugs. "We're on the road. Why pay rent when I'm barely here?"

Gray goes on to talk about how they still don't feel like they've "made it" and how all they really want is to make noise that's interesting. I'm so at ease, when the drummer asks to see the rest of my tats, I take off my hoodie altogether. By the time the promoter lets us know that the band has to get going, we've been talking for an hour, but I feel like I could do this forever.

After they leave, Talia swoops in from the booth to give me a hug. "You did awesome! You didn't seem nervous at all."

My smile is as wide as it gets when I ask, "When can I do the next one?"

The only thing that would make this better? If I could share it with Jess.

Chapter 13

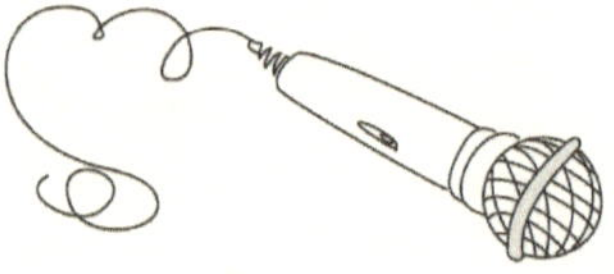

Don't miss WBAR's annual Bleeding Hearts concert this weekend at the Ratt in Kenmore Square with headliners The Colourfield and Dexy's Midnight Runners. Tickets available at Ticketron.

JESS

I manage to make it to the station only a few minutes late. There's a different receptionist at the front than there was the other day, but after a few unsuccessful tries at getting Jones on the phone, the woman gives up and points down a hallway. Unfortunately, this place is a bit of a rabbit warren. After a few turns, I find myself in a hallway lined with closed doors. I try to retrace my steps, but I end up in what seems like a different hallway, also lined with closed doors.

Now fifteen minutes late, I'm wondering if I'm actually asleep and having a nightmare. Telling myself that I won't ruin the broadcast if I'm super quiet, I pick a door and turn the knob.

When I pull it open, a man falls through.

CAL

Still riding the high of a successful interview, I head to the music library to put my research away before we edit the tape. Arms full of folders stacked on top of my crate of albums, I turn around to open a door with my back, but it disappears behind me so fast I stumble through the opening. Instinctively protecting my precious cargo with both arms, I land on my ass with a thud. I save the albums, but the folders and their contents scatter across the floor.

"Oh my god, I'm so sorry." A mass of dark corkscrew curls hides the face of a petite woman as she stoops to gather up the papers, but I sure as hell know that voice.

"I'm so stupid," she mutters. "I'm trying to find the promo booth. I swear I can get lost anywhere."

I don't think. Without even getting up, I take both of her hands in mine.

She looks up, drops the papers, and gasps. I never put my hoodie back on after the interview, so my tats and my scars are exposed. Her eyes take it all in, from my hands, to my arms, to my neck, my jaw, left cheek, and finally to my eyes.

What I see in hers about kills me. It's the usual suspects.

Surprise. Horror. Pity.

Boom, boom, boom.

I squeeze her hands once before releasing them and giving her my crooked smile. It's not a flirty thing. It's the only one I've got.

Eyes on the spill, I quickly sweep everything up, give her a quick nod and get away as quickly as I can, hoping the lit Recording sign in the studio will keep her from following me.

It's only when I'm safe behind the closed door that I wonder what the fuck she's doing here.

Chapter 14

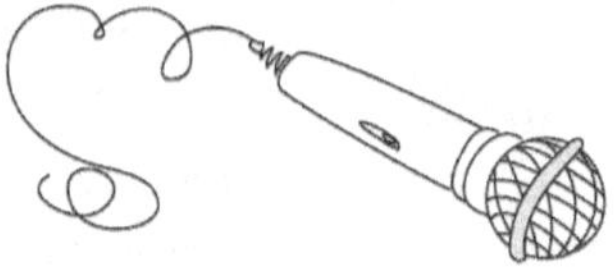

Brought to you by the station that fits you to a T, WBAR 101.7 FM, Boston.

JESS

I'm not sure how long I sit on the floor after the mystery man leaves.

When I do manage to stand, my legs are shaky. I feel like I just saw a ghost. No, not a ghost. More like one of those guardian angels from that movie *Wings of Desire*. But the warm, firm hands gripping mine said otherwise. Not to mention broad shoulders that looked like they held the weight of the world. Or muscled arms strong enough to do the most challenging choreographed lift.

The scars molding and stretching the planes of his face looked painful. Angry, even. But they weren't what brought on my tears. It was what I read in his eyes. In seconds, I saw an entire life story.

Desire. Rage. Despair.

Boom, boom, boom.

On top of that, I'm such a weirdo that all I wanted to do was touch his skin. And see more of it. Images of the back of his left hand, his neck, his jaw are seared into my brain. Marbled swirls of ridged and pulled skin on one hand, glorious, inked colors on the other. Somehow the imperfect pieces of his puzzle added up to a whole that just said *yes*.

Who was that guy?

And how do I find out?

I can't exactly go around asking, *Hey, I ran into a guy who has terrible scars on one side of his face while the other is the most beautiful I've ever seen. Can you tell me his name?* He was wearing a pale blue T-shirt with the sleeves cut off and black jeans. Black curly hair and tawny brown skin. Wideset hazel eyes framed by dark lashes. A well-kept goatee. If asked, I could describe every detail.

Eventually, I remember that I'm here to do a job, if only I could find the people I'm supposed to be working with. Thinking maybe that guy could give me directions if I could form words to ask, I carefully open the door again, only to find another dim hallway. At least there's a window at the end of this one. When I get closer, not only do I see that the hall actually doglegs at the window, but there's a brightly lit stage on the other side of the glass. On it, a man wearing a black hoodie sits behind a big mic. The Recording sign is lit, so I don't want to disturb him. An exit sign beyond the curve beckons to me, so I drift in that direction, thinking it might lead to the other studios or to Jones's office.

As I pass, I peek at the man onstage.

It's him.

Before I can open the door next to the window, I hear Cal's voice through the speakers above my head. His words match the moving lips of the man on the other side of the window. The man who fell through the door—that guardian angel—is *my* guardian angel.

But Cal doesn't work in the afternoon. Is it possible Jones set this whole thing up? Would he hire me to record an inane set of announcements anybody could read on a day that Cal happens to be working a day shift as some sort of crazy meet-cute?

The idea takes me on a rollercoaster of feeling from hurt to hope to just plain mad. This girl does not like to be manipulated.

THE EXIT DOOR to the left takes me to another that leads me to Jones's office. When I find him, my mouth launches right in. "Is Cal working right now?"

He just sighs.

"This is probably super unprofessional, but I have to know."

Jones drops his head, shakes it once, meets my gaze and nods.

"How long is he here for?"

"I don't know. He's here to do an interview."

I check the clock on the wall. It's almost three. I have to leave at four to get to Chichester in time to get ready for the show tonight. I take a deep breath. I have spots to record and I have no idea how long it'll take to do them. That has to be my priority. "I'm sorry I'm late but I've been wandering around lost for the past half hour. Can we get started?"

"You sure?"

"Well, I am wondering right now if you brought me in here for some reason other than my talent, but you know what? I really need the work, so let's do it."

After a brief moment where he looks like he's going to confess to playing Cupid, he ushers me down yet another hallway and into a recording studio that's about a tenth of the size of the one Cal was in. Jones adjusts the microphone and gives me headphones—which I put on correctly, thanks to Marnie—then settles in on the other side of the glass next to an engineer who moves sliders around and pushes buttons as I recite the copy. Once the levels are set, Jones gives me direction. "Let's go for a brighter read. Like you're telling a girlfriend about a party that she can't miss."

I do multiple takes of each short spot, so many that I've lost count. He and the engineer don't seem frustrated, so I guess I'm doing what they want. It's crazy how many different ways you can say the same two sentences.

I don't let myself watch the clock. Jones knows that my out time is four, and I have a feeling he'd like me to talk to Cal before I leave. Unfortunately, the whole crazy scenario has tension creeping into my shoulders and neck, so I have to keep shaking out my arms and rolling my head around to get rid of it. Despite the fact that the work seems to be going well, the nervous buzz behind my solar plexus won't go away.

I want to talk to Cal, and it's the last thing I want to do. I'm afraid I'll fall for him. I'm afraid the whole perfect fairy tale will fall flat if we actually spend any time face to face. But that moment between us was filled with more spark than anything I've ever felt for any man. At least in real life.

But *is* it real life?

Finally, I must give them what they're looking for. Or rather, listening for. When Jones gives me a salute and a thank you, I grab my stuff and sprint out the door.

This time, my body seems to know the way to the heart of the station, to the studio where my own personal superhero was perched on a stool in front of the mic that gives him his power.

But when I get there, he's gone.

The place is empty.

When I turn around, I almost run smack into Jones. I didn't even know he was on my heels.

Before he can say anything, a woman appears and hands Jones a stack of While You Were Out slips. "The two on top need callbacks before five." She tips her head at the glassed-in studio. "Talia said Cal did an amazing job with the interview, so you've got to hear that, too." She winces. "And don't kill the messenger, but I'm supposed to tell you that you're an asshole."

Jones nods, his mouth pinched, and then turns to me. "I guess I deserve that."

I take a deep breath, mirror his grim expression. "Thank you. For the work, that is. I appreciate it."

The big hand clicks forward. "I have to go," I say to Jones.

I'll be back, is what I say to myself.

IT TOOK every bit of the self-control drilled into me during years of ballet to get through tonight's show. Now, butt back in my car for the drive home, I turn up the heat and the radio and debate whether I should go home or to the station.

Seeing him this afternoon rocked my world. The drive north helped me calm down a bit, and my preshow rituals got me focused. Mostly. Performing this nutty play is probably as good a way as any to channel the crazy mix of feelings set off by seeing Cal in person for the first time. By feeling the surge of electricity when his hands touched mine.

When his voice comes through my car speakers, those feelings perk right up again, and it's suddenly crystal clear that I need to talk to him. In person. Having seen his scars, I get that they might be what's had him keeping me at a distance. I'm sure he's had some bad experiences because of it.

But...

I didn't go to law school like my brother, but dinner at my family's table growing up was like being on the debate team. Let's just say I have a lot of *buts* to argue with by the time I pull into the station lot.

The station's front door is locked, however. It is almost eleven o'clock. Remembering what Cal said about the volunteers who deal with late-night visitors, I push the button by the squawk box until a giant of a man answers the door, so fierce-looking he probably moonlights as a bouncer at one of the clubs down the street.

All my arguments for Cal won't work on this guy, but I have other tools at my disposal. The only good thing about a body like mine is that it makes men stupid.

Tipping my head to the side and crossing my legs, I let a lazy smile spread across my face. I give him a breathy "Hi" and then bite my lip.

He frowns. "Can I help you?"

"I hope so." I do a little wiggle as I unzip my coat and lean against the door frame. After his gaze drops to check out the maracas, I go on. "I was here earlier today recording some promos." This is where it gets tricky. I don't think I'm getting past this guy if Cal told him he doesn't want to see me.

Bringing a hand to my brow, damsel-in-distress style, I shake my head like it's the end of the world. "I can't find my wallet, and I think it might've fallen out of my purse when I was in the booth. I have to work early tomorrow, so I'd really like to get it now." I top of the speech with pitiful puppy eyes.

Any director would laugh me offstage for this performance, but desperation has me pulling out all the stops.

He blinks slowly and then looks over my shoulder into the parking lot like maybe I brought back up. His lips flattening, he sighs. "All right. But everything's locked up down at that end. I'll have to escort you down there."

Hands fly to a prayer position over my heart. "Thank you so much."

Once I'm inside and he's turned the deadbolt behind me, he heads down a hallway I haven't used before. Whoever designed this building must've use Boston streets as inspiration. I play Chatty Cathy as I follow him, finding out that his name's Big Bob, he's worked here for four years, he's a security guard but he also drives the station van to special events, and that he's studying sound engineering at a community college. When he opens the door to the recording studio, I manage a nice little sleight of hand while he turns on the lights. Covering my actions with a swoop of my hair, I chuck my wallet in the corner. Then I look for it in the opposite corner.

"Is that it?" Big Bob asks, pointing to my wallet.

"Oh my gosh! You're my hero."

Leading the way out, I head in the opposite direction of the way we came. "Thank you so much, Big Bob."

Before he can say anything about my choice of route, I turn around and walk backward. "Jones was going to show me the listener line lounge earlier, but I had to run." This is a total lie, but I do remember Cal saying once that the lounge is next to the broadcast studio. I keep walking, talking over my shoulder. "It's this way, right?"

"Uh, yeah, but—"

I grab his hand. "I won't make any noise; don't worry. I know you have to be quiet around the booths. Believe me, when somebody slammed a door while I was recording earlier, that was so frustrating."

I bat my eyes at him, ask him a few questions about his studies, and let him lead the way since I really have no idea where I'm going. When Bob opens a door and ushers me inside a large room filled with assorted seating and a handful of half-asleep humans, we're greeted by a woman with magenta hair, square-framed glasses and a wary smile. "Aren't you going to introduce your friend, Big Bob?"

Stepping away from me, his round cheeks turn pink. "Oh no, she's not my friend."

I reach out a hand. "I'm Jessica Abraham. I dropped my wallet when I was here earlier today."

The woman's penciled-in brows rise. "Jessica, huh?"

My smile is hopeful. "Yep."

"I'm Talia." She draws a circle in the air behind her, indicating the volunteers. "I'm in charge." Her Southie accent really kicks in on the last word. I know I'm facing the real gatekeeper when she crosses her arms over a generous bust and looks me up and down, taking inventory. "And you're Jess. From the phone."

Suddenly warm, I take off my coat. "Guilty as charged."

Flirting's not gonna get me through this door, so I spit out the truth. "I'd really like to talk to Cal before I leave."

Her eyes narrow further.

Before I can say anything else, I hear him. Cal's voice cuts through the murmur of volunteers on the phones and goes right to my heart.

That voice may still be coming through wires, but, discounting our collision earlier today, the man is closer than he's ever been. As I listen, every single reservation about whatever it is between Cal and me fades away. "Please," I whisper. "I need to talk to him. Face to face."

Slowly, her gaze tracks from me to the speaker on the wall and back again. "Yup. I think you do." Talia tips her head at the door to our left. "This way."

Big Bob steps in our way. "Talia, Cal said no visitors."

Talia's no shorty, but even she has to crane her neck when she turns to face him. "Big Bob, when does Cal smile?"

"Uh, never?"

"No. There's one occasion when Cal always smiles."

A volunteer hangs up a phone and pops a pink bubble. "When Jessica calls, duh. You can hear it in his voice."

Big Bob looks at me, then at the door. "I don't know..."

Talia puts a hand in the middle of Big Bob's wide chest and pats it twice. "Someday you'll get it, sweetheart." Before he can say anything else, she adds, "If this goes south, it's on me."

He shakes his big head slowly. "All right. But I don't want anything to do with it." Both hands up in surrender, he turns and walks away.

Talia puts an arm around me. "You're a heck of lot prettier than I thought you'd be. Maybe that's part of the problem. But don't give up. We're all rootin' for ya." She opens the first of two doors that lead into the recording studio. When I hesitate, she gives me a little shove as she whispers, "In you go."

Taking a big breath, I make what feels like the most important entrance of my life. Problem is, the first door only takes me to a small buffer chamber between the lounge and the actual studio. The bravado that got me to this point falls away, and I can't quite get myself to open the second door. All I can seem to do is wait at the window and hope that he invites me in.

Chapter 15

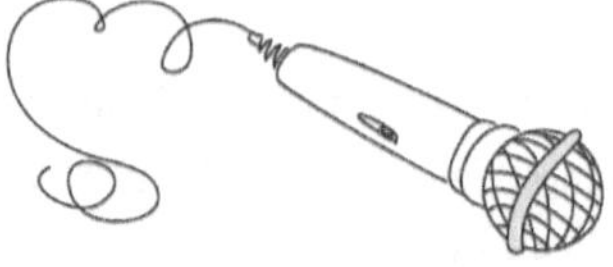

What's happening out there this fine winter evening, Boston? Tell me what you're up to. All I know is it's exactly thirty-two degrees and not a cloud in the sky to blot out that full moon. Be safe out there and watch out for werewolves.

CAL

There's a shadow on the other side of the window in the studio door. If it were Talia, she'd already be inside. Even though it's possible for Jess to have finished her show and made the drive back here, I can't believe it'd be her. If it is, she's probably just here to try to apologize for how she reacted when she saw my scars—or worse, try to convince me that she doesn't care about them while she secretly pities me.

I know what I saw in her eyes, so I stifle any surviving shreds of hope for a real relationship with her and solder my focus to the tasks at hand. After all, it's time to check the rack and make engineering notations. Then I really should line up carts for the next round of commercials.

But I can only hold off for so long. Now that I've encountered the woman behind the voice, all I want is to inhale the scent that I didn't get anywhere near enough of and touch the soft skin that I barely brushed, even as I'm taunted by the fact that her beauty puts her so far out of my league even the idea of romance between us is a cruel joke.

Despite all the reasons why I shouldn't, I turn my head. The person on the other side of the glass is a tiny thing. Not Talia, that's for sure. I'd trust her next to me in a pub brawl. This creature, this delicate vision with a halo of curls, needs protecting.

The drive to open the door and pull her into my arms is doing its best to drown out protests from my frontal lobe when a red blinking light from the telephone reminds me that I do have a job to do here. Rolling my chair over, I tuck the phone receiver between shoulder and ear and punch the button, even as I keep one eye on the window. "This is Cal, what can I play for you?"

"This is Talia. You need to invite that girl in and talk to her, or I will stop screening calls for you and you'll have to talk to anyone and everyone, including the idiots requesting country music."

"You know I don't allow visitors in here," is my last attempt at self-preservation. Letting this woman rock my world feels more dangerous than going back under the knife.

"What I know is that you're acting like an idiot," Talia says in her mom voice. "Get over yourself."

It takes me a moment to clock the dial tone blaring in my ear. Setting the receiver back in the cradle, my heart plays a heavy baseline in my chest as I take my time putting away albums I played earlier, slipping them into the far end of the box before pulling one from the Heavy Rotation section. Spinning the cover, I try to skim Jones's notes about the preferred track, but I just keep reading the same words over and over. Giving up on that part of my job, I slide the record from the sleeve. For the first time ever, my hand shakes as I place the needle, and I almost scratch the fucking record.

This is why I can't have visitors.

"Hold My Life" by the Replacements is winding down—something I need help with, it seems. Sliding my headphones back on, my hands go through the familiar motions to slip-cue from one track to another: set the needle, check the volume, fade out on one and in on the other as I release the record so it can join the spin of the turntable. The sequence complete, I look over my shoulder.

She's still there.

For five songs, three calls and two commercials, it takes every one of my brain cells to get my job done.

When I risk another look, she's so still I think I might be imagining her for a moment, but then the light catches the left side of her face.

Great, just great.

I've made a beautiful woman cry.

JESS

I'm not sure how long I've been standing here watching Cal. It could be days, it could be a handful of seconds. All I know is that I can't take my eyes off him. I don't want to miss a step of the choreography unfolding before me or a note of the story he spins with his song choices. Some part of his body is always in motion, keeping time with the beat. His eyes, when I get to see them, flash with emotion. Concern for a woman who's on the side of the road at a payphone, lost somewhere in Somerville. Patience as he finds a map and gives her directions. Wry amusement when a group of drunks calls begging him to play "Rock Lobster."

All I can do is watch as his fingers dance over a dizzying array of knobs and buttons and albums and turntables and his lips caress the microphone the way I want them to touch me.

A tap on my shoulder has me nearly jumping out of my skin. Somehow I manage to clap a hand over my mouth to muffle a startled squeal. Talia eases me to the side, opens the door to his domain and drops something on a desk inside. She mumbles a curt good night to Cal before doing a nimble do-si-do with me so that I'm inside and she's outside.

Even though I suddenly feel like I'm in enemy territory, I muster the courage to ask, "Why are you being so mean to me?"

CAL

I don't hear tears in her voice when she whispers the question, but when I glance over, I can see them reflecting in the dim light. Unbelievably, brimming eyes make her even more beautiful. No puffy, blotchy cry-face for this girl. She really is a princess.

"You have no idea" is what comes out of my mouth. Not quite a question, not quite a statement.

She surveys the booth. Not like she can't stand to look at me, but like the answers might be in the racks of albums behind me or in the carousels of carts or on the bulletin board choked with everything from tattered autographed photos of rock stars to postcards for shows from three years ago.

When her eyes meet mine again, she swipes tears from her cheek. I have to admit, the way she looks at me isn't what I'm used to. She neither avoids the scars nor tries to pretend they don't exist. Instead, she looks through them, through all of my skin, making me want to know what she sees beneath it all.

She drops her head, shakes it, then faces me again. "I mean, I'm guessing it's about your… appearance."

A harsh laugh barks out of me. "You think?"

Stubborn-as-hell lips press together as she settles in for an argument. Gesturing up and down her body, she asks, "So is that how it is for you? Is it all about how *pretty* I am?"

Most of my brain is wondering about the ugly way she just called herself pretty, but a corner of it registers that "Sowing the Seeds of Love" is about to end. Raising one finger in her direction, I run the other down my log before pulling albums and lining up the next three songs. Checking the time, I do a quick station ID. Then, eyes still on the equipment in front of me, I answer her question. "Of course not."

"So, you can like the me that you know from the phone, but I'm not allowed to do the same?"

"No, but—"

"What's the problem then?"

"The problem is that I look like this and you look like that."

"So it is all about what's on the outside."

"People don't cover their kids' eyes when they see you, Jess."

"Maybe not, but they sure as hell make assumptions about me. You don't have to be blonde for people to call you a bimbo, you know."

"It's not the same."

"No, it's not the same. But I'm not talking about other people, I'm talking about you and me. Why do I have to pay for every terrible thing other people have said or done to you?"

My heart, panicking inside the walls of my chest, is so loud I can barely hear the music. I can't tell if it's trying to get away from her or get to her.

One thing I am sure of: I can't have this conversation and do my job at the same time. It's too much.

Something catches my ear and I remember that this track is mixed on the high side, so I reach back to adjust the volume on the output. Sliding the last album I played back in its sleeve, I note the date on its grid and slide it onto the rack behind me, in line with the others I've played tonight. I pick up another from the rack and realize I haven't been making notes since Jess showed up on the other side of the glass an hour ago.

Fingers tented over closed eyes, I blow out a breath before dropping my hands to face her again. "This is a complicated conversation because of me and how my life has gone so far. It's got nothing to do with you and how much of a good person you are." I wave a hand around the studio. "I'm making mistakes here. If we keep talking, I may as well walk out. I know it's not the end of the world if songs aren't playing on the radio, but it is my job."

She takes an abrupt step back. "I'm sorry. You're right. I shouldn't have—"

God help me, I grab her hand. It's a risk, because I may not be able to let go. "Jess. It's okay. When I'm talking to you on the phone, I can handle all this, no problem." I rub a thumb over the soft skin of her hand. Softer than anything I've ever felt. "But for this conversation, I need all my focus. Can we do it another time?"

The expression "face like an open book" could have been coined for her. Disappointment, frustration, anger and resignation march right across it, one after the other. Suddenly, she grabs my other hand and grips both fiercely.

"I'll wait." Without breaking eye contact, she points to the lounge on the other side of the glass. "I'll be out there when you're done tonight."

She releases my hands and turns to leave, but before I move an inch, she's back, hands on the arms of my chair. Her lips meet mine, a whisper-soft brush followed by a firm press that melts any resolve I thought I was hanging onto.

She pulls back, straightens and points at the clock behind me. "No sneaking out without me."

This time when she turns to go, she doesn't stop.

Me? I've fallen, and I don't *want* to get up.

THE REST OF MY SHIFT, time is a slippery concept. After Jess leaves, the clock hands stop, but before I know it, they read one forty-five. Then the final fifteen minutes stretch out for years. When Wayne steps in for his shift, all I've been able to do during the final song of my set is stare at the disc spinning on the felt. My closing tasks are a mountain I can't seem to climb. I put things in the wrong place, get the dates and times wrong on my notes and generally stumble around until Wayne orders me out because I'm harshing on his groove.

Mumbling an apology, I stagger out to the lounge. At first I don't see her, but then I find her curled up on one end of the couch, my dog snoring away at her feet. Moving carefully so as not to disturb either of them, I perch on the coffee table to take her in. She *is* the girl in the neon-green dress. I knew she'd be pretty, but this sleeping beauty makes a mockery of the word. She's so captivating I could sit here for the rest of my days. I could die right now and be happy.

But my dog has other ideas. Once her one eye opens, she's ready to go. Poor thing needs her walk. Speaking of which, Phil's waiting on me. So instead of shushing Blondie, I let her whining and wriggling wake Jess.

"Hey, princess."

She must've been completely out. After her eyes bat open, she looks around the space in confusion.

"Sorry to wake you, but I've got to get somewhere."

She sits up quickly. "But you said—I waited—"

"You can come with me if you want, but I have to go. My friend Phil has food waiting for me, and I don't want it to go to waste."

Standing, I hold out my hand. When she takes it, I swear I hear music—and it's not whatever weird shit Wayne's spinning. A melody soars inside my chest, and for once, I am the prince in a fairy tale.

JESS

The outside air is bracing after the stuffy warmth of the studio. After he closes and locks the back door, Cal takes my hand to tuck it in his coat pocket along with his own. His other hand holds a leash connected to a dog that I'd assumed was some sort of company mascot. After the dog does her business in a patch of snow, he tips his head away from the building. "You coming?"

I have an audition tomorrow morning. I should be in bed. But it seems worth the risk of giant eye circles to say yes to this offer. I get the feeling it doesn't happen often. If ever. So I follow.

"You hungry?"

Momentarily muted by the charge sizzling from his hand to mine, I finally manage, "Is anything open?"

"Only if you have connections," he answers before turning into an alley I'd never think of venturing down on my own. Cal is a guardian in more ways than one. I knew he'd be sexy the first time I heard that voice, but I didn't expect wide shoulders and a muscled build on a guy who sits in front of a mic for a living. Of course, I couldn't have known that he never stops moving when he's spinning.

Moments later, we've arrived at a nondescript building with a neon sign proclaiming "BAR." Cal ushers me and the dog inside. It's after hours, so no one else is here, but when as sit at the bar, a voice calls from the kitchen. "Be there in a sec, Cal."

When a barrel-chested man steps in from the kitchen carrying a covered plate, the expression on his face confirms that a date on Cal's arm is rare, maybe even a first.

"Phil, this is Jessica. Jessica, Phil."

I reach out to shake Phil's hand. "Nice to meet you."

"Likewise." He sets down the plate in front of Cal. "Uh, we're closed, officially, but I may be able to locate a beverage for you that someone forgot to serve. Like this beer here." He sets a sweating pint glass in front of Cal.

I study the rows of bottles behind him and the taps down the bar. In the summer, I'm a G&T girl but it's a bit cold for a cocktail. "Maybe a glass of red wine?"

He nods before turning around to peruse the shelves. Selecting a bottle, he holds it up to the light before emptying the remaining contents into two glasses, handing me one and lifting the other in a salute before taking a sip himself. "This'd be no good by tomorrow. Can't let it go to waste." He tilts his head toward the kitchen. "Can probably find some eats for you if you'd like."

"Thank you, that'd be nice." I didn't feel like eating before the show tonight, so I am pretty hungry. After Phil disappears, I raise my glass. "Thanks for giving me a chance."

Cal clinks with me and takes a sip without losing eye contact. "You're pretty damn stubborn."

"Thank you."

Instead of dousing the flames of desire lighting up every corner of my body, the wine spreads the heat faster. I end up shoving my hands under my thighs so I don't grab him by the collar and crawl into his lap. That glancing kiss back at the studio only made me want more.

When Talia pushed me into the studio earlier, I was fired up for a debate. Now my brain's hazy from the nap I took, so when Phil slides a mouth-watering plate of food in front of me, I dig in and Cal does too. Before I can say anything, he beats me to the punch.

"I know I have a face only a mother could love."

"Cal—"

"Let me get this out. Please."

It's not easy for me to back down, but I do.

"But you were right back in the studio. It is hard for me to wrap my head around the idea that someone who looks like you would want to even be seen with someone who looks like me."

This is obviously difficult territory for him, so I clamp my lips together and keep listening.

"You're also right that it's pretty obnoxious of me to think that'd be all you care about, but I've lived in this fucked-up body for a really long time. So I know that for me, normal is not possible. You've got an imagination. Picture what it'd be like for you to be out in public with me."

"I'm used to people staring, Cal. People have stared because of my so-called exotic beauty my whole life."

"I'm sorry, but it's not the same."

"How do you know? You say that I can't know what it's like to live in your skin. Logically, the same is true the other way around." The zing of winning a point is immediately tamped down by shame. I mean, I am right, but he is too. I can't imagine the pain he's suffered, both physical and psychological.

"When you saw me for the first time, your face said it all."

Shaking my head, I push my empty plate away and turn to face him. "You startled me."

"Your face told a very clear story. One I've read before."

"I don't know what you think you saw, but I do know about projection. My mother teaches psychology. People often see what they expect to see."

"Exactly. People would see you and me and be like, 'What the fuck is a monster like him doing with a gorgeous woman like her?'"

"What do you care what assholes like that think?"

"Because it fucking hurts, that's why I care. It hurt when you saw my face and you were afraid."

"I wasn't afraid. I wasn't expecting you. Or anyone. I mean, you fell through the door."

"I saw your thoughts, Jess. You may have been startled at first, but then it was the same thing I get every time. Your face is expressive, you know."

"That may be so, but—"

"Sorry, guys," Phil interrupts us. "But I've got to clear out the place. Don't want to give the cops any reason to sniff around." He sets two bags full of takeout containers on the bar next to Cal. "Nice to meet you, Jessica. Hope to see you again."

Before I know it, we're back out in the cold. This time Cal's hands are full, so I have to shove my hands in my own pockets.

"I'll walk you back to your car, but then I have to deliver these."

"To whom?"

"Some homeless guys. Phil hates waste, and I don't like people to go hungry. Plus, I get why some people don't want to be out in the world."

I'm suddenly too tired and too cold to argue anymore. Tonight, anyway. This man is a saint compared to the guys I usually go out with, but it's going to take some time to convince him of that. I might've met my match on the stubborn front, but now that I know the reason why he's kept me at bay—which doesn't seem to include him being a player or married—I'm not giving up until he gives us a chance.

Before I know it, we're back at my car. I unlock the door and turn around to make one last plea, but Cal reaches around to open it for me. "Time for princesses to go home."

"Only if you promise me that this isn't the only time I'll see you, that this isn't some kind of magical"—I swoop my hands in the air between us—"time warp that you'll pretend never happened."

He nods slowly. "I promise."

I can't stop the yawns. "Okay, but only because I have a five-show weekend to face." Placing a hand on his chest I add, "And only if you'll let me do this."

The urge has been nipping at my heels for the past hour, so I take him by the hoodie and pull him close to finish what I started back at the studio. A tightness around his mouth gives me pause, so I whisper a quote from *Othello*. "I know a lady in Venice would have walked barefoot to Palestine for a touch of his nether lip."

When his mouth quirks in a half smile, I bring my "nether lip" to his. Once, twice… and before I get to the third, his hands are in my hair and our lips are locked in a conversation all their own.

CAL

The melody that began playing in my head when this woman brushed her lips over mine hours ago swells into a full-on orchestral arrangement when our mouths meet again. Horns and strings and resounding percussion.

Her lips are even softer than her skin. God help me, I want to feel them pressed to every inch of mine. When a mew of a moan widens that gorgeous smile of hers, my tongue accepts the invitation. Thank goodness her curls have taken my fingers prisoner because otherwise they'd be ripping our clothes off, no matter that it's below freezing out here.

When a dumpster slams shut and Blondie barks, we jump apart. Clouds of breath fog the space between us. I'm shaking with desire, but she's shivering in her thin coat. Taking her by the shoulders, I guide her to the driver's seat of her car.

Once she's got both hands on the wheel, staring ahead like she's as shocked as I am by that kiss, I lean in to whisper in her ear, "Good night, princess. Call me tomorrow?"

When I get a shaky nod, I close her car door and step away. As she disappears around the corner, a big old chunk of my heart goes with her.

Chapter 16

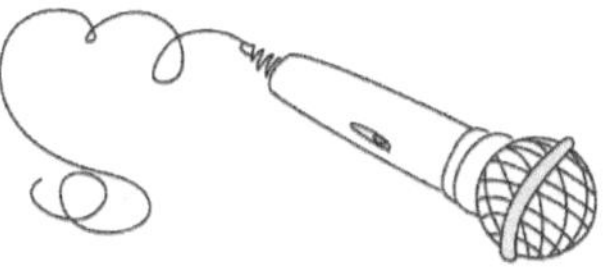

Your morning traffic update on WBAR is being brought to you by Pilgrim Cellular. Car phones! Want to try one out for free? A car phone for free! Three months! No installation fee, no obligation to keep it after three months. Yep, just call Pilgrim Cellular in Woburn.

JESS

When Cal put me in my car last night, I didn't think I even had enough energy to make it home, but the nap at the station and the late-night dinner must've messed with my circadian rhythms because it took forever to fall asleep.

Replaying the kiss over and over may have had a part in that too, I suppose.

Even though I make it to my audition this morning within a half hour of my appointment time, I still have to wait forty-five minutes to get called in. But the real shocker? I find out they've brought me in for the role of a mom. Of a nine-year-old. I mean, of course I could have multiple kids under ten without even having had them as a teen, but still. Am I really in that category now?

Worse, there's not a kid in the waiting room who looks anything like me. There are little blondes, redheads and even one adorable black girl, but not a single part-Russian Ashkenazi, part-Moroccan Sephardic Jew.

Despite the odds being totally stacked against me, I give it my best shot. Hey, maybe the eye wrinkles that seem to be breeding like rabbits will make me more mom-like.

When I get home, five free hours stretch before me before I have to leave for the weekend up in Chichester. I'm kicking myself for forgetting to get Cal's home phone number. Again. We could've hung out today. During daylight hours. Instead, I buckle down and spend the time getting organized, working out, and packing up food. The theater feeds us between shows, but I can't afford to eat breakfast out every day like I did last weekend. Then I leave with plenty of time to spare. It's a Friday and the mountains got snow this week, so the roads will be clogged with skiers heading to New Hampshire and Vermont. It's one thing to be late for an audition or a date, but for a performance? Unforgivable. Plus, getting to Chichester early will let me get settled in at the house.

Somehow, I make it through the Friday night show without thinking of Cal. There is a niggling worry at the back of my mind that he won't take my call, so when his "When can I see you again?" lands in my ear on the kitchen phone back at the house, I sigh out loud in relief.

I filled the guys in on what's going on, but I can't monopolize the kitchen for too long, so I do my best to get to the point. "Well, I'm up here through Monday morning. My friend Bella's coming up to see the show Sunday night, and she's going to sleep over. She's got a kid but her mom's babysitting, so we're having a girls' night."

"How about lunch Monday?"

"Monday, hmm." Pulling my dayplanner from my bag, I flip it to next week. "Damn. I'm actually teaching a new class at a studio in Cambridge, the place where I teach Monday and Tuesday nights."

"So when are you free?" He doesn't sound impatient but I wouldn't blame him if he were.

"Well, I'm free tomorrow afternoon. You could come up and see a show. We have one at four and one at eight."

"I don't think I can. I have to spin at Nine Landsdowne tomorrow."

"So, Monday night, I guess?"

"I thought you had class Monday nights."

"Yeah, but I'll be done before you even get started."

"Come to the studio, then? You can hang out till I'm done. Or take a nap again till I'm done. I'd really like to see you."

How can I say no to that?

"I'll see you Monday."

"Good." The smile in his voice is crystal clear. "It's a date."

IN THE LAST scene of the Saturday afternoon matinee, I somehow snag a button of my cardigan on the doorframe as I make my exit. Luckily, it doesn't bring the set down or anything, but I do lose the button. After the curtain call and a fruitless search backstage, I go to the costume shop to see if they have an extra.

I'm surprised to find Anya there instead of our usual dresser. "Her son is sick, so I'm your substitute today," she tells me, her Slavic accent making her words sound more romantic than they are. Patting the workbench, she says, "Leave it here; I'll take care of it."

"Thank you, Anya. Sorry about that."

She waves down my apology, but says, "Can I ask you something, my dear?"

Something in the tone of her voice has me stepping back inside the shop. "Of course."

When she doesn't say anything, I step closer. "Is everything okay?"

Her brow wrinkles in either concern or some sort of pain.

"Are you okay?" I ask.

"Yes, yes, dear," she says. Sighing, she turns off the iron she'd been pressing shirts with and comes to stand in front of me. "This is not my place, but I am concerned about you. We've had to take in the waistline of your skirts. Twice."

Masking my emotions as quickly as I can—anger, guilt and shame battle for control of my face—I muster a polite smile. I'm sure Anya is just being motherly, so I keep things light as I say, "Don't worry, Anya. I'm not sick or anything. My exercise routine has changed, and I've had a crazy schedule, but I'm fine."

She takes my hands in hers. "Very well. Please let me know if there is anything I can do for you."

"I'm fine, Anya."

She nods and then steps back to the workbench to pull out a container filled with buttons. "I'll have your sweater mended for tonight's show," she says, her tone distant.

I thank her, but indignation powers my steps as I head to the green room to eat my dinner. Every morsel of it. How dare she accuse me of... *I do not have a problem.*

Anymore.

I'm fine.

ANYA'S CONCERN picks at me the way I used to pick at scabs when I was little. Rough spots drive me nuts, whether they're on my skin or parts of my day. I do what I can to smooth things out, so when I see her later, I apologize for being short and reassure her again that I'm fine.

I almost tell her my past history with weight loss, but that'd make her worry. Unnecessarily.

When I was a teenager, in addition to my academic challenges, I struggled with the changes my body was going through. Well, "struggled" is probably too tame a word. Ballet was my first love, and you could say we had a pretty fucked-up relationship. So I *hated* the changes, especially the breasts that seem to get bigger by the day. I tried to stop them from growing by taking in fewer and fewer calories. I got thinner, but while the boob growth slowed a bit, it didn't work. I no longer had the proportions of a ballerina.

I auditioned for Ballet Boston anyway, hoping that my talent would outshine my shape, but despite trying three times, I never made it into their apprentice program. Other girls from my studio did. I was as good as they were, I worked as hard or harder, but unlike the naturally lean girls, I eventually had to accept that I'd never be able to pursue a career as a professional dancer.

The third rejection letter sent me into a spiral that ended in hospitalization, force-feeding and a psychiatrist accusing my parents of neglect. The whole thing almost broke my mom and dad, and I'll never forgive myself for the hurt they suffered. It was bad enough that *I* felt like a failure. They didn't have to join me.

Anorexia was the diagnosis, but it never felt right to me. I didn't have the same thought patterns as the other girls in group therapy. I actually like food. Not eating was a poorly-thought-out attempt to return my body to its original shape. I wasn't trying to control my universe.

I probably should've lobbied for a breast reduction instead. I still think about trying to do that, but I don't have the money. Even though lots of my friends got nose jobs at sixteen, my parents said no to plastic surgery for me.

It took a few years, but I was finally able to make peace with dance and bring her back into my life as a friend. Granted, she can be a harsh and overly critical companion. When I look in the mirror, I'm never happy with what I see, and dance concurs. We both miss the beautiful lines of preadolescent Jessica too much.

But I'm not anorexic. I'm not restricting calorie intake. I'm just running around so much that sometimes I literally don't have time to eat properly. I probably do need to work on that now that the show has opened.

I'm still wrestling with these worries Sunday night when Bella comes over. My preoccupation must be pretty obvious because once we're in our jammies and lying on the twin beds in my actor house room and she's complimented my performance, she narrows her eyes at me. "Something's off with you."

Throwing my arm over my eyes, I groan. "Not you too."

"What do you mean?"

"Everybody's momming me."

She tips her head from side to side. "I don't think I'm momming. I'm girlfriending."

Blowing out a breath, I get to my feet. "Okay. Be honest. Am I too thin?"

When she opens her mouth but doesn't say anything, I add, "Or too fat?"

"Jesus, no. Ugh." She scrubs her hands over her face and then shakes them out, mumbling something to herself.

"Are you okay?"

"Yes. No. I hate talking about this stuff. But I love you, so…" She sits up straight and slaps her hands on her thighs. "I'm going to spit it out. You *have* lost weight since last summer and I *have* been worried about it but it's not my place to say anything so I haven't but it has really been bothering me so I'm glad you brought it up." Totally out of breath by the time she speeds through these words, she takes in another to say, "There. I said it. Don't hate me."

I sink onto my bed. "Okay."

She winces. "Okay? That's it?"

I nod slowly. "I was treated for anorexia when I was a teenager, but I always thought the doctors were wrong. Maybe they were right and it's back." I get up and stand in front of the full-length mirror, turning to the side to check my profile like I always do. Like always, it looks wrong. "I don't know how to tell. I mean, we all have to watch our weight, but I eat pretty normally. For an actress." Gesturing up and down at my body, I try to explain. "I mean, my breasts are freakishly big, but I don't think I'm fat." Eyes back on the mirror, I shake my head at the lumpy shapes that make up my torso. "I'm not sure I know what normal looks like."

She doesn't say anything, and when I meet her eyes, it seems like she wants to say more.

"Just say it."

She winces. "I wish I knew what to say, but I don't know what's helpful. All I know is that this industry can really fuck with your head and get a girl to justify all kinds of unhealthy behaviors." Hugging her knees and resting her chin on them, she sighs. "Being pregnant taught me to listen to my body, to what feels healthy. I don't think mirrors ever tell the truth."

Making myself smile, I wag a finger at her. "Except when you tip them the right way."

Following my playful lead, she gasps and claps her hands to her cheeks. "Like those ones they have in department stores that make you look totally awesome!"

"Yeah, I've never stood in front of one of those." Attempting to lighten the mood is too exhausting, so I flop back onto the bed with a groan. "Why can't I be normal and enjoy having a boyfriend?"

She throws a pillow at me. "What? You have a boyfriend? Why am I the last to know? Wait," she gasps. "Is it the DJ?"

Sitting up, I can't help the grin that takes over my face when I think about Cal. Catching her up on what happened puts a smile back on her face, too.

When I finish the story, she grabs her pillow back and hugs it as she sits cross-legged on her bed. "You've had a lot of change in the past couple of months. Maybe you need to acknowledge that and give yourself a break? You can stand to gain some weight back, so you could enjoy doing that. Plus you've got a cool guy in your life." She moans into the pillow. "Trying so hard not to be jealous."

Things feel better when we settle back against the headboards. I shared some of my crazy with Bella, and she didn't even blink. In fact, it felt like she had something to share too. Maybe she's not quite ready, though, because she moves on to talk about her daughter and Shakespeare Boston instead. Eventually, we're echoing each other's yawns, so we get under the covers and I turn off the light.

It's been quiet for a bit, so I'm not sure if she's asleep when I whisper, "Love you, Bella," but she whispers back, "Love you too, girl."

There's a smile on my face when I fall asleep. Not only do I maybe have a new best friend, tomorrow I get to see Cal again.

Chapter 17

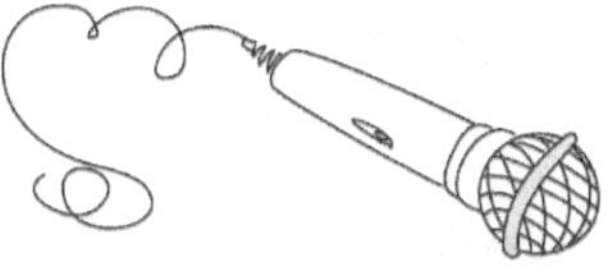

Grace Traynor wrapping up my time tonight with Suzanne Vega and "Left of Center" from the *Pretty in Pink* soundtrack. And if you want *me*, you know you can find me here weeknights from six to ten. At least for the time being.

CAL

"Special delivery for Cal Alonso." Monday night at ten fifteen p.m., Talia sticks her head in the door. "Hey, doll. I'm heading out early tonight, but I think this one can get your coffee. Maybe even read the weather."

Before I can say anything, she disappears and Jess tentatively steps inside. My smile's as wide as it can go, which isn't far, but for once the stretch feels good. "I was thinking maybe I dreamt last Thursday."

After the door closes behind her, she hovers on the threshold like last week, but without the tears.

"Just a sec, and I'll get you a seat." The song's winding down, so I put a finger to my lips. When I catch her nod out of the corner of my eye, I punch up my mic. "That was Concrete Blonde with 'Dance Along the Edge.'" I have to actually check my notes since everything I had planned seems to have left my brain. "Going out to Stu in Medford heading out for the late shift, here's 'Mad World.'" After I fade the mic and slip-cue from one track to the next, one part of my brain watches my hands slide the album into its sleeve, write today's date on the sticker and store it on the rack. Another part checks the clock. Two hours left on my shift. And then what? Any other guy would find a way to get Jessica back to his place so he could explore every inch of her gorgeous body.

Not only am I as atypical a guy as you can get, but there's something special here that I literally don't want to fuck up. I think it might kill me if I did. Going a whole three days without seeing her was painful enough.

She's still standing, so after a glance at the board to make sure everything's set, I get up, a little creaky from sitting too long. "I'll be right back."

Panic pales her cheeks. "You're leaving me alone with this?" she whispers.

"Don't worry. It'll run on its own for the next couple minutes."

I hustle into the listener line room to grab a chair. A volunteer looks up from a copy of *Rolling Stone*. "Everything okay, man?"

At my nod, he holds up the bong sitting next to him, a question on his face. Tempting, but I shake my head. Need to have all my wits about me if I'm going to be able to work while sharing space with Jess.

A song's about to finish, so I have to hustle. After dropping the chair next to her and cueing up the next one, I spin to face her.

"Are you sure it's okay for me to be here?"

"Didn't I tell you how Gracie practically has parties in here?" Heart racing, I gesture to the still empty chair. "Anyway, like Talia said, you're my substitute producer."

"You mean your coffee fetcher." Smirking, she perches gracefully on the seat edge.

"Like I said, producer."

"All right, then." Crossing her arms over her chest and one

purple-tight-covered leg over the other, her short corduroy skirt slides up to expose muscled thighs. "Produce."

I'm grinning like a fool as I check the clock—not only because I'm counting the minutes till this shift is over but because it's about time for a station check.

Jess fills the next one hundred and twenty minutes with a gazillion questions about what I'm doing. She apparently fully digests each bit of information because each follow-up question builds on the previous one, sometimes on ten questions back. Two hours later, she *could* be a producer. More importantly, when she leaves to grab us sodas, the room feels empty without her.

Thankfully, I don't make too many mistakes. More than I'd usually make because I really, really want to kiss her again, but I'm afraid if I do, I'll lose all ability to function. By the time Wayne shuffles in for his shift—a raised eyebrow the only indication that Jessica's presence is a surprise—I can't wait to get out of here.

Only problem is, I'm not sure what to do next.

JESS

At the station's back door, Cal helps me into my coat as he says, "Wind's supposed to pick up." After zipping up his hoodie and shrugging into his jacket, he hesitates before opening the door. "We, uh... didn't really discuss the plan here."

Usually the guy asks *Your place or mine?* But something tells me Cal won't want to move that quickly. I'm not sure that I do either. "This is your time of night. I don't even know what's open right now."

He looks at the door, then back at me. "Phil's bar is closed Mondays, so I usually go home after work. I guess we could go to Buzzy's or the Waffle House but I'd have to take the dog home first."

"Let's go to your place."

He clears his throat. "No expectations."

I nod. "Right."

"I'm right around the corner and parking sucks there. You want to leave your car here? I can walk you back."

Pushing past him and out the door before either of us can change our minds, I simply say, "Sounds good."

Like last time, he takes my hand and tucks it inside his pocket. It is blustery outside, so I pull up my own hood. Both Blondie and I have to trot to keep up with his long strides. He wasn't kidding about being around the corner. Within minutes, he's guiding me toward the back door of a large warehouse-type building. The moment we step inside, a blast of heat has us both unzipping coats. The lights are dim in the small foyer, and I follow him to an elevator that takes us to the top floor.

Cal gives me that crooked smile before he unlocks the door. "Prepare yourself for an enthusiastic greeting from my roommate." A puff of a laugh escapes his lips. "And like me, he's nicer than he looks."

As I'm wondering what the heck I've gotten myself into, he turns the knob and Blondie launches herself through it. By the time Cal closes it behind us, an enormous cat is yowling even as it rubs the side of its face against Blondie's jaw.

"Who is this?"

It's only when Cal sweeps the cat into his arms that I notice it's missing a leg. And a tail. And its ears have chunks taken out of them. "This is my buddy Cash."

"Like money?"

"Like Johnny. The Man in Black?"

"What happened to him?"

The cat keeps yowling, and Blondie adds to the cacophony with a few howls. "Sorry, I've got to feed these two before they wake up my neighbor."

As he does so, he explains that he found Cash by the side of the road on his way home one night. He'd been hit by a car. The people at Tufts veterinary school managed to save his life but not his leg. "He's a Manx, so he never had a tail."

"And what's Blondie's story?"

"She was a police dog. Lost the eye when she got shot in the line of duty. Her handler was killed, and his family didn't want to keep her. I actually got her when I brought Cash home from the vet. They'd bonded while they were in recovery. I knew a little something about that, so I didn't want to split them up."

"I actually meant why is she called Blondie when she's a brunette?" I ask, stroking the German shepherd's soft fur.

"Well, Deborah Harry isn't either."

"Good point."

"But I didn't name her, so I don't really know. Maybe the cops were fans."

He gestures to the rest of the apartment. "Make yourself comfortable. Can I take your coat?"

"I think I'll keep it on for now."

"Sorry. I keep it kind of cold." He steps behind me and turns on a space heater. "This should help."

"Thanks." I'm dying to poke around, but I don't want to violate his trust, which seems like a pretty big deal to him. So I rein in my curiosity, even as I take in the open space. There's not much furniture: a couch and a TV in one corner, weights and a punching bag by the window, a bed at the far end.

I'm tempted to crawl into his bed, but I head for the couch instead. When I get close enough, I realize that shelves line the space under the big windows. There must be hundreds of albums here. I don't see a big, fancy stereo setup, though. Instead, there's a rack like the ones at the studio with a turntable and some other equipment. "Where are the speakers?" is all I can think to say.

He points to the corners of the high ceiling. "My brother helped me hang those. And outfit the rest of the place." He shrugs. "It was an empty box. Used to be a printworks."

"It's very cool."

Slapping his hands against his sides, he seems a bit lost without buttons to punch and sliders to slide. He points to the couch. "Have a seat." The dog's already curled up on one end, and when I sit down, she growls.

Popping back up, I whisper, "She didn't do that at the station."

"Blondie." His voice is sharp, but he seems surprised. "Sorry. She's not used to visitors."

This shouldn't make me as happy as it does. I mean, I hate to think of him living like a monk. But I also don't like the idea of sharing him.

I take his hand. The tattooed one. I'm still not comfortable touching his scars without permission. "Maybe we can let her see that I mean you no harm."

"Good idea. Come on, I'll make something to eat."

Following him back to the kitchen area, I slide onto a barstool at the counter. He pulls a few items from the fridge, including two bottles of Heineken. He holds one up, a question in his eyes. My first thought is that I don't need the calories, but then I remember my talk with Bella. Since the alcohol might help me calm down, I nod.

The jangly feeling behind my solar plexus is not a familiar one. Usually, once I've decided to go home with a guy, the next steps are clear: the removal of clothing, a bit of tongue hockey, way too much attention paid to my breasts, and if I'm lucky, an orgasm.

But something's different here. I'm not sure how to act as he pulls out a cutting board and arranges some cheeses, a bowl of cute little pickles, another of olives. After fanning a sleeve of crackers along the edge, he looks at it for a moment before pulling a couple of knives out of a drawer. After sliding the work of art toward me and resting his elbows on the counter, his eyes hold a shyness that mirrors my own.

"It's so pretty I don't want to mess it up."

"Agh." He waves a hand in the air. "It's a snack. Eat."

When I'm out with a guy, I'm often very conscious of what I eat. Guys can be weird about it, like it's a turn-off if you have too much. The other night at the bar, Cal scarfed down his burger and didn't seem to care that I did too. So I make a little sandwich of pickle and cheese. He waits for me to pop it in my mouth and then asks, "Is that actually good?"

I nod enthusiastically, my mouth full, and he tries the combo. He makes a face, but he swallows it. "Not for me. I like 'em separated by beer."

After clinking my bottle with his and taking a sip, I encourage the muscles of my shoulders to relax as I enjoy the food. Nails click on the floor, and Blondie appears, obviously begging for a treat. I raise my brows as I pick up a chunk of cheese.

"She can have a little piece."

Nothing like bribing your way into the heart of your boyfriend's dog.

Hm. Have to file that thought for perusal later. Second time in two days that I've used a word I generally avoid. I go on dates, and I sleep with guys. I keep things light and my options open.

But there's something about this man. I want to worm my way into that hidden heart of his. And if the path includes sucking up to the girl who got there first, I have no shame.

The dog is a bit intimidating, like she could take my arm off without even thinking about it. I need to let her know we're on the same side, so I hold out the treat and trust her to take it.

Which she does, almost delicately, before wolfing it down, revealing big sharp teeth, but I leave my hand out. After swallowing, she sniffs my hand and gives it a lick before meeting my gaze with a hopeful look. I pet the surprisingly silky fur on the top of her head and slip her a cracker, too.

When Cal laughs at my sneakiness, it transforms his face. Yes, his skin is uneven in color and texture. Yes, his left ear doesn't quite match the right. But his sincere smile softens the scars and reveals part of what's beneath the outer layers—delight, warmth, kindness— making me want to see more.

His thumb wipes my cheek. "What's the matter?"

I check the other cheek. "Oops. Guess I'm leaking."

He just raises his good eyebrow.

I let out a little laugh of my own. "I'm not really kidding. Some- times I get so full of feelings that they overflow."

Suddenly this counter between us is a problem, so I slide off my stool and shrug off my coat. Taking a big breath, I walk around the island so I can take his hands, both of them. "Listen. I like sex. A lot.

But I like you more. The more time I spend with you, the more I want to. I don't want to mess that up. I want to have sex with you, but I want us to really be ready." His gaze has dropped to the floor so I squeeze his hands. "Okay?"

"What does that mean, exactly?"

He seems genuinely confused, so I choose my words carefully. "For me, it means I don't want to have a one-night stand with you. Which is, frankly, what I usually do." My heart's pounding all of a sudden, and not with desire. With fear, I guess. That he'll judge me. "Sorry."

He squeezes my hands back, a pout on his face. "Does this mean I don't get laid tonight?" When my jaw drops, he releases my hands to raise his in the air. "I'm kidding. Of course. I agree, I think, but I'm not sure I get what you want. Do you want to go home?"

"I don't; I just want to take it slow. Or maybe, it's…" Taking his right hand, I wrap it around my left wrist. "You let me know when and where you're ready to be touched. When you place my hand on your skin, I'll take that as permission, that I have license to touch you on that spot whenever I want."

"Okay. But you have to do the same."

Unexpected, his words are like a pinprick to my heart. It answers, *You have scars too, Jess.*

Releasing my wrist, he wraps my hand around his. "You have to tell me where and how *you* like to be touched. Starting now."

Before the fear of exposure can stop me, I place his palm on the side of my face. His warmth immediately begins to ease the tension in my jaw. When he strokes my cheek with his thumb, I want more, so I guide it across my lips before moving his hand to the back of my skull. As I'd hoped, he grips my curls and pulls my lips to his.

And the dance continues.

Even as I guide his hand down the back of my neck and around to my collarbone, I move in adagio. Neither ripping off my clothes in a breathless rush nor doing a sensual striptease would be right here. Either would be an act, even more so than with other guys. In fact, it's slowly becoming clear that I've been playing the part of a turned-on woman for years, because right now every spot he comes in contact with lights up like I'm a virgin who's never been touched by a man. Maybe on some level I am, because the way Cal touches me goes beyond the simple boundaries of skin-on-skin.

I'm more keyed up right now than I've ever been, and we haven't removed a single item of clothing.

When he takes my hand to draw it across his left cheek, there's a searing warmth in the center of my chest that blurs the border of pleasure and pain, melting my worries from the inside out.

Before, my fingertips had been curious, wanting to know what the scars felt like. Now, all they can do is grasp both sides of his face to pull his lips back to mine.

There's no way I'll ever get enough of this man.

CAL

I don't know if I can do this.

I mean, obviously, I can. My dick's harder than it's ever been, and she's soft in every way that I'm not.

But this feels like driving off a cliff.

So I hit the brakes, breaking the kiss before I do something she'll regret.

"Did I hurt you?" she pants.

I have to grab onto the counter to keep from grabbing her.

"Cal?"

God, I love how she says my name. Unable to get words past my lips, I shake my head. When that doesn't wipe the concern from her face, I take her hand and press it to my chest, even as my heart threatens to break free of its cage. Begging it to trust me—trust her— I ask, "Would you stay here tonight?" Before she can say no, I add, "Not to have sex. To sleep, to… be together. In person."

"Okay." Her smile is shaky, but what I hear is relief.

"Good." Nodding, I take purposeful strides across the loft to hide my disappointment. Did I really expect her to rip off my shirt and demand to be ravaged? After she screams in horror at the scars on my back and sides, which make the ones on my face blush in comparison.

Taking a deep breath, I corral my words into submission. "The facilities are in here." I rifle through the cabinet in the tiny bathroom. "I've got an extra toothbrush, courtesy of the dentist, that hasn't been opened."

"Thank you."

I hustle to clean up the kitchen while she's doing her thing. Then I go through my drawers to grab pajamas for me and a soft T-shirt for her. I let her know it's there and that I'm taking the dog out.

After Blondie and I have both taken care of business and I reappear, pajama-clad, she's snuggled up in bed. My cat, who hates everyone, purrs loudly as she strokes him from nose to stumpy tail, a sound I'm not sure I've ever heard from him before.

I pause at the edge of the bed, the "One of These Things (Is Not Like the Others)" song from *Sesame Street* running through my head. She's too damn beautiful to be here with us.

When she turns my way, a sleepy smile on her face, I do my best to accept that she seems to think otherwise. "You, uh, got everything you need?"

She nods and lifts the covers.

Fuck it. It is my bed. I climb in.

She tries to kiss me, but a yawn gets in the way. "I'm sorry. It's way past my bedtime."

I kiss her on the forehead. "Go to sleep, princess."

She turns over and curls into a ball. "Good night, Cal," she sighs.

I turn on my side to face her back, close enough to share my warmth but far enough away that she can't feel how much I need her.

JESS

"Are you hiding an elf who really wants to be a dentist somewhere?"

Cal blinks at me as I take the bowl he's handed me and hold it up to the others in his cabinet. None of them match and most of them have chips or cracks. Like he found them on the side of the road.

"It's like the island of misfit toys in here. A one-eyed dog, a three-legged cat. What else have you got?"

Even though he's obviously not a morning person, he grants me a lazy half smile. "I don't think you need any coffee, missy."

"I'm sorry; that was probably rude. I tend to wake up in go mode."

"I've heard worse." He juts a chin at the small bowl of berries and yogurt in front of me. "You sure you don't want anything else?"

I shake my head. "I usually eat after I work out." There are a lot of reasons I don't do sleepovers with guys. One, I need to move in the morning. I'm used to taking or teaching a class first thing. Or at least doing the barre.

And while it was surprisingly comforting to fall asleep next to Cal —even as a tiny chunk of my brain worried that he was mad I'd said no to sex—when my eyes fluttered open at seven a.m., doubt was already wide awake and whispering in my ear.

Cal sets his coffee mug on the counter and shuffles over to me. The careful movement reminds me that he got out of bed slowly too. Maybe the scarring makes him stiff in the morning.

Drawing a line over my furrowed brow, he asks, "What's going on in there?"

Escaping his too-penetrating gaze, I press my head into his warm chest. After blindly setting my bowl on the Formica behind him, I wrap my arms around his ribcage. When I hover awkwardly, suddenly worried about hurting him, he sets his chin on top of my head to rumble, "You can hug me as hard as you want. It actually feels good."

So I do. Resting my cheek against the soft cotton covering his chest, I soak up his warmth as we simply hold each other. I want to find my way not just under his clothes, but under all of his scars. I have a feeling that the ones in his head and heart are even thicker than the ones I can feel right now through the fabric of his shirt.

Something I might know a little bit about.

Unfortunately, that can't happen right now. Discipline is a harsh mistress, but we serve each other well. Putting my body through its paces is the only way I know how to stay sane. "I kind of have to go," I mumble.

Before I can take another breath, he slips out of my embrace and starts putting dishes in the sink, so I add, "Can I come back tonight?"

"You don't have to, Jess. You can call me anytime, but…"

"Do you not want me to come over?"

When he glances back at me, his eyes are shuttered. "I don't want—"

Hands up in the air, I interrupt his excuses. "Is this because we didn't have sex last night?"

He stiffens. "No. Jesus. Why would you think that?"

"Then what is it?"

His head slowly shaking from side to side, right before my eyes, his face hardens into a mask. "I don't know, Jess. I can't see…" He gestures back and forth between us as if that's an answer.

I shrug. The little bit of yogurt I ate churns in my belly. "Okay, well… I have to go." I grab my bag from the floor. "Thanks for…" I wave my hand around the loft. "Everything."

For some stupid reason I'm crying, which I never do over guys, even though I cry about every other thing in the world. I've almost made it to grab my coat when he catches up to me.

"Jess—"

"I'll talk to you later. On the phone if that's easier for you." I give him a real-as-I-can-fake-it smile and slip out the door.

Chapter 18

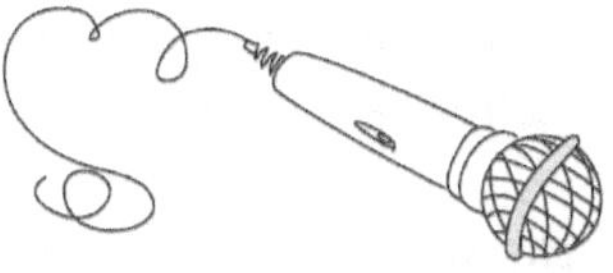

You can get a dozen roses for just eight ninety-nine at Star Market today, folks, so head on over before they run ou
—*SCREEECH*

CAL

When the door closes, I'm too confused to move. I'm also too wired to go back to bed, even though I barely slept a wink lying next to Jess. I spent those precious hours memorizing the scents and sounds and feel of her in case it never happened again.

Good thing I did because it didn't take her long to figure out that she doesn't belong on my island of misfits. Why would she want to hang out with a circus freak when she could have any guy she wants?

A whine from Blondie is the reality check I need right now. Taking care of these creatures is often the only thing that makes me take care of myself. Outside, it's early enough that the streets are quiet, so we go on a longer walk than usual to make up for skipping it after work. When we pass the diner where I usually pick up breakfast, I decide I may as well grab it now.

After I push my way through the door, still squinting from the brightness of sun reflecting off snow, the counter guy greets me with a pointed look at his watch. "Isn't this when you get your beauty sleep?"

When I don't answer, he grins. "Don't worry. I've screwed up on this stupid holiday, too. Get her some flowers and chocolates and beg forgiveness."

"I guess I'm still half asleep because I'm missing something here."

He hooks a thumb at the calendar on the wall behind him. "February fourteenth?"

I can barely think two words in a row, but two words do eventually pop into my brain and fall out of my mouth. "Valentine's Day?"

"Tell me you didn't wake up next to a beautiful woman and forget to at least *say* happy Valentine's Day."

"Man. I didn't even know it was Tuesday."

He winces. "Only a miracle is going to get you laid tonight."

I cough out a pitiful laugh. Having sex with the woman I pretty much drove from my apartment less than an hour ago? That'll take more than a miracle. More like an apocalypse.

AFTER BREAKFAST AND A WORKOUT, I've worked up the courage to call Jess and ask for a do-over when I realize that I've never gotten her number. Since there are loads of Jessica Abrahams in the Boston phone book, I can either spend all day calling them hoping to find her or I can ask Jones if he has it.

I knock on his door half an hour later. Tipping his head at the window, he asks, "What are you doing here? It's light out."

"Can I have Jessica Abraham's home number?"

"You still don't have it?"

I kick the floor. "Long story."

He raises a brow but flips through his Rolodex without pressing for more. The phone rings while he's in the process of copying the number from the card, so he tips his head at it. For some reason, the station can't seem to hold on to a receptionist for more than a week or two, so you never know if a call is routed to the right phone. Jones hates to do more than one thing at a time, so I answer the phone and tell the person—who, miraculously, is looking for Jones—that he'll be with them in a moment. After I press the hold button, I hold out the receiver, intending to make a trade, but he holds the pink slip hostage. "Don't fuck this up. I'm thinking about offering her a regular gig."

"Can I tell her?"

"No." He rolls his eyes. "Even I know girls don't want a job offer for Valentine's Day."

When he finally hands over the damn piece of paper, I stare at her number. *Now what?*

"Get out of here, you. I have to take this call, and you need to make one."

I do. But first, I need some advice. And I can only think of one place to get it. It'll be painful, but Jess is worth it.

I'D HAVE no privacy if I telephoned from the radio station, so I go home before dialing my sister's number. When she answers the phone, I let out a tiny sigh of relief.

"Hey, what's up?"

"I… need some advice."

"From me?"

"No, from baby Danny. Yes, from you. You're who I called."

"Don't go all jerkhead on me. I'm surprised is all. You never ask me for advice."

"Well, it's a girl thing. And you're the only girl I know. That I trust."

"Awww, Cal. That's so sweet and not at all like you."

"Shut up."

"You shut up."

Our oh-so-mature conversation is interrupted by a loud squawk in the background. "What the heck was that? Did you guys get a parrot or something?"

She sighs. "That is your nephew. He's found his voice, and it ain't pretty. Hang on, I'll get him some Cheerios."

The phone clunking on the counter is followed by several more ear-splitting screeches. When Penny picks up the phone again, she's breathless. "Okay. You have at least two minutes, five if you're lucky."

I blow out a breath.

"Come on, come on. He's vacuuming those suckers up."

"Okay." Pacing in a circle, I swing the phone cord as I work up the courage to spit it out. "I forgot it's Valentine's Day."

"Oh, that's sweet. But you don't have to do anything for me."

I cough out a laugh. "Not for you, you idiot. A girl."

"I am a girl."

"Yes, but you have your own boy."

"Who will likely forget."

"You're already married. It doesn't count."

"Oh, ho. Now there's where you're wrong."

"Penny, I need your advice."

"Okay, sorry. Is it the girl on the phone?"

"Yeah."

"That you still haven't brought to Sunday dinner?"

"I only met her in person the other day. Don't you think that's enough of a horror show for one week?"

"All right," she sighs. "So what's the problem? The day's not over."

"Well, I woke up with her, and I didn't even say happy Valentine's Day."

"Cal! You dog."

"She just slept over; we didn't—"

"I don't want details. Gross."

"Anyway. What's the best Valentine's gift you ever got? Do I do the whole Whitman's sampler and red roses thing?"

"Well, that's nice. But honestly? The best one I ever got was last year when I was so pregnant I could only waddle and I had to pee constantly and had hemorrhoi—"

"Ew, talk about gross."

"Anyway. Daniel made me a coupon book."

"Like that thing that mom has? To organize coupons?" That does not sound romantic, but maybe women are really into them.

"No, you idiot. I mean, those things are cool, but that's like a stocking stuffer or something. I mean a construction-paper book he cut and pasted with his own two hands. Inside were coupons for stuff like a foot rub and doing the dishes without me asking, and dinner out not at a sports bar. Stuff like that."

"You think she'd like that more than chocolates?"

"I think anyone would prefer something handmade over something any jamoke can pick up on the way home."

Something crashes on her end of the line.

"Shit."

"Everything okay?"

"Yeah, just a giant mess a tiny kid made. Gotta go. Good luck. Love you, you big dummy."

"Love you too, brat."

Chapter 19

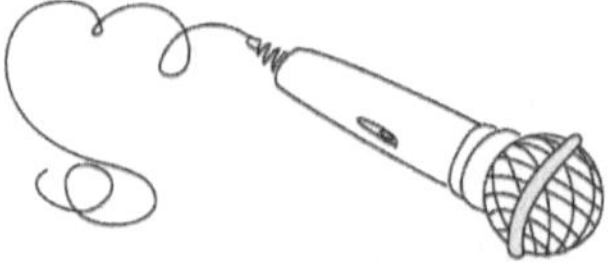

It's fifteen bleepin' degrees at nine oh three p.m. on this Valentine's Day. If you're all alone, fear not; Gracie's here at WBAR to warm you right up with some rockin' tunes, starting with the Talking Heads' "And She Was."

JESS

When I get home from teaching another new dance class Tuesday night, my apartment seems extra cold and empty. I wonder if I could manage to take care of a cat. Cal's cat was like my own personal heater when he snuggled next to me on the bed. Sleeping between the two of them, I was toasty warm.

Unfortunately, I seemed to have screwed things up. I really thought Cal was okay with us not having sex last night, but maybe that's not possible for a guy.

Shuffling through my mail, my heart catches when I see a big red envelope. But when I open it, it's a Snoopy Valentine's Day card. From my dad. Sweet. But not what I was hoping for.

Who am I kidding? Of the guys that I've dated in the past year, which of them is going to call me his valentine? I can't really expect anything from Cal. He doesn't even know my address.

At least my answering machine is blinking. Somebody loves me. Or wants something from me.

BEEP. Jess, it's Bella. Happy Valentine's Day! I hope it doesn't suck for you as much as it does for me. I miss you, girl. Call me. And hey, do you want to be my date to opening night of Hamlet? You're going right? Call me.

BEEP. Jessica, it's Marnie Farrell. I've got an audition for you for Thursday. Happy Valentine's Day. God, I hate this holiday.

I laugh. Misery does love company. Another beep from the machine is followed by silence and then some shuffling. I'm about to push delete, figuring it's a wrong number, when a familiar voice says my name.

Jess. I'm sorry things were weird this morning. Can you call me when you get in? I would really like to see you tonight. You can come to the station or to my place or whatever. Okay. Bye.

CAL

My shift's almost over and still no call from Jessica. I played "Jessica" by the Allman Brothers at eleven and "Jessica" by Rick Springfield at midnight. At one a.m. I even played "Jessica" by Seals & Crofts. A volunteer had to dig through the forbidden zone of the music library for half an hour to find their *Diamond Girl* album, but nothing seems to have gotten through to her.

The stupid thing I made with the red construction paper and glitter that Talia insisted on running out and buying for me—before skipping out for dinner with her boyfriend—will go to waste, I guess. Worse, now I'll have to tell her *and* my sister what a loser I am.

Wayne finally shuffles in to relieve me, a milk crate of albums under one arm and a girl running a hand through his mullet under the other. I make a quick exit. Seems every-fucking-body but me has a Valentine.

When I push out the back door, a woman screams in my face, and all hell breaks loose. Blondie's barking and arms are flailing. As I try keep us all from slipping on the icy steps, she clocks me right in the solar plexus with a hammer of a punch. I manage to make out Jess's face through the stars in my eyes, but I can't seem to catch my breath.

"Oh my god, are you okay? I can't believe I hit you. I didn't think the door would open but I tried it anyway and then it swung right at me and scared the crap out of me."

I wave at her and shake my head in an attempt to communicate. Pressing hard on my thighs, I push away from the cold, hard handrail behind me.

"Cal? Should I call 911?"

"Just got the wind knocked out of me," I finally manage. "You've got quite a hook." Once my lungs get some oxygen, my brain slots back into working order. "You didn't call."

She flaps her hands at her sides. "I fell asleep. I woke up like twenty minutes ago. Since it was almost the end of your shift, I figured I'd try to catch you."

Before I can ask her if she'll come back to my place for a do-over, I remember that it's Tuesday. Well, it's Wednesday technically, but the point is, it's a night when I regularly make the rounds. Problem is, Jess isn't dressed for that. "Listen, Phil and the guys will be expecting me to deliver dinners, but it won't take too long. Would you wait for me at my place?"

Shivering, she looks over at her car. "We can do it another night. I don't want to screw up your plans."

Plans. "Shit! I forgot something."

After pulling her back inside the building so she can wait in the warmth, I hand her Blondie's leash and promise, "I'll be right back."

No way I'm letting all that glitter go to waste.

JESS

When Cal returns, he doesn't say what it was that he forgot. It's too cold to stand around outside talking, so I let him wrap his scarf around my head and neck before hustling us both to the bar, where he picks up bags of to-go containers, and then back to his place, where he hands me Blondie's leash again. "If you could feed the pets, I'll be back before you know it." He pulls a manila envelope out from under his jacket. "This is for you. Make yourself comfortable."

Coming from most of the guys I've dated, that would mean *I expect you'll be in bed naked and primed for sex by the time I get back from this errand that's more important than you.* I'm still not sure what happened between us this morning, but I'm really hoping Cal means… what he said.

I do wonder if I'm supposed to open the envelope.

When I step inside the apartment, Cash appears out of nowhere to wind around my ankles. With his black fur and quiet paws, he'd be very sneaky if his yowls weren't so loud. I pick him up and carry him to the kitchen. Neither animal waits patiently while I find their food and dish it out, but we manage. Once that's done, I settle on the couch with a blanket around my shoulders, still not sure what to do with the envelope.

A yawn takes over my face, so I get up to pace around the apartment in an effort to stay awake. Sifting through the albums, I reason that if I put some music on low, I probably won't wake the neighbors.

Music playing softly, I take advantage of the open space of Cal's loft. Slipping in and out of shafts of moonlight streaming through oversized windows, I make myself comfortable the way I know best.

CAL

Part of me feels bad for hurrying through my visits with the homeless guys, but at the same time, Walt seemed happy that I trusted him to distribute the meal to the other camp as well as his own. Thing is, now that I'm back, standing outside my own apartment, I'm not sure what I was thinking.

I want her. More, I want her to want me, even though the idea defies all logic.

Snuffling noises from Blondie interrupt my brooding. If I don't open the door quickly, she'll wake up the artist who lives in the loft downstairs.

When I do, it's awfully nice to be greeted by music playing softly and a feminine scent filling the air.

"Jess?" I call softly. "I'm back."

"I'm here." Gliding in and out of shadows, her hips sway languidly.

As I step closer, I see that she's got someone in her arms. "Are you dancing with my cat?"

She giggles. "He likes it."

"That cat doesn't like anything." Guess she's got him under her spell too. After shucking off my outer layers, I move in on my cat. "May I cut in?"

He yowls in protest when I remove him from her arms, but her smile lights up the entire apartment. "But of course."

"I'm not much of a dancer, but I think I might be on par with the cat."

After she places my right hand at her waist and the other in her right, we sway back and forth, grinning goofily at each other. I'm not sure how I managed to get her back in my arms, but I'll take it. "Does this really count as dancing?"

"It's way better than cotillion, I'll tell you that." There's a dreamy quality to her voice that I haven't heard before.

"What's cotillion?"

"A way to torture hormone-drunk junior high school boys and girls."

"Ah. I didn't do that."

"You didn't miss much."

"Did the boys get to do this?" I brush my lips behind her ear, eliciting a surprisingly guttural moan.

"Uh-uh."

"Poor kids. What about this?" Brushing my lips across her brow, I draw a teasing caress across her lower back.

"Nope," she whispers as she trails her lips along my right jaw, landing a hairsbreadth from my lips. "Or this."

And finally, we're kissing again. I've been thinking about getting my lips back on hers all fucking day. Hell, I could kiss her for the rest of my days.

When we pause for breath, she's shaking, so I ask, "Are you—is everything okay?"

She shakes her head, then nods it, then bobs it in a circle. "I don't know… I, uh… sensation overload."

I can't help it, I have to draw a finger along her hairline, the perfect frame to her perfect face, but then I get my shit together.

"You're probably hungry. Let me make us some food." I head for the kitchen. "Do you want anything to drink?"

"Um, I'd take a glass of wine if you have it," she says, following me.

Luckily, I picked up a bottle before my shift, remembering that she drank red the other night at the bar. I set out some vegetables and dip and a box of chocolates and pour two glasses of wine. I've probably gone overboard, but I need all the help I can get.

Cash jumps up on the counter, trying to get in on the action. When she sets him on the stool next to her, he crawls into her lap. "You are such a sweet boy," she purrs, stroking his fur.

Suppressing a snort—"sweet" is not a word anyone's ever used to describe my cat—I slide the chocolates closer to her and hand her a glass before lifting my own. "Happy late Valentine's Day."

"Oh. Thank you." She clinks her glass to mine. "Happy Valentine's Day." She takes a sip and opens the box of chocolates. "Is it late?"

"Well, it is the fifteenth by now."

"Oh, right." She smiles but seems uncertain. "You didn't have to get me anything. It's not like we're…" She gestures between us with her glass before taking another sip.

No way I'm jumping into that minefield.

We move to the couch and eat in silence, sharing the chocolates as well as the healthier stuff. She doesn't want the coconut or toffee but does like the fruity ones, so I'm thinking we're a perfect match. I don't have enough experience with this kind of thing to know if the silence between us is awkward, but as I'm wondering why things are so much easier with her on the phone, she clears her throat. "So, when I was feeding the pets, I couldn't help noticing that you don't have a stove. How come?"

"Are you going to use a coupon on that question?"

"Coupon?"

I point to the envelope sitting on the coffee table. "You didn't open it?"

She shrugs. "I wasn't sure if I should."

"Well"—I hold it up—"*this* is your official valentine."

When she leans forward to put her glass on the table, Cash slips off her lap, complaining loudly.

"Sorry, Cash."

Watching him stalk off, I envy his confidence. My stomach literally feels like birds have hatched inside it. As I watch her unclasp the envelope and slide out the booklet I made, glitter scattering everywhere in the process, it's official. I am a complete and total loser.

"What the…" she whispers. When she finally looks up, her cheeks are pink and her smile is wobbly.

Goddamn it. I've made her cry again. It seems to be a superpower of mine. "Is it… Are you okay?"

She shakes her head, then nods it. "This is the sweetest thing ever, Cal." Running a finger over the cover of the booklet, a grin blooms on her face. "I'm very impressed by your glitter creations."

Trying to suppress what has got to be the sappiest smile ever, I shrug. "I worked pretty hard on those."

Taking her time, she studies my childlike printing. Missing huge chunks of elementary school for surgeries does not make for good penmanship.

"Do I have to use them in order?"

"Nope. Any order you like. And there's no expiration date, as you can see." I point to that detail on the back. Pretty clever, if I do say so myself.

"Good to know." Taking a deep breath, she points to page three. "I'll use this one." She covers the page as if I'm going to steal it from her or something. "But I'm not ripping the coupon out or anything. I don't want to ruin it."

My smile fades. Distracted by her delight, I'd forgotten why I'd prodded her to open the gift in the first place. "Uh, what exactly was your question?"

"You have a full kitchen here but no stove—" Her eyes flicker to the left side of my face, and she seems to realize what she's asking. Eyes back on the coupons she says, "Or I could use a different one."

Taking her hand along with a deep breath, I say, "It's not a big deal. I mean, I want to know everything about *you*, so..."

The pupils of her Disney-princess eyes almost eclipse the honey-brown of her irises when she meets my gaze. I have to tamp down a flare of panic. No one outside of my family and a few doctors knows my whole story, but I need her to accept all of me. The good, the bad, and the ugly.

Pressing her palm to my left cheek, I draw it over my jaw. Then I kiss it before clasping her hand in both of mine.

"When I was four, I wanted to be like my older brothers. We had a new baby in the house—who I resented, I guess—and I didn't think I should have to go to bed early like her when they got to stay up and watch movies.

"One night, something woke me up in the middle of the night. Lying there, I got the idea that I could show them what a big boy I was. I didn't like to wear pajamas because they were itchy and tight, but I was cold when I got out of bed, so I grabbed the blanket I liked to wear like a Superman cape. Then I snuck down to the kitchen, climbed up on the counter and got out a package of Jiffy Pop." My heart pounding, I push through the rest. "I'd watched my mom make it tons of times and thought I could do it, but when I turned on the gas flame, the blanket caught fire. And so did I."

She sniffs loudly, and I realize that I've got her hands in a death grip. I release them to swipe at her wet cheeks with my thumb. "So I don't cook."

"I'm sorry," she whispers.

I shrug. "Not your fault."

She nods. "I'm sorry that happened to you."

"Could've been worse. Our dog woke up my parents, and they got the fire out. I'm lucky that we lived close enough to Boston that I could get treated at Mass General. It had the best burn center in the country at the time. At any other place, I might not have survived."

"Well, I'm glad for that." She squeezes my hand and takes a swallow of wine. After a few moments, she points at the coupon book. "Can I use another one?"

I don't like overhead lights, but the one lamp I usually leave on isn't quite enough, so I turn on another before sitting a little closer to her. "You don't have to use them all tonight."

"You went to all this trouble. I don't want them to go to waste."

Pointing to the coupon for a foot massage, she raises a brow.

"Very well, madam." I hold up a finger. "I'll be right back."

After fetching the mineral oil I use to massage my scars, I refill her glass before settling on the couch again. She holds up one boot and then the other for me to unzip, kicks them off and then uses her toes to slide her socks off before putting her feet on my lap, where she points and flexes them.

"What the fuck?" I can't quite believe what I'm seeing. "Are you sure you want a massage?"

She stares at her feet like they belong to someone else. "Yeah, they don't hurt anymore. In fact, I can't feel anything in some spots." With ridiculous flexibility, she folds herself into a pretzel and sniffs her toes. "Not too stinky."

Gently, I draw the gnarly, knobby beasts back onto my lap. Her toe joints are red and look swollen, but when I touch one, it's hard as a rock. Some toenails are greenish black; others seem to have disappeared completely.

As I trace over the shapes, I hear a tiny sigh escape from her lips. For once, I can't quite read the expression on her face.

"Why would you do this to yourself?"

"It seemed worth it at the time."

The edges of her heels are like sandpaper, but not as regular as sandpaper. More like the surface of a clamshell. "But it wasn't?"

She slumps sideways against the back of the couch. "When I was really, really little, my mom took me to the ballet. From that moment on, it was all I wanted, to be a part of that picture." Her hand loops in the air. "To make those shapes and lines. To become one of those perfect beings.

"And I did—I was. For years, I was one of them. The day I got my pointe shoes"—her feet arch under my hands, lengthening, as her toes fold away—"it was a high, a drug I couldn't get enough of. No matter how much it hurt, it was worth it."

"What happened?"

"These happened." She grabs her breasts, but not the way I'd want to grab them. Her hands serve them up like they're leftovers that've been in the back of the fridge too long. "My body betrayed me, wouldn't bow to my will anymore, couldn't make those perfect shapes." Angry tears trickle down her cheeks. "I know it probably seems stupid and"—her hands fly from her breasts, flapping— "trivial, especially considering what you've been through, but it was the only thing I was good at. And then it was gone."

"But what about other kinds of dance?"

She swipes a palm across her cheek. "Modern and jazz, they were the silver and bronze to ballet's gold. I would've tried, but I had some… other issues." She sniffs and seems to rearrange her face. "Whoa. Way to bring the room down."

"Don't do that." Gripping both feet, I squeeze until she meets my gaze.

"Do what?"

"Minimize your pain."

Her lips flatten. "My corns and bunions and dead toenails have nothing on your scars."

"It's not a competition."

"It isn't?"

"If it was, you'd lose, princess."

She scrubs her palms over her face. "I know; I'm sorry."

"Jess, I mean it. It's—it's good. I know I want to be skin to skin with you"—she peeks at me between fingers, and I raise one of her feet as evidence—"but we have a lot of scars between us. And, I guess…"

Since I can't seem to find the next word, I flop back to stare at the ceiling, hoping something might be written there that'll express what I want to say. What I'm afraid to say. That I'm half in love with her already, and I'm terrified of fucking this up and losing her. Of scaring her away.

No words on the ceiling, but two little feet find their way between my thighs while I'm looking for them.

"What're you up to, missy?"

When I tickle her feet, she doesn't even flinch. So I haul her over to my lap. A delicate moan hums behind her lips. A not-so-delicate groan crosses mine. When I try to stop her wiggling by wrapping my arms around her, she drops her head on my shoulder with a sigh.

My heart pounds heavily in my chest, but I'm not exactly sure what it's afraid of. Her compact body feels like it belongs right where it is, and I don't ever want her to leave the protection of my arms. I'm wishing I knew how to move forward—what to do next that will let her know I want her without rushing things—when her thumb trails across my goatee. Pausing at the transition from the area on my chin where I can grow a beard to the scarred skin where the hair won't grow, she asks, "Can you feel that?"

"I can, but connections are spotty around the plastic surgery." Covering her hand with mine, I press it into the ridges. "A firmer touch feels better than a glide."

"Got it," she whispers as she explores, fingertips kneading in and over the tightly pulled skin from cheekbone to jawbone.

My eyelids droop and tension drains from my shoulders. Her touch doesn't pry, doesn't poke, nor does it pity. It… cares.

When her fingers get close to my ear, I cover her hand with mine again and pull her palm to my lips to kiss it.

Turning my head as far as I can to the right—which isn't far since my range of motion is limited—I point to a place behind my ear where I can't stand to be touched, the place I have to remind the barber about every time I get a hair cut. "If you can avoid this spot—there; it's kind of like when you're driving out of range of a radio station. The sensation goes in and out. Drives me crazy."

She nods, but I cup her cheek with my palm and brush my thumb over her bottom lip. "It's a lot, I know."

Her mouth curves slightly as she drags her lips against my thumbnail, a simple movement that lights up all my nerve endings. In a good way.

And yet. It *is* a lot. And even though I want to be inside her more than I've ever wanted anything, rushing hasn't worked for me in the past. If I'm not completely ready, things fall apart quick.

Still, her hand is warm on my left cheek, and her lips soft on my right hand. I think I might be ready to go further, when she yawns.

"I'm sorry," she groans over another yawn.

"No, I'm sorry," I say over a yawn of my own. "We've both been up since…"

"Seven."

"Yikes. It's after three now, so that's like…"

"I know. I'm too tired for math too."

That's it, then. Scooping her into my arms, I carry her to the bathroom door. "You do what you need to do, I'll take Blondie out one last time, and I'll meet you back in my bed."

When she opens her mouth like she's about to argue, another yawn takes over her face, so she smiles again. "Okay."

Drawing a finger across her brow, I say, "I want to savor getting to know every inch of you, and"—taking a deep breath for courage, I finish—"I want us both to be ready for you to see every inch of me."

JESS

On his way out the door, Cal calls, "Feel free to take one of my shirts to sleep in. Second drawer."

So, after grabbing my makeup bag from my purse and rushing through brushing my teeth, cleansing, moisturizing and using the toilet—my body shedding warmth quickly in the chilly space—I shuck off my clothes except for my undies, slip into one of his soft T-shirts and dive under the bedcovers. Surrounded by the scents of him, my mind skitters over what just happened between us.

I've never, *ever* had a guy put the brakes on. Now Cal's done it twice. Usually, having sex with a guy without getting too close keeps fears at bay. All kinds of fears. Not being able to sustain more than the initial flash of desire. That he'll see through the fragile facades I maintain. That I'm not... enough.

I'm terrified. The only thing keeping me here, besides the connection we built up talking on the phone, is that what I see in his eyes and feel in his caress is new. So new that my defense systems are overwhelmed. Even so, somewhere deep inside, a voice is telling me to give in. To trust.

Maybe there is more to me under the surface that a man could actually be interested in. Maybe Cal could be the one thing I fall for that doesn't get taken away.

I'm drifting down to sleep when he returns to spoon me, wrapping his big, warm body around mine. Rubbing his hand over my side, he whispers, "Oh my god, you're freezing."

Not quite awake, I mumble, "Bad circulation."

"I tend to be hypersensitive to heat, so I keep it pretty cold in here," he says, chafing up and down my side until I capture his hand and pull it under the covers as I wiggle back into his warmth.

When he folds a leg over mine and rubs my feet with his, the erection pressing between my cheeks wakes me right back up. "Are you sure you want to take it slow?" I ask, shifting my hips. "You seem... ready to go."

Stilling me with a palm he growls, "I can't imagine not being ready to go if I'm pressed up against you. You're Baskin-Robbins, and I love all the flavors."

"No talking about cold things," I whine. "Only warm things. Like a nice, toasty fir—"

As I try to swallow my unfortunate choice of words, he nuzzles under my hair to kiss the curve of my jaw. "It's okay. You can say the word 'fire' in front of me. I won't freak out. Anymore."

I turn to face him, moving carefully so as not to let any cold in. "Will you tell me, though?"

"Tell you what?"

"If something bothers you?"

"You're going to use up all of your coupons."

"Yeah, I know the guy that makes them. I might be able to convince him to issue a few more."

"You think so?"

"I know so."

"Maybe you need to issue a few coupons of your own."

"I don't think I'm as gifted with glitter as you, but I bet I could come up with something."

His forehead rests against mine, and my body decides it's okay to relax. My eyes flutter closed, and my brain gives it up too.

An arm snakes under me and pulls me in so I can nestle into his shoulder. The heat of him wraps around me like a cozy blanket. As I'm sliding into dreamland, he draws one of my hands under his shirt, pressing it against a ridge of scarred skin. I spread my palm, reveling in his trust as I sink toward sleep.

Chapter 20

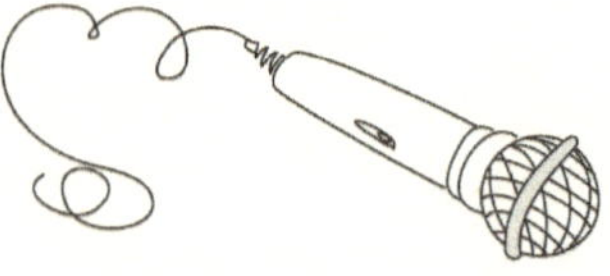

**SQUAWK. Rock and roll, Polly wanna rock and roll.
SQUAWK. Wake up. Wake up. Polly want you to wake up
and drive to work. SQUAWK.**

JESS

Even though Cal has blackout curtains, my biological clock wakes me at seven again. I don't have an audition today, but I suddenly remember that I do have a call at the radio station at noon to record with "Porky and Rocket," whatever that means. When Jones called me with the offer yesterday, I was over-the-moon excited.

Interesting that the evening with Cal erased it from my mind completely.

The problem with pretending that you know what you're doing? You end up not knowing what you're doing. Why didn't I ask Jones more about this job so I could prepare? What if there are long scripts I have to read?

Anxiety has me itching to move, so I sneak out of bed, wishing I'd brought some extra clothes with me. If I had a mat and sweats, I could do a floor barre here. Maybe I should go home.

Cal's still sleeping, so I write him a note and get dressed as quietly as I can. But as I'm setting it on the nightstand next to him, a hand reaches out to grab my wrist. "Are you sneaking out on me?"

"I was trying to let you sleep."

"Come back to bed, and I'll remind you of why you should stay. Then I'll make you breakfast."

After kissing him on the cheek I whisper, "Go back to sleep. I'll see you"—then I remember that I actually have a performance tonight, something I usually keep front of mind—"um, soon."

"If I let you go now, will you come back tonight?"

"I have a show."

"After your show?"

Work, dance, sleep and skincare are typically numbers one through four on my priority list. Men fall somewhere between numbers ten and twenty. But being with Cal and talking with Cal and kissing Cal… I mean, we haven't even had sex yet and already it's all so very different than my experiences with other guys that my priorities are all confused. "I don't know if I can stay up till the wee hours three days in a row and do five shows this weekend. I'm thirty, not twenty. I need sleep. Like, at least five hours in a row."

With a groan—which I hope is because his scars give him pain, not me being a pain—he sits up and rifles through his nightstand drawer, then places a set of keys in my palm and closes my fingers around them. "If you come here after your show and hang out with Cash or go to bed, I promise to not wake you. Then you can wake me any way you want—any time you want—tomorrow."

Before I can answer, he loops both arms around me and pulls me close. Squeezing my butt and kissing his way up my neck, he murmurs, "Please?"

How can I say no? I have a feeling he's let me in further than he has anyone. He's taking a chance. And since my work today and tomorrow is either on the radio or playing a character that the costume designer has worked hard to make unattractive, who cares if I have giant bags under my eyes and dull skin?

I take a deep breath and whisper, "See you tonight."

BECAUSE I'M ME, it takes me just as long to get dressed and do my hair and makeup to go record at the station where no one will see me as it does to get ready for an audition or a date or anything other than dance class. So as usual, I'm running late. And that's before I get lost. Not on my way to the station, but inside the fucking building.

At Shakespeare Boston, they're used to me always being a wee bit behind, and up at Chichester, the traffic has been my excuse when I run late, but even I know that showing up late for a brand-new gig is not a great way to start.

Somehow, I've ended up in a room full of cubicles where every-one's on the phone. I've about decided to retrace my steps instead of waiting for someone to be free to ask directions, when a man takes me by the elbow and steers me toward a desk. "You're late."

"I—I know; I'm sorry, but—"

"Don't want to hear it. Phones are off the hook. You're there"—he points at a desk—"and company directory's in the drawer."

"But I'm not here to—"

"I don't care what the temp agency told you, I need a receptionist. And I need one now." When I don't move, he jabs a finger at the phone, where several lines are lit up. "Do I need to call the agency back?"

I'm so confused at this point that I'm about to turn tail and go home, when a voice behind me asks, "Hey, isn't that our new girl?"

When I turn around, a human string bean offers me his hand. "Jess, right? I recognize your voice from the tape Jones made. I'm Porky."

"Porky?" Never has a person been so ill-named.

The guy who thinks I'm the receptionist sneers at him. "Peter, get back to your cage. I'm trying to run a business here."

"Can't do it without the talent, Alan." Porky/Peter nods slowly. "Heh-heh, that almost rhymes."

Still gripping my elbow, Alan rolls his eyes. "Are you going to answer the phones or not?"

Relieving him of my arm, and taking a step towards Porky—or Peter, whatever his name is—I beam a winning smile at Alan. "I'm afraid you've made an incorrect assumption"—*and a sexist one* I want to say, but no need to burn bridges on my first day—"I am, indeed, talent, but I got lost."

"Come on, Jess, I'll show you to our cage." With a courtly little bow, he gestures in the direction of a door I hadn't noticed before. "I'm Pete, by the way, but you can call me Porky. Everyone does." He tips his head back at Alan, now seated at the desk and answering the phone himself. "Only that dickhead calls me Peter."

Even though his movements are unhurried, Porky's legs are twice as long as mine, so I have to jog to keep up. After ushering me into a recording studio crowded with so much equipment that it seems smaller than it is, he introduces me to Jonny "Rocket" Rogers. Jonny's voice is higher pitched and a little nasal, and he's the portly one.

"Jones told us you were coming today," Rocket says, crossing his arms over his chest and leaning back in his chair. "But he didn't tell us what to do with you."

"Oh." Today is really turning out to be a disaster. First, the front office dude assumes I'm a receptionist because I'm a girl, and now I'm here only because Jones wants to make Cal happy.

"That's not true," Porky drawls. "He said we need to expand our appeal to the fairer sex. So he got us a representative."

Rocket huffs. "What voices do you do?"

"Voices?"

"You know, characters. Looney Tunes, Hanna Barbera, TV shows..."

"Well, I'm an actress, so I—"

"Oh, for crying out loud. Not an actress."

"Don't be an asshole, Rocket. Let's get in there, and we'll figure it out as we go."

Looking around the room like someone else might emerge from behind a speaker or the electric piano, I have to ask, "Is it really only the two of you?"

Rocket frowns. "What, we aren't enough for you?"

"No, I... I thought it was a whole troupe recording the routines." WBAR is known for its comedy bits, especially the hilarious song takeoffs. They've turned "Electric Avenue" into "Electric Barbecue" and "Beast of Burden" into "I Can Smell Your Pizza Burning." They also play fake commercials, kind of like the ones on *Saturday Night Live*.

Porky dips his head at me. "I'll take that as a compliment."

"Uh-huh." Rocket purses his lips, then juts his chin at mic stands crowded into the corner like a flock of flamingos. "Before we record, we write. And before we write, we research."

My gut clenches, and it's not because I was so behind schedule that I skipped breakfast. I've never written anything in my life. And research usually involves reading.

This day just gets better and better.

"When Jones said he was bringing you in, I recorded a bunch of TV—prime time and daytime. Let's see what we can find." Rocket shoves a cassette into a VCR/TV combo and presses play. Instead of skipping the commercials like you normally would, he skips the show and plays the commercials—the ones with women in them, that is.

"It's like a whole new world of things to make fun of," Porky says, rubbing his hands together as Rocket fast-forwards through ads for Dunkin' Donuts and Jordan's Furniture muttering, "Did that, did that."

When he plays the L'eggs ad for Sheer Energy where a stewardess walks off the plane and then dances around the tarmac, both guys giggle like boys on the first days of ballet classes. Before they figure out how hard it is.

Rocket plays the section where she caresses her legs and talks about how the pantyhose "stimulate" her legs over and over, until he can imitate her perfectly.

Shaking my head in wonder, I say, "I don't think you guys need me."

"Nah," Porky says. "Rocket can only do a falsetto for so long before his voice gives out."

"This is a possibility, but let's keep at it." Rocket makes a note of the time stamp of the L'eggs ad, singing the tag line, "Nothing beats a great pair of L'eggs" to himself before continuing the hunt.

Next up: an Arrid Extra Dry ad.

"This has potential," Rocket says as he sharpens a pencil. "First things first, we have to come up with another name for the product, unless we want to get sued."

"So we want something that sounds like Arrid but isn't?"

"Exactly," Porky nods.

"Huh." A laugh puffs out of me. "You know, I never thought about it, but 'arid' with one 'r' means dry, so it's like the deodorant is called 'Dry Extra Dry.'"

"Arid means dry?" Porky stares off into the distance like this has blown his mind.

"Yeah," I say. "So we need another word that means dry?"

"Or something that rhymes. Sometimes that's better. Our listeners aren't as smart as you. Let's do a speed round." Circling between us with his finger, Rocket explains. "Say the first word that comes into your head until we find one that seems good. Got it?"

This is like one of my favorite warm-ups from college improv, so I nod. Porky starts with "dry," and then we continue to rattle off words. Some don't make any sense at all in the context, but I know that you have to "Yes, and" to get the juices flowing. So when I say, "bone dry" and Porky follows with "boner," I don't object or even roll my eyes, I just say, "stoner." Eventually we come up with a list of potential Arrid replacements that Rocket thinks could work: Desert, Barren and Torrid.

When we play the commercial again, the guys jump around the small room, imitating the couple onscreen. Suddenly, Porky turns to me. "Do chicks really care about how guys smell?"

"Wait." Rocket pauses the video. "Is this about how the guy smells or how the girl smells?"

"It's weird to watch people smell each other," I say. "That guy is creepy enough sneaking up behind her, but on top of that, does she want a guy who *likes* that she smells like a baby?"

Rocket points at me. "You've got something there. You could do the woman's lines like in the real commercial about the patented formula, blah-blah-blah, then I could go 'Hey, baby, I noticed you smell like a baby now. That really turns me on.'"

"And then I could do the announcer wrap-up," Porky says. "Arrid Extra Dry—or whatever we end up calling it—with the baby-fresh scent. A surefire weirdo detector."

Rocket's head tics back and forth like a metronome. "Maybe. Let's keep at it. But write that down."

Next, Rocket sits at the keyboard and—without any sheet music or anything—begins to play the "Get a little closer" jingle while Porky makes notes. I'm feeling useless again until I notice that Rocket has accidentally replaced the "get" in the lyrics with "come."

This gives me an idea, I sing along. On "Come a little closer," I crook my finger at Porky, who steps behind me like the guy in the real commercial does and murmurs, "Hey, baby, you smell great."

Without planning to, I whirl around like a Charlie's Angel and mime squirting him in the face with a can of deodorant, shouting, "Too close! Back off, buddy." Then I turn to Rocket and pretend to holster the can. "Doubles as pepper spray."

Rocket claps once. "I love it. With a spray sound effect and Porky screaming his head off. Let's do it."

And we do. After choosing "Torrid" as our replacement brand name, an engineer materializes from somewhere to set up the mics, and we record the little scenario. Then Jones comes in to remind us that we have some actual commercials to record, so Rocket goes somewhere else to mix sound effects and music into the Torrid spot, while Porky and I record the things advertisers are paying top dollar for.

I'm so relaxed with these guys that I don't hesitate to ask Porky to read the script to me. When he asks why and I explain about my dyslexia, he asks, "So I read it to you once, and then you remember it?"

"Well, I have to pay attention and repeat it in my head a few times, but yeah."

"That is so cool. It's like you have a superpower. Bet you wouldn't have that if you could read better."

"Huh. Maybe not."

I do have a show to get to, so after we record the Newbury Comics and Ground Round ads, it's time for me to go. Rocket returns from the mixing room and stops me on my way out, pointing a finger gun at me. "You're coming back tomorrow, right? I want to do an *National Enquirer* takeoff, and I need you to be the girl who wants to know."

"I'll be here," I say with a smile.

The day has definitely taken a turn for the better because I only get lost once on my way out of the building.

Chapter 21

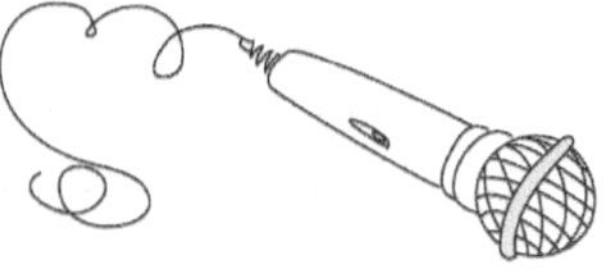

Weird Wayne here at WBAR. I don't know what time it is, but I've got "Time" for you. Whoa, like, that's, like, cosmic man. Take it away Mr. Waits.

CAL

When I sneak into my apartment in the wee hours of Friday, having handed off the meals to Walt again, and see the sleeping beauty in my bed, I really, really want to wake her with a kiss. But I promised I wouldn't, and I'm not a fairy-tale prince anyway, so I slip in next to her without even disturbing Cash, who's curled up at her feet. Her heat-seeking butt wiggles close, but the only sound she makes is a soft little sigh.

Next thing I know, I'm waking to the sweet scent of Jess on my pillow—some coconutty thing she must use in her hair. Smiling, I rub crusty eyes open, but there's no Jess in the bed. Turning my head with caution, as sometimes the left side gets cranky, I'm relieved to see her on the floor doing some sort of exercise routine. My morning boner swells with happiness, so I tiptoe to the head. When I return, Jess is back in my bed and greets me with open arms.

Hugging her tightly, stroking her smooth curves and breathing in more of her heady scent is driving me closer to the edge of need. Even though she doesn't seem disturbed by the parts she's seen so far, battle scars from previous encounters with women have me gun-shy. I'm not sure which was worse, the ones who were turned on by my scars or the ones who couldn't even look at them.

While I'm trying to figure out how to talk about all this, she trails a figure down my right arm and asks, "Will you tell me the story of these?"

"How do you know there's a story?"

"The images are connected literally, but I feel like they're connected figuratively, too."

It's not that I forget how smart she is, but when a sentence like that is served up in her raspy morning voice, it's sexy as hell. Like everything about her.

"You're gonna have to explain some of those words." I knock on the side of my skull. "Not much going on in here."

"Well, that's total bullshit," she snaps, her tone shifting again.

"Okay, but I didn't go to college to learn about… what is it that you studied?"

"Dance and theater. It's not like I'm some erudite scholar."

"You definitely know bigger words than I do. What exactly does 'figuratively' mean? Like, figures?"

She goes back to tracing the outlines of my tats. "It means metaphorically, standing for an idea or something other than what it is."

"Uh, okay. I guess I get it."

"Anyway"—she kisses the center of the purple Aster on my shoulder—"all these delicate flowers covering these hard-as-rock muscles. That contrast tells a story in and of itself."

My brain's not quite awake, but maybe it's better that way. Easier to let the words escape when my guard's down. "They're reminders."

"'There's rosemary, that's for remembrance.'" When I raise my eyebrows in question, she adds, "That's what Ophelia says. In *Hamlet*. She has this whole speech about the meanings of flowers."

I've never explained my tattoos to anyone. Not even the artist that created them. All he wanted was pictures to work from.

Sitting up and stuffing a pillow behind me, I rotate my arm so she can focus on the ink. I want to trust Jess with all the scary parts of me, so maybe this is a good place to start. "After the fire, I had to spend a lot of time at the hospital. For the first couple of months—"

Her hand on my forearm interrupts me. "You were there for *months?*"

"Yeah, the first time I was there for about five months."

"Oh my god."

"Oh, it gets worse. The treatments were—I can't even describe how horrific they were." Swallowing past the taste of bile that thinking about that time always brings up, I search for a better way to talk about this. "But there were things, and people, that made it bearable. Barely. Like my mom, who spent as much time as possible with me, even though she had my baby sister to take care of. One of the doctors who always took the time to answer my questions. Some of the nurses were especially kind. And then there was this framed picture of flowers on the wall right by my bed. Staring at those flowers helped me kind of leave my body. Without that, the pain was intolerable."

"Didn't they give you, like, anesthesia?"

"They did not. I've heard that these days they keep people in a controlled coma for the first weeks or months of treatment. Back then, they didn't. Not even painkillers. I guess they didn't have research on how those meds would affect kids, so they were afraid to use them."

"That's unbelievable," she whispers.

"Anyway, when I got to leave the hospital the first time, I guess I threw a major tantrum until my mom talked them into letting us take the picture with us. I've kept it by my bed ever since." I point at the wall behind her.

Even now, I like knowing that it's there. I can't look at it for too long, though, so I focus on the flowers on my arm instead.

"Over the years, I learned the names of the different flowers and what they represent. When I turned eighteen, I decided to get a tattoo so I could carry them with me everywhere." Pointing to each one, I recite, "The aster means patience. Something I had to learn. These are bluebells, which stand for both humility and gratitude. The cherry blossom has a lot of meanings: renewal, the ephemeral nature of life—and beauty."

"Pretty big words for an uneducated guy."

"I looked them all up."

"No roses?"

I shake my head. "Roses are for love and passion. I haven't had a whole lot of that in my life."

She's silent for a few beats before she points to my inner arm. "This is a lotus, right?"

"Yep. It also has multiple meanings, but rebirth is the one that means something to me. Every time I had to go under for surgery, I'd get really afraid."

When I don't continue, she asks, "What scared you?"

I've never told anyone this. Not even my mom. "I was afraid that I wouldn't wake up. And I was afraid *to* wake up. Because of the pain."

"I'm sorry." There are tears in her eyes and in her voice.

"I did wake up each time, obviously, but it was like a rebirth. New scars and new skin I'd have to break in. It was painful, but I survived. Anyway, I told you I don't want you to feel sorry for me."

Resting her cheek on my chest as she wraps an arm around my ribcage, she's quiet for so long that I think she's gone back to sleep. When she speaks again, her voice is different. Softer, but stronger at the same time.

"There's a difference between empathy and pity. I feel things around me. That's empathy. I don't feel sorry for you. I feel the story you told me. And tears don't always mean I'm sad." She wipes her tears onto my skin. "I cry at museums a lot. Sometimes beauty is so" —she draws a jagged shape in the air—"*that,* and I get overwhelmed and I leak."

She nestles in even closer somehow, so close that I can almost imagine the skin separating our bodies—the scars, too—melting away.

"So please don't take it personally," she whispers.

JESS

I've never felt so comfortable and so confused at the same time. I could lie here cuddling and talking with Cal forever, but I can't let go of the worry. Does he not want more? Cal is letting me in, inch by inch, but at the same time, he's not pressing for more from me physically.

It does kind of make me wonder if I've been doing sex wrong all this time. I mean, I've read all the articles in *Cosmo*. I know how to get a guy off, and myself too, but often sex is simply another workout after which all I want is to get home and shower and sleep in my own bed. Maybe sex with someone I've taken the time to get to know, to share secrets with, will be different.

There might be a little tiny corner of my heart that's been holding out hope for a happy ending for myself, that someday a prince will come along and sweep me off my feet and I'll hear heavenly music when we make love instead of a clock ticking in the back of my head.

A fingertip tracing its way over my brow brings me back to the here and now. Without thinking, I put on a happy face.

"Please don't do that," Cal says.

"Do what?"

"Hide what you're really feeling."

I can't help it; my hands fly to cover my face. Speaking into my palms, I confess, "I don't know what I'm doing here."

A kiss lands on my hairline, a little brush. "Do you want to leave?"

My palms press more firmly into my cheeks and over my eye sockets. All I can do is shake my head. One emotion after another gallops through me, and I'm afraid for him to see any of them. Suddenly this moment feels so important and I don't want to screw it up, but I'm so out of my depth I don't know what else to want.

A muscled arm snakes under my torso and scoops me up so that my body covers Cal's. Both arms wrap around my lower back but not in a way that feels like a trap. His heart thumps against my hands, giving them permission to let go. With a sigh, I pull my hands away from my face, nestle my cheek into his broad chest, and let myself just be here with him.

CAL

In this moment, Jess feels like a wild bird that flew in the window to perch on my chest. I'm dying to explore the textures of its soft feathers, but I don't want to frighten it away. I want it to decide to stay. So I hold her, but not too tightly. I have a feeling she's rarely still for this long when she's awake, but I could stay here forever.

When a shaky sigh shudders through her torso, I draw small circles in the space between her shoulder blades, trying to communicate that it's okay to feel whatever she's feeling. For the first time, self-consciousness about my scars isn't what's keeping me from seducing a woman. I want to make love to her right now more than I want my heart to keep beating, but like her, I feel like I don't know what I'm doing.

"Maybe we need to be okay with that," I whisper.

She raises her head to meet my gaze. "With what?"

"I'm so nervous about getting this right with you that I feel like I've never… been with a woman before."

The tiniest glimmer of understanding in her eyes has me plunging forward. "Maybe I never really have, because every second that I'm touching you feels like nothing I've ever felt."

Her smile grows.

"So I don't want to rush—"

Her smile dims.

"But I don't want to put it off any longer either."

Her head drops, and she rolls her forehead across my sternum as a groan spills past her lips. Worried that I've scared that little bird off, I hold my breath until she shifts, gracefully and deliciously dragging her body over mine so that her forearms frame my face and her nose brushes over mine, once, twice… and then she kisses it. When she pulls back so that I can see her eyes, I'm rewarded with a happy gleam.

When her lips play across my right cheek, over my brow and down my left, I feel her desire in every cell of my body. Desire to know, to honor, to trust. And it makes me want to return it all in spades.

So I let my hands listen, let my lips worship, let my brain go. For the first time ever, my worry about how a person will react to my scars? I let *that* bird fly right out the window.

JESS

My lips and fingertips absorb so much information as they explore the terrain of Cal's body that it's all I can do to simply take it in. Our bodies are still separated by T-shirts and underwear, but that feels like a good thing. I feel safe with my breasts hidden away, and maybe he feels the same having most of his scars covered. Even with clothes on, there's so much to learn, and I don't want to miss a thing. Still, his palm skimming down my spine has my sex clenching with the need to feel him inside me as well as outside.

Be patient, I tell it.

"I'm doing my best," Cal murmurs.

"Oh, I wasn't talking to you." My grin is wide as I frame his face with my hands and rub my chin across his goatee. "I was talking to my vagina."

Laughing, he says, "Maybe you can give a pep talk to my penis while you're at it."

The image has me giggling, and I don't even care. It does confirm how much I've been performing when I've had sex with other partners. Pressing my pelvis into his, I whisper, "Maybe they can have a conversation of their own?"

Slipping his palms under my shoulders, he bench-presses my chest away from his and pointedly looks down at the space between us for a moment. Then he meets my gaze. "He says yes."

"Well, then." Grasping his wrists, I slide his hands to my ribcage and use the momentum of his lift to scoop my tailbone under so that my butt lands right on the spot he just checked out. "She says, 'Come on in, the water's fine.'"

The flirty half-grin drops, and the eyes that meet mine are solemn. "Are you sure?"

Shaking my head and then nodding, I match his tone. "I've never been more sure and less sure of anything."

His grin is back, but it's not playful, it's simply beautiful. "I hear you." Without breaking eye contact, his right arm reaches for the bedside table, pulls out a string of condoms, and holds them up between us. "Ready if we need 'em."

I have no idea how many minutes or hours we spend in mutual discovery. All I know is that with every touch, I want more. With every glance, I want more. Every moan of his is met with an equally needy one of mine. My skin is slick with sweat, but my sex is wetter, and I swear it sighs with relief when he finally finds his way inside.

The only time I've ever lost control of my body was in the hospital when I was fifteen. Then, control was wrenched away from me.

Now, when Cal's thrusts pick up speed, letting go is a gift I give myself. Waves of sensation expand from my core out to the universe and back again until all that energy gathers to a point of excruciatingly pleasurable pain.

Before it explodes.

Chapter 22

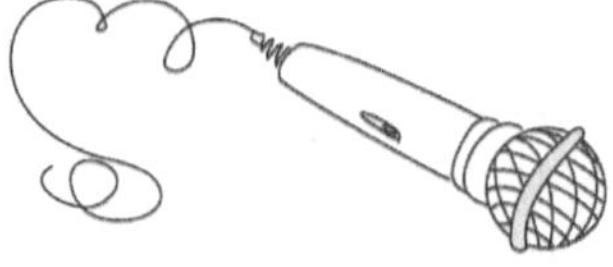

Faster than a speeding Buick, more powerful than a monster truck, able to leap small children in a single bound, it's the only DJ with a mouth of steel: Motor. Weekday afternoons, only at 101.7 W-B-A-Rrrr. *RRR. RRR. RRR.*

CAL

The high I'm still riding from making love to Jess for the first time— followed shortly by the second and third—has me floating all the way to the station to interview the Godfathers, a British band I've followed for a couple of years. When you've made the most beautiful woman in the world weep and laugh at the same time as you rock her world, who gives a fuck what a bunch of rock and rollers think of you.

No one asks about my scars, but I give the spiel about the fire anyway. And then the ball's rolling. We talk about everything from their time touring with the Ramones, to why they choose to dress in suits and ties—unlike most bands these days who might throw a leather jacket on over a T-shirt and jeans—and the origin of their name. Turns out they really are godfathers. Not the criminal kind, but the Irish-Catholic family kind.

After a laugh at that, they record a short acoustic set and are on their way, promising to visit again the next time they come through town.

Jones stops me in the hall when I'm on my way back to the studio to work with the engineer to cut the interview into smaller bites we can play over the course of my slot. "Hey, man. I heard the tail end of that. Great questions. You totally loosened them up." His chin drops, and his brows rise. "You're good at this, you know."

Rolling my eyes, I can't help but grin. "Yeah, yeah. You told me so. Now get out of my way; I got work to do."

Then for the first time ever, Jones claps me on the left shoulder, hard. Like he does everyone else.

FRIDAY NIGHT. Good thing: Jess can call in right after her show because she doesn't have to make the drive home first. Bad thing: she's not coming back to Boston until Sunday.

Even though I know her commute is only minutes, I'm still flooded with relief when the Jessica sign appears in the booth window. Like I am every time. Relief that she's okay mixed with disbelief that she's calling again.

There're only seconds left in the Smithereens' "A Girl Like You," but I punch the phone line and say, "I'm here, I miss you, but I need a minute to line up some songs."

"Got it," she breathes. "I miss you too."

The lyrics of the song—which express how I feel about Jess right now, including the fact that I'll do anything to win her love—echo in my head as I punch in a cart with part of today's interview, followed by the acoustic version of the Godfathers' "Just Like You."

When I punch back into the phone line, Jess squeals, "You did such a good job on that interview! Did you do that today?"

"Yep." I can't hide the pride in my voice. "And how about you? Was tonight's show better than Thursday's?"

She sighs. "It was. We found our rhythm, thank goodness."

"I'm going to miss your rhythms." My voice is more gravelly than usual as I confess, "I'll miss you next to me tonight."

"Me too," she whispers. "Wait. Are you sure you're not broadcasting this conversation?"

I fake a gasp. "Oops."

"Oh my god. Are you?"

"Nah, I'm kidding."

She laughs, and I can almost feel her shove me as she says, "You jerk. You about gave me a heart attack."

"Sorry."

"You're not sorry."

"No, I'm not." I'm grinning so wide I'm sure Talia would think I was on something if she walked in here right now. "But I'm not kidding about missing you." Normally, after sleeping with a girl, everything feels so awkward that I avoid seeing them again. With Jess, I don't want to waste another second apart from her. "When will I see you next?"

"Um, Sunday night, maybe? I'll be wasted though. It's a long weekend. You could come up here, though. See the play and sleep with me."

Springing what's between us out of the cocoon of my place and the station is terrifying, but I'm almost ready to risk it. Still, obligations are an issue.

"I'm spinning at Axis Saturday night. But maybe I can another weekend. I'd have to get someone to take care of Blondie."

"The Sunday night show starts earlier, so I'll be done at nine."

"I'd love to have you come to my place. I'm not working Sunday. I have dinner with my family, but I'll be home before you're done."

"That might work."

There's a hesitancy in her voice. I don't want to push too hard and scare her off. "Maybe we can talk tomorrow and figure it out."

After I give her my home number, she says, "I'll call you before I go to the theater, like at one o'clock."

"Sounds good, princess."

"'Good night, good night. Parting is such sweet sorrow, that I shall say good night till it be morrow.' But I won't"—she switches vocal gears from floaty ingenue to world-weary broad—"because I need sleep and you need to get back to work."

Forty-eight hours. Such a long time. But then I get an idea for how to fill the time.

AFTER WORK, when Phil slides a beer across the bar, he's got a funny look on his face.

"What?"

He frowns. "What do you mean, what?"

"I mean, spit it out."

"For someone who hides his own face all the time, you're pretty good at reading them."

"Yeah, well, when you're a target, that's a survival skill. What's the bad news?" I lift my glass. "No more late-night beers for Cal?"

"You haven't sat on that stool all week." He juts his chin at the bags of to-go containers on the bar next to me. "You pick up the food and skedaddle out of here. I figured you had something better to do with your time. Or someone better to hang out with than me."

"As a matter of fact, I have." I can't stop the cocky grin that takes over half of my face.

Phil crosses his arms over his chest, tatted biceps bulging. "So what happened? She break up with your sorry ass?"

"She's busy tonight. So *you* have to deal with my sorry ass." I lower my chin and raise my crooked brows. "What is it you need to tell me?"

Elbow on the bar, he blows out a breath. "I think it's actually good news. I've been talking to some people at St. Francis House. It's a homeless shelter over in the Combat Zone," he clarifies. "Anyway, we're expanding what you and I started here. They're talking to the health department, and I'm recruiting other restaurants. They've got a van and volunteers ready to go."

It's selfish, but it feels like Phil's taking something away from me. "You think Walt and his buddies are going to deal with the health department? Or people demanding that they pray before they can eat?"

"The social worker at the shelter said they've had success with making contact—like you've been doing—by bringing meals. Then they turn the trust they've built up into helping these guys get off the street. At the very least, giving them a choice. They don't have to go to church or anything."

"That's hard to believe. I mean, it's called St. Francis."

"I think they're good people with good intentions. More important, they can feed more people than you and I can alone."

I take a sip of my beer. Rationally, I know he's right, but delivering food made me feel… worthwhile. Not a good reason to stand in the way of the guys getting a chance at something better, though. "Guess I'll have to hang up my superhero costume."

"You don't have to be the lone caped crusader, Cal. You can help in other ways. Talk about it on the radio, maybe."

"Maybe."

"And now you've got a girl to spend your nights with."

"Until she gets tired of hiding in the shadows with me."

"Or maybe you'll get tired of hiding in the shadows?"

I gesture at the empty bar. "You're one to talk."

He rolls his eyes. "Drink up. I'm ready to close up."

"I'll miss you, Phil."

"Maybe you'll come in some night at a normal time."

"Yeah, and maybe the Sox'll win the World Series again someday."

He sighs, a dreamy look on his face. "Wouldn't that be nice? Break the curse of the Bambino."

"Got to have hope for the impossible, huh?"

"Shut your mouth." He snaps a bar towel my way. "And get out of here with your last delivery. The van's taking over Monday."

Chapter 23

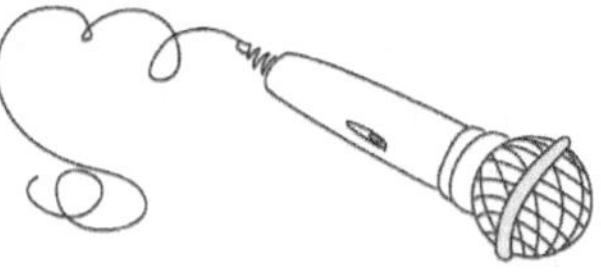

We'll return to part forty-four of this Saturday's Million Dollar Movie, *Elvis meets Costello*, right after this.

JESS

I totally feel like a teenager right now. For one thing, after getting Cal on the line, I stretch the phone cord to its limit and hunker down in the pantry so I can have a little privacy, like I did growing up. And two, I have that giddy feeling in my tummy about talking to a boy, one I don't think I've had since I was twelve.

When did I get so fucking cynical about romance?

"So, tell me. Did you want to be a DJ since you were a kid?" I ask.

He grunts out a laugh. "Actually, I thought I wanted to be a fireman."

"Seriously?"

"Yeah, it seemed like the right thing to do. But when I was in high school, I tried to interview the fire chief at our local station for some class project, but the crew showed up fresh from fighting a fire, and I couldn't be in the same room with them. The smells were... too much."

"So then you decided to be a DJ?"

"That was more of a winding road. I got into a program my senior year of high school where instead of going to regular classes, we did internships. One of them was at a radio station, and I fell in love with the equipment. I've always loved music, ever since I was in the hospital the first time—"

"Wait. How many times were you in the hospital as a kid?"

"I'm not even sure. At least once a year from the time I was four till I was fifteen."

"That seems like a lot."

"It was, but it was necessary because as you grow, normal skin grows along with the rest of your body. But scarred skin doesn't make new cells, so they have to keep creating grafts to keep up."

"Oh." Picturing him as a little kid, having to go through surgery over and over again breaks my heart.

"Anyway, the first stretch—the time where I stared at the picture of the flowers—the ward was a really quiet place. I was little, so I don't remember too much except that it was lonely. I didn't see other patients. But when I went back for skin graft surgeries, I was on the other end of the ward, surrounded by other kids. When I whined to my parents that it was still boring, my older brother gave me his Close 'n Play and a stack of 45s so I could listen to music."

"That was nice of him."

"Well, he did get a nicer player out of the deal. Anyway, I wanted to listen all day long. It helped distract me from the pain, the itching, and having to lie still. It was always something. But you can only listen to one 45 over and over so many times before you go nuts. I'd push the call button to get a nurse to turn the record over for me, which of course drove them crazy, so at some point an actual stereo appeared on the ward. Some nurse convinced the powers that be that it was calming for everyone. They'd stack LPs and let 'em play one after the other. The staff had some pretty eclectic tastes. You never knew what you were going to get."

"But it helped?"

"There are some songs from that era that I can't listen to. They're locked up with memories I can't... I don't want to revisit."

Picturing my nieces going through something like this? I can't even imagine it. "Maybe that's why you like newer music."

He huffs out a laugh. "I definitely couldn't work at an oldies station. I'm thankful for those songs, though. They kept my heart beating, my lungs moving the air in and out."

"I get that. Like your organs moved in rhythm with the music. I feel that when I get lost in choreography. It's not the same, but—" There's a knock on the pantry door, and Tim sticks his head in.

"Do you still want a ride to the theater? Bus is leaving in five."

"Oh shit. Sorry, Cal, I have to go." To Tim, I whisper, "Yes, please."

When I haul myself up off the floor, I make a very unladylike sound.

"You okay?" both Tim and Cal ask.

"Yeah, I think my butt fell asleep."

I wave Tim out of the way as I head back to the kitchen.

"Can we talk tonight?" Cal asks.

"Won't you be at the club till late?"

"Right. So… will I see you tomorrow night? Will you come to my place after your shows?"

Gripping the receiver in both hands, I bounce on the balls of my feet, partly to wake them up, but partly because this man makes me feel giddy. "I will."

"Good. I miss you, princess."

As I follow Tim down the front steps, he says, "I think I need to hear all about whoever it is that put that blush on your cheeks, girlfriend. Someone's not going to need any makeup this afternoon."

OUR SATURDAY MATINEE audience is much more enthusiastic than usual, so when I get a message from the stage manager that friends are waiting for me, I have an inkling I know who they might be. When I find a whole carload of Shakespeare Boston actors in the lobby, I'm totally *verklempt.* "You guys, it was so sweet of you to drive all the way up here."

Trying to hug everyone at once turns my tears into a giggle fest. Eventually I learn that half the *Hamlet* cast had to attend some sort of academic conference, so the younger cast members—meaning all my friends—got the day off. Since I need to eat in the hour before the next show and they have to refuel for the drive back to Boston, we decamp to the coffee shop down the street.

When I shiver on the walk over, Randall puts an arm around me. "It's colder here than down in Boston."

"Tell me about it. The actor housing heat is useless. I had to bring up extra blankets."

Will steps in on my other side. "Ah, 'the icy fang and churlish chiding of the winter's wind.'" After a slight pause he adds, "Duke Senior, *As You Like It*."

An answering quote to pop into my brain from a poem that's haunted me for years. "'Call it winter, which being full of care, makes summer's welcome thrice more wished, more rare.' Sonnet fifty-six."

"Nice one," Will allows. "And so appropriate. We need you back this summer, you know."

"That's not exactly under my control."

"We do have some news about the season," Randall says. "But let's get inside. It's too damn cold to yammer out here, no matter how poetic you two make it sound."

By the time we've ordered and taken over a couple of couches in the back corner, the others are primed to gossip.

"There's some sort of history between Mira and Nick," Mike tells me. "They were going at it during a preseason production meeting."

"You mean like kissing?" I try to picture that happening in one of those meetings. They're usually so boring that I struggle to stay awake.

"No, no." He shakes his head, laughing. "Like fighting. Disagreeing. Sniping at each other about anything and everything."

"There is some history, but even Ben doesn't know what it is," Will adds. Ben and Mira were college besties and have remained friends since. She's the one who brought him to Shakespeare Boston last summer. "He thinks it happened when Mira was studying in London her junior year."

Randall sits back, putting his feet up on the coffee table. "Whatever it is, those two in the same room?" He makes a blowing up noise and mimes an explosion.

"I guess I'm missing a lot," I pout.

"Which is why you better get your butt to the summer season auditions," Will says, elbowing me. "The shows are *The Tempest* and *Comedy of Errors.*"

I slump back into the couch cushions and blow errant curls out of my face. "I'm too old for Miranda."

Will sits forward. "That's the cool thing—and one source of the battle between Mira and Nick. She wants the casting for *Tempest* to be totally out there. So you can audition for anyone. *I* might even audition for Miranda."

"What the heck is her concept?" I ask.

Mike throws up his hands. "Who knows? But she's had success with crazy casting before, so she'll probably get her way. I think I'm going to try for Trinculo. And maybe Ariel." He nods at me. "Of course, you'd be a great Ariel. But that might be too obvious."

"Not feeling terribly sprightly at the moment," I grumble, realizing that this means I'll have to actually reread the play now. "But I'll do my best. When are they?"

"Next Saturday," Will says.

"Ugh," I whine. "I have two shows that day."

"I thought you closed this weekend," Will says.

"It's selling well, so they extended."

Randall points at me. "We open the following Wednesday, so I hope you have that free."

"Okay, okay." They're right; I am being a baby about this. "I miss you guys. And it's been a nice little visit with contemporary theater, but I miss Mr. Shakespeare too."

AFTER THE EVENING SHOW, my new actor friends help me brainstorm audition possibilities over a glass of wine back at the actor house. No more whiskey for this girl. Then I have a great idea. "You guys should audition! I mean, they don't usually bring actors in from out of town, so I'm not sure if they'd offer housing…"

"But it would be nice to get out of New York for the summer," Earl finishes my sentence. "What are the plays?"

I tell them what I learned over coffee earlier, and not only do the guys promise they'll drive down with me to audition if I get them appointments, they encourage me to really go for it and audition for the role that intrigues me the most. In a normal world, I'd never even be considered for it. But in Mira's world, who knows?

Not Prospero. I don't have the maturity to play that. *Yet.*

But when I was in college, I had an assignment to work up a monologue from a role opposite from my type, and I chose Caliban from *The Tempest*. It was an exercise, but I remember connecting deeply with the words. The curses of a slave at his master echoed how I felt about the prison of my body. The longing for all he'd lost mirrored my grief at the loss of my dream of being a ballerina. The feeling of being trapped by circumstances beyond your control made total sense to me.

I'd never audition with a Caliban speech in any other scenario, but this seems like an opportunity to step out of my own shadow.

Playing irritable, clueless, frumpy Prudence. Getting paid to goof around at the radio station. Risks are paying off so far. Playing Juliet one summer and Caliban the next would prove that I'm more than an aging ingenue.

Chapter 24

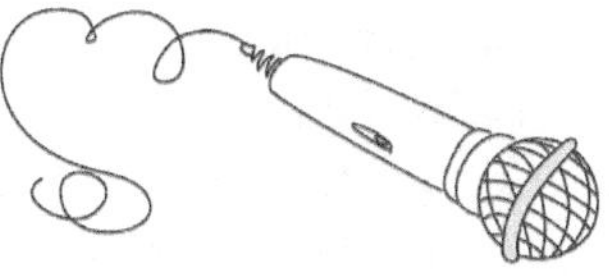

The following is an ad for Peter University. PU. Why pay thousands of dollars at MIT or BU for a stinkin' piece of paper? Come on down to our open house this Saturday to get a whiff of what's on offer at Peter University, next to the fish market under the overpass right here in downtown Boston. Get the essence of an education without the effort at PU.

CAL

Enlisting my contractor brother to help me build a ballet barre over the weekend costs me—in teasing and nosy questions as well as dollars. It gets worse at Sunday dinner because, of course, he tells the rest of the family. Now they all want to meet the woman I'd do something like that for.

But when she leaves Monday morning to work out at her own apartment, even though I offer up my washer and dryer to her so she can catch up on laundry without having to go to a laundromat, I know it was a smart move. I can't wait to finish it and get it installed so she'll have a reason to spend more time at my place.

She doesn't have shows Monday through Wednesday nights, but I have to work late. She has auditions and classes during the day, as well as recording promos and comedy bits with Rocket and Porky at the station. Unfortunately, her schedule at the station doesn't line up with mine at all.

Except on Mondays.

So as soon as the music meeting is over, instead of going straight home to work out, I stop by the promo studio. It used to be called Studio C, but the guys decided that was too boring. So they made a new sign one day out of a pizza box and now it's called Studio Pizza.

Makes no sense to me, but they like it.

As I round the corner, Jess is stepping out the door. "See you guys Wednesday."

"Later, skater," Porky calls.

Jess stops short when she sees me. "What are you doing here?"

Hands up, I take a step back. "I was hoping to catch you. The music meeting's over."

With a glance behind her, she takes my elbow and walks further down the hall. "I'm sorry, but I don't want people to think that I got this job because I'm… because of you."

The word job catches my ear. "Did they offer you a regular gig?"

She grins but keeps me moving away from Studio Pizza. "They did. Three afternoons a week. And the money's good enough that I don't have to get a temp job when the show's over."

Breaking away from me, she spins down the hall. It makes me dizzy to watch, but when she stops, her bright eyes fix on mine. Then she plants her hands on her hips. "I still feel like I have to prove myself, though." She gestures down the hall behind me. "Those guys are off-the-charts talented. I can barely keep up."

"I think I know how you feel. It's a little bit like you choosing to be with me. Like, how did I get so lucky?"

Her smile softens, and she takes a step back to me. Wrapping her arms around me, she whispers, "I'm the lucky one."

But then she steps back. "I mean that, but I'm late."

"Will I see you tonight? After your classes?" I've got her schedule memorized, lovestruck fool that I am.

"I'd like to, but I don't think I can. Bella and I are going to work on our pieces for Shakespeare Boston tonight, and then I've got an early audition Tuesday."

"I have a surprise for you."

"Another coupon book?" She tips her head to the side. "I haven't even finished using up the first one."

"I think it's even better than a coupon book."

She bites her lip. I don't want to push too hard. Plus, if I wait till tomorrow, my brother can help me install it. "No rush. It'll be there Tuesday night if you want to come over."

After checking the hall in both directions, she goes on tiptoe to give me a lingering kiss. "It's a date," she whispers.

Sliding my hands into her curls, I pull her lips to mine and give it everything I've got. After I release her, she executes a complicated set of twirls down the hall. Before stepping through the exit door, she blows me a kiss.

I pretend to catch it, but I know I'm the one who's caught... in a web of this girl's charms.

WEDNESDAY MORNING–WELL, what counts for morning for me; it might be past noon—I wake up to a most beautiful sight: Jessica doing ballet exercises.

When she found the barre here last night, she was so excited she called me at the station and about burst my eardrums. I tried not to wake her up when I got home, but she rolled over and greeted me in the best way possible: arms wide and naked. Except for her bra. I think she has some sort of hang-up about her breasts that she doesn't seem ready to talk about. I'm doing my best to pretend it isn't a big deal, even as I wish I could show her how much I love their soft curves.

Of course, I haven't taken my shirt off, either, so I can hardly complain.

Right now she's got most of her clothes back on, but watching her muscles work is mesmerizing. She'd be an amazing boxer; she's got so much control. I could watch her point and flex her little feet and sweep her arms in graceful arcs all day long.

Even as I relish the sight, worry simmers in the back of my heart. I don't know how much longer I'll be able to keep this beautiful bird entertained inside the cage I've erected for myself.

I've been captivated by her since the moment I first heard her voice on the phone. I've let her see more of me than anybody, even my family. They know what I've been through physically, were there for the bullying and the loneliness. Thing is, I think they still see the broken little kid me.

Jess knows the here-and-now me. She's peeled back layer after layer and hasn't yet run screaming. Instead, she makes me laugh with her goofy voices as she shares stories from her day. Every time her eyes spill over, her tears wash away some of my grief. And only buried deep inside her have I felt a release that has my soul singing.

My thoughts are interrupted by her musical voice calling across the open space of the loft. "I'm almost done, but I'm sweaty."

"I know a way to make you even sweatier."

She cocks her head to the side, an impish grin on her face. "I know you do. And I'm looking forward to that. Right after"—she kicks her leg out sharply—"I'm done with this."

By the time she pulls off her ballet slippers and does a few flying leaps across the room, I'm wide awake and readier than ready for her. Leg warmers and leotard and sweatshirt and tights go flying. She's still in her bra and underwear, but when I try to pull her on top of me, she resists, reaching for the hem of my shirt. "Can I?"

"Are you sure you want to?" is my immediate response, but then I make myself meet her gaze. As they have every step of the way, her eyes tell me she's curious, not judgmental.

She still hasn't seen the worst of my scars—the ones that spread across the left side of my torso and back. Seeing and touching the minor scarring of the donor sites on my butt and thighs had her shaking, her empathy runs so deep. Seeing the swaths of skin I gave up on might be too much.

"Cal." Kneeling by the bed, her eyes find mine. "I want to be able to love all of you. I can't do that if I can't be here with all of you."

It's the L-word that does it. Trusting her the way I want her to trust me, I draw my shirt over my head and chuck it to the floor. Her eyes sweep over my shoulder and down my side, then she crawls behind me. For what seems an eternity, all I can hear and feel is my own heartbeat. When her arms encircle me from behind to squeeze me tight, I can't help it, I shudder with relief. With her cheek pressed to my left shoulder blade, I feel loved.

After she whispers, "Thank you" in my ear, I let out a breath I didn't know I was holding. Then I turn around and do my best to show her how much *I* love *her*.

JESS

Sex with Cal makes me experience my body in a way that I truly didn't know was possible. Guys have always appreciated my looks way more than I have, from the junior high boys who literally drooled over my brand new boobs to that asshole Charles who acted like he was starring in a porn film as he praised my "tight pussy" even as he wanted me to "suck his cock with my pouty lips." I still can't believe I even let that guy touch me.

The only way I can deal with the fact that I slept with guys like him is to file them away in a drawer that's labeled… I don't know, Copulation Because I Was Bored. Or maybe Fucking Because I Didn't Know Any Better.

I've always thought "making love" was a silly term. In my experience, sex was about giving a guy who'd bought me dinner a polite thank you. If I used my imagination and thought about Patrick Swayze or Richard Gere, I might have an orgasm, but I usually turned in a mediocre performance that got good reviews as long as the guy got off.

Cal has educated me. He claims that he doesn't have a lot of experience with sex, but from where I'm sitting, that doesn't matter. With his eyes, his touch, his words, he worships every bit of me, from my gnarly feet to my crazy hair.

Except for my breasts, which is worrisome. On the phone, way back in the early days, he said he was a breast man, but he hasn't demanded that I take off my bra like other guys have. He's touched them and kissed them through the fabric, but moves on quickly. Is that because he finds them as repulsive as I do?

The need to get moving pushes my concerns aside. I wish I could be the kind of girl that could lie around all day, but after a barre workout and sex, I need to drink water and I need to pee. Lately, I can't seem to do enough of either. I should pick up some cranberry juice because I really don't have time to deal with a UTI right now.

Leaning over to give him a quick kiss, I whisper, "I'll be right back. Can I get you anything?"

"More time with you," he murmurs.

A few moments later, I'm back with water for both of us. After I set the glasses on the bedside table, he tries to pull me back into bed, but I dig in my heels. "If I could fit more hours in the day, I would definitely spend them next to you."

"I know you have to get going. Just a few more minutes of snuggling and I'll make you breakfast while you shower."

"You don't have to get up."

"I'm awake. I'll even take you out to breakfast if you want."

"I really have to go home and shower so I can deal with my hair. But I have another ten minutes." After dutifully downing a good eight ounces of water, I curl up next to him. I'm going over the long list of things I need to get done today and wondering if Cal has fallen back asleep when he speaks.

"The Shriners called the station yesterday and left a message for me."

"You mean the guys in the red hats and little cars?"

"Well, someone from that organization. They want me to help them with a fundraiser."

"Why did they call you?"

"It's for the Shriners' Burn Institute. For kids. Here in Boston."

"Is that where you…?" All my plans for the day suddenly feel unimportant. I get the feeling Cal has told me more about his burn experience than most people. He let me see the rest of his scars this morning. Maybe he's ready to bare a little bit more of his heart, too.

"It's where I was treated. Sort of. The first two years of treatment were at Mass General, but they didn't have a burn unit specifically for kids. When I went in for surgery a couple years later, the Shriners had created a mini-hospital for children inside MGH. Then they built a whole separate building. All my treatments were there from then on—surgeries, therapies, everything. And it was free. We didn't pay a cent. They do that for all the kids who go there. It's the best treatment, too, the most cutting-edge. So I guess they need the money. And I guess you could say I owe them."

Turning over to face him, I wish I could smooth his pain away. "What do they want from you exactly?"

He rolls onto his back and talks to the ceiling. "I don't know. I'm afraid to call them."

I nod, not wanting to push.

"I can't go back in there."

"To the hospital?"

"They saved my life, but the pain—the anticipation of the pain—was… indescribable." He takes my hand. "That's why my back is so hideous. I couldn't take it anymore. I refused to go back."

His face has lost all its color. I want him to know that I feel for him. I don't pity him; I never have. I'm in awe of what he's survived. All I can do is show him, so I snake my arms around his torso. Before squeezing him tight, I ask. "This okay?"

"It's very much okay," he says, his voice thick.

I open my mouth to tell Cal about the reason why I understand his fear of hospitals, but my experience seems to pale in comparison to his. They may have strapped me in a chair and force-fed me, they may have messed with my head, but they didn't torture me. So I simply whisper, "I don't think you have to call them back if you don't want to. You don't owe them anything."

He sucks in a breath and hugs me back.

Chapter 25

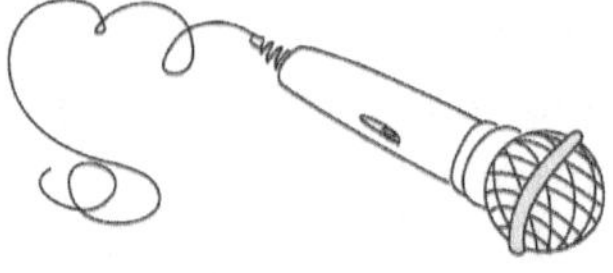

This week's episode of *Family Ties* is entitled "Til' Her Family Takes the T-bird Away." Last week's was called "My Best Friend's Girl." Did Alex start a band or something?

JESS

Cal and I have found a weeknight rhythm, even if it means less than four hours of uninterrupted sleep for either of us, but the weekend continues to elude us. He has commitments that mean he can't see my show, let alone come up for the whole weekend. When I get an idea for a way to sneak in some extra time together, I worry that it might be rushing things, but it's the only one I've got.

Friday morning—well, what counts for morning for Cal—after I do my barre workout and shower, I wake Cal with a kiss and float my idea.

"Since we're both working every night this weekend, what would you think of meeting me at my parents' for brunch Sunday? I promised my mom I'd come down because I haven't seen them in a while. They're in Bedford, so halfway between Boston and Chichester."

"You want me to meet your family?"

His frown seems concerned rather than horrified, so I plunge on. "Yeah, why not?"

"We've only been together for like a couple weeks."

"But we've been talking since the beginning of the year. So, like, almost two months."

"Are you sure? They won't freak out?"

"Why would they?"

He suddenly sits up and takes my hand. "Thank you."

I meet his eyes, even though I feel like a fraud for not sharing all of my ugly bits, the way he does with me. Sidestepping the real issues, I shrug. "I mean, they won't love that you're not Jewish, but I think we can get around that."

"How?"

"Well, technically, if we were to have kids, they'd still be Jewish. And that's what really matters to them."

"Us having kids?"

Now I'm blushing. "I'm not—I'm not saying we should have kids or anything, I don't even—"

"Stop, Jess. I'm giving you a hard time. Two months or two weeks, it's too early for that kind of conversation." He pulls me onto his lap. "I mean, come on, though, our kids would be gorgeous."

Shifting to straddle him, I nuzzle his ear. "Someone's ego's about to get too big for his britches."

"That doesn't even make sense."

Giggling and grinding into his lap, I whisper a quote from one of my favorite sonnets, "'Love is not love which alters when it alteration finds.'"

Hands on my butt, he pulls me even closer. "I'll show you some alterations."

After kissing him behind his right ear—not his left, that's a taboo area—I whisper, "'Men have died from time to time and worms have eaten them, but not for love.'"

Apparently taking that as a challenge, he flips me over and tries to kill me with orgasms. Some time later, when we're panting next to each other, he says, "It might help if you prepare them."

My brain's truly scrambled, so it takes me a minute to realize that he's talking about my family. "Prepare them?"

"About my scars."

"Oh, okay. What should I say?"

"I think it's best to keep it simple. Something like, 'He was in a fire as a child, he has visible scars, but he's fine.' At least on the outside. Well, don't say that last part."

Rolling to face him, I press my hand into his chest over his heart. "I think we're pretty equally fucked up on the inside, Cal."

"I don't know. I might give you a run for your money on that."

Not a debate I'm ready to have. So I deflect. "Well, either way, I'll definitely come over Sunday night after my show. But now, I should get going."

Kissing my hand, he promises, "I'll see you Sunday. In Bedford."

CAL

Late Sunday morning, I wait in my car until I see Jessica's car pull up in front of the Bedford address she gave me. After I give her a greedy kiss, she takes both of my hands in hers. "I apologize now if the family gets super nosy." She makes a face. "I haven't exactly brought a guy home recently. Like, maybe since junior high."

This I was not expecting. "What am I supposed to tell them? About us?"

"Whatever you want." She shrugs as she turns to head up the front walk.

My gloved hand slips out of hers when I don't move. "I'm not sure this is a good idea."

"Cal, it's simple." Returning to capture my hand again, she walks backward, pulling me along as she continues. "You're important to me, and they're important to me. And I think when you meet people's families, you get to see another side of them."

"I feel like this is a big deal now."

"It's not, really; I—"

Before she can finish, the door opens and a woman who can only be Jessica's mother greets us with a smile. "I was wondering why the dogs were barking. What are you two doing standing around out here?"

And then it's a whirlwind of introductions and taking coats. I'm glad to get rid of mine because I'm overheating fast. I rarely take off my hoodie with people I don't know, but something has me going for it. Her sister's gaze is the first to flick over the scars. I remember Jess said that she's a doctor of some sort, and I recognize the quick, professional rearrangement of features. Doctors and nurses who work with burn victims don't even flinch when they see someone like me, but on the rare occasion that I see a regular doctor, it usually takes some effort for him or her to hide the shock and concern.

She knows something about burn survivors, though, because she immediately turns to a thermostat on the wall and turns down the heat.

Jess pulls me further into the house, where I'm offered coffee and peppered with questions about my job.

"And are you responsible for Jess getting all this new radio work?" Mrs. Abraham reaches out to touch my arm to get my attention, but quickly folds her hands together instead.

"Not on purpose. Maybe by accident."

Jess, deep in conversation with her father, is obviously a daddy's girl. He's barely spoken to me. I don't think it's because of the scars, though. It's that instinctive thing fathers have, like if we were cavemen, he'd be challenging me to a fight. Jess is completely at ease, though, like she knows that in his eyes she can do no wrong.

"We were concerned when she quit teaching," her mom continues. "It's good to have some sort of regular paycheck."

I laugh. "Since I've made more mistakes since meeting Jess than I have in the past ten years at the station, I might be the one looking for a job soon."

"Oh, dear."

"I'm kidding. Though she is a bit"—I jut my chin in Jess's direction as she makes a dramatic gesture with her hands—"distracting."

Mrs. Abraham raises an eyebrow, exactly the way Jess does when she's amused.

"That's how she got called in to the station in the first place," I explain. "We were talking on the phone and I pushed the wrong button and our conversation played on air instead of the song on the turntable. I didn't even notice."

Before Mrs. Abraham can respond, the dogs start barking again. "Oh, the girls must be here—my grandchildren. They had Sunday school," she explains.

Two tiny females barrel down the hall and go straight for Jess, practically tackling her with demands for her attention.

When one of them turns and sees me, she emits a bloodcurdling scream.

Jess's sister steps between me and the girl and grasps her by the shoulders. "Tamara! Stop it."

The girl buries her face in her mom's ample chest for a few moments, but then curiosity seems to win out over terror.

As she peeks at me over Esther's shoulder, I get down to her level to whisper, "It's okay. Sometimes I scream like that when I look in the mirror."

Both girls giggle. Esther's hands go to her hips. Her face is flushed with embarrassment. "Stop that, Tamara. Apologize to Mr. Alonso. Now."

The girl's lower lip sticks out in a pout. "I'm sorry."

I nod. "I'm sorry I scared you."

Esther clamps her lips into a line, like she doesn't want to let her off the hook.

I wave a hand through the air. "How about we have a do-over?" Everyone stares at me like I'm crazy. "Come on. Let's do it over. This time you won't be surprised by the weird-looking guy, and you can say hi like it's all normal."

Tamara narrows her eyes at me momentarily like she's not sure I'm serious, but then lifts her chin. "Okay."

After running back to the front door, she recreates her entrance right up to the moment when she noticed me. This time, instead of screaming she says, "Hi, Aunt Jess's friend. Who are you? I'm Tamara, but you can call me Tami."

Then she marches up to me and holds out her hand, which I shake.

"Very nice to meet you, Tami. I'm Callihan Alonso, but everybody calls me Cal. And who did you bring with you?"

She introduces her older sister Abigail and her father in a tone that manages to balance prim with bossy. She's definitely cut from the same cloth as her auntie.

This performance seems to shake out the discomfort for everyone. When Mrs. Abraham announces that brunch is almost ready and I ask for directions to the bathroom so I can wash up, Jess shows me the way.

"I'm sorry, Cal. I told my parents about you, but I guess the message didn't make it to the kids."

"It's okay. I'm bigger than Tami. I knew I could take her if I had to."

She rolls her eyes but then adds, "I'm also sorry for ambushing you about the other thing. That you're the first boyfriend I've brought home."

I run a finger lightly across her lips. "Did you just call me your boyfriend?"

She raises her chin. "Yes, I believe I did."

"Well, that makes it all worth it." After checking to make sure we're alone, I lean down to kiss her, to get a taste of the only thing I'm hungry for of late. But I have to keep it brief or I'll never stop, so I pull back and murmur, "Thank you."

Her brows arch in question as she meets my gaze.

"For"—my hands flap at my sides as I dig deep—"for all of it."

When the smile that feels like it's made for me takes over her face, she's so beautiful my heart stops. Probably because all the blood in my body's fled south. I need to be skin to skin with this woman. As soon as possible. "Will you come over tonight after your show?"

Somehow, her smile grows even wider. "I'd love to." Then she gives me another quick kiss before skipping down the hall away from me.

Skipping.

This woman.

JESS

After Cal leaves my parents' place, after a brunch that went relatively smoothly despite what could've been a disastrous start, my sister catches me on the way out the door.

"Are you doing okay, Jess?"

My dad already grilled me about my finances, and I was happy to be able to report that I'm mostly back on track. But my sister's concern seems to be about something else. "Listen, I know Cal isn't Jewish, but he is special to me, so please let's not argue about that yet. It's pretty new, and who knows where it'll go. I mean, we did talk about it, and he did say something about how beautiful our kids would be—"

Esther stops my babbling by circling my wrist with her thumb and forefinger. "I'm worried about your weight. Are you... getting into bad habits?"

Sometimes I feel like my family watches me like I'm some sort of zoo animal. It's hard not to get defensive, so I count to five and paste on a smile before answering. "I'm fine, Es. I have to stay trim—"

"But you're not dancing professionally, Jess."

"Not for that." My tone comes out harsher than I meant it to, and I have to make an effort to soften it. "I know you don't really watch TV, but if I want to land a national commercial or a guest spot on a movie or TV show shooting here, I have to be competitive. And that means being thin. The camera adds twenty pounds or something."

Her frown says she's not convinced.

"But I am eating healthily."

When she sighs, she sounds like our mom.

"I promise. Now stop mothering me."

"I'm sorry. I can't help it." She pulls me into a pillowy, motherly hug. "You scared me when you were fifteen. A lot. I'm always afraid it'll happen again."

"It's okay," I whisper, to her and to myself. "I'm fine."

If I didn't feel like she'd haul me off to do a bunch of tests I'd confess to my sister that I have been feeling a bit under the weather. Anyway, my dressing room buddy Lanie was battling some sort of stomach bug last week, so it's probably that. Losing weight because I'm too nauseous to eat does not mean I'm anorexic again.

For once in my life, I'm actually really happy. If only my family, and my body, would let me simply enjoy it.

Chapter 26

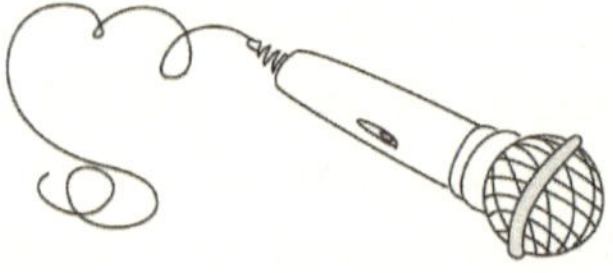

**It's Special Kay on WBAR with your quote of the week.
This is from the philosopher Nietzsche. 'Without music,
life would be a mistake.' Wow, like just, wow. That old
German dude rocks, man.**

CAL

For the past few weeks, my primary focus has been showing Jess in every way possible how much I care about her, whether that's building her a ballet barre, meeting her family, or making her body soar. So not only am I late to Monday's music meeting, but I'm unprepared. I don't have new music to fight for, and I am in no way expecting the bomb that Gracie drops.

"It's official. I'm leaving, kids."

By the reactions around the room, seems like I'm the only one that didn't see this coming. "What are you talking about?"

"She's been up for a slot in a midday show at an LA station for weeks, you idiot." Kay throws an empty coffee cup at me to punctuate her insult. "Someone's lost in the love canal."

Not sure I want to even begin to address that metaphor, I give Gracie my congratulations. "So, when do you go?"

"Three weeks," she says with a grin. "Enough time to say goodbye to all the guys in Boston."

The meeting continues like any other, with no word from anybody as to who is replacing her or what's happening with the schedule. Not that I'm going to lobby for it. I've never wanted the higher profile an earlier spot would bring, nor the tighter control on what's played. I'd have to play what the ad guys, the stockholders, and the so-called prime listeners want.

I'd be abandoning the people that really need the music. Like me.

However, I do have someone in my life now. Someone who would probably like it if I came home at ten instead of starting work then. I'm gearing myself up to talk to Jones about it after the meeting, when Motor makes an announcement.

"The station's getting an uptick in homophobic, menacing calls and mail, and somebody followed me home the other night." It's only when he stands that I see that his suit's more rumpled than usual and he's got deep bags under his eyes.

Jones clears his throat. "We're working on tightening security. From now on, nobody comes in the back door after five o'clock and nobody comes in the front door without prior authorization."

"This is bullshit," Guy says, sitting forward. "How can the guys over at BST get away with siccing their dogs on you?"

"Their name is basically bullshit," Nigel drawls. "Perhaps that's all they know how to serve up."

"Maybe somebody needs to teach them a lesson," Big Bob growls.

"Sinking to their level is not going to solve anything." Jones says. "The hate they're stirring up for anyone who's not a white heterosexual male won't be tempered by adding more of the same."

"Guess we'll have to love them to death," Nigel mutters.

The fresh memory of Jess's niece screaming at the sight of me sharpens my anxiety. If the shock jocks set their sights on me—and Jess—they could do a lot of damage. Not only do I not relish being paraded around as a freak, negative publicity could affect her career. Moving slots no longer seems like a good idea. So when the meeting's over, I duck out of the room before Jones can even ask.

WEDNESDAY AFTERNOON, after a quick workout with my free weights, Blondie and I head over to the station. I'm hoping to catch Jess at the end of her session with Porky and Rocket to see if she wants to have lunch.

Lucky for me, they're running over, so I sneak into the booth with the engineer to watch the trio work. Somehow, Jess even makes headphones sexy. Unfortunately, Blondie cuts my time playing audience short. When she hears Jess on the studio speakers, she barks. It's awesome that she's as in love with this woman as I am, but it has the engineer pointing at the exit. Catching Jess's eye before we leave, I give her a sheepish wave.

She's kind of pissed off when she finds us in the break room. "You can't sneak in and watch. I'm still figuring it out, and it totally threw me off."

"I'm sorry. I had no idea. You seem so confident—"

"Well, I'm not, okay!"

Blondie makes a noise I've never heard before. It doesn't sound like a happy one, though, so I take a step back. I'm not sure if she's feeling protective of Jess or me.

Before I can say anything, Jess shakes out her arms and makes a face. "Sorry, I'm a little on edge."

My sister has trained me well, so I don't ask if she's on her period… though I haven't ever seen a sign of her having a period, come to think of it. That's a question for another time. "I, uh, I wanted to see if you'd have lunch with me."

She wipes a hand over her face like she's erasing a chalkboard, and when she's done, her expression has shifted. "I could do that."

I shove my hands in my pockets, feeling awkward all of a sudden. "I figure we'd get takeout and have it here."

"You don't want to go somewhere?"

"Eating out can be weird for me." Before she can argue, I add, "Plus, I've got Blondie."

She crosses her arms. "I'll get lunch with you if we walk to get it and bring it back here."

At the word *walk*, Blondie barks. "Blondie, enough."

Jess squats and strokes both sides of the dog's furry face. "Poor girl. You're not getting enough walks these days, are you?" Blondie whines. "You used to walk her—"

"Stop saying that word. You're making her crazy."

"Sorry, sweet girl." Standing, she pokes me in the chest. "You used to take her out after your shift, right? Now she's not getting the exercise she used to. That'd make me squirrelly."

That word gets Blondie going too. "Oh my god, stop talking. Okay, we can W-A-L-K to a Thai place on the other side of the Fens."

Smile back on her face, Jess loops her arm in mine. "Perfect."

Outside, the sun, warm with the promise of spring, has lured lots of people out. When Jess demands that we cut through the Fen gardens rather than stay on Boylston Street, I'm happy to do so, thinking we'll avoid human traffic that way. I enjoy watching both of my girls running around outside so much, I don't notice until too late that the path takes us right by the playground at Mother's Rest. Before we can get past it, a little girl comes running straight at us, her mother a few steps behind.

When she gets close, the girl looks me right in the face. "Can I pet your dog?"

Caught off guard at the question, I mumble, "Um, sure. Hang on. Blondie, sit."

The moment my dog's butt hits the ground, the girl's tiny hand reaches up to stroke her scruffy neck. The mom's gaze flicks to my scars briefly, but she's obviously more concerned about the proximity of her child's hand to the jaws of a German shepherd than she is with the state of my face.

By the time Blondie's rolled over to expose her belly, she's got them both charmed. Studying the dog's face, the girl asks, "Why does she only have one eye?"

I join her and scratch under Blondie's chin. "She was a police dog, and she got injured in the line of duty."

"Poor doggie. You must be very brave," the girl coos. Then she looks at me. Her brow wrinkling, she asks, "Did you get injured in the line of duty too?"

Letting down my guard seems to have erased the prepared speech from my brain. "No, I, uh—"

"Jenny, I think that's enough," the mom says. Mouthing "sorry" to me, she pulls her daughter to her feet. "Say thank you."

"Thank you," Jenny says obediently. Then, patting me on the arm, she continues, "You must be very brave too."

Chapter 27

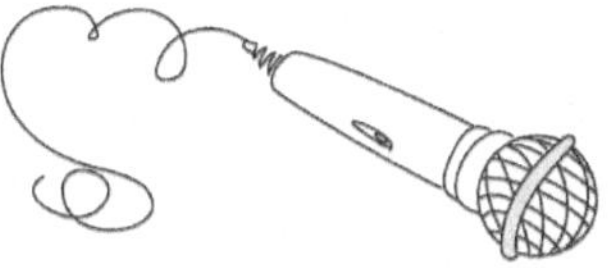

And now, the WBAR corporation is proud to present another instant-classic super spectacular, a little-known Shakespearean tragedy: "Henry the Eighth." Whoa, dude. Heavy. Right, man. Don't lose your head over it.

JESS

Wednesday night, when I find Bella waiting for me in the lobby of Shakespeare Boston's winter home, I give her a big hug and whisper, "It's a good thing you bought the tickets ahead. Only the thought that I'd be wasting your money got me here tonight."

She puts on a pouty face. "Standing me up wasn't enough?"

"I can't even tell you how tired I am," I moan.

"Jess, I suffered through months of dealing with a baby that never slept more than three hours in a row. You have no idea what tired looks like."

"Damn. You always win with the mom card."

"So, what's got you so tired? Hot sex every night? This is where I lose with the mom card, you know."

Her smile tells me that she's kidding. Mostly. Bella only drops hints about what she calls her "checkered past." But this is not the time nor place to be flapping dirty laundry about.

"Tickets?" When we hand them over, the usher recognizes us, and her smile shifts from professional to personal. "Oh, how nice to see you girls. I'm so sad you're not in this play."

"Nice to see you too," we echo, giving the older woman a hug.

"I suppose you two can find your way to your seats."

Once we're settled, Bella elbows me. "So? Hot sex? C'mon, you know I live vicariously through your sexcapades."

"Well, I have to admit that is part of it. But mostly it's that his schedule and mine do not match up. He doesn't get home from work till after two a.m., and I can't seem to sleep past seven. Plus, I'm running all over town trying to make an actor living."

"We're only young once, though, right?"

"I guess youth is relative." Scanning the program, Rhonda's name jumps out at me. "Oh, to be twenty-two again."

"Uh-uh." Bella shakes her head. "You couldn't pay me enough to go back there."

Before I can argue, the lights dim, and she whispers, "Hope it's good. I don't want to have to fake it when we talk to them after."

"Me neither."

When I hear the first words of the performance, I send up a thank you to the director for cutting the script. There's no way I'd last through a four-hour *Hamlet*.

I'm also entranced. The play shifts back and forth between highly theatrical bits that almost have the feel of Greek tragedy—starting from the top with the entrance of the king's ghost—to hushed, furtive intimacy. Will is fantastic, as are pretty much all of the play-ers. Eva Marie as Polonius blows my mind. It's not that she's playing a male character. It's that she's playing the role like her character is putting on an act, and it works. Everyone in the world they've created is always playing a role, so none of them can trust each other.

When Hamlet raises a dagger to stab Claudius, the scene blacks out with a boom of thunder, and the entire audience gasps.

After the lights come up, signaling the intermission, Bella grabs my arm. "Suddenly, I can't remember. Does Hamlet kill Claudius at this point?"

I shake my head. "No, but they made it pretty convincing. That's a brilliant spot to take the break." Fanning myself with my program, I slump back in my seat. "Wow. Unless they totally fuck up the second act, we won't have to lie at all when we tell them 'good show.'"

"Not at all," Bella agrees

"Even Rhonda," I pout.

Bella whacks me. "Come on, girl. It's not a zero-sum game. When you're talented and work hard—both of which apply to you—the work will be there. It may not be what you think you want, but it'll be what you need."

"Okay, Yoda. I've got to run and pee before intermission is over."

BY THE TIME the lights come up at the end of the show, my body feels like half the characters onstage: dead. Between my ever-present exhaustion, throbbing pain in my lower back that's been bothering me for a few days—exacerbated by sitting in uncomfortable theater seats for three hours—and the emotional journey of the play, all I want is for Scotty to beam me up so I can crawl into bed.

We can't leave without congratulating our friends, however, so Bella and I follow the rest of the crowd to the lobby, where we find Lucy, along with Kate, Will's fiancée.

After giving Kate a big hug along, with my congratulations on their engagement, I turn to ask Lucy where Ben is.

"He's in rehearsals in New York," she says. "So I'm Kate's date."

Bella hooks her arm in mine. "Girlfriends are often the best dates, anyway."

Kate laughs. "Agreed."

Lucy leans forward to whisper, "I'm glad I had Kate to explain what was happening. I did get a little lost at times. I still don't really get what those guys with the German names were all about."

"Rosencrantz and Guildenstern?" I ask.

Lucy nods. "Those guys."

"Don't worry. Nobody really does," Bella stage-whispers.

By the time the actors appear, the four of us have laughed so much that the grief of the play has washed out of me and I'm ready to give the cast hugs and tell them how well they did.

If I were more responsible, I'd go home to my apartment, but I can't say no to the prospect of Cal's warm body next to mine—even if it's only for a few hours. So I steer my little car in the direction of his place instead. Good thing his voice coming through the speakers warms me from the inside out because the heater in this beater is useless and the warmth of the day's sunshine has disappeared. Spring in Boston is an elusive creature.

When he plays an old song by the Boston band Human Sexual Response called "Guardian Angel," it turns my yawn into a huge smile. I do like having my own personal DJ.

In the quiet of his apartment, though, grief catches up with me. I've been a Shakespeare Boston company member since its inception five years ago, and I've acted in every single production. Until tonight.

Sitting in the audience instead of being part of what was happening onstage felt strangely like the first time I saw my sister hold baby Abigail—like my family was moving on without me.

When Cash hops up on the bed to snuggle with me, I am reminded that not working at Shakespeare Boston actually brought good changes to my life. I fall asleep to the sound of his comforting purr with a smile on my face.

Chapter 28

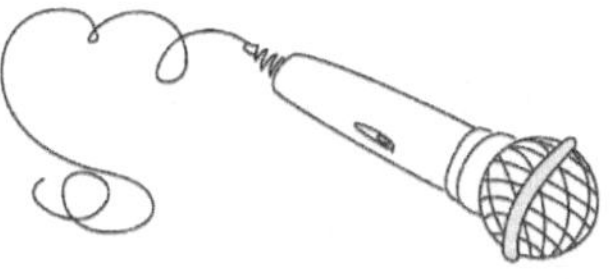

This is Bobcat Goldthwaite, and you're listening to Motor on WBAR. Keep listening, okay, or they won't let me leave this place. *BAM. BAM.* Hey, guys. *BAM. BAM.* Hello? Anyone there?

CAL

Friday afternoon I kiss Jess goodbye before she leaves the station to drive up to Chichester for the show's final weekend. As I watch her drive off, I sort through our plans for the next couple of days, doing my best to tamp down anxieties. Since we met, Jess has been easing me out of rigid routines and out of my shell. I know on some level it's good for me, but the changes are still unsettling. I am looking forward to seeing her in the play, but since I've left it to the last minute, I now have to deal with meeting people at the closing party afterward if I want to stay overnight with her.

At least she won't be making that drive anymore. I still worry until I know she's home safe. Plus, she's pushing her limits with her schedule. I hope she'll slow down a bit when it's over, take a breather before the next new challenge.

Can't worry about her at the moment, though, because I'm late for a meeting with Jones. And Motor, for some reason. I've heard that attacks on him have escalated. I don't know why people give a shit who he sleeps with or what that has to do with the music he plays, but now it's not only assholes leaving messages with foul slurs, it's thugs confronting him in person.

In Jones's office, the mood is lighter than I'd expected. Motor's actually laughing. When I walk in, Jones gestures to the couch. "Hey, Cal. Thanks for coming in early."

Sitting on the edge of his desk, Jones crosses his arms. "As you know, changes are in the works for the schedule."

"Chang*es*?" I ask, emphasizing the last syllable. I thought there was one change—replacing Gracie.

"I'm moving on, too," Motor says.

My spine stiffens. "Are you kidding me? You're caving to pressure from those assholes over at WBST?"

He sighs. "That's part of it. But not all of it. I'm getting a little too old for this"—he makes a helicopter-like circle in the air with a finger—"circus. I've been offered a management position over at the Comedy Stop."

"Wow." Slumping back into the couch cushions, I blow out a breath. "Uh, congratulations, I guess?"

He nods, his smile wider than I've seen in some time. "I'm actually pretty stoked. Not that hanging out with you assholes hasn't been great, but it's a good move."

As my gaze pings back and forth between the two men, unease grows in my gut. "So why am I here?"

"Because I really want you to take my slot," Motor says.

"As do I," Jones adds.

Honestly, I've been trying to work up the courage to ask for Gracie's six-to-ten so that I can spend more time with Jess. But taking on Motor's two-to-six would be a whole other ballgame. The drive-time slot garners a *lot* more attention. "Uhhh" is the best I can come up with.

Jones is all business as he leans forward. "To be honest, I had my reservations at first."

"What changed your mind?"

"A popular part of Motor's segment has been the live interviews. The comics have been fun, but I'd rather get bands in here. If you're on in the afternoon, you could interview them the day of their gig, live, right before they head to the venue. It could have a behind-the-scenes, you-only-hear-it-here feel."

I open my mouth to protest, but he cuts me off with a hand up. "You've got the relationships with the musicians already. You do a great interview. And I think I can use that to make the case to the guys up the food chain."

I turn to Motor. "Why do you care if you're out of here?"

He launches himself off the couch to pace, his long legs and sudden burst of energy making the room seem smaller than it is. "Corporate has a couple of jocks they're grooming to move up. The guy that they want to send up for my spot is basically a gay-bashing asshole. He's not as obvious as the guys over at BST, but people I trust have warned me about him. I don't want him even coming to town."

Jones shakes his head. "Nor do I."

"Plus, I know you'll play good shit." Motor sends a sly smile in Jones's direction. "Push back against management."

My gut churns at the thought, but something makes me ask, "If I were to say yes, what happens next?"

Jones picks up a headshot of a woman with a big smile and bigger hair. "It's more complicated than a baseball trade. We can get this woman from Atlanta for Gracie's slot but only if we also take her partner on for your late-night slot."

"So I'm the DFA in this scenario?"

"Kind of, but in this case I need to actually designate your assignment. We don't have any free agents here. If your spot's part of the deal, I have a stronger case for the Atlanta couple. But if we make the change one at a time, corporate can argue that we need their picks ratings-wise." Jones sits on the arm of the couch across from me. "This'd be a good shake-up all around. We get a black couple in here, which will diversify our sound and our roster. Plus you get an opportunity to change things up."

"I'd have to play what corporate wants me to play?"

"Yes and no. Partly because of you, we have a reputation of finding up-and-comers before anyone else. If you can build on that by getting them in here for exclusive interviews, that's as valuable as playing the tried and true that the advertisers think they want." He shrugs. "It's all a balancing act."

"Which is why I'm glad I don't have your job," I mutter before meeting his gaze. "Can I think it over?"

"I can give you a week. No more."

"Okay."

When I stand to shake Motor's hand, he claps me on the shoulder. "You can do it, man."

"Thanks, Motor. Don't be a stranger."

"Any stranger than I already am?" Releasing my hand, he points a finger at me. "Same to you. You and that gorgeous girlfriend of yours are welcome at the Comedy Stop anytime."

That gorgeous girlfriend of mine. Yet another reason to face the music. We'd get to have a semi-normal life together. As I exit Jones's office, the possibilities have my heart racing, not with fear, but with anticipation.

If you'd told me a few months ago that any of the shit going down right now was even a remote possibility—from an amazing woman in my life to a high-visibility slot at the station—I'd have told you to go get your head examined right before you go jump in a lake.

Perhaps my life could have a fairy-tale ending after all.

AS I HEAD for the exit door, planning to go home and hit the bag to work out some of the questions in my head, as well as get my ass in gear, one of the sales managers catches me.

"Cal, a woman's here from the Shriners' organization. She says she's been trying to get in touch with you."

"Yeah, and I've been avoiding her," I mutter.

"Don't they help kids like... uh..."

I'm pretty sure this is the guy who assumed Jess was a temp on her first day at work with Rocket and Porky, so I don't let him off the hook. "Kids with massive burns all over their bodies? Like me?"

"Well, yeah." He nods, his face reddening. "We're always looking for quality charities to partner with, so—"

I put a hand up between us. "Save it. I'll talk to her."

May as well get it over with. Obviously, the Shriners are not going to let it go.

The sales guy ushers me to an office where a blonde about my age waits. When she sticks out her hand to shake mine, I can't help but notice that it's covered in scars. "Sharon Clemmons. I'm a recipient of the Shriners' charity, as well as an advocate," she says by way of introduction.

"Nice to meet you," I lie.

For the next half hour, Ms. Clemmons bombards me with statistics and batters me with arguments. She doesn't breathe a word about what the organization did for me personally, the thousands of dollars of bills they footed for years of surgeries and therapies. She does tell me about the kids from all over the world whose lives they've saved and the new therapies and techniques they are on the forefront of developing.

When she finally takes a moment to breathe and her left hand traces over her right hand's scars, something about the movement jogs a memory. "I believe you, like me," she says, "received care early on that would be considered barbaric now. In fact, I believe that we may have heard each other beg for mercy."

It's then that her name drops in, and the face of a girl a couple of years older than me flashes in my mind. "Sharon from Vermont?"

She nods and her professional smile softens. It's only then that I notice a slight pull in the skin around her right eye. She must've hung in for more plastic surgery than I did because if memory serves, her facial scarring was more extensive than mine.

"Remember playing keep the balloon off the ground?" she asks.

Picturing inflated surgical gloves bopping in the air as we dove and swatted them with bandaged limbs, competing to keep them from touching the hospital floor, I shake my head. "I can't believe it's you." Laughing as another memory hits me, I shake a finger at her. "I remember you starting a massive food fight. Do the Shriners know what a troublemaker you were?"

"Why do you think they hired me?"

As she draws me into shared memories, for the first time ever, I'm saddened that I wasn't able to maintain the bonds forged in the burn treatment trenches. We played together and ate together, and as Sharon said, we heard each other cry. But when a kid left, you never saw them again unless their follow-up surgeries happened to overlap with yours. I never wanted to dwell on my time there, so I never sought anyone out, either.

"So, I guess there's a reason they sent you to talk to me," I finally say.

"Yes, there is. But believe it or not, I don't mean to use childhood memories as leverage."

"It's not a part of my life that I have any desire to revisit, that's for sure. And honestly, I don't know why you'd want me as a poster boy." I draw a line between her face and mine. "Why not you?"

"My range of experiences make me a strong advocate. But you have an audience. You literally have a megaphone in there," she says, pointing in the direction of the studio. "You reach more people in one hour than I can in a month."

"But if they want to trumpet their successes, wouldn't they want someone who looks better? You barely notice the scars on your face. Mine are still a mess. And my back is worse."

Sharon continues to make her case, doing her best to get me to see the other side of each of my arguments. Finally, she seems to sense that I've had enough. She extends an invitation to come and tour the hospital to see the improvements they've made as well as their plans for the future, which include creating a summer camp for burn survivors.

As I walk her to the exit, she makes one last plea. "I understand your reticence, believe me. But please think about it, not only for them—the kids who'll benefit—but for you." She hands me a video-tape. "Watch this? I'll think it'll help you see how connecting with other survivors can change your life. I know it saved mine."

Chapter 29

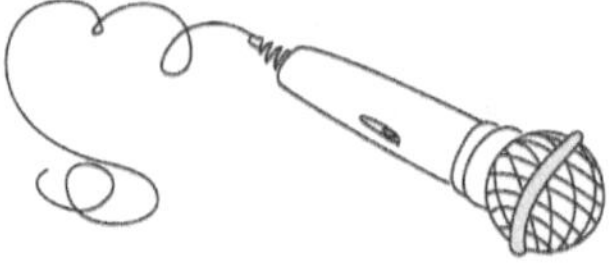

**I've got tickets for the third caller to see the Rolling Stones
live at the Cape Cod Coliseum this Saturday, compliments
of Boston's best rock station, WBAR.**

JESS

Saturday morning I have to be back in Boston for a ten o'clock audition appointment, which means I have to get up at six to get ready. Jack and Earl are driving down with me, which is nice, but it kills me that they literally roll out of bed fifteen minutes before we have to leave.

By the time we make it to the theater and park, my bladder feels like it's going to explode, so I ask the guys to sign in for me while I run to the ladies' room. By the time I make it to the waiting area, I'm late for my call.

Luckily, the directors are running late too. As I run my audition monologues in my head, I do my best to stretch out the kinks in my tired body. For the first time in years, I'm nervous for a Shakespeare Boston audition, so nervous that I'm downright nauseous. Since my reign as the company ingenue is over, this is my shot to convince the powers that be that I can do other things.

As I take slow, deep breaths to counter the fight-or-flight response churning in my belly, I remind myself that I've had successes away from the womb of this theater. This place may have been my first professional home, but it won't be my last. No matter what happens this morning, I'll find work. I've talked myself into not worrying about it when another wave of nausea hits. Along with the need to pee again.

Bella walks in the door as I'm running for the bathroom. "Hey, you're still here; I—"

"Hold that thought; I have to pee."

"I'll come with you."

I grab her hand and pull her down the hall. "I don't have much time."

On the way back from the bathroom, Bella tells me she's decided to read for Trinculo as well as Adriana, and I confess that I decided last minute to read for Luciana in *Comedy of Errors*, instead of the lead role. Adriana is the kind of role I'm known for, but Luciana's speeches are a better balance to Caliban's.

The moment Bella and I settle down in a corner, I'm finally called in. I'm a little dizzy when I hop up from the floor, but Bella catches me from behind so I don't land on my butt.

"You okay?"

"Yeah, just lost my balance."

She squeezes my hand. "Have fun in there. Break legs and all."

I blow out a breath. "Thanks."

Once I'm inside, Mira and Dave really put me through my paces. I figured I'd perform my pieces and that'd be it, but both directors give me direction and have me go at them again.

Dave asks me to add another layer to what I'm doing with Luciana. "What if she starts out berating her sister, but then gets caught up in a fantasy of the perfect man?"

Going for it, picturing Luciana as a corseted spinster who gets carried away, I'm dizzy with desire by the time I get to "Men, more divine, the masters of all these," and I let that play all the way through "are masters to their females, and their lords" but then turn on a dime and wrestle it all back under control for the final line, "Then let your will attend on their accords."

Which earns me a bellow of a laugh from Dave.

Mira suggests I play with the vowels and consonants in Caliban's speech. Shakespeare's words often carry meaning through sounds, so this makes sense. In practice, when I open up the vowels in the section "thou strokedst me and madest much of me," my voice howls with deep mourning. Then when I really hit the consonants in "Cursed be I that did so! All the charms of Sycorax, toads, beetles, bats, light on you!" I'm spitting evil spells.

By the end, I feel like I'm flying.

"I think we've seen enough," Dave finally says. "Nice work, Jess. You've grown since last summer."

Shoving aside the temptation to make a joke about my age, I curtsy. "Thanks. I've been busy."

He tips his head to the side. "Is that you I've been hearing on the radio?"

"It is. Those guys are insane. Most of the time, I'm trying not to laugh."

"I think you're giving them a run for their money," Mira says. "I had no idea you were so funny." She taps her pen on the pad in front of her. "And good work with Caliban. You really nail the 'beauty is in the eye of the beholder' concept."

"Well, I could stand here and soak up your praise all day—"

"But we do have other actors to see," the stage manager cuts in.

"And I have to get back up to Chichester. So I'll get out of your hair."

Stoked by the praise, I simply enjoy time with my old friends as I wait for Jack and Earl to finish up. I have to pee *again*, but I guess that means I'm doing a good job of staying hydrated.

When I return to the waiting area, Bella catches me by the arm and leans in close. "Listen, I didn't want to say anything before you went in, but… are you sure you're not pregnant?"

My hands press my belly. "Do I look pregnant?

"No, not at all. But nausea on top of feeling like you need to urinate constantly… I'm sure you're careful and all, but those are kind of telltale symptoms."

I shake my head. "I don't think—"

"Check it out, okay? Believe me, I know from experience that birth control doesn't always work."

And just like that, my post-audition high comes crashing to the ground.

CAL

Nothing like waiting till the last minute. My mom would say I take it to an art form. I'm so late for the final performance of *Beyond Therapy* that the theater lot is full. The closest spot I can find is blocks away. Even though I jog back, they're closing the house by the time I make it inside. A grumpy woman ushers me to a spot at the back of the dim theater. While some guy gives a speech in front of the curtain, I melt into the shadows.

The seat is uncomfortable and the auditorium overheated, but the moment Jess steps onstage, all that falls away. I can't take my eyes off her. The force of her natural beauty is blunted by the poorly fitting costume, frizzy hairdo and even her posture. The character she plays is awkward, rude, and kind of mean, but every little movement is fascinating. Every shift tells a part of this woman's story. The stuff she's been recording at the station has been entertaining, but I had no idea that Jessica is a truly gifted actress.

When it's all over, I'm wrung out, but in a good way. I feel like I went through some crazy therapy with these people. On top of that, I laughed harder than I have in a long time.

Out in the lobby, the bar is open and quite a few people are hanging around drinking and chatting, so I find a spot in a corner to wait for Jess. When the actors finally emerge, each of them looks a bit different than they did on stage, but none more so than Jess. She's redone her hair and makeup, and she's in a curve-hugging dress. I'm halfway across the room before I know it.

JESS

The need to remind the world—especially the artistic director of the theater, who has the power to bring me in for future roles—that I don't really look like Prudence powers me through fixing my hair and makeup after the show. But only seeing Cal waiting for me gives me the energy to sprint across the room and into his arms.

After I give him a long, lingering kiss, I whisper, "Thank you for coming. It means a lot."

When we separate, he looks around at the crowd—like he's a little surprised at the PDA—before he grins and twirls me around.

"Are you checking out my butt?"

"You betcha," he says with a grin. "I need to soak in all of you. You were too good as Prudence up there. I almost forgot what you really look like."

Blushing, grinning like a fool, I go up on tiptoe, give him a peck on the left cheek, and whisper, "The sooner you meet my friends, the sooner you get to meet my bed."

I prepped everyone ahead of time so they wouldn't react like I did the first time I met Cal, and no one bats an eye at his scars. The giddy energy of a cast that's completed a really good run pulls him right in. When we move the festivities back to the actor house, he relaxes even more when everyone tells funny stories. He even contributes a few of his own.

As I step out of my heels and sink gratefully into a chair next to him, I'm glad he's here. I may not *need* a guy next to me, but having this guy in my life comes with more bonuses than I ever expected. Taking his hand and leaning my cheek on his shoulder, I'm happier than I've ever been, even though I've never felt so bone-tired in my life. Yet another problem with aging: I can't run this body on fumes like I used to.

If I could just sleep for a week or so, my life would be perfect.

As long as I'm not pregnant, that is.

WITH CAL next to me in my actor housing bed, I wake up much later Sunday morning than I usually do, but I don't feel rested. I'd love to go back to sleep, but we have to be out by noon. I'll be sad to say goodbye to Jack, Earl and Timothy, but at least it'll be quick since I don't have much time to pack up.

When I wake Cal with a kiss, he tries to pull me back into bed. "How 'bout a quickie?" he asks with the crooked grin I've fallen in love with.

Yes, I said that word. In my head. Not quite ready for prime time, though.

"There's no such thing with you." At his pout, I add, "That's usually a good thing, but right now we have to clear out. House-keepers will be here any minute to get this place ready for the next crew of actors."

He groans when I pull him up to a seated position. As he moves through the stretches he needs to do every morning to maintain mobility, he asks if I want to go with him to his parents' house for Sunday dinner.

I stop shoving my clothes into a suitcase. "Really?"

"Really. I think it's about time my family met the woman I'm in love with."

His words—words I was too chickenshit to utter moments ago—have me literally dropping everything. With the side that anyone would call gorgeous in my left palm, the side that I find beautiful for all it represents in my right, my lips caress his, telling him the best way I can how much I love him.

When his hands get frisky, however, I have to push away. "Later, you. After I meet your family."

And after I have a nap.

Back at my apartment an hour later, I try to sprint up the stairs to the bathroom, but my legs feel like they're made of lead. I've needed to pee since I hit Route 128, but when I sit on the toilet, hardly anything comes out. Cal followed me here in his car so we can drive together to his parents' house, and he uses my phone to call them and let them know we're coming as I change into something parent-worthy. Running on adrenaline, my tummy feels a bit off as I settle into the passenger seat of his car.

"Are they going to like me?"

His bark of a laugh is full of honest surprise. "Jess, I've never brought a girlfriend to Sunday dinner. When they see how I look at you, they'll know."

"Know what?"

Taking my hand, he pulls it to his chest. "That you're the only girl for me. That the past few months with you have been the best of my life." With a quick glance my way he adds, "Sorry."

"Sorry about what?"

His grin is so wide I'm afraid it's straining his scars to the point of pain. "Now that I've said it, I can't stop saying it." When he presses my hand to his chest, his heart beats a tattoo against my palm. "I love you, Jess."

This time I'm ready. Curling my other hand around his bicep, I rest my head on his shoulder to whisper, "I love you too, Cal."

Chapter 30

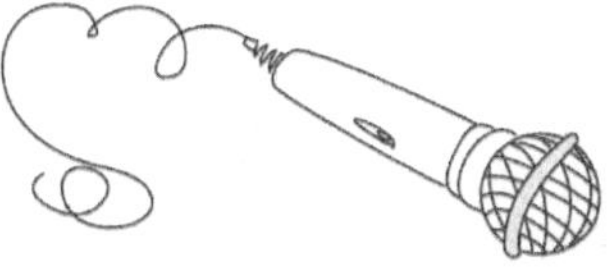

CAL

Jess falls asleep on the short drive to Worcester and doesn't wake up when I stop the car in front of my parents' house. I'm wondering if she's sick, if I should turn the car around and take her home, when her eyes flutter open.

"We don't have to do this today, princess."

It seems to take her a moment to figure out what I'm talking about, but then she sits up. "Are we here already?"

"Yeah. Are you sure you're okay?"

Her smile seems a bit dimmer than usual when she squeezes my hand, but she says, "I think I'm a bit run-down. It usually happens when a show closes. But I really want to meet your family, and we're here." She looks around. "Right?"

A little concerned that she's asking the question when I just gave her the answer, I give her a kiss on the forehead so I can sneak a check of her temperature. Her brow seems a bit clammy, but it's not hot. "We can leave anytime you want to. Let me know, and we'll go."

"I will."

"Alright," I say as I open the door. "Brace yourself. My family's kind of a zoo."

JESS

The minute we step inside Cal's family home, I know this was a mistake. Everything feels off. My skin feels tight and dry, the nausea is back, and in addition to a constant need to pee, a persistent pain prowls through my lower back and pelvis. Bella's question from yesterday rears its ugly head again.

Meeting your just-told-you-he-loves-you boyfriend's family while wondering if you're pregnant? Not ideal.

There are so many of them. Brothers and at least one sister, nieces and nephews and maybe a cousin or two? A sea of faces and names I can't quite hold onto.

I *always* remember names. But right now...

I'm onstage in a play that I forgot to learn lines for.

I'm not even sure what role I'm supposed to play.

My costume feels too hot and then too cold.

The audience won't stop talking.

And I want this nightmare to be over.

CAL

When my mom finds me in the backyard throwing a ball with my nephew and Blondie, she pulls me aside to tell me that Jess doesn't look well. Something tells me this isn't good, so I ask my mom if she'll keep Blondie another night and go looking for my girl. When I find her slumped against a bookshelf nodding listlessly at whatever my cousin who teaches high school English is talking about, I swoop in, scoop her up and bundle her back into the car. This time when I brush my lips over her brow, she's burning up, so after I start the car and get the heat going, I run back into the house to get some Tylenol from my mom.

Jess takes it without a word and then falls asleep before I get to the Mass Pike. I decide to take her to my place so I can keep an eye on her. When I park the car, she doesn't wake up. As I gather her into my arms, our foreheads touch. Hers is still too warm, despite taking the medicine. Hustling inside, I peel her coat off.

"I can do it," she mutters, pushing me away and stripping right there in my living room till she's in nothing but her underwear. Suddenly, shivers shake her body. "Cold."

"Shit." Picking her up again, I carry her to the bed.

"Tired."

"I know, princess." When I brush the hair off her face, her forehead's clammy. "You're sick."

"I always get sick after a show," she groans, turning on her side. "Burn candle at both ends... Sorry, didn't mean to..."

She falls asleep mid-sentence.

After tucking her in, I give Cash some attention along with fresh water and food and then pace around the loft, not sure what to do. Hoping that Jess can fight off whatever she's got with some rest, I settle in front of the TV to watch whatever football is on with the sound off. I doubt it'd wake her, but I want to make sure I can hear if she needs anything.

When I wake up, it takes me a few moments to figure out where I am. The apartment is dim, the TV's on with no sound, and there's a heavy weight on my chest. Then I hear the sound that must've woken me up. Someone's throwing up. Cash yowls when I sit up and dump him off the couch, so it wasn't him.

Coughing from the bathroom.

Jess.

I find her slumped on the ground, her head on the edge of the tub. "So hot."

Touching the back of my hand to her forehead, I wince. "Oh my god, you're burning up."

She dives for the toilet and retches, but nothing comes out. When she turns to face me, she looks so small and pitiful. "I'm sorry," she whispers. "I hope I don't get you sick."

Fever means infection. Infection can kill a burn victim, so I go into panic mode. Jess isn't a burn victim, of course but it still freaks the shit out of me. "I'm worried about you, Jess." It's Sunday, so the only doctor I could take her to is the emergency room of the hospital. I haven't been to a hospital in fifteen years. Even when my sister had the baby, even when my dad had hernia surgery. I couldn't go.

"It's okay," she moans. "I always get sick after a show."

"You said that."

"Oh. Sorry." Pushing her hair out of the way, she tries to sit up. When I put my arm around her waist to help her up, she gasps, and I almost drop her.

"Did I hurt you?"

"Not you." She winces. "*It* hurts." Gingerly touching her right side, she blows out a long breath.

"What can I do? I feel like this is not something you can sleep off."

She gasps, pressing into her side, and a tear runs down her cheek. "I guess"—she squeezes her eyes shut—"what time is it?"

"Hang on." I run to the kitchen to check the clock. "It's eight thirty," I call as I grab a glass of water and a bottle of Tylenol.

When I return, she's hunched over. "Can you call my sister?"

"Of course."

By the time I'm back with the cordless phone, she's on the ground, curled up in a ball. Sitting next to her, I brush the hair out of her face. "It'll be okay, princess. I'm here." She whispers her sister's phone number. Once I get her on the line and quickly explain what's happening, Esther asks to talk to Jess.

Jess mumbles answers into the phone and then hands it back to me.

"She needs to go to the ER," Esther says without preamble. "If my sister is admitting she's in pain, it's bad. It's hard to tell over the phone, but it could be her appendix or even an ectopic pregnancy. Either one could be fatal if it's bad enough."

The closest hospital is Mass General, good for Jess because it's the best. Bad for me because the worst moments of my life took place there.

"I'll call ahead," Esther's saying, "see if I can get her bumped up the line. Hopefully, I know someone who's on tonight. And I'll meet you there." She hangs up without even saying goodbye.

Even though I pick Jess up as gently as I can, she bites her lip to suppress a cry of pain. I carry her over to the bed and then scrabble around until I find some soft sweats in the drawer I cleared out for her to keep clothes in. Getting them on her is like dressing a doll. She fights me when I try to get her in a coat, so I bring it along. Moments later, we're back out the door and on our way to the hospital.

JESS

I thought I'd dealt with pain before. I've worked my muscles until they scream with pain. My feet ache every morning. I've pushed aside a throbbing pain in my lower back for weeks, not wanting to even think about the ways my body might be failing me. But the ride to the hospital, being carried in by Cal and then whisked away to an exam room, the entire time I wished I'd pass out, the stabbing pains were so awful and so relentless.

I guess I finally did because now Cal's gone and I'm alone. Unfortunately, the pain's still with me.

As I turn onto my side, shivering in the gown they put me in, even the crinkly paper under me hurts my skin. Squeezing myself into a ball, I beg my body to stop punishing me, promising it that I'll be nicer if it'll stop.

It doesn't listen.

SOFT BLANKET. *Eyes open. Panic. Where am I? Pain.*

"You're in the ER, sweetie."

My sister.

Pain stabs. Eyes shut. Hide again.

"I'm trying to get someone in here as fast as I can. Can you tell me what's going on?"

I... can't.

WHERE AM I?

Sharp scent, hushed quiet. Tube in my arm.
Hospital. Pain dulled.
Esther asleep.
Where is Cal?

A NURSE POKES and prods at me, measuring and counting and adjusting the tubes and IV attached to my arm. She explains that my sister had to go but she'll be back.

A woman in a white coat enters, trailed by more white coats with young faces. The one in charge picks up my chart and rattles off words. The only ones that sink in are "kidney" and "infection."

I get a brief smile and a nod before she exits, doctor ducklings trailing behind her.

I guess I'm not pregnant.

Hopefully not dying.

I feel like shit, but the pain has dulled to a low roar.

Wooziness is taking over again. I try to hang on to my brain because something's—some*one*...

My brain cells keel over, but when I open my eyes, I see him.

Cal.

There he is.

Cal.

Stop.

Don't leave me.

Chapter 31

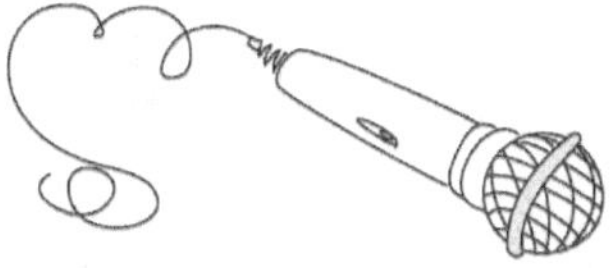

You're listening to 101.7 WBAR on this beautiful Sunday night. Live music in Boston this week: upcoming R&B artist Karyn White headlines at the Channel, Phish is at the Paradise, and the Dropkick Murphys are at the Avalon Ballroom. Get out and hear some live music or stay home and watch reruns, the choice is yours.

CAL

I managed to drive to the hospital, find Esther and hand Jess off. I even managed to get my car out of the loading zone and into a parking space.

Then I freeze up. I need to know that Jess is okay but re-entering that place might actually give me a heart attack.

The image of Jess's unnaturally pale face as they wheeled her away from me gets my ass out of the car and my feet walking back toward the doors. If something happens to her and I'm not there, I'll never forgive myself. It's bad enough that I didn't see how seriously ill she is.

Concentrating on putting one foot in front of the other while trying not to let the hospital scents enter my nose, I make it to the check-in desk. When I ask about Jess, however, all the woman will tell me is that they've moved her. I'm not related to her, so that's all the information I can get. I can't remember her sister's last name, so they can't even page her for me.

I walk away from the desk, and before I know it, I'm in the hallway leading to the burn unit. Once my brain finally gets in gear, it occurs to me that someone there might be willing to help me find Jess.

The moment I see the sign announcing that I've entered the wing, my heart stops slamming against my breastbone. In fact, it stops all together as I face doors I vowed I'd never pass through again, no matter what I ended up looking like.

Worry for Jess restarts my ticker and shoves my fear aside. What happens on the other side of those doors has nothing to do with me today. Visiting hours are over, so I slip through them as quietly as I can. Taking the first right, trying to keep the sounds of pain and the smells of antiseptic from shutting me down completely, I pass rooms where I know kids are likely awake, positioned to heal and too uncomfortable to sleep.

Before I can find help, a nurse finds me. "Can I help you, sir? Visiting hours are over."

I'd recognize that voice anywhere. Drill sergeant on the outside, marshmallow on the inside. "Nurse Angie?"

She frowns. "Do I know you?"

"It's me. Cal Alonso."

A hand flies to her heart. "Say that again."

"Cal Alonso?"

Hands on hips, she narrows her eyes at me. "Say it like you say it on the radio."

A laugh puffs past my lips, but I obey. "This is Callihan, coming at you from 101.7 WBAR."

There are tears in her eyes as she grabs my hand and pulls me toward a door I was never allowed to pass through as a kid. We may have had wheelchair races in the halls and played hide-and-seek everywhere else, but the nurses' break room was strictly off-limits.

When we burst inside, several faces turn our way, some I recognize. "People, it's Cal. Cal Alonso."

Suddenly, I'm overwhelmed with hugs and introductions and exclamations. Apparently, I've got loyal fans here in the burn unit.

At some point, Nurse Angie must realize that I'm probably not here for an impromptu reunion. "Obviously, we're happy to see you, but—" She breaks off to study my face. "What happened?"

"I brought my... my girlfriend to the ER." Panic rises again. People lose their lives here. I cannot lose Jess. "But after I moved my car, they wouldn't tell me where she was. I wanted to see if you could help me find out what's going on with her."

Nurses run this place, so it doesn't take long for them to find out where Jessica is. Before giving me directions to her room, however, I have to promise to come back. "It'd mean the world for these kids to see you, to see how successful you are, despite..."

For once, Nurse Angie is speechless.

"Despite looking like they do?"

She nods curtly.

Being here isn't easy—halls I played in and rooms I suffered in—but I made it through once, so I guess I can do it again. "I'll try."

"I'm here till five a.m. Check in before you leave so I know she's okay?"

After getting a nod from me, she kisses me on the cheek—the left cheek—before sending me on my way.

FIFTEEN MINUTES LATER, I find the nurse's station in the renal unit, which does not seem like a good place for Jess to have landed. When I give my name, the RN in charge doesn't hesitate to take me to her, so I send up a quick thanks to Angie. Once things settle down, I will go back and see what I can do to help.

But when I see Jess, all hope for a happy ending to this story withers. She's dwarfed by the hospital bed. Machines with tubes and wires coming and going surround her—are possibly keeping her alive. I've about worked up the courage to get closer to her when someone grabs me by the elbow to pull me back into the hall.

I turn to protest, to tell whoever it is that I have permission to be here, but Jess's sister beats me to the punch. "How could you not know she was sick?"

"I… she didn't seem—I mean, she was tired, but her schedule was pretty crazy. It wasn't until today—"

"Are you sleeping with her?"

Jess is a grown woman, but her sister's tone makes me feel like I've done something really bad. "Do you have a problem with that? It was completely consensual."

"That's not what I'm talking about." Jabbing a finger in the direction of the room where her sister lies, her life possibly in danger, she hisses, "How could you sleep next to that body and not know that she's dangerously underweight?"

"Is she going to die? What is wrong with her?"

Hands on hips, Esther swerves into doctor mode. "She has a severe kidney infection, which is being treated by intravenous antibiotics. She's also receiving much-needed nutrition via her veins because it looks like my sister has been starving herself again."

Starving herself. Again. The words twist in my gut—how did I not know this? How did I not notice? "But she's going to be okay?"

"It depends on what you mean by okay. Yes, she will survive this infection. But the fact that she's anorexic again is a major problem."

Stepping back, I stumble into a chair and let myself fall into it since I don't think I can hold myself up and think at the same time.

Esther stands in judgement over me. "She's practically skin and bones. How could you not notice?"

"Well, let's see." Pulling my hoodie down, I point to my scars. "There are more where these came from. The ones you can't see are much worse. Because of that, I've only been naked with a handful of women, so I'm no expert on women's bodies." Buttons pushed, I can't help but add, "Nor am I a doctor like you."

The woman looks at me like I'm a piece of dog crap on her shoe. "When she was fifteen and was dancing seriously while struggling with this eating disorder, she almost starved herself to death. Remember Karen Carpenter? That's what happened to her. If Jess doesn't make some major changes to her life, she won't survive either."

Shame washes over me, but it's rage—at Esther, at doctors and their failures, at Jess for hurting herself, but mostly at myself for not being able to protect her—that has me on my feet and heading for the exit.

Before I push through the doors, I turn back to make my position clear. "When she wakes up, tell her I love her." Swallowing past the boulder in my throat, I add, "And that I'm sorry I couldn't save her."

WHEN I DROVE Jess to Mass General I don't know how many hours ago, I was worried that I literally wouldn't be able to walk through the hospital doors.

Now I can't seem to leave.

Instead, I wander the hospital basement. Memories lodged down here aren't quite as painful as those up in the burn unit. The main hospital is connected to the Shriners' wing through these shadowy underground hallways. The most rebellious of us used it as our personal playground. Challenging each other to explore its darker corners, we thought it was the height of adventure. It seems strange to me now that nobody ever chased us out of here. Maybe they felt that sorry for us. Or were happy to have us out of their hair. Probably both.

Esther's words chase each other around in my head as I pace the length of the building and back again. *She's practically skin and bones.* Jess is thin and she does forget to eat sometimes, but she seems so on top of everything and sure of herself that...

Fuck. Did I not *want* to see?

The thought stops me in my tracks. She's helped me through so much, challenged me to stretch my wings. What have I fucking done for her? Sucked her dry, apparently. She gave in to my demands that she come to my place night after night, even though it meant she never got a full night's sleep. I thought I was helping by building her a barre at my place, but maybe she took that as a signal that I thought she needed to exercise more.

She won't survive.

Obviously, I have no fucking idea how to watch out for Jess, even though I tried every which way I know how. Seems I'm only capable of taking care of a three-legged cat and a one-eyed dog. A two-legged princess? I not only don't deserve her, I'm a danger to her.

If I tell her that, she'll deny it.

When I was fifteen, I told my parents that I would rather kill myself than go through another surgery. I meant it. I thought about suicide a lot then. The look on my mother's face when I said it aloud —I couldn't do that to her. I couldn't leave my family with that kind of guilt.

I've moved on from that level of pain, but maybe I haven't moved far. I've let Jessica prop me up these past few months, and it almost killed her. If we're to have any chance of survival as a couple, I have to be enough of a man to stand on my own two feet.

Maybe it's time I faced my own demons. If I can conquer them, I can help Jess conquer hers.

First stop: facing my nightmares. Which happen to live right here in this building.

IT'S after two in the morning when I make it back up to the burn unit. The atmosphere is hushed and the overhead lights are off, but a hospital never completely shuts down. When I knock softly on the break room door, a nurse opens it with a frown, but when she sees it's me, she pulls me inside.

"He's back," she announces to the group sitting around a coffee table playing cards and drinking coffee.

"This is what you do in here?" Shoving my hands in my pockets, I suddenly feel like a little kid again.

Angie gets up and ushers me to a spot on the couch beside her. "Have to stay awake somehow so we can answer the damn bells when the little brats need something." Angie always had a backhanded sense of humor. I was kind of scared of her until I was old enough to get it.

"So how's your girlfriend?"

The word pricks my heart, but I'm not here for comfort. I'm here for information. "She has a pretty bad kidney infection, but her sister —who's a doctor—told me she's going to be okay." *As long as she stays away from me*, I remind myself.

Pushing self-pity aside, I press ahead. "Listen, I want to know some things, and I think you're the only people who can tell me."

Angie's brows come together, but she nods. "What do you want to know?"

"Do you think it's right? That you save kids in this place by torturing their bodies, only to have those same kids end up living a life that's tortured up here?" I finish, tapping my temple.

The room is silent. Maybe I'm out of line. But after a tense few moments, Angie places a hand on my shoulder. "He's right. When Cal was here, the treatment was torture. There's no other word for it." She clears her throat. "We take an oath to save lives—"

"But is it right to do that, when you know you're sentencing us to a life of pain? Inside and out?"

She lifts her chin. "It's all I know how to do, Cal. We didn't know better then. We know a little more now."

"So we're lab mice in some experiment you're running here?"

Angie gives me the *look*. The one that says, *I don't like this any more than you do, but we've got to get through it*. When I don't back down, she pats my shoulder before getting up to pull something from a bookshelf.

Sitting next to me again, she opens what appears to be a scrapbook.

The pages are filled with Polaroids and newspaper clippings. She flips through quickly until she gets to a section filled with photos of me, age four to age fifteen.

"I always wondered why you took those pictures," I murmur.

She bumps shoulders with me. "So we wouldn't forget." She points to the first picture of me, where I barely look human I'm missing so much skin. "And so we'd know we were making progress."

On the next page, instead of photographs, there are Christmas cards and letters in my mom's handwriting and clippings from the *Phoenix* and *Boston Globe*—announcements of when I was spinning at clubs, even an article from the Worcester paper that ran when I first got a DJ slot at WBAR. Taking the book from her, I page through it. The photos of other people are hard to take in. Some kids I recognize, many I don't. There are obituaries, but also marriage announcements.

When I raise my head, not only do I find that the room has emptied except for Angie and me, I notice that this isn't the only scrapbook on the shelf. It's stuffed with them. "So many kids."

"So many," Angie echoes. When she faces me, her eyes are shiny. "All we can do is our best."

A breath shudders through me, and I take her hand. "I know. I'm sorry."

"Things are better now, Cal. Both in here and out there." Her hand moves vaguely toward the door, but I get what she means. The treatment is better and kids are adapting better.

I shake my head. *Is it too late for me?*

"It's never too late to heal, Cal," Angie whispers.

I didn't mean to say the words out loud—I didn't even know I felt them—but I'm glad I did. Facing the fear that it's too late for me seems like the first step, but it's a doozy.

"I wonder," Angie says, "if there's any way you could get away for a couple weeks later this month? There's a retreat, kind of a training for burn camp counselors. We could probably get you a spot."

"What's with this burn camp?" I remember Sharon from the Shriners saying something about one. "Send kids away so their parents get a break?"

"That's a benefit for all families when kids go to summer camp. But for burn survivors, like other kids, it's time to have fun and gain independence. It's also time with other kids who know what they've been through. Getting to take risks without worrying about being bullied, it gives them confidence, so when they go back home and to school, they have inner resources. Every kid who comes here after that experience is stronger, inside and out."

Inside and out. To be whole, *in here and out there,* is that even possible for me?

She takes the scrapbook from me and returns it to the shelf before turning back to say, "I hear counselors get even more out of it than campers."

Chapter 32

**Motor here at WBAR kicking off your Monday drivetime
lineup with "We Care a Lot" from Faith No More.**

JESS

When I finally wake up for real, I'm alone. The pain has subsided to a
dull roar in the background. I feel less flu-y, but I'm so, so tired. I
don't feel like I'm going to fade away again, but I'm also not sure I
can get up. I've got tubes coming and going, neither of which is
pleasant. I'm starting to feel panicky about being trapped in the bed
when a nurse comes in.

"You're awake. Good." All business, she checks the IV and takes
my vitals.

"Um, can I go to the bathroom?"

She lifts up the sheet to point at a bag at my side. "We've got you
on a catheter at the moment, but as soon as the doctor gives the go
ahead, we'll remove that and help you to the toilet."

"Okay, thanks."

This lack of power, lack of control, is what I hate about the hospital. One of many things. "Um, what time is it?"

She checks her watch. "Five thirty."

"P.M.?"

"Mm-hm." Before I can ask, she smiles. "And it's Monday."

Okay, not too bad. I've only lost twenty-four hours.

"Dinner will be coming soon." She checks my chart again. "Do you feel like eating?"

And I'm fifteen again. Nurses and doctors asking me over and over if I want to eat, if I can eat, if I will eat. But I'm not fifteen. I'm a thirty-year-old woman. I can do this. I am in control of some things.

I don't want to lie to myself, however, so I take a moment to pay attention. Without the nausea that's been plaguing me lately, I am hungry. Really hungry. "Yes. Yes, I do."

It's only when she's halfway out the door that I sum up the courage to ask, "Has my—um, my boyfriend been here?"

Her brow wrinkles slightly, a crack in her professional demeanor revealing what looks like pity, but she says, "Sorry, sweetheart, I just clocked in an hour ago, so I can't tell you."

WHEN DINNER FINALLY SHOWS UP, I'm so ravenous that I'd probably eat it if it were mystery meat with a side of Jell-O salad. But it's actually not bad. Bland, but edible. I even manage to wrangle an extra dessert.

I'm licking the spoon to get the last bit of butterscotch pudding when my sister walks in, followed by a doctor.

Esther's face softens when she sees that I'm awake, then practically glows when she takes in the empty food tray. Before I can ask about Cal, the doctor introduces himself and adds that he and my sister went to med school together.

Good news, I'll get extra attention. Bad news, they'll gang up on me.

He checks my chart and talks some medical gobbledygook to my sister, to the point that I have to clear my throat. "I understand that I have a kidney infection. That's it, right?"

The doctor pulls up a rolling stool and sits down next to me. "Yes and no." He meets my sister's gaze briefly before returning to mine, making me feel like a child. "Your low BMI, low blood pressure and heart rate, in combination with your history, have us a bit concerned about how we got to this point."

Taking in a deep breath, I do my best to tamp down my emotions. Losing it at the doctor will not help. "I understand your concern, but I am not anorexic. Normally, I eat healthy meals, but I was super nauseous the past couple of weeks and had a pretty taxing schedule." I catch Esther sighing in the corner of my eye, so I turn to her. "I though I was getting a UTI, but I didn't have time to go to the doctor. I was planning to get it checked out this week if it didn't get better."

The doctor listens patiently to my explanation but doesn't look convinced. "Sometimes it's hard to tease out what's really going on when you're in the thick of it." He pats my hand. "We'll have the catheter removed, but I want you to stay overnight so we can monitor your kidney function. Your systems have been stressed, and we need to make sure everything bounces back once we've got the infection under control."

"Okay. Thanks." I don't like it, but what am I going to do? He's in charge.

Esther walks to the door behind him.

"Are you leaving?"

"I'll be back."

In the meantime, a nurse comes and removes the catheter and helps me to the bathroom. Despite the fact that they're pumping fluids into me, I'm feeling a bit dizzy, so I'm glad for the help. She's getting me settled again when Esther returns. As soon as the nurse leaves, I start in.

"You're reading way too much into this."

Esther shakes her head. "Do you not get how serious this is? You've stressed your kidneys. You need them. To live."

Tears spring to her eyes, not something I'm used to seeing, and I'm swamped with guilt. I hold out my hand, and when she takes it, I squeeze hard. "I'm sorry if I scared you."

"You're damn right you scared me." A sob hiccups over her words, but doesn't slow her down. "And if you think I'm going to sit by and watch you try and kill yourself—again—you have another think coming."

Breathe in, breathe out. Count to ten. "Esther. I get why this has you freaked out, but I'm not sick like that."

Shaking her head, eyes on the ceiling, a half-laugh, half-groan of disbelief chokes out of her.

"Es, I swear it's not the same. I'm not the same person. I ate dinner. They didn't have to strap me in a fucking chair and pry my jaws apart and force food down my throat."

She meets my gaze, her eyes wide. "That's what they did back then?"

"Yes, Esther. That's what they did. And they made mom and dad feel like it was their fault, which about killed me." And now my tears have started. "I know… I know I have some problems. But it's not the same. You have to believe me. I can't go through that treatment again."

When she opens her mouth to argue I add, "You weren't here."

Tears streaming down her face, she shakes her head. "I know. And I hate that I wasn't. I hate that I wasn't there for you. That I didn't know." Her head drops like it weighs a thousand pounds, and her shoulders cave in. "And I hate even more that I didn't know this time."

"It's not your fault, Es. Or your responsibility."

"But I'm a doctor. I should've noticed."

Closing my eyes, dropping back into the pillows, I give in. "Okay, I admit it. I sometimes hide how much I eat or don't from you and mom. I don't want you to worry, and I hate to argue about it."

I make myself meet her gaze. She's not judging me. She's just worried. "I'm an actress. I can't get fat."

"You're not—"

I raise my hand to stop her. "I know I'm not fat. I understand that I pushed myself too hard and that I got too thin." I have to swallow around the lump of fear in my throat to keep going. "I do think… I think I may have a problem knowing how to judge, or... seeing myself clearly."

Esther narrows her eyes and turns away, like she's scanning through something in her head. "Dysmorphia," she finally whispers.

"What?"

"Maybe it's body dysmorphia." She starts to pace. "Maybe you were never anorexic, or maybe it's a combination."

"What are you talking about?"

"There is a condition, one psychologists are only beginning to understand, where the patient has difficulty seeing their body as it truly is. Or something like that. It's not always about weight; it can be one area of the body." Talking to herself, she heads for the door. "You might have to talk to someone from psych before they'll let you go, so I want to look into this to make sure they consider it as a possibility."

This actually makes sense to me. "Okay."

She's out the door before I can take another breath, but I need to know, so I shout, "Where's Cal?"

Her mouth is tight when she pops back in. "He left."

"What do you mean?"

She shrugs. "He left after he dropped you off."

I shake my head. "He was here." Hoping I wasn't hallucinating, I press on. "In the doorway. I saw him."

"He was. He said he was"—she makes air quotes—"'sorry he couldn't save you,' and he left."

When I open my mouth, she holds up a hand. "Jess, you can't be in a relationship when you literally"—her hand gestures at the hospital bed—"can't stand on your own two feet. It's not healthy—for either of you."

I want to protest, I want to argue, but I'm suddenly so tired.

And I know she's right. I can't burden Cal with my crap. He's got enough of his own to deal with. So I nod.

"I'll be back," she says.

And I'm alone again.

WHEN I WALK into my chilly, dank apartment after almost a week away, I have to admit it was nice to hole up at my parents' and let my mom take care of me after I got out of the hospital. I'm so grateful that I have my family's support. Like me, my parents were wary at first about this new diagnosis because of the blame foisted on them by doctors when I was a teenager, but body dysmorphia, as bizarre as it sounds, makes more sense to all of us.

I don't quite understand it yet, but it seems that being bullied because of my reading struggles were a contributing factor. The crisis point most likely hit when I lost my ballet body. Feelings of failure sent me into a tailspin, resulting in misapprehensions and obsessions around the size of my breasts. Even though it's all pretty new, the psychologist I talked to at the body dysmorphia disorder clinic at Brown University convinced me that it's worth taking some time to work with them intensively. She's pretty confident that once they get me on the road to recovery, I can work with a therapist locally to continue the process.

Running my hand along the smooth surface of my ballet barre, I can't help checking out my silhouette in the mirror. Obsessively checking one's appearance is apparently part of the disorder. I never really thought about how much time I spend looking in mirrors. I mean, when you take ballet seriously, you're surrounded by them. Monitoring your form in the mirror is part of the process.

My parents' house doesn't have any full-length mirrors—I don't know how my mom gets dressed without one—and the bathroom mirror at the hospital was one of those tilted, blurry things where you can barely see well enough to brush your teeth. It's been a weird mix of relief and anxiety to be away from *my* mirrors. A slightly different mix of relief and anxiety to look at my reflection now. My breasts look the same—ugly. Leaning in, I'm not sure if the wrinkle situation is the same or not. I'm actually not sure if I can believe anything I see. I know I don't have a ballet body, but I'm not sure of anything else.

I guess that's why I am turning my life upside down to go to Rhode Island. Closing my eyes, I remind myself of the list of tasks I need to accomplish so I can leave town. When I open them, I avoid my reflection as I draw the curtain to hide it.

The shudder that goes through me once I can no longer see myself is a familiar one. I never thought about the ritual I go through every day when I open and close that curtain. Yet another thing to delve into, I guess.

Before I can do that, though, I need to sit down and listen to the answering machine messages that have built up over the week. The little red light is practically strobing, it's blinking so fast. Thinking about what might be waiting for me on that tiny little cassette has the spot behind my solar plexus clenching, so instead of pushing the button, I bustle around packing clothes and cleaning out my fridge until there's only a half hour left before I have to leave for Providence. If I'm going to make it in time for check-in, it's now or never.

Part of me wants to erase it all, but my curiosity must be stronger than my fear of the unknown because my finger pushes play.

BEEP. Jessica, darling, it's Mira. I hope you're feeling better. Bella let us know you were in the hospital. I want you to know that we are happy to consider you for both shows without a callback and will get back to you with casting as soon as we can. Take care of yourself.

The next couple messages are about auditions that I missed this week. I already called the casting directors in town to let them know that I won't be available for the rest of March, so I don't need to deal with them. I got my dance classes covered while I was at my parents' house too.

BEEP. Jessica, this is Dave. We are happy to offer you the roles of Luciana in Comedy of Errors and Caliban in The Tempest for the summer season. I'm not sure if you're out of the hospital yet, but if you can give the office a call when you have a chance to let us know

*if you accept and can start rehearsals mid-May, that'd be great.
Looking forward to working with you again.*

Pressing pause, I celebrate winning the roles I wanted with a little jig. However, I have no idea how many messages are left and the clock is ticking down, so I make myself start the machine again.

BEEP. Jess, this is Richard Jones from WBAR. I got the message that you're out sick this week, but Rocket and Porky are wondering when you're going to be back in. Can you give me a call as soon as you know?

My brain races through possibilities as I listen with half an ear to the rest of the messages, most of which are from friends. Dance and theater friends I've neglected while I've been running myself ragged trying to be too many places at once the past few months. Bella came to see me while I was in the hospital and I've talked to her on the phone, but I guess everyone else will have to wait.

No message from Cal. Of course, I haven't called him either. I was angry that he left me at the hospital, but I also get how hard it must've been for him to even walk in there in the first place. On top of that, my sister can be pretty intimidating when she's in doctor mode or protecting her little sister, so the combination may have freaked him out. But if he loves me, wouldn't he at least reach out to check on me?

Only fifteen minutes left before I have to leave, so I call the Shakespeare Boston office and leave a message accepting the job. What I don't say is that I'm not positive that I'll be well enough to do it. Hopefully, knowing I have work will be the incentive I need to get through whatever is in store for me down in Rhode Island. Like Prudence, neither of these characters is defined by their beauty, so maybe playing them won't be a danger to my mental health.

Calling Jones is trickier, so instead of making that call, I rerecord my outgoing message five times trying to hit the right tone.

"Hi, you've reached the answering machine for Jessica Abraham. I am out of town with limited telephone access, so I won't be checking messages or returning calls until after March twenty-seventh."

Time's up. I need to get out the door, but I stare at the machine for a few moments anyway as I try to figure out what to say to Jones.

I love Cal and I want the best for him, but I also need to work. The regular gig at the station is not something I'm going to walk away from. I think I can behave professionally, even with a broken heart—I'll be in therapy, so hopefully that'll help—so I make the call.

The receptionist puts me right through to Jones's office.

"Jones's office, Cal speaking."

"Cal?"

In the beat before he answers, I remember that Jones's office is a regular way station for the DJs since they don't have their own.

"Jess?"

"What are you—" I begin.

"How are you—" he says at the same time. "Sorry. No, wait. I'm not sorry. I need to know. Are you okay?"

My heart's bouncing from my throat to my belly, and I'm gripping the phone like it's a lifeline. *Am I okay?* "I'm... the infection is under control, but I'm—I have some stuff to deal with. Mental issues."

An audible sigh is all I get, so I keep talking.

"I will be okay, though. I promise. I—I actually need to leave, like, right this minute, and drive down to this special clinic in Rhode Island to begin the work I need to do, and I'm running late as usual. I'm returning Jones's call about my work at the station, but I don't—I mean, I don't want things to be awkward for you. I need the money, so—"

"Jess. It's okay. You should keep working here. I'm really glad you're okay, but more important, I'm so sorry that—"

He breaks off, sniffs and swallows. I want to let him off the hook, tell him it's fine, I'll be fine, I understand if he doesn't want to deal with all my crazy shit. But I also want to hear his apology.

So I wait.

"Sorry, I uh… Phew. I want you to know I'm sorry I didn't realize you were sick. I'm sorry I didn't take care of you better."

"Cal, it's not—"

"Let me finish, okay?"

"Okay."

"I love you, Jess. I love you more than anyone I've ever known. But I don't think I can be with you until I figure some things out."

Heart pounding with dread, I make myself ask, "And if you can't?"

He sniffs again. "I will. Because I don't want to lose you."

"I have a lot to work on too."

"I don't want to put any pressure on you. Maybe we… Fuck. I'm so out of my depth here I don't even know how to say it."

Now I'm sniffling too—surprise, surprise. "I don't know either, Cal. But I love you. I want to get better too, and I have to do that before I can decide about anything." As I swipe the snot from my nose, my gaze lands on the clock over the stove. "I really have to go. Can you, um, give Jones the message that I'll be back the twenty-seventh and I'd like to come back to work then? Is that okay?"

He doesn't say anything for a beat, and I'm about to tell him that I'll figure something else out if it's going to mean we can't be together when he says, "It's very okay. I'll tell him. Take care of your-self, Jess. I mean it."

"You too, Cal. Bye."

"Bye, princess. See you soon."

CAL

The dial tone in my ear is interrupted by Jones's voice. "Hey, Cal. Was that for me?"

Wishing I had a recording of the conversation with Jess, wishing that we'd talked face-to-face so I had a better idea of what is happen-ing, I do my best to file away the memory word for word as I put the phone back in its cradle.

Then I face Jones. "It was." After giving him Jess's message, I add, "I'm actually here because I need to talk to you."

"Good," he says as he crosses to the other side of his desk. "I need to talk to you too." He sits and gestures for me to do the same. "I'm really hoping you're here to say yes to the new lineup because we need to act now to avoid losing this couple in Atlanta. Charlotte is making a play for them, but I'm pretty sure our offer is better. If you're in?"

Pushing aside worries that working during the day would be awkward if Jess and I can't work things out, I shake my head. "I'm in, but I really need to do this… thing. Which involves leaving town. Is there any way I can take off the last week of March?"

"Well, let's see what we can do." After pulling out the master schedule, he gets the Atlanta station manager on the phone. The whole thing seems to take forever, especially the long stretch that he's on hold while the manager checks with his DJs. Finally, Jones wraps up the conversation, hangs up the phone and lifts his hand for a high five.

"We got 'em. And they can start the last week of March. So as long as you can get Motor to stay through then, I think we've got you covered." He points a finger at me. "But you have to be back for April first. Don't want to miss the Fool's Parade."

Hope blooms in my chest as I stand. "I wouldn't miss it."

BACK AT MY APARTMENT, I start making phone calls.

First, to Motor. Thankfully, he agrees to stay on through the end of March, as long as I cover some of his shifts for the next couple of weeks. It'll mean some long days, but it's worth it.

Next, to the Phoenix Society, where I confirm that I can make it to the burn camp counselor training intensive at the end of March. After that, I call Phil at the bar to check in on how things are going with the food deliveries. If I'm making this change, there's no way I can go back to delivering late-night meals, so his positive report takes a huge weight off my shoulders.

"We don't need you anymore, Cal," Phil confirms. "It's going great. But Walt did ask if you'd come visit St. Francis House. He and a couple others now spend nights there, but for some reason they miss your ugly mug."

I miss them too. And Phil. My life may be heading in a better direction, but that doesn't mean I have to leave everything behind. "I'll do that. And maybe I'll be in for dinner tonight."

"Meatloaf special."

"Well then, it's a date."

"See you later, Cal."

My final call is to Sharon at the Shriners Foundation. If I got anything from that phone call from Jessica, it's that I need to do more than go away to camp for a week. Sharon is the only person I can think of who can help me figure out what that means, exactly.

After I run some ideas by her for a concert fundraiser, I pause, trying to figure out what to say. She must sense my hesitation because she asks, "Was there something else?"

"Yeah, actually. So, you said something the first time we talked that I've been thinking about. I'm actually going to do a counselor training at a burn camp down in Pennsylvania later this month."

"That's great, Cal," Sharon says. "I think you'll be great, and like I said, I think you'll get a lot out of it, too."

"Um, that's the part I wanted to ask you about. I'm wondering if there's anybody that you, uh, see here. To talk about..." I don't even know the words for this stuff, so I don't know how I think I'm ready to do it, but I have to at least try. I want to be better. For Jess and for myself. "You know, mental stuff."

"Like a counselor? Or a therapist?"

"Either, I guess. Someone to help me figure out how being burned has fucked up my head."

She doesn't say anything, so I add, "I mean, you seem pretty together, so I figured you must have seen somebody."

"Oh, I have. You should probably interview a few people to see if they—"

"Listen," I interrupt her. "Did they help you with your… issues around your, uh, accident? And the treatment and everything after?"

"He did."

"Then that's all I need to know. I don't want to waste any more time."

Chapter 33

Be sure to catch all the live coverage and full-color commentary of the one hundred and fifty-fifth annual Fool's Parade on Boston's own Landsdowne Street, this coming April first, only at WBAR, 101.7 FM. *Waah, waah, waah.* What did you say? It's only the fifth annual? But it says here—*Waah, waah, waah.* No, I'm the one who looks like an idiot. Yes, I know they can't see me, but—You know what? You're so smart, you read the damn thing. I quit. *SLAM.*

JESS

It's been a great week back at the station. When I finally talked to Jones—which I had to do as a part of my treatment—he was very accommodating about me taking time off. In some ways, asking was the hardest step. Asking for help, asking for what often feels like special treatment, takes me back to school and all the times teachers shook their heads or sighed with impatience when they heard from my parents that I'd need extra attention. They weren't all like that, of course, and I realize now that they were likely overworked and underpaid. But at the time, it made me feel like a problem.

So I stopped asking.

I'm starting to get, however, that asking for help doesn't make me weak or needy. It makes me human.

I still have a lot of work to do, but the stint at the body dysmorphic disorder clinic both blew my mind and jump-started the journey of putting it back together again. I'll be making bi-monthly trips down there for some time to continue the cognitive behavioral therapy as well as meeting with a local therapist. The big difference is, unlike the anorexia treatment I went through at fifteen, this work makes sense to me. I mean, it's fucked up that my brain can somehow pull a fast one on my eyes, but knowing that I'm not the only person who thinks like this? It's a massive relief.

It's been especially nice working at the station again because it's really the only thing I'm doing. Besides helping me wrap my mind around the fact that my breasts are not my enemy, my therapist is trying to get me to accept that I don't have to go at everything at full speed all the time.

On top of all that, the goofiness level around here has risen to an all-time high as we get ready for the Fool's Parade. Tomorrow, April first, is the biggest day of the year for Porky and Rocket. They've pulled out all the stops creating promos and writing the script for the parade, in which we'll do color commentary as if we were watching a parade marching down Landsdowne Street. Of course, there is no parade; it's one giant April Fool's joke, but it's become quite the tradition. This year, I get to be a part of it.

Still, it's not the same without Cal around. We haven't talked since I left for Rhode Island weeks ago. I was not only surprised that he wasn't here when I got back, I was disappointed. I had myself all worked up to have a big talk and start figuring things out now that I'm on the path to better mental and physical health. I even wrote him a couple of letters while I was away, also part of the process of working through some of my fears. But he's gone away to summer camp, according to Jones. Which is odd, considering it's still March.

When I enter the breakroom to stash my lunch, I'm surprised to see that they've added a mailbox slot for me. There's even mail in it.

Like, a lot. I'm hit by a flash of anxiety at the thought of all the reading that'll mean, but drawing on my new CBT practices, I slow my breath and rearrange my thoughts. I don't have to read them all right this minute.

Curiosity gets the better of me, though. I have time to at least look through them since I'm actually early for my call time. It's amazing how easy it is to be on time when you don't cram too much into your day or spend hours changing clothes to try to change your silhouette. So I sit at the table to see if there's anything in this pile that's from a certain someone.

CAL

It's a beautiful spring morning—a time of day I've begun to actually enjoy. On our walk to the station, Blondie and I take a long-cut through the Fens, where she's greeted lovingly by the fans she accumulated before we went away to camp. From retirees working in garden plots to kids at the playground, everyone's happy to see her again and accept her doggy kisses.

There's a buzz behind my solar plexus, but it's a good one. Excitement about starting anew. My steps quicken as we turn onto Landsdowne Street. I want to do some more research before my interview with the band members of R.E.M. later today. And of course, there's the big "parade" tomorrow, which'll happen during my timeslot for the first time ever.

Reminding myself to check my mailbox—not only am I expecting an EP a friend overnighted from a station in Seattle, but I've got new burn camp pen pals I'm hoping to hear from—I cut left instead of right when we enter the front doors of the station. Suddenly, Blondie whines and sprints ahead, startling me enough that I drop the leash.

When she darts into the mailroom ahead of me, I hear a voice that has me sprinting to catch up.

JESS

I'm sorting through the envelopes, searching for Cal's name in the upper left-hand corner, when I hear a dog's whine and the skittery clicks of nails on tile. Shifting in the chair, I don't have time to get up before Blondie launches her upper body at me and covers my face with kisses.

"Whoa, whoa. I missed you too, sweet girl."

And then the face that I've missed more than I could ever have imagined appears in the doorway.

"Jess," he breathes.

"Cal." Suddenly feeling uncertain, I'm grateful for the large dog in my lap.

"Blondie, off," Cal says sharply. With a whine, she obeys.

So much for the buffer between us.

After making her sit, he asks. "Did you get my letter?"

Scooping up the pile of envelopes Blondie knocked out of my hands, I get to my feet. "I was going through these. It'll take me a minute." Shrugging off the habitual wave of shame, I say. "Slow reader, you know." Dragging my eyes away from his smile, I point at the other mailboxes. "There should be a few for you from me, but you have to promise not to judge me for any spelling mistakes."

Shaking his head, he takes a careful step toward me like he's afraid I might disappear. "I missed so much school I doubt I'd catch any errors." Taking another step, he asks, "Maybe we could skip the reading and tell each other what we wrote instead?"

"As long as it's not a Dear John." Eyes on his, which tell me that he didn't write to break up with me, I close the gap between us. "I like that idea."

"I'll go first," we say at the same time.

Grasping each other's hands, almost as if entranced, we continue to mirror each other. "You go first."

"I really want to kiss you," is the last sentence we utter in unison before our giggles break the spell. Still smiling, I drop my forehead to his sternum with a sigh. After reveling in his familiar, comforting scent for a few moments, I raise my eyes to meet his. "I do—I really do want to kiss you and… everything else.

"But I need you to know something first," I continue. Pressing his big, strong hand over my heavily thumping heart, I draw on the tools I've begun to learn and give myself permission to speak my truth to the man I love. "You do not bear any responsibility for how I take care of my body. Or don't—or didn't. My sister told me how she read you the riot act. She was wrong to put any blame on you. What's wrong is all up here." I knock on my skull with our joined hands, unwilling to let go for even a moment now that I've got hold of him again. "The only thing wrong between us was our opposing schedules, and I think that's something we can figure out."

He nods slowly, takes a breath and then pauses for a moment, mouth open, brows raised.

I nod. "I'm done."

He clears his throat. "My letter thanks you. For breaking through the armor I'd built up. For waking me up. Shaking things up. Rocking my world and spinning it round. You spin me. In all the good ways." Bringing my right palm to his left cheek and holding it there, he squeezes my left hand as he takes another big breath. "I don't want to go back in that shell. I won't, whether you're with me out here or not. But I would like to move forward with you next to me, if you'll have me."

Before I can say anything, he drops my hand. "Here. Let me show you something." Then, without a shred of self-consciousness, he takes off his hoodie as well as the tank underneath it. I'm so busy swooning at the sight of his sculpted chest that I don't notice what's new until he points to a spot over his heart.

There, curving over his pectoral muscle and blended into the edges of his scars in a way that's truly a work of art, is a tattoo of a red rose in full bloom.

"I got it the day after we talked," he says. "The day after you left for Rhode Island." Rubbing the tattoo with his right hand, he adds, "You're the love of my life. You've brought me back to life. You're my Rose Red, princess."

My bottom lip trembles. For once, I have no words. Even if I did, I don't think I could get them past the lump in my throat. All I can do is nod, so I do it over and over again until his palms cup both sides of my face.

He waits patiently while I try to calm down. Not to get myself under control—I'm beginning to understand that forcing my body to do anything isn't healthy—but following my breath gives me at least a glimpse of what it means to simply be present with the love of my life. When I find stillness, a relaxed smile blooms on my face, mirroring the one on his.

"Now how about that kiss?"

Epilogue

As you most likely know, all little princes and princesses must take the journeys set before them.

They must fight the fire-breathing dragons along the way, whether those dragons are along the path or in their hearts.

It's not always the case that a prince and princess find true love. Sometimes a prince finds a prince, for example. Sometimes a princess decides she doesn't need a partner.

Even when true lovers find each other, the road of life, the hills and valleys of a relationship, may tear them apart.

Oftentimes, the Good Faeries of Therapeia help princes and princesses forge a path through the dark forests of the mind and the trials of the heart so that when they make it to the other side, they are equally vulnerable and steadfast.

And that, dearest reader, is what happens to princess Jessica and her guardian angel Callihan.

Afterword

Thank you for reading Jess & Cal's story.

Every book in the Boston Classics series is a standalone and you can read them in any order, but I'd recommend picking up *Child of Mine* next—Bella's Secret Baby story. You can find links to all retailers at books2read.com/COMKGrey.

And, to get a free novella along with deleted scenes from this book and other bonus material, sign up for my newsletter by visiting followkarengrey.com.

If you loved this Boston Classics novel, leaving a review is the absolute best way to support an author. You can leave one wherever you downloaded the book, or on Goodreads or Bookbub.

Also by Karen Grey

What I'm Looking For: *The course of true love never did run smooth*, but in this smart and sexy retro rom-com with a finance-nerd heroine and a drama-geek hero, returns on love can't be measured on the S&P 500.

Forget About Me: An underwear model, a best friend's little sister, and a dog who steals the show make for an unforgettable mix in this bittersweet romantic comedy.

Child of Mine: A single mom gets a job offer she can't refuse but has to work side-by-side with the one-night stand that doesn't know he's a father. Of her daughter.

You Get What You Give: When a fiery redhead and the guy she thought was a one night stand turn out to be rivals, his family feud causes shockwaves bigger than the surf stirred up by the latest hurricane.

Hold On To Me: In this slow-burn, boss-assistant, entertainment biz romance, a bad cop movie production chief takes on a sexy assistant who challenges her every assumption.

I Want It That Way: She's a driver to the stars who just wants to get her tubes tied. He's a former child actor who needs to get back behind the wheel. A fake relationship seems like the perfect solution.

When I Come Around: When two besties work together on a movie out of town, a secret friends-with-benefits deal seems like a good idea. Until their friends weigh in.

For Fork's Sake: Grumpy, nerdy soil scientist Sam finds passionate, idealist Diane interviewing his grandma for her YouTube channel. Feathers fly between these farm business rivals!

The Single Dad's Guide to Recreation: He's the new-in-town single dad tasked with cutting costs at Climax Parks & Rec. She's the program director with classes on the chopping block. It should be easier for them to keep their hands off each other.

Acknowledgments

Although I started this book in 2019, most of it was written during the Covid-19 lockdown of 2020, and it's releasing in the spring of 2021. Taking this journey with not only my fictional characters but with all the generous people I encountered while researching what might have been Jess and Cal's realities, kept my brain active during the long winter of 2020. More importantly, this couple's efforts to not just survive, but to thrive—both as individuals and as a pair—feels important to me as we move into a more hopeful spring.

The usual suspects supported me during the process—friends and family—but I especially need to thank my husband for giving me space in which to write (and let me steal his stories) and for my friends Melissa and Laurie. Our walks and drinks around bonfires kept me sane this winter.

This book wouldn't be the same without the painstaking work (and endless cheerleading) from my editor Sarah Pesce and proof-reader Jax Garren.

Research-wise, heartfelt thanks go to Carter Alan. Not only was his book *Radio Free Boston* an invaluable resource, he spent time on the phone with a total stranger to answer her niggling questions. Burn survivor Kelsey Pandiani likewise shared her time, experiences and invaluable insights with me, following up as a sensitivity reader. Finally, Dr. Bruce Cairns not only helped me get through AP Physics in high school, he got me access to medical journals articles from the 1960's and 70's. (He also pours a great deal of energy into running the NC Jaycee Burn Center.) Psychologist Dr. Berta Summers clarified the finer points of a Body Dysmorphia Disorder diagnosis, and BDD patient Florence Launay served as a sensitivity reader. Finally,

Christie Scott Hill and my dad both helped me with the details on Jess's kidney infection.

Any errors are entirely mine.

Finally, to WBCN and WFNX DJ Nik Carter: thanks for taking my calls way back in 1993.

RESOURCES

Flashback Girl by Lise Deguire, Psy.D
    Reason for Living by George E. Pessotti
    Trial by Fire by Scott James
    Radio Free Boston by Carter Alan
    We Want the Airwaves director Jason Steeves
    Alisa Ann Ruch Burn Foundation
    Phoenix Society for Burn Survivoers
    Shriners Hospitals for Children
    Body Dysmorphic Disorder Foundation

About the Author

KAREN GREY is a *USA Today* bestselling and award-winning author of vintage romantic comedies with smart heroines and hunky heroes. Drawing on a long career as a performer, her retro 80's and 90's romances are populated with characters working both on- and off-stage in theater, TV and film. When not reading or writing, she's lounging at the beach or hiking in the mountains. Or dreaming about both with an IPA in hand and a dog or a cat nearby.

(Author photo: Celestial Studios)

For the latest news and bonus materials, join her free VIP club at:
followkarengrey.com

facebook.com/karengreyauthor

instagram.com/karengreyauthor

goodreads.com/karen_grey

bookbub.com/profile/karen-grey

tiktok.com/@karengreyauthor

www.ingramcontent.com/pod-product-compliance
Lightning Source LLC
Chambersburg PA
CBHW031649100726
47898CB00006B/2035